MARVEL SUPER HERO ADVENTURES

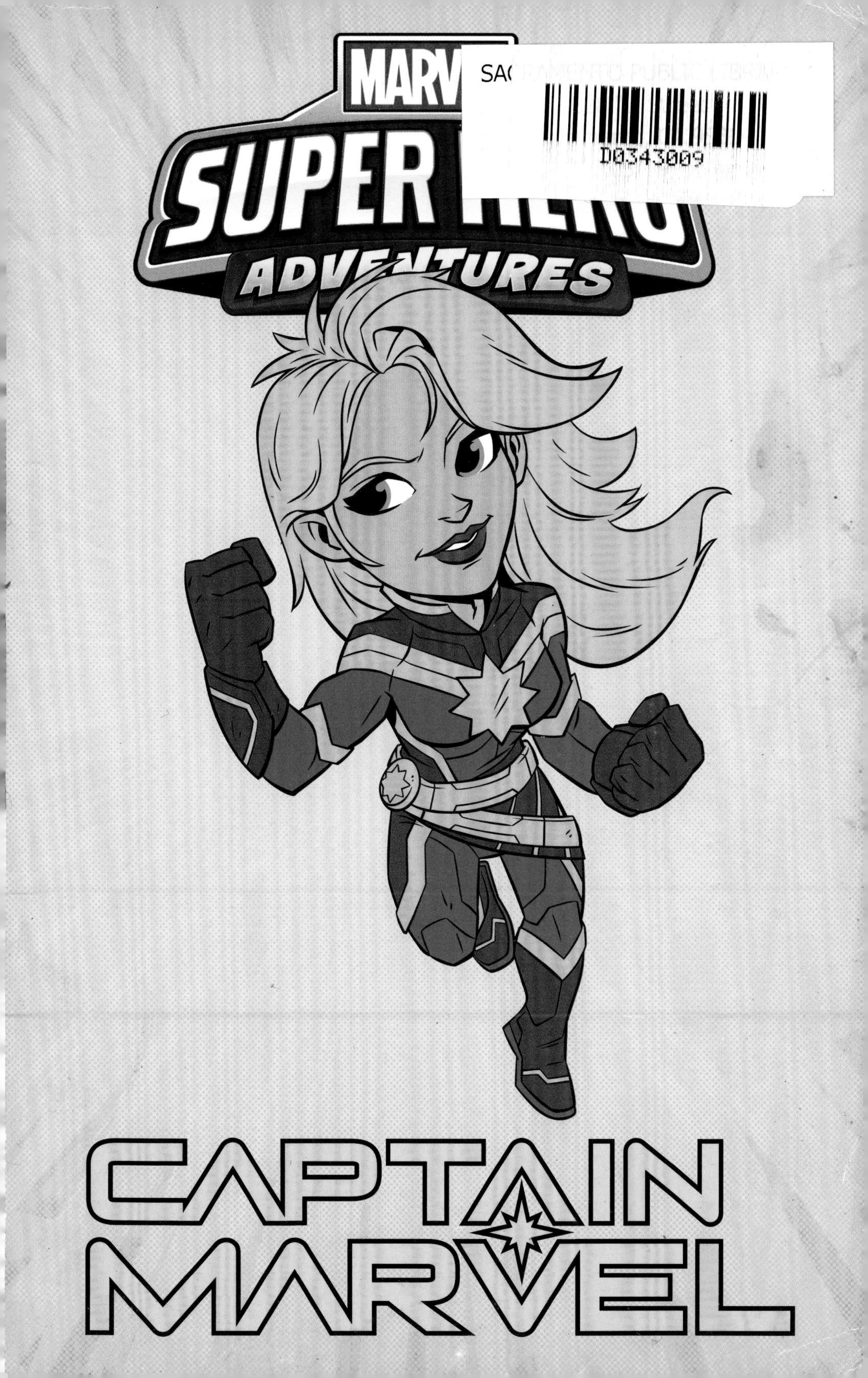

CAPTAIN MARVEL

Cover by Paulina Ganucheau

collection editor Jennifer Grünwald
assistant editor Caitlin O'Connell
associate managing editor Kateri Woody
editor, special projects Mark D. Beazley
vp production & special projects Jeff Youngquist
svp print, sales & marketing David Gabriel

editor in chief C.B. Cebulski
chief creative officer Joe Quesada
president Dan Buckley
executive producer Alan Fine

MARVEL SUPER HERO ADVENTURES: CAPTAIN MARVEL. Contains material originally published in magazine form as MARVEL SUPER HERO ADVENTURES: CAPTAIN MARVEL — FIRST DAY OF SCHOOL #1, MARVEL SUPER HERO ADVENTURES: CAPTAIN MARVEL — HALLOWEEN SPOOKTACULAR #1, MARVEL SUPER HERO ADVENTURES: CAPTAIN MARVEL — MEALTIME MAYHEM #1, MARVEL SUPER HERO ADVENTURES: CAPTAIN MARVEL — FROST GIANTS AMONG US #1 and MARVEL SUPER HERO ADVENTURES: MS. MARVEL AND THE TELEPORTING DOG #1. First printing 2018. ISBN 978-1-302-91569-8. Published by MARVEL WORLDWIDE, INC., a subsidiary of MARVEL ENTERTAINMENT, LLC. OFFICE OF PUBLICATION: 135 West 50th Street, New York, NY 10020. Copyright © 2018 MARVEL No similarity between any of the names, characters, persons, and/or institutions in this magazine with those of any living or dead person or institution is intended, and any such similarity which may exist is purely coincidental. **Printed in Canada.** DAN BUCKLEY, President, Marvel Entertainment; JOHN NEE, Publisher; JOE QUESADA, Chief Creative Officer; TOM BREVOORT, SVP of Publishing; DAVID BOGART, SVP of Business Affairs & Operations, Publishing & Partnership; DAVID GABRIEL, SVP of Sales & Marketing, Publishing; JEFF YOUNGQUIST, VP of Production & Special Projects; DAN CARR, Executive Director of Publishing Technology; ALEX MORALES, Director of Publishing Operations; DAN EDINGTON, Managing Editor; SUSAN CRESPI, Production Manager; STAN LEE, Chairman Emeritus. For information regarding advertising in Marvel Comics or on Marvel.com, please contact Vit DeBellis, Custom Solutions & Integrated Advertising Manager, at vdebellis@marvel.com. For Marvel subscription inquiries, please call 888-511-5480. **Manufactured between 11/2/2018 and 12/4/2018 by SOLISCO PRINTERS, SCOTT, QC, CANADA.**

10 9 8 7 6 5 4 3 2 1

MARVEL SUPER HERO ADVENTURES

CAPTAIN MARVEL

FIRST DAY OF SCHOOL
Writer: Sholly Fisch
Artist: Mario Del Pennino
Color Artist: Java Tartaglia
Cover Art: Agnes Garbowska & Chris Sotomayor
Special thanks to Derek Laufman

HALLOWEEN SPOOKTACULAR
"Spidey's Super-Scary Stories"
Writer/Artist/Colorist: Jacob Chabot

"Sanctum Spooktorum"
Writer: Jeff Loveness
Artist: Mario Del Pennino
Color Artist: Matt Yackey

MEALTIME MAYHEM
"Slice of Life"
Writer: Seanan McGuire
Artist: Irene Strychalski
Color Artist: Jim Campbell

"Thankful"
Writer: Sean Ryan
Artist: Mario Del Pennino
Color Artist: Jim Campbell

FROST GIANTS AMONG US
"Snow Day"
Writer: Joe Caramagna
Artist: Mario Del Pennino
Color Artist: Jim Campbell

"Ahoy, Spidey!"
Writer: Leah Williams
Artist: Ty Templeton
Color Artist: Keiren Smith

Daily Bugle Funnies
Writer/Artist: Ty Templeton
Color Artist: Keiren Smith

Spider-Man Word Search & Maze
Written & Drawn by Owen McCarron
Colored by Andy Yanchus

Letterer: VC's Joe Caramagna
Assistant Editor: Lauren Amaro
Editor: Devin Lewis
Supervising Editor: Sana Amanat

MS. MARVEL AND THE TELEPORTING DOG
Writer: Jim McCann
Artist: Dario Brizuela
Color Artist: Chris Sotomayor
Letterer: VC's Joe Caramagna

Cover Art: Jacob Chabot
Editor: Sarah Brunstad
Consulting Editor: Sana Amanat
Special thanks to Derek Laufman

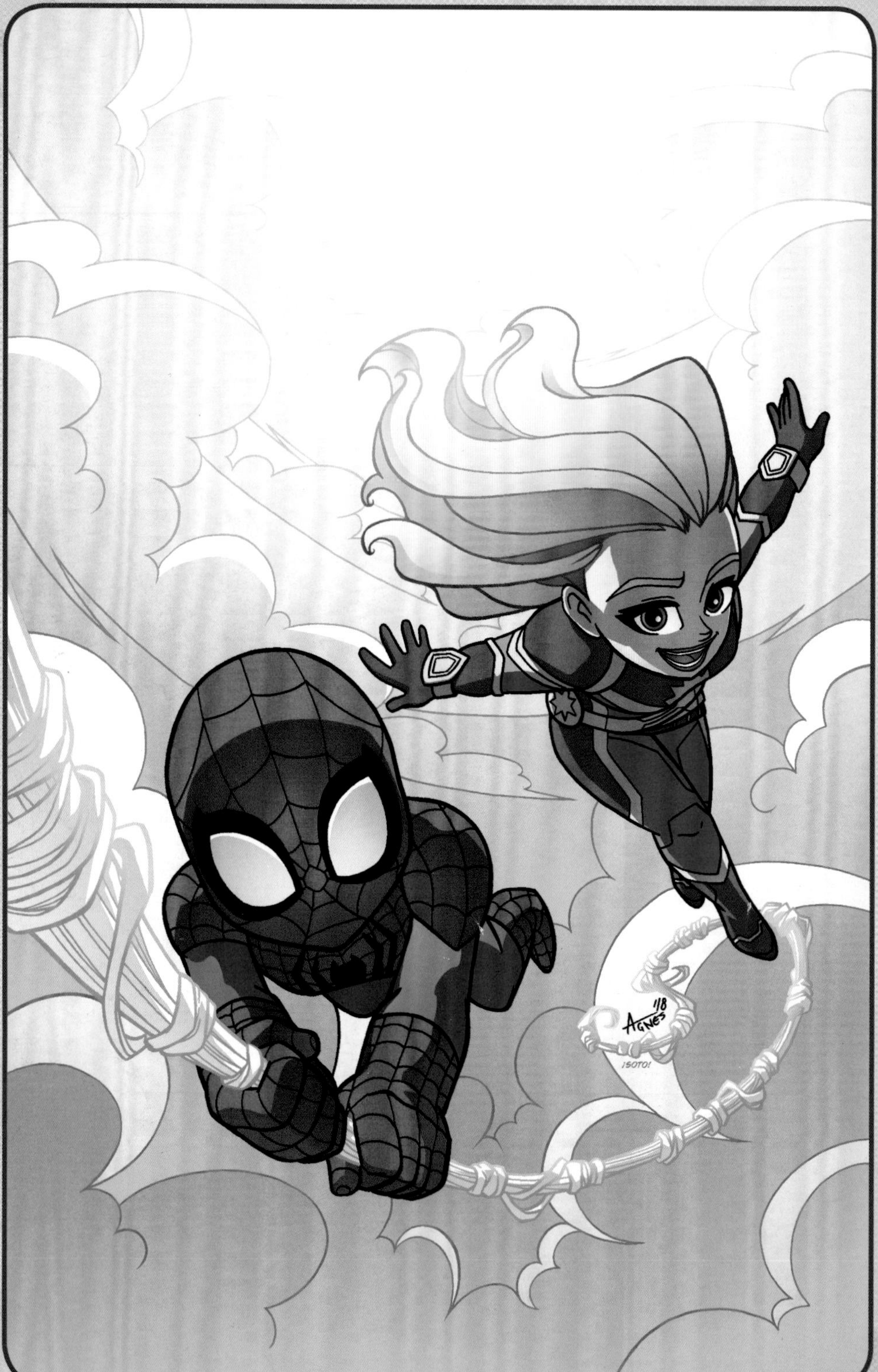
AGNES '18
¡SOTO!

First Day of School

cover by Agnes Garbowska & Chris Sotomayor

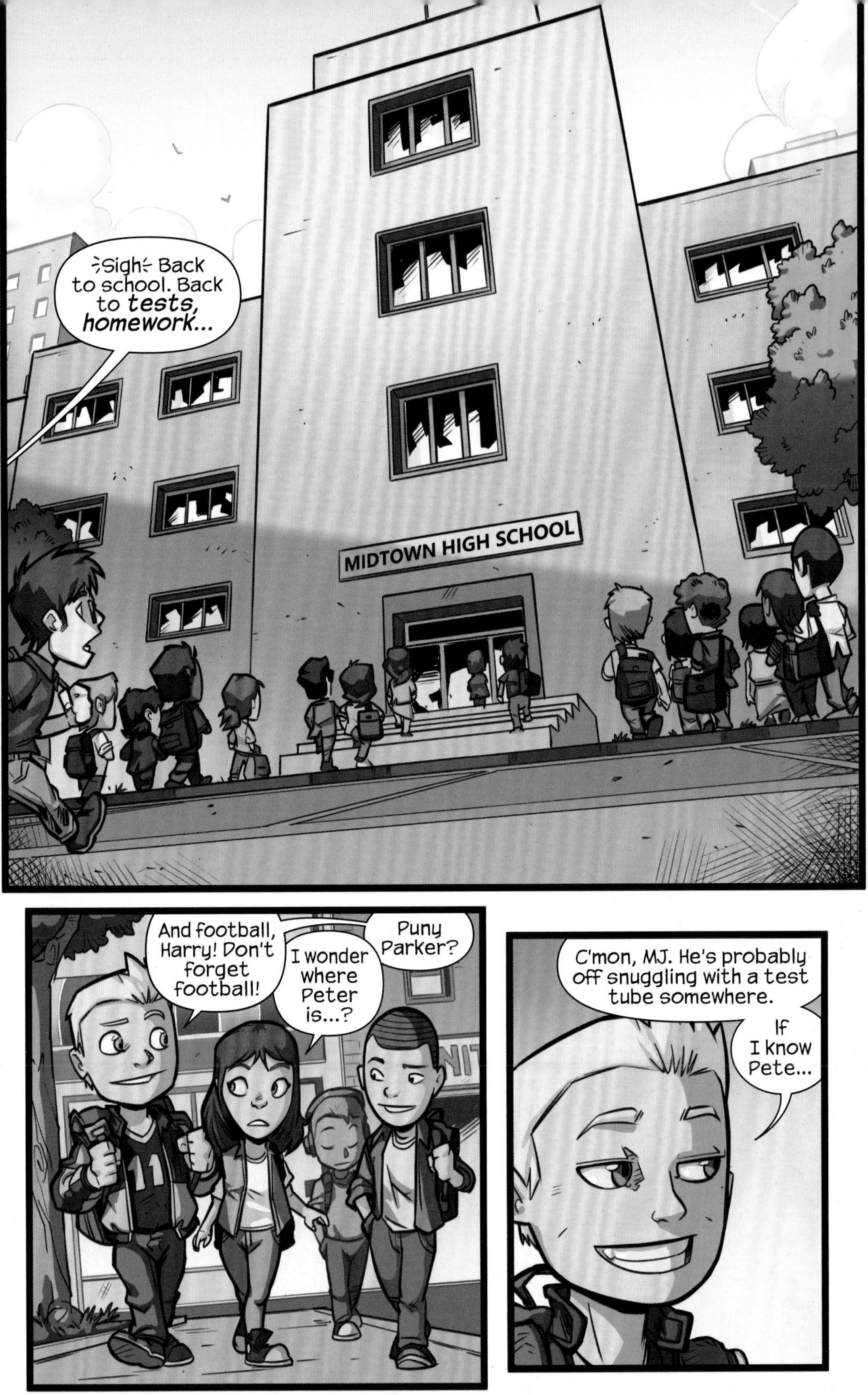
Sigh Back to school. Back to *tests, homework...*
MIDTOWN HIGH SCHOOL
And football, Harry! Don't forget football!
I wonder where Peter is...?
Puny Parker?
C'mon, MJ. He's probably off snuggling with a test tube somewhere.
If I know Pete...

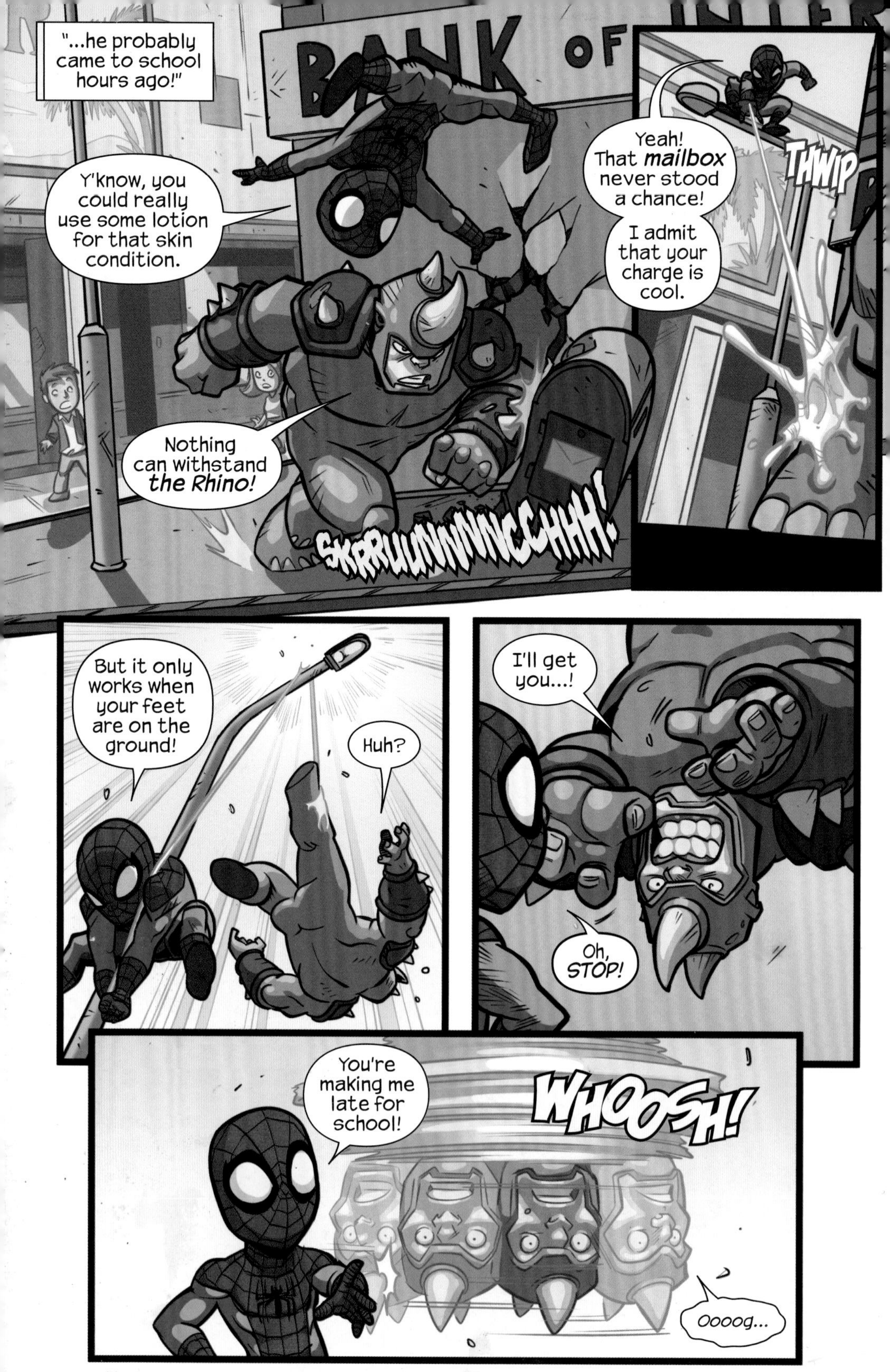
"...he probably came to school hours ago!"
BANK OF
Y'know, you could really use some lotion for that skin condition.
Nothing can withstand *the Rhino!*
SKRRUUNNNNCCHHH!
Yeah! That *mailbox* never stood a chance!
I admit that your charge is cool.
THWIP
But it only works when your feet are on the ground!
Huh?
I'll get you...!
Oh, STOP!
You're making me late for school!
WHOOSH!
Oooog...

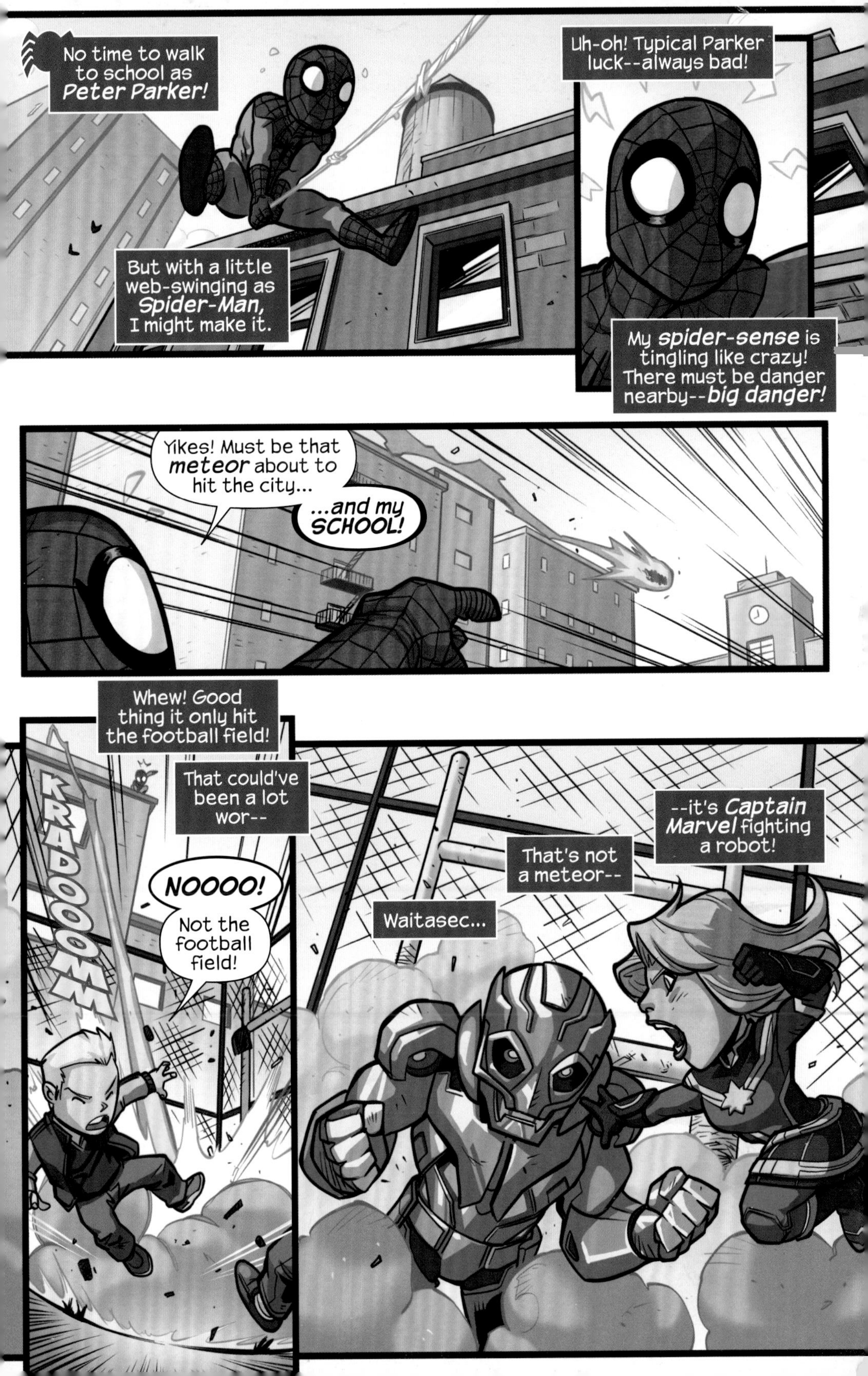
No time to walk to school as Peter Parker!
But with a little web-swinging as Spider-Man, I might make it.
Uh-oh! Typical Parker luck--always bad!
My spider-sense is tingling like crazy! There must be danger nearby--big danger!
Yikes! Must be that meteor about to hit the city...
...and my SCHOOL!
Whew! Good thing it only hit the football field!
That could've been a lot wor--
KRADOOOOMM
NOOOO! Not the football field!
Waitasec...
That's not a meteor--
--it's Captain Marvel fighting a robot!

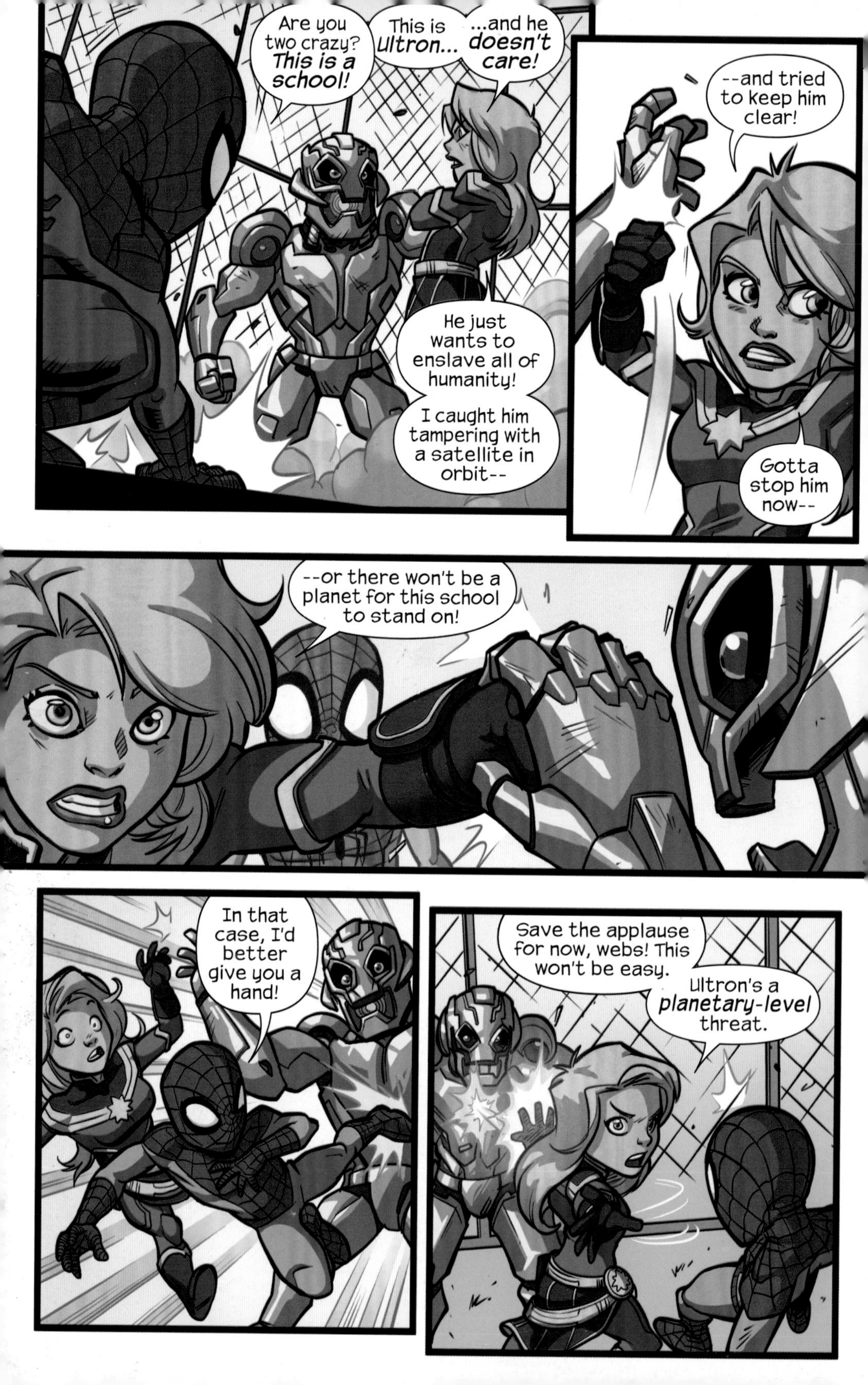

Are you two crazy? This is a school!
This is Ultron...
...and he doesn't care!
He just wants to enslave all of humanity!
I caught him tampering with a satellite in orbit--
--and tried to keep him clear!
Gotta stop him now--
--or there won't be a planet for this school to stand on!
In that case, I'd better give you a hand!
Save the applause for now, webs! This won't be easy.
Ultron's a planetary-level threat.

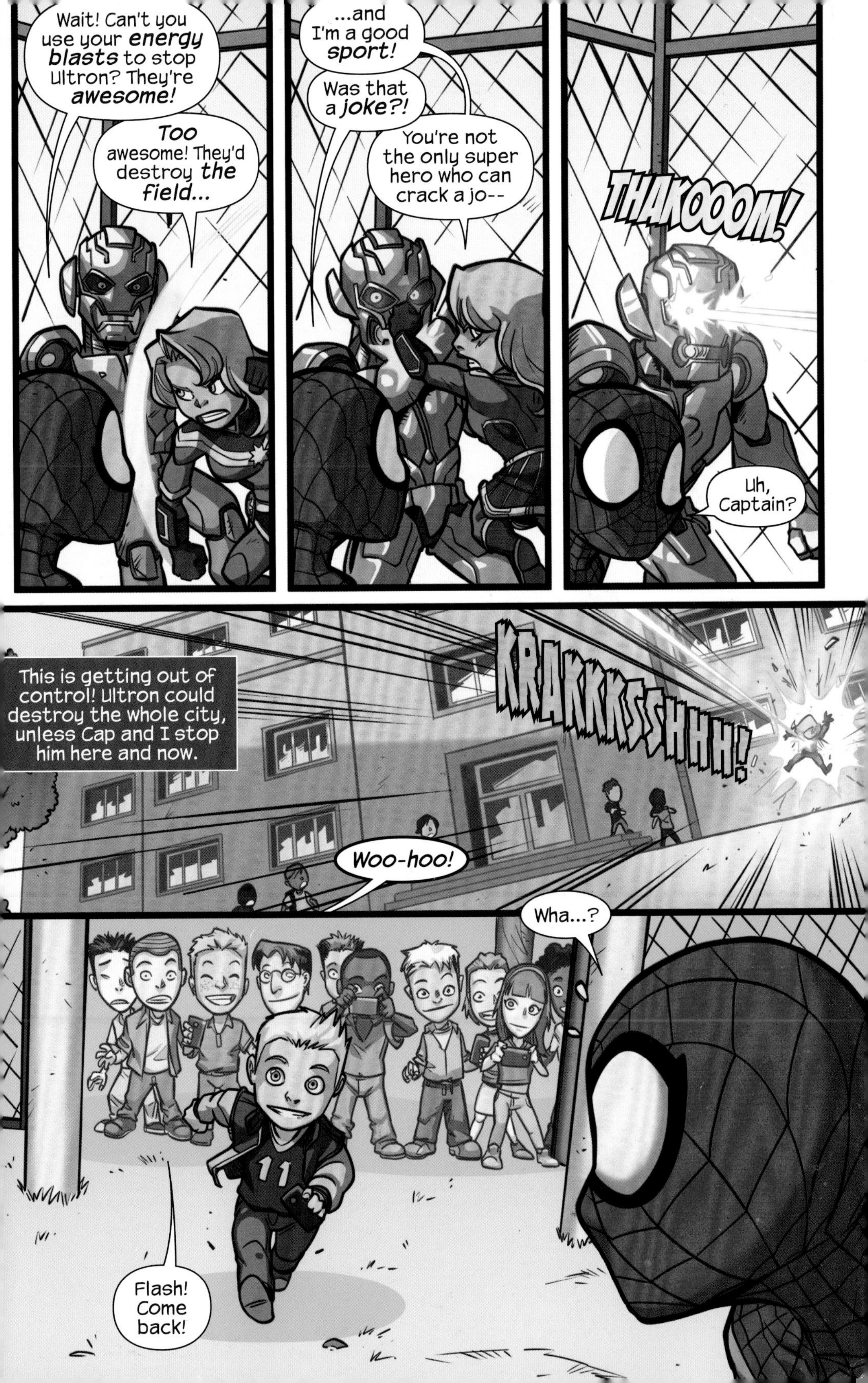
Wait! Can't you use your energy blasts to stop Ultron? They're awesome!
Too awesome! They'd destroy the field...
...and I'm a good sport!
Was that a joke?!
You're not the only super hero who can crack a jo--
THAKOOOM!
Uh, Captain?
This is getting out of control! Ultron could destroy the whole city, unless Cap and I stop him here and now.
KRAKKKSSHHH!
Woo-hoo!
Wha...?
Flash! Come back!

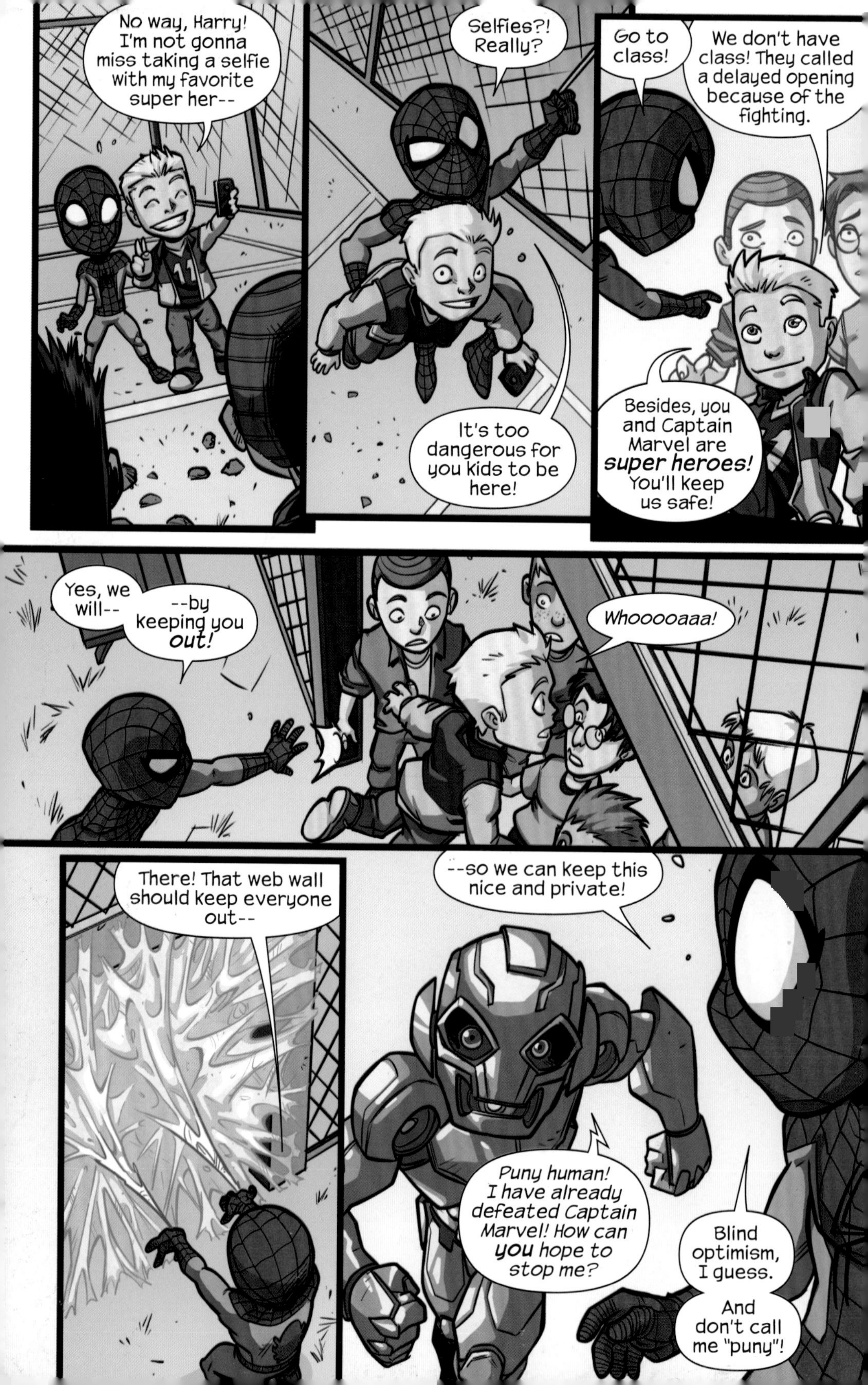

No way, Harry! I'm not gonna miss taking a selfie with my favorite super her--
Selfies?! Really?
It's too dangerous for you kids to be here!
Go to class!
We don't have class! They called a delayed opening because of the fighting.
Besides, you and Captain Marvel are super heroes! You'll keep us safe!
Yes, we will--
--by keeping you out!
Whoooooaaa!
There! That web wall should keep everyone out--
--so we can keep this nice and private!
Puny human! I have already defeated Captain Marvel! How can you hope to stop me?
Blind optimism, I guess.
And don't call me "puny"!

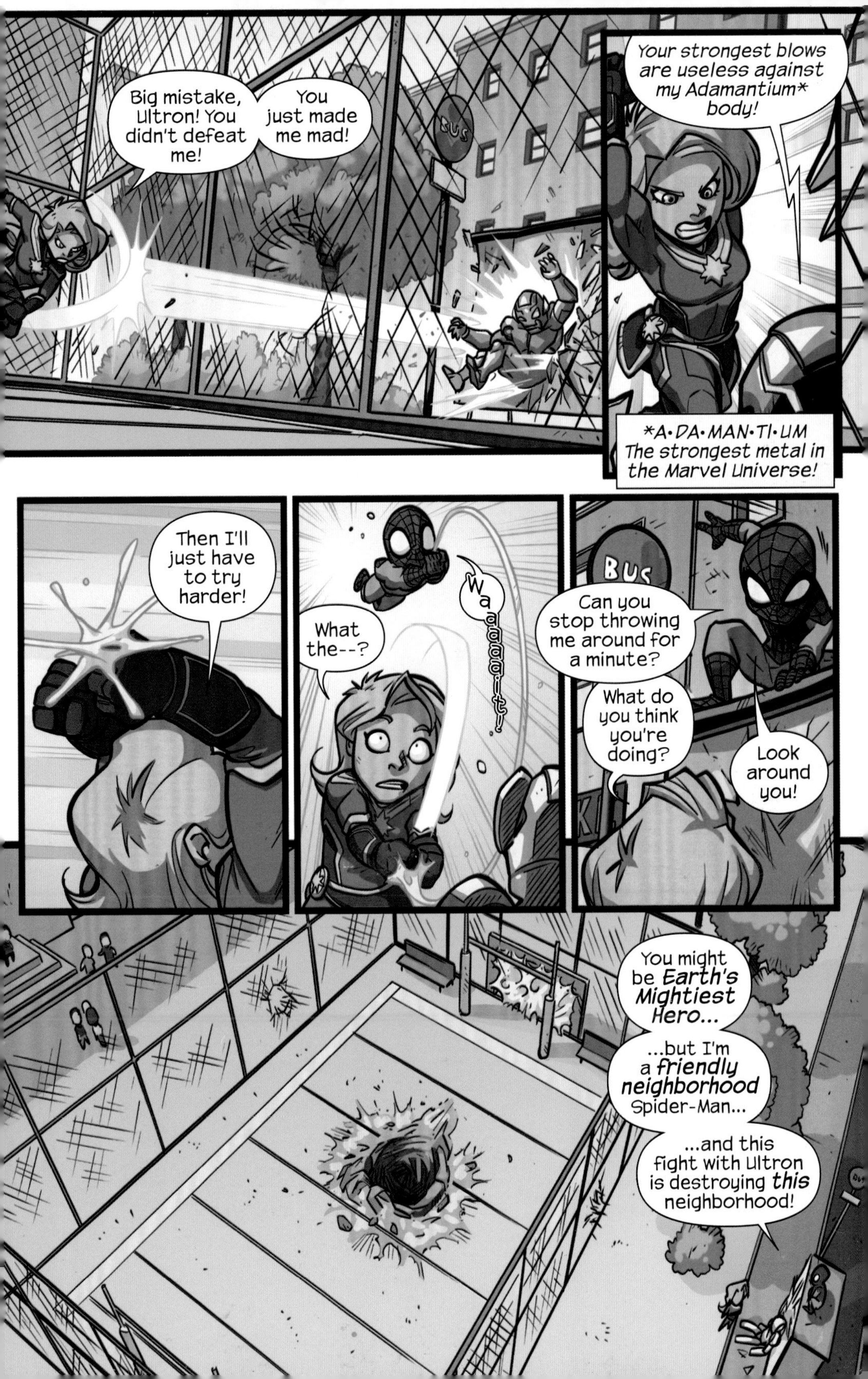
Big mistake, Ultron! You didn't defeat me!
You just made me mad!
Your strongest blows are useless against my Adamantium* body!
*A•DA•MAN•TI•UM The strongest metal in the Marvel Universe!
BUS
Then I'll just have to try harder!
What the--?
Waaaaaait!
Can you stop throwing me around for a minute?
What do you think you're doing?
Look around you!
You might be *Earth's Mightiest Hero...*
...but I'm a ***friendly neighborhood*** Spider-Man...
...and this fight with Ultron is destroying ***this*** neighborhood!

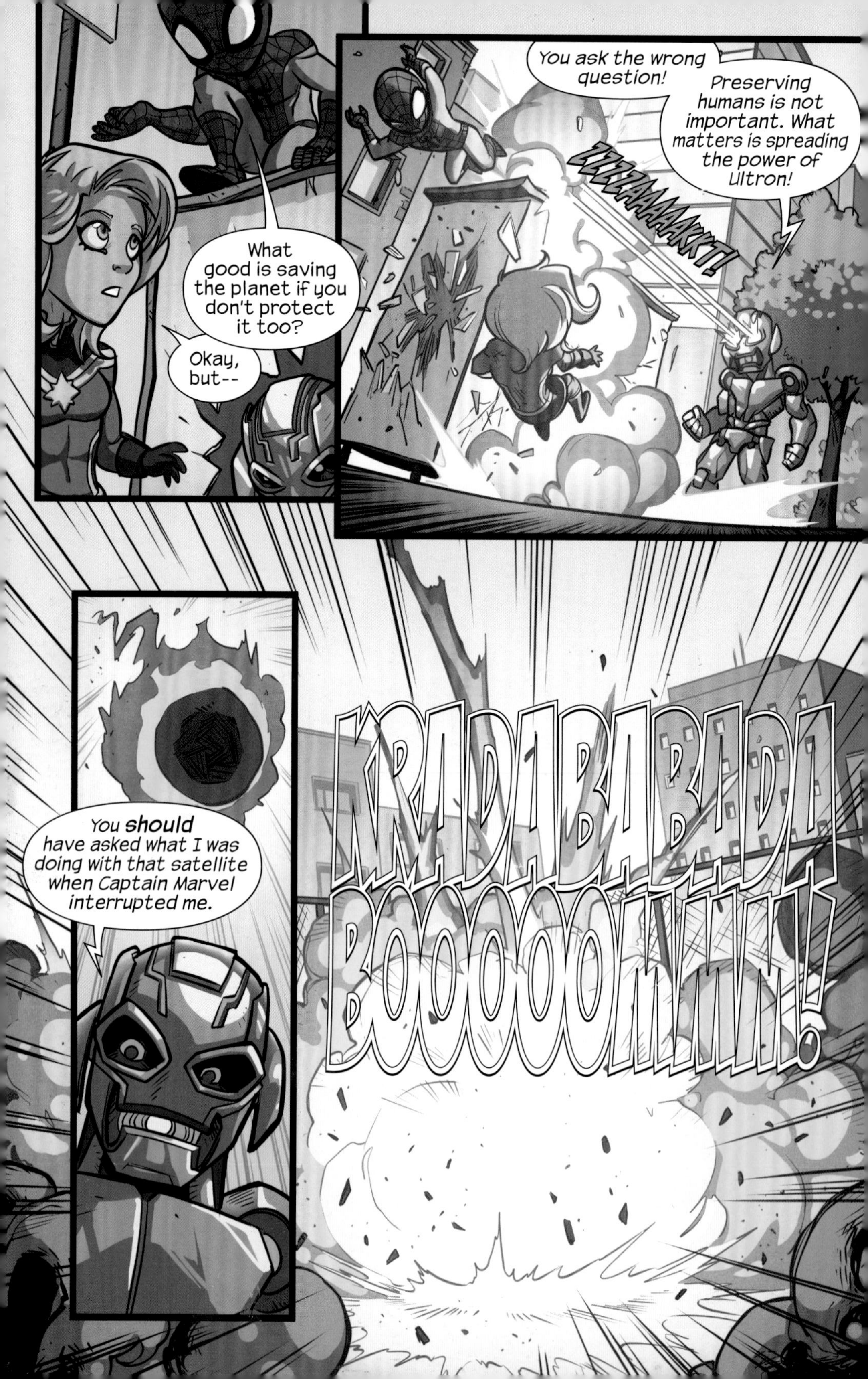
What good is saving the planet if you don't protect it too?
Okay, but--
You ask the wrong question!
Preserving humans is not important. What matters is spreading the power of Ultron!
ZZZZAAAAAKKT!
You **should** have asked what I was doing with that satellite when Captain Marvel interrupted me.
KRADABABADI BOOOOOOMMMM!

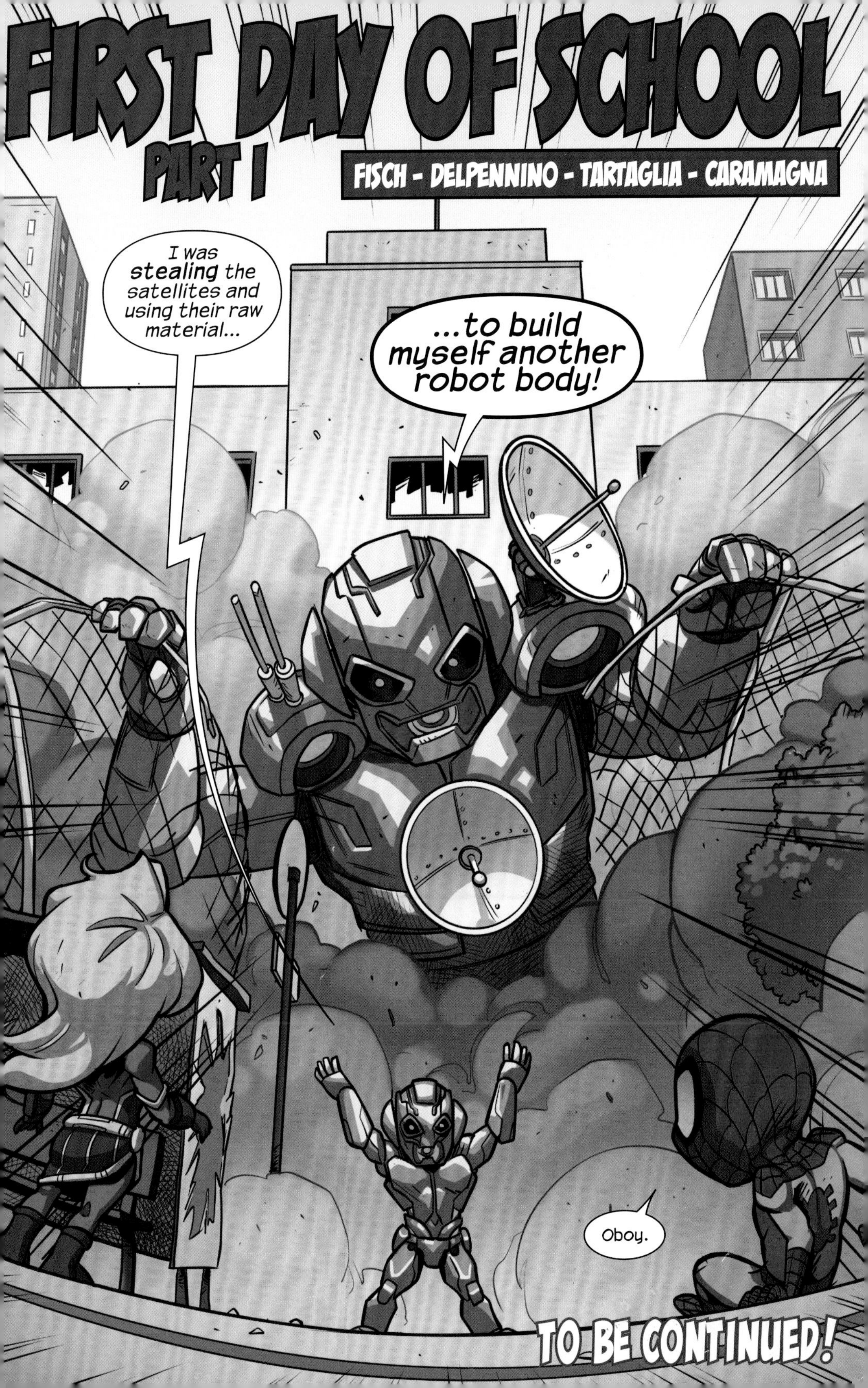
FIRST DAY OF SCHOOL
PART 1
FISCH - DELPENNINO - TARTAGLIA - CARAMAGNA
I was stealing the satellites and using their raw material...
...to build myself another robot body!
Oboy.
TO BE CONTINUED!

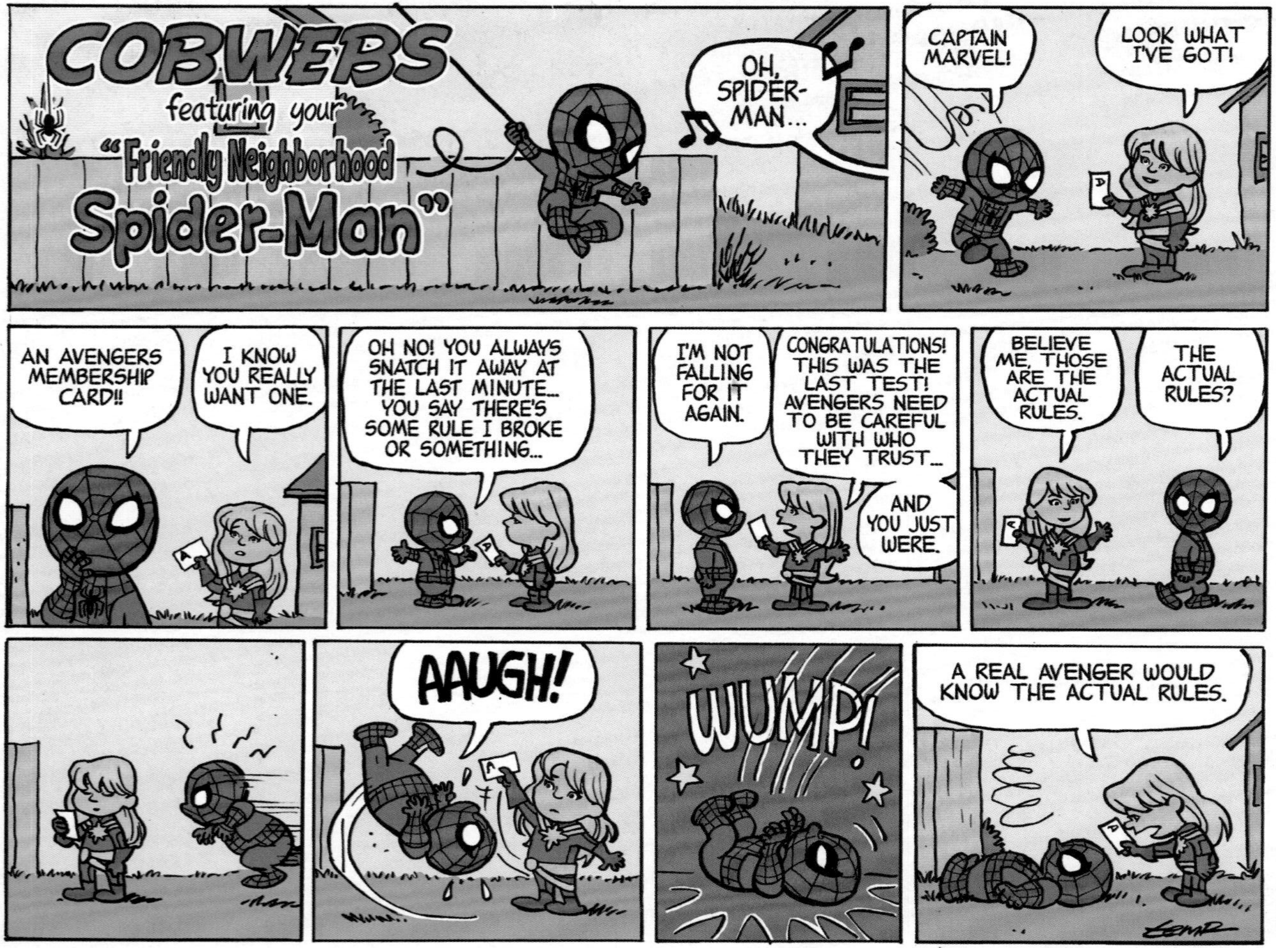
COBWEBS
featuring your "Friendly Neighborhood Spider-Man"
OH, SPIDER-MAN...
CAPTAIN MARVEL!
LOOK WHAT I'VE GOT!
AN AVENGERS MEMBERSHIP CARD!!
I KNOW YOU REALLY WANT ONE.
OH NO! YOU ALWAYS SNATCH IT AWAY AT THE LAST MINUTE... YOU SAY THERE'S SOME RULE I BROKE OR SOMETHING...
I'M NOT FALLING FOR IT AGAIN.
CONGRATULATIONS! THIS WAS THE LAST TEST! AVENGERS NEED TO BE CAREFUL WITH WHO THEY TRUST...
AND YOU JUST WERE.
BELIEVE ME, THOSE ARE THE ACTUAL RULES.
THE ACTUAL RULES?
AAUGH!
WUMP!
A REAL AVENGER WOULD KNOW THE ACTUAL RULES.

DAILY BUGLE

NEW YORK'S FUNNIEST DAILY NEWSPAPER

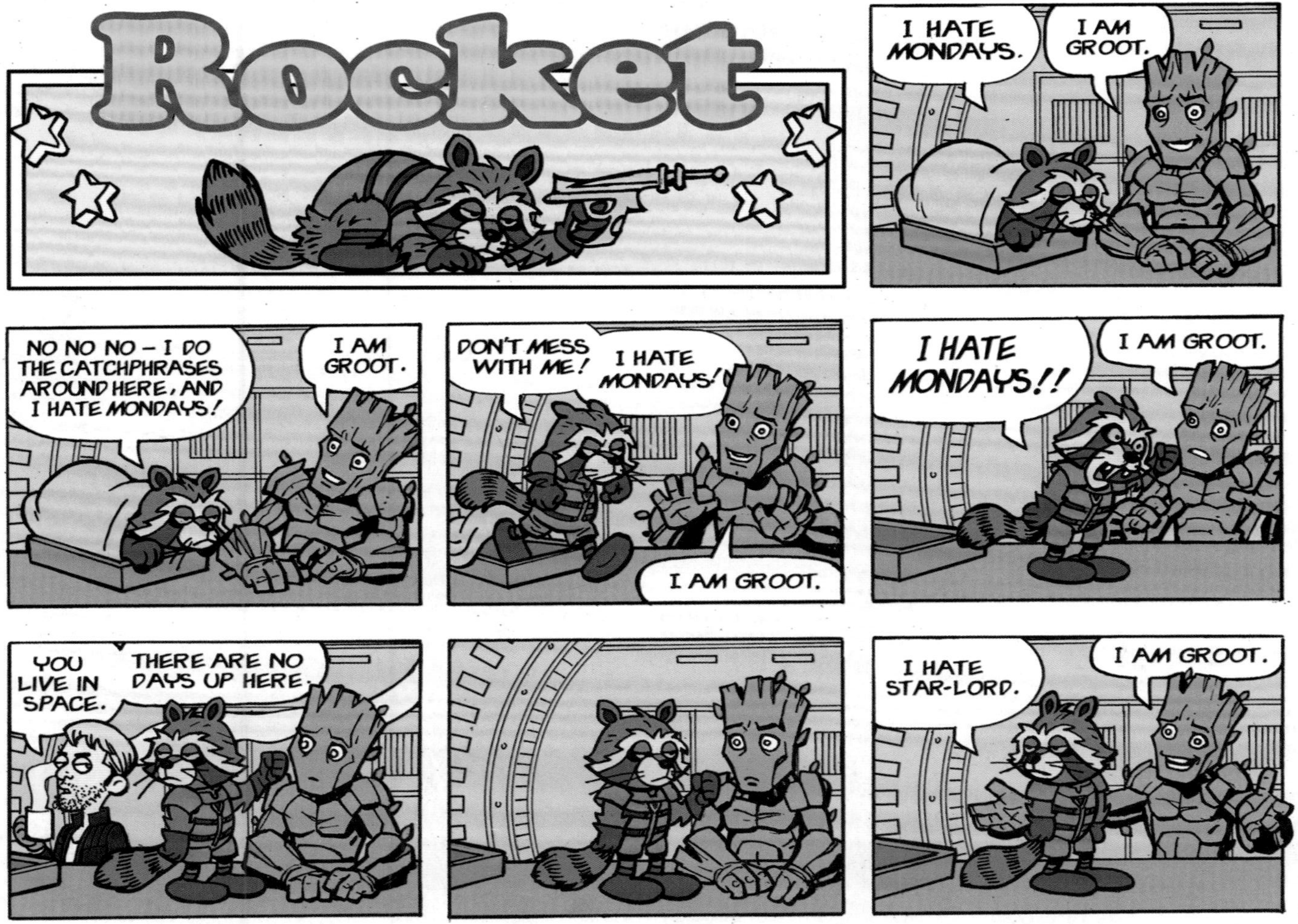
Rocket
I HATE MONDAYS.
I AM GROOT.
NO NO NO – I DO THE CATCHPHRASES AROUND HERE, AND I HATE MONDAYS!
I AM GROOT.
DON'T MESS WITH ME!
I HATE MONDAYS!
I AM GROOT.
I HATE MONDAYS!!
I AM GROOT.
YOU LIVE IN SPACE.
THERE ARE NO DAYS UP HERE.
I HATE STAR-LORD.
I AM GROOT.

DAILY BUGLE
NEW YORK'S FUNNIEST DAILY NEWSPAPER

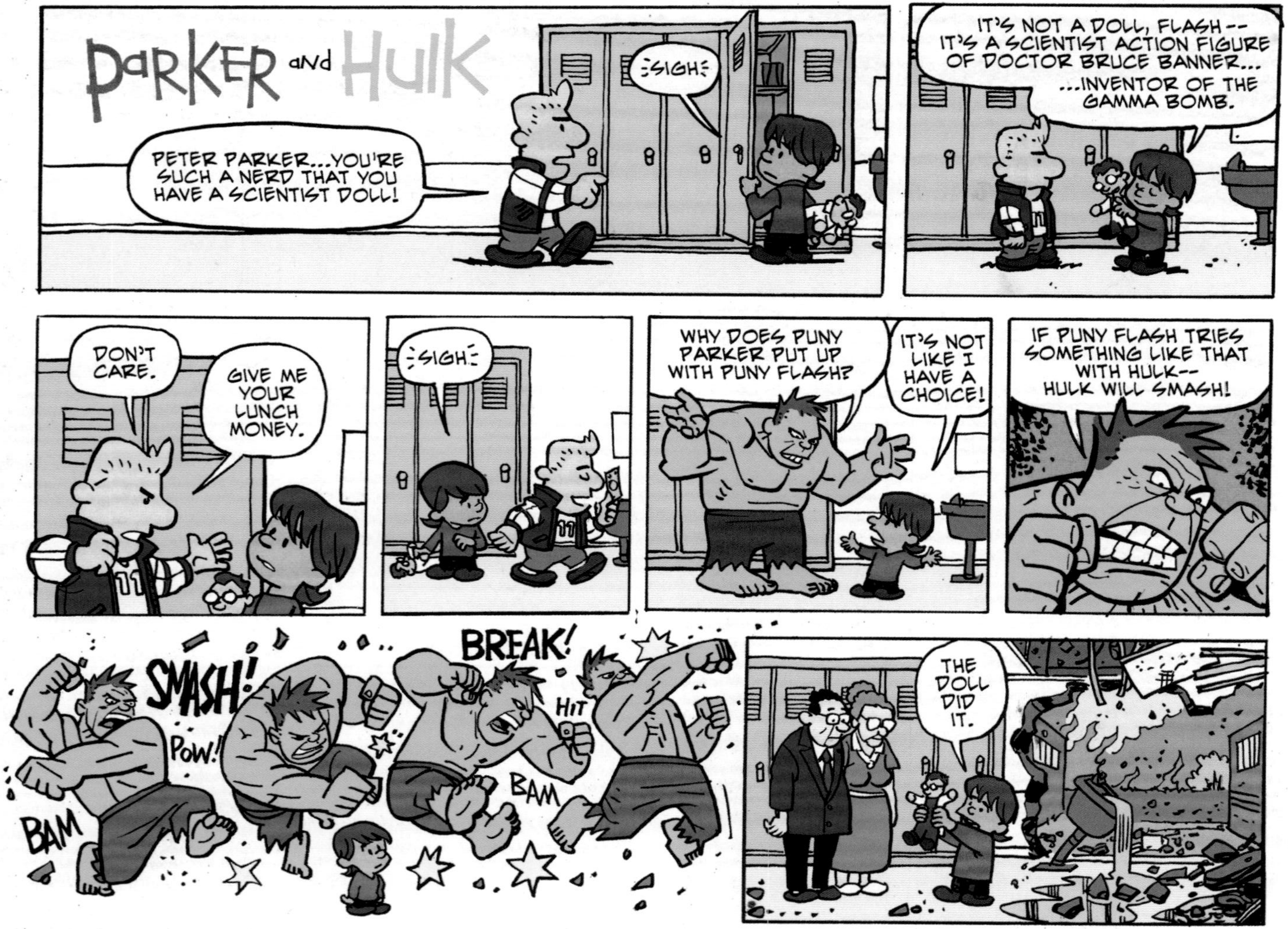
PARKER and HULK
PETER PARKER...YOU'RE SUCH A NERD THAT YOU HAVE A SCIENTIST DOLL!
SIGH
IT'S NOT A DOLL, FLASH -- IT'S A SCIENTIST ACTION FIGURE OF DOCTOR BRUCE BANNER...
...INVENTOR OF THE GAMMA BOMB.
DON'T CARE.
GIVE ME YOUR LUNCH MONEY.
SIGH
WHY DOES PUNY PARKER PUT UP WITH PUNY FLASH?
IT'S NOT LIKE I HAVE A CHOICE!
IF PUNY FLASH TRIES SOMETHING LIKE THAT WITH HULK-- HULK WILL SMASH!
BAM
SMASH!
POW!
BREAK!
HIT
BAM
THE DOLL DID IT.

the Strange Side

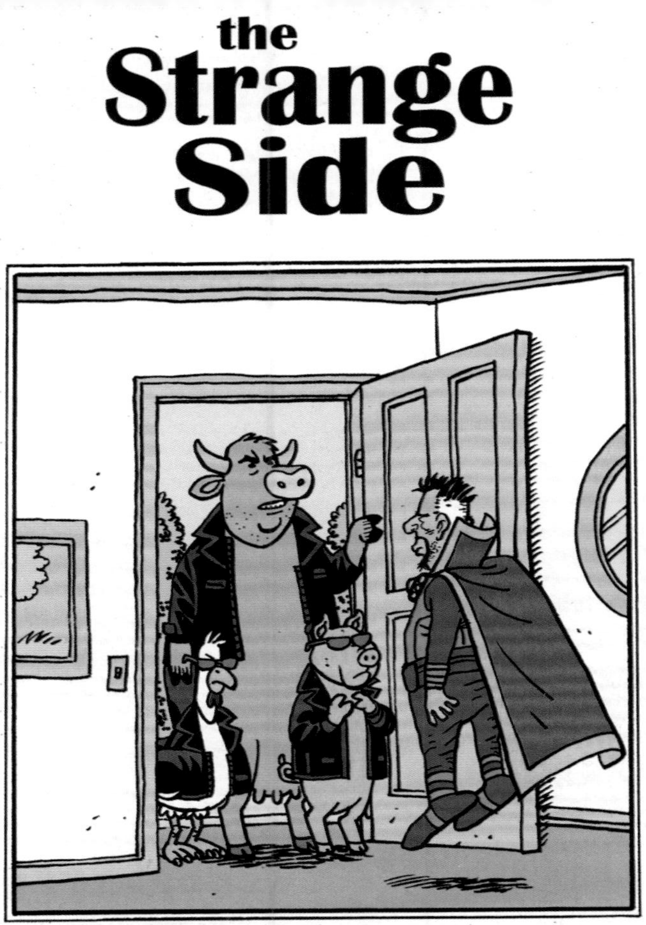

"We're from the farm next door.
You were spell casting in your sleep again."

The Villainy Circus

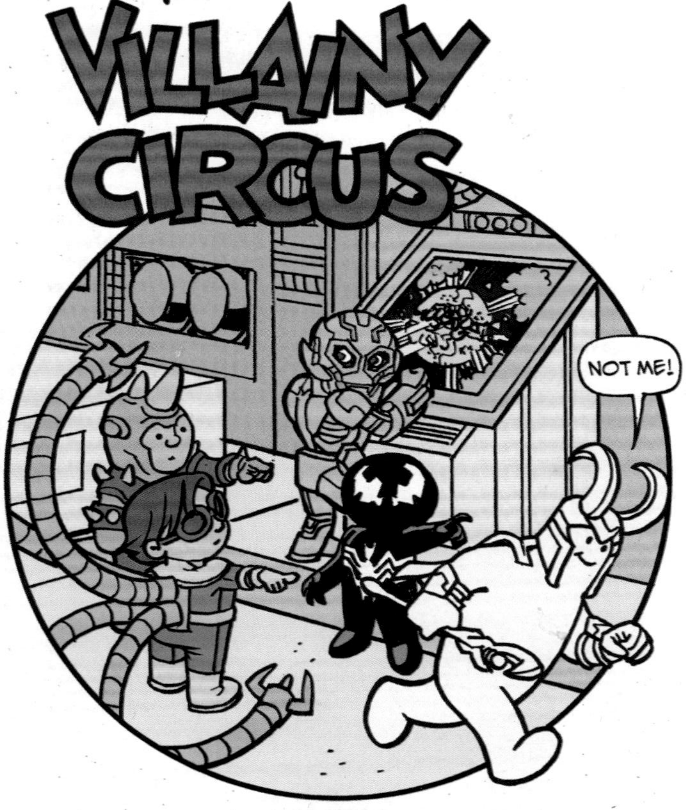
NOT ME!

"All right, WHO set off
my doomsday device?"

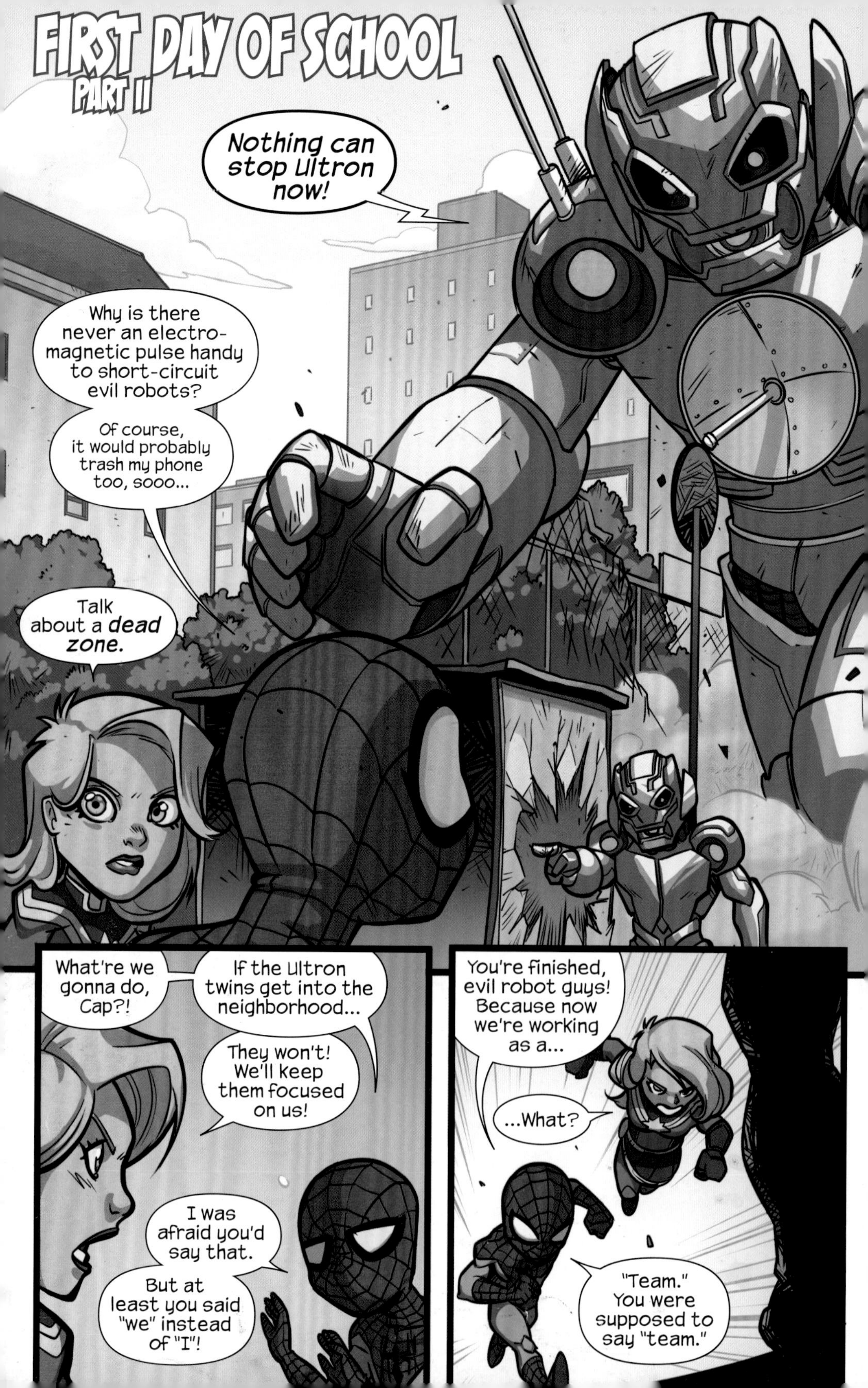
FIRST DAY OF SCHOOL
PART II
Nothing can stop Ultron now!
Why is there never an electro-magnetic pulse handy to short-circuit evil robots?
Of course, it would probably trash my phone too, sooo...
Talk about a dead zone.
What're we gonna do, Cap?!
If the Ultron twins get into the neighborhood...
They won't! We'll keep them focused on us!
I was afraid you'd say that.
But at least you said "we" instead of "I"!
You're finished, evil robot guys! Because now we're working as a...
...What?
"Team." You were supposed to say "team."

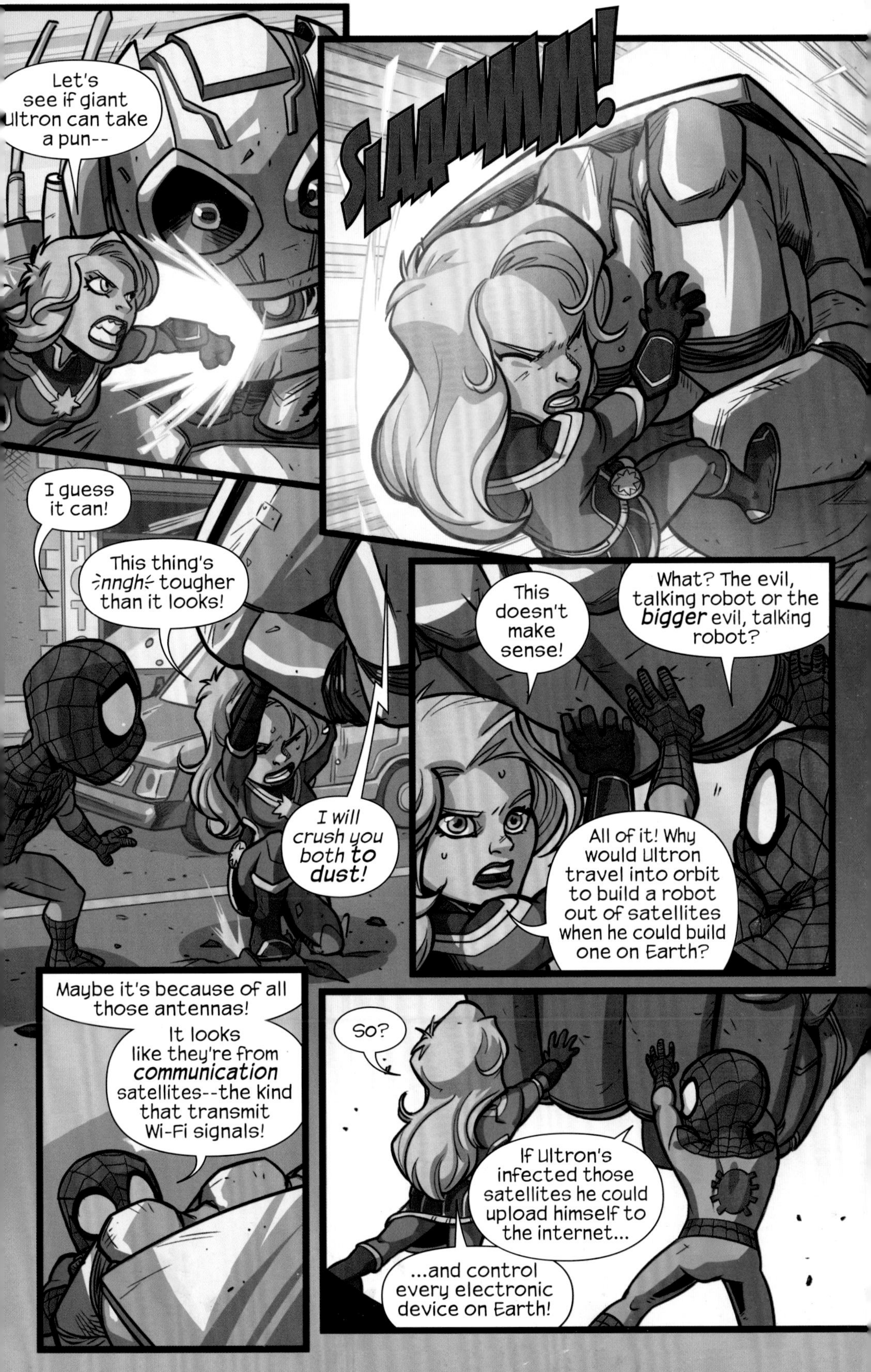
Let's see if giant Ultron can take a pun--
SLAAMMM!
I guess it can!
This thing's -nngh- tougher than it looks!
I will crush you both to dust!
This doesn't make sense!
What? The evil, talking robot or the bigger evil, talking robot?
All of it! Why would Ultron travel into orbit to build a robot out of satellites when he could build one on Earth?
Maybe it's because of all those antennas!
It looks like they're from communication satellites--the kind that transmit Wi-Fi signals!
So?
If Ultron's infected those satellites he could upload himself to the internet...
...and control every electronic device on Earth!

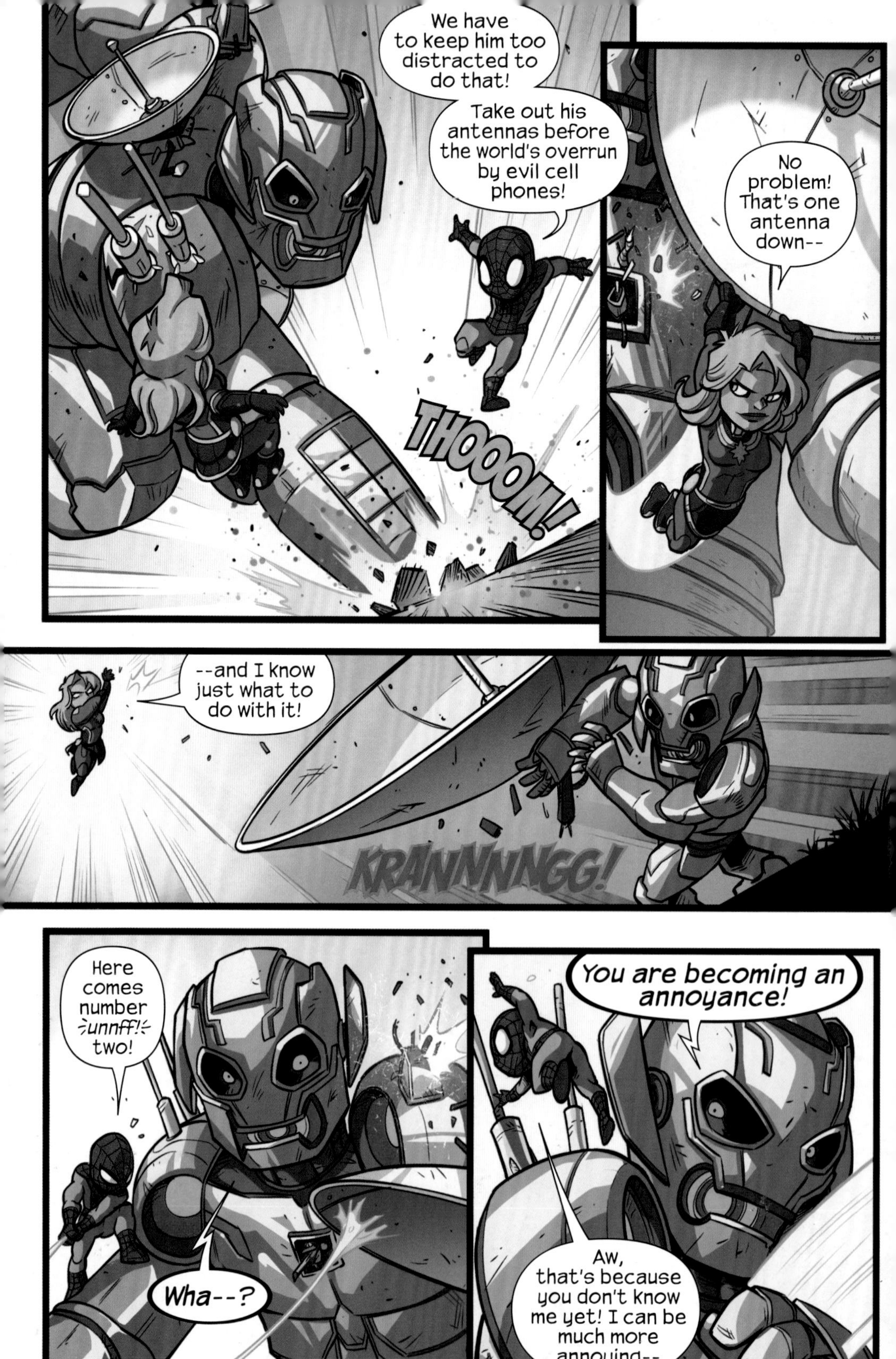
We have to keep him too distracted to do that!
Take out his antennas before the world's overrun by evil cell phones!
THOOOM!
No problem! That's one antenna down--
--and I know just what to do with it!
KRANNNNGG!
Here comes number unnff! two!
Wha--?
You are becoming an annoyance!
Aw, that's because you don't know me yet! I can be much more annoying--

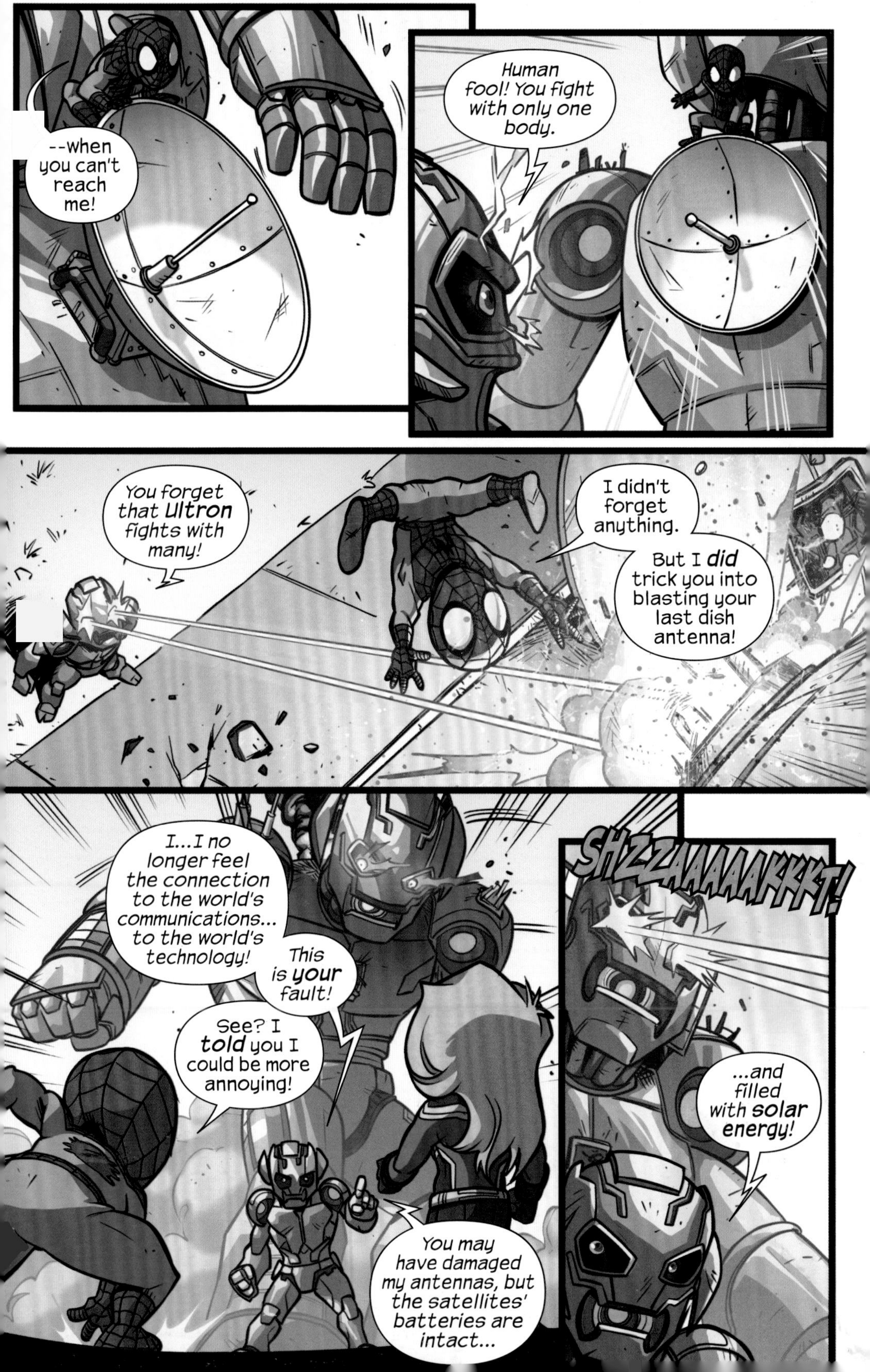
--when you can't reach me!
Human fool! You fight with only one body.
You forget that Ultron fights with many!
I didn't forget anything.
But I did trick you into blasting your last dish antenna!
I...I no longer feel the connection to the world's communications... to the world's technology!
This is your fault!
See? I told you I could be more annoying!
You may have damaged my antennas, but the satellites' batteries are intact...
SHZZAAAAAKKKT!
...and filled with solar energy!

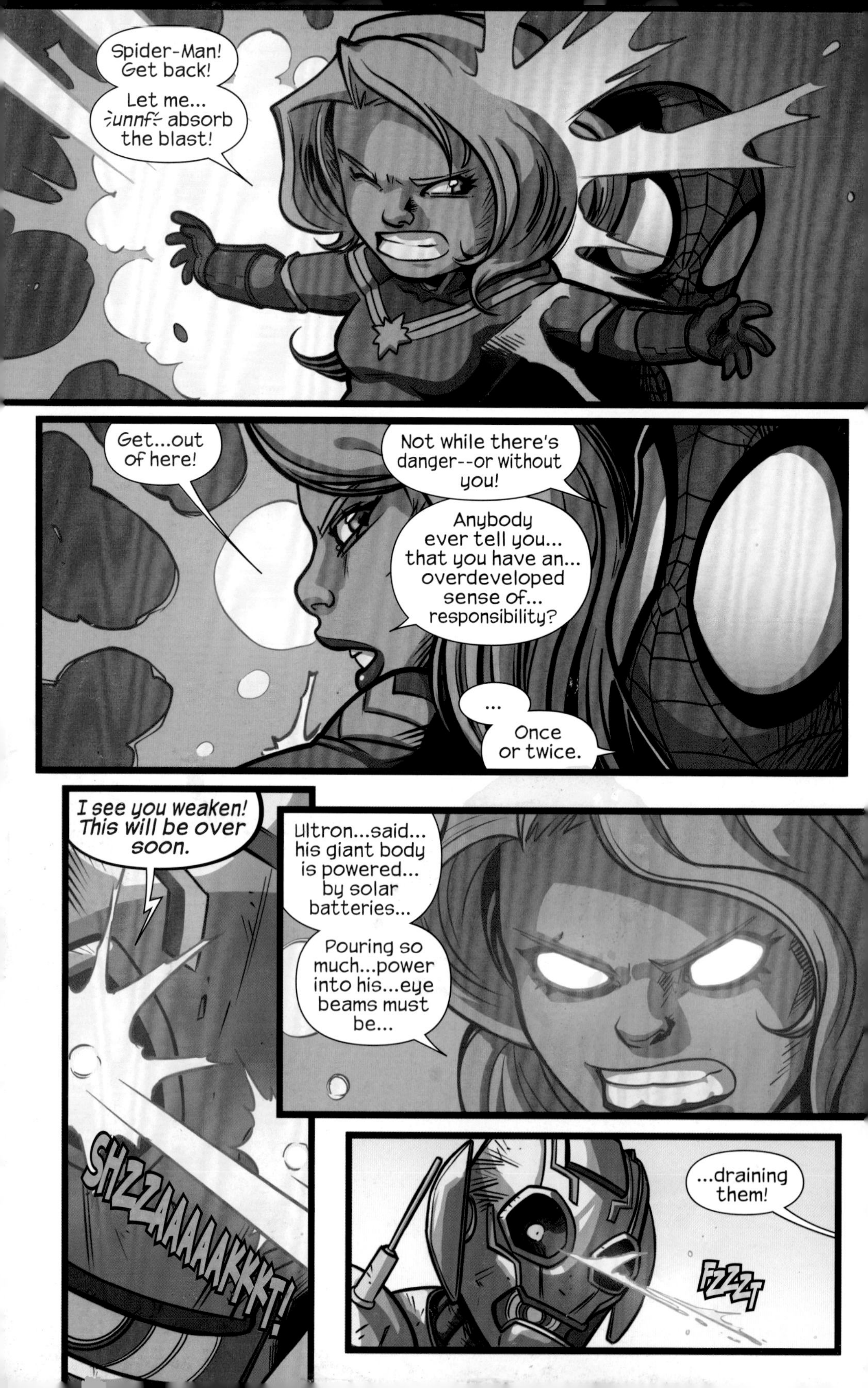
Spider-Man! Get back!
Let me... -unnf- absorb the blast!
Get...out of here!
Not while there's danger--or without you!
Anybody ever tell you... that you have an... overdeveloped sense of... responsibility?
...
Once or twice.
I see you weaken! This will be over soon.
Ultron...said... his giant body is powered... by solar batteries...
Pouring so much...power into his...eye beams must be...
SHZZAAAAAKKKT!
...draining them!
FZZZT

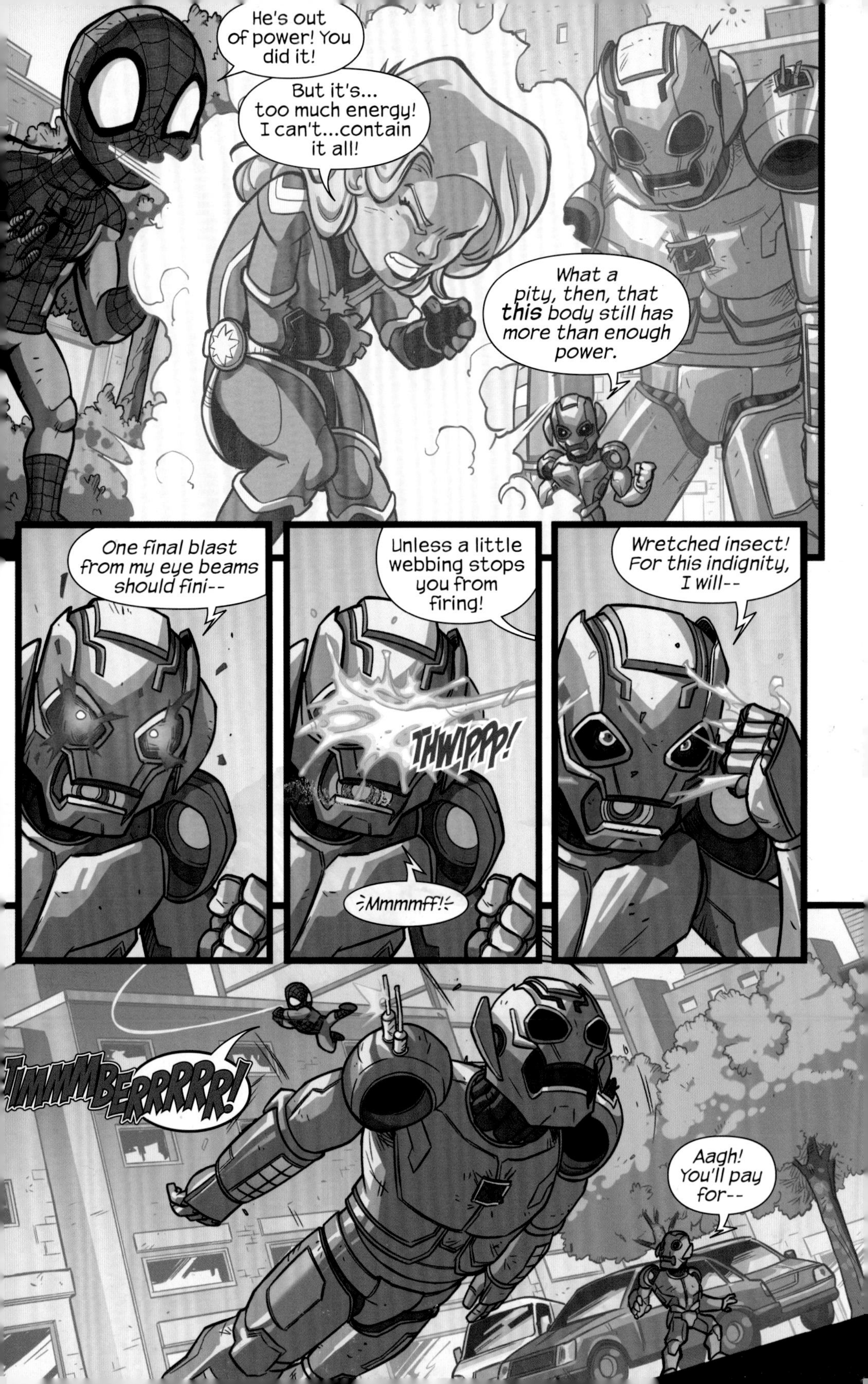
He's out of power! You did it!
But it's... too much energy! I can't...contain it all!
What a pity, then, that **this** body still has more than enough power.
One final blast from my eye beams should fini--
Unless a little webbing stops you from firing!
THWIPPP!
Mmmmff!
Wretched insect! For this indignity, I will--
TIMMMBERRRRR!
Aagh! You'll pay for--

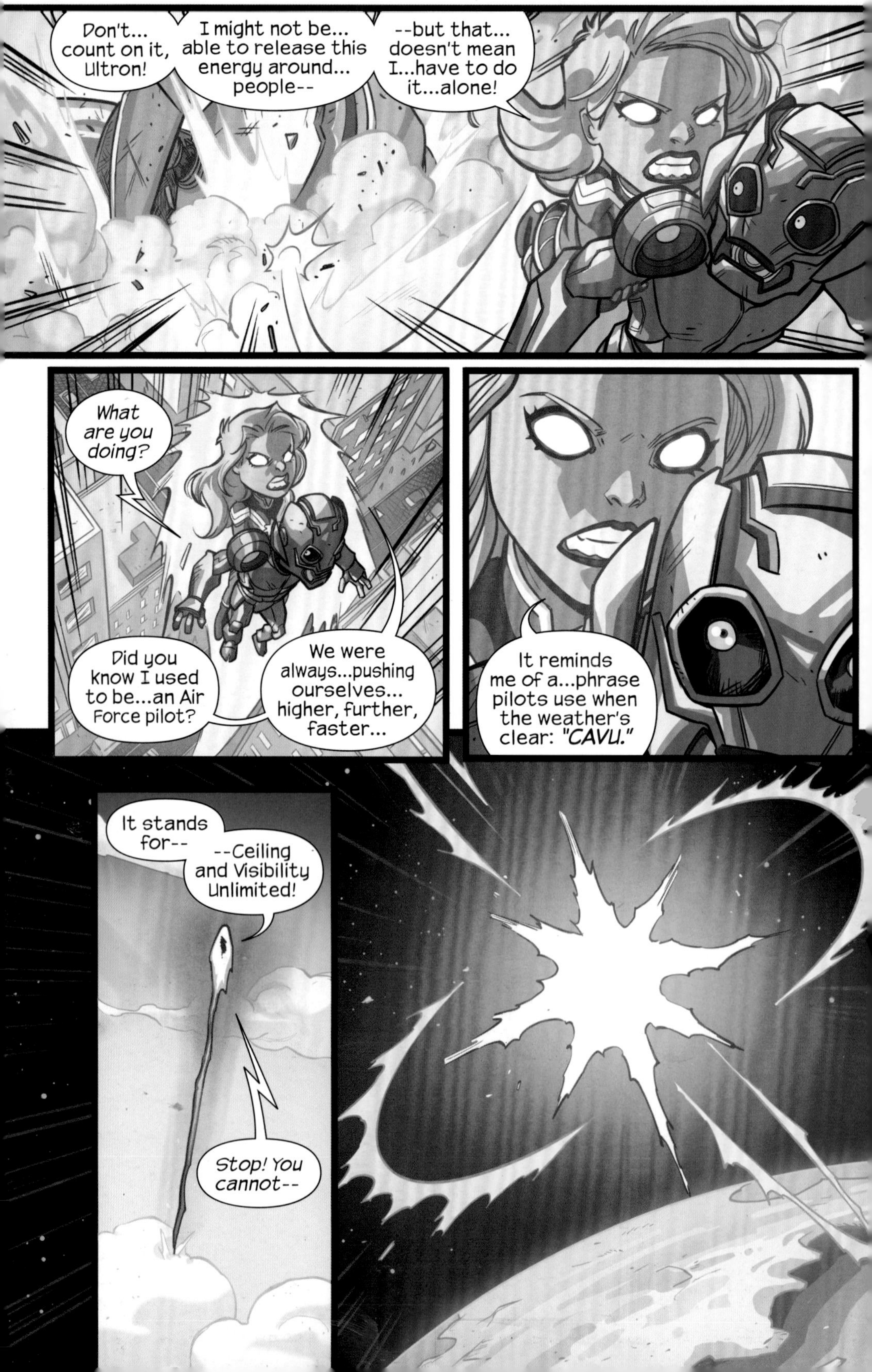
Don't... count on it, Ultron!
I might not be... able to release this energy around... people--
--but that... doesn't mean I...have to do it...alone!
What are you doing?
Did you know I used to be...an Air Force pilot?
We were always...pushing ourselves... higher, further, faster...
It reminds me of a...phrase pilots use when the weather's clear: "CAVU."
It stands for--
--Ceiling and Visibility Unlimited!
Stop! You cannot--

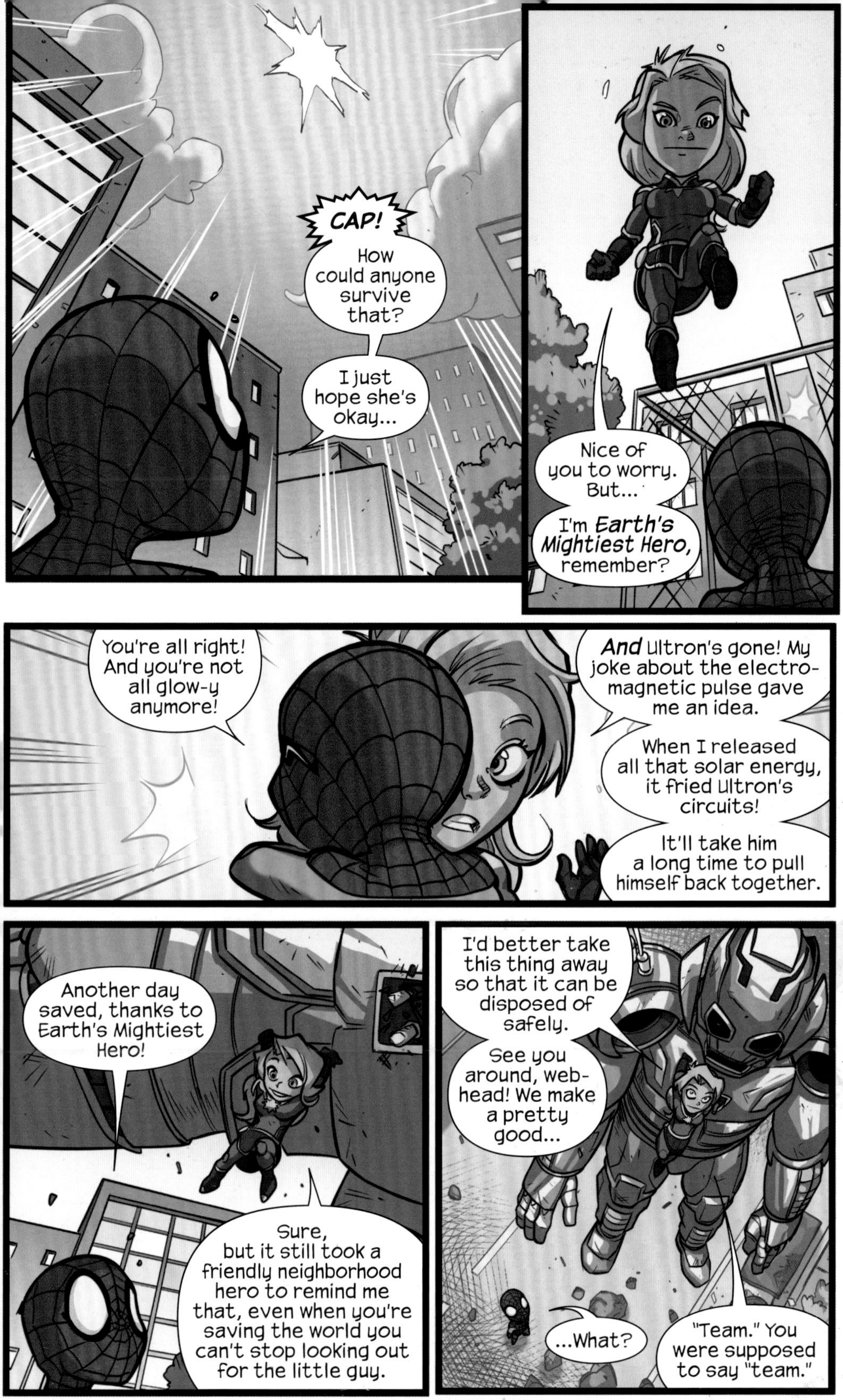
CAP!
How could anyone survive that?
I just hope she's okay...
Nice of you to worry. But...
I'm Earth's Mightiest Hero, remember?
You're all right! And you're not all glow-y anymore!
And Ultron's gone! My joke about the electro-magnetic pulse gave me an idea.
When I released all that solar energy, it fried Ultron's circuits!
It'll take him a long time to pull himself back together.
Another day saved, thanks to Earth's Mightiest Hero!
Sure, but it still took a friendly neighborhood hero to remind me that, even when you're saving the world you can't stop looking out for the little guy.
I'd better take this thing away so that it can be disposed of safely.
See you around, web-head! We make a pretty good...
...What?
"Team." You were supposed to say "team."

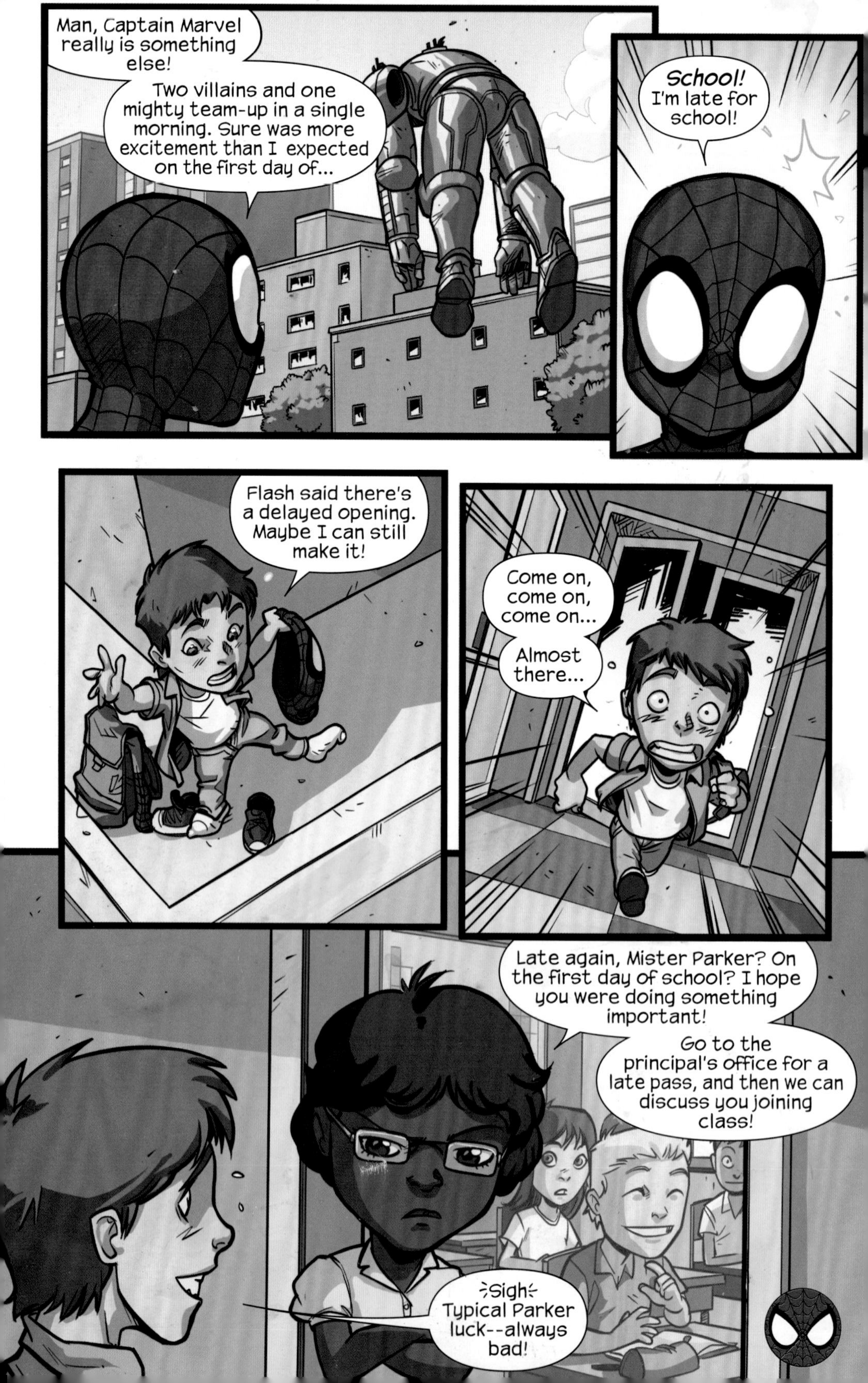
Man, Captain Marvel really is something else!
Two villains and one mighty team-up in a single morning. Sure was more excitement than I expected on the first day of...
School! I'm late for school!
Flash said there's a delayed opening. Maybe I can still make it!
Come on, come on, come on...
Almost there...
Late again, Mister Parker? On the first day of school? I hope you were doing something important!
Go to the principal's office for a late pass, and then we can discuss you joining class!
Sigh
Typical Parker luck--always bad!

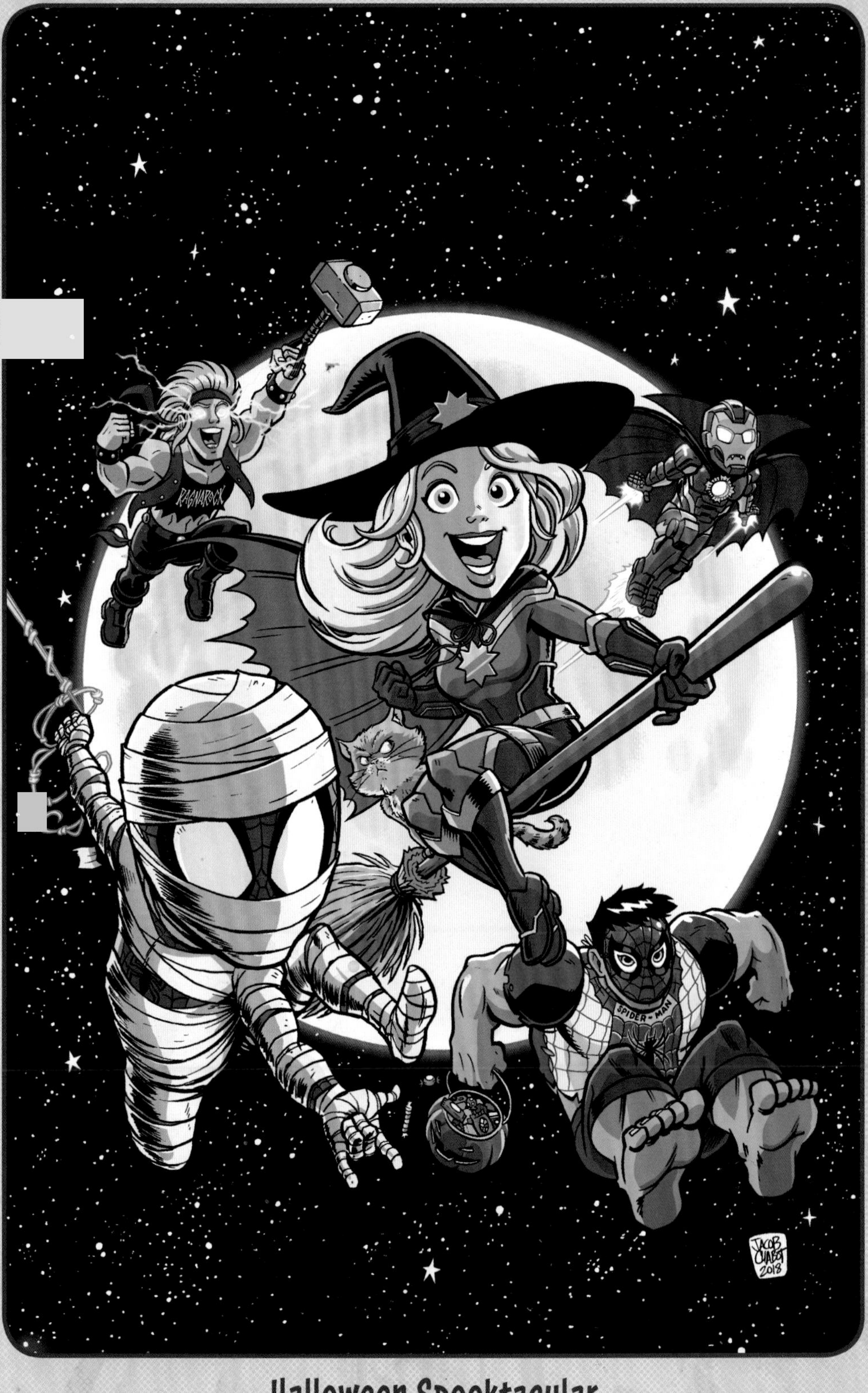
RAGNAROCK
SPIDER-MAN
JACOB CHABOT 2018

Halloween Spooktacular

cover by Jacob Chabot

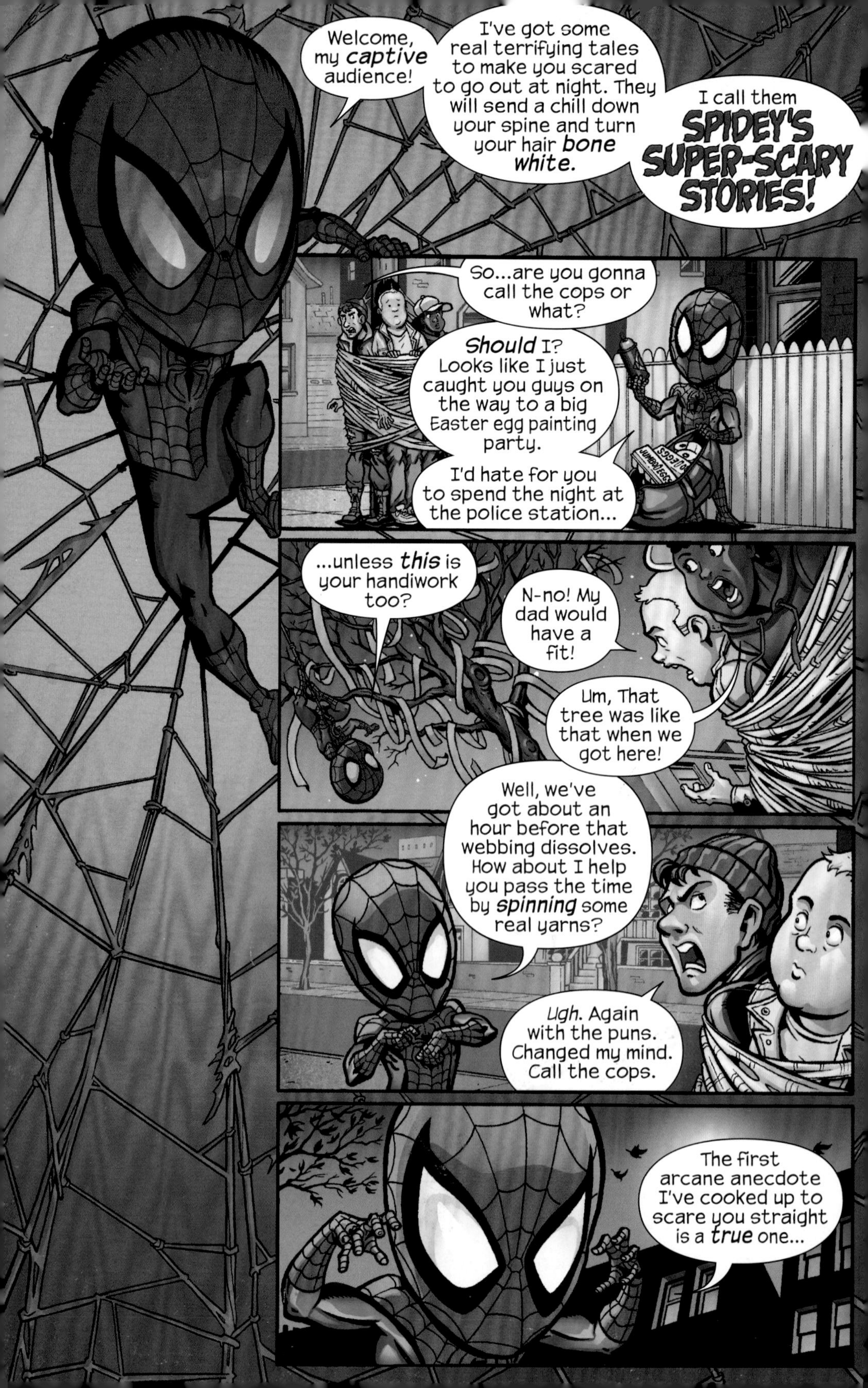
Welcome, my *captive* audience!
I've got some real terrifying tales to make you scared to go out at night. They will send a chill down your spine and turn your hair *bone white.*
I call them SPIDEY'S SUPER-SCARY STORIES!
So...are you gonna call the cops or what?
Should I? Looks like I just caught you guys on the way to a big Easter egg painting party.
I'd hate for you to spend the night at the police station...
...unless *this* is your handiwork too?
N-no! My dad would have a fit!
Um, That tree was like that when we got here!
Well, we've got about an hour before that webbing dissolves. How about I help you pass the time by *spinning* some real yarns?
Ugh. Again with the puns. Changed my mind. Call the cops.
The first arcane anecdote I've cooked up to scare you straight is a *true* one...

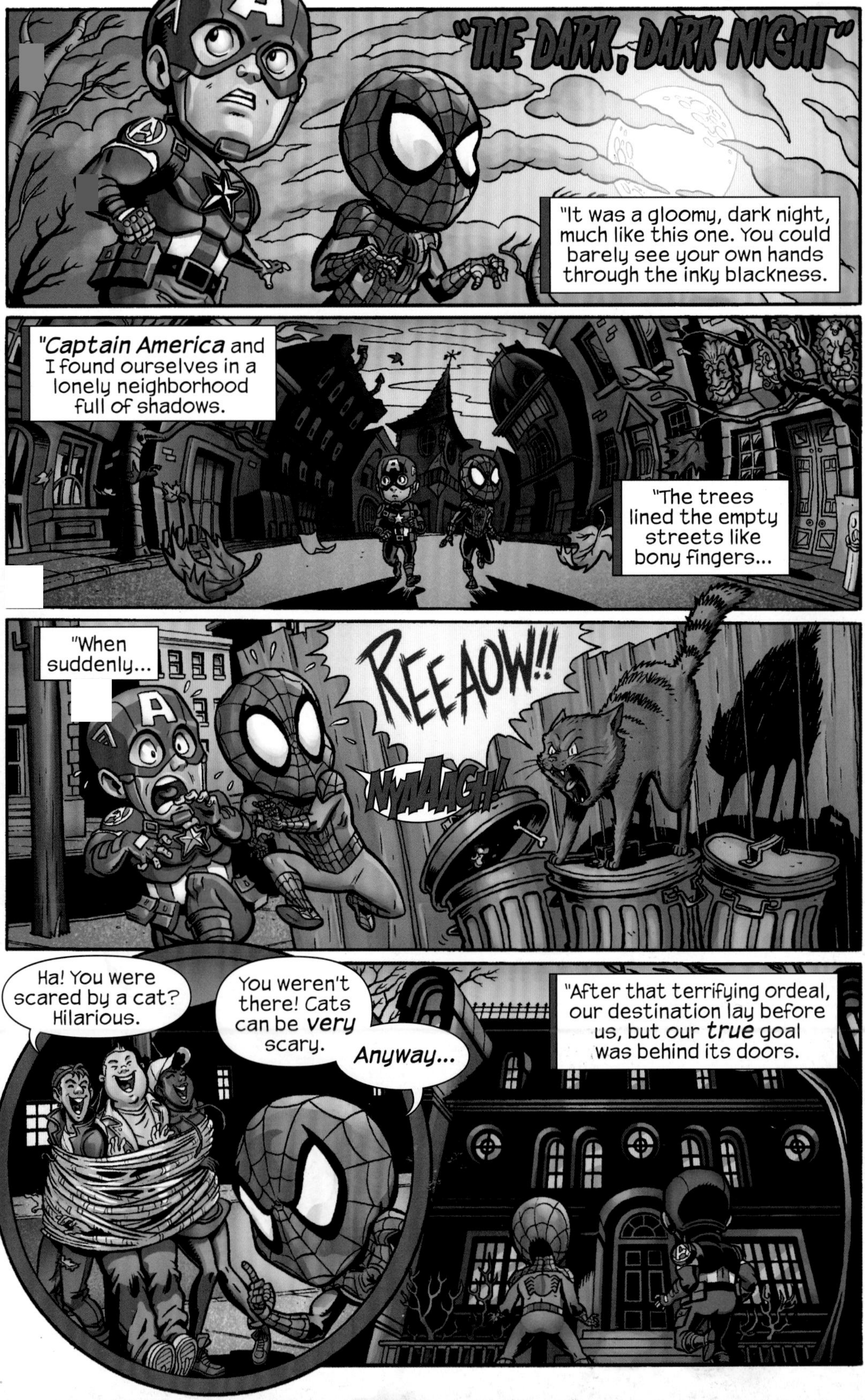
"THE DARK, DARK NIGHT"
"It was a gloomy, dark night, much like this one. You could barely see your own hands through the inky blackness.
"Captain America and I found ourselves in a lonely neighborhood full of shadows.
"The trees lined the empty streets like bony fingers...
"When suddenly...
REEAOW!!
NYAAAGH!
Ha! You were scared by a cat? Hilarious.
You weren't there! Cats can be very scary.
Anyway...
"After that terrifying ordeal, our destination lay before us, but our true goal was behind its doors.

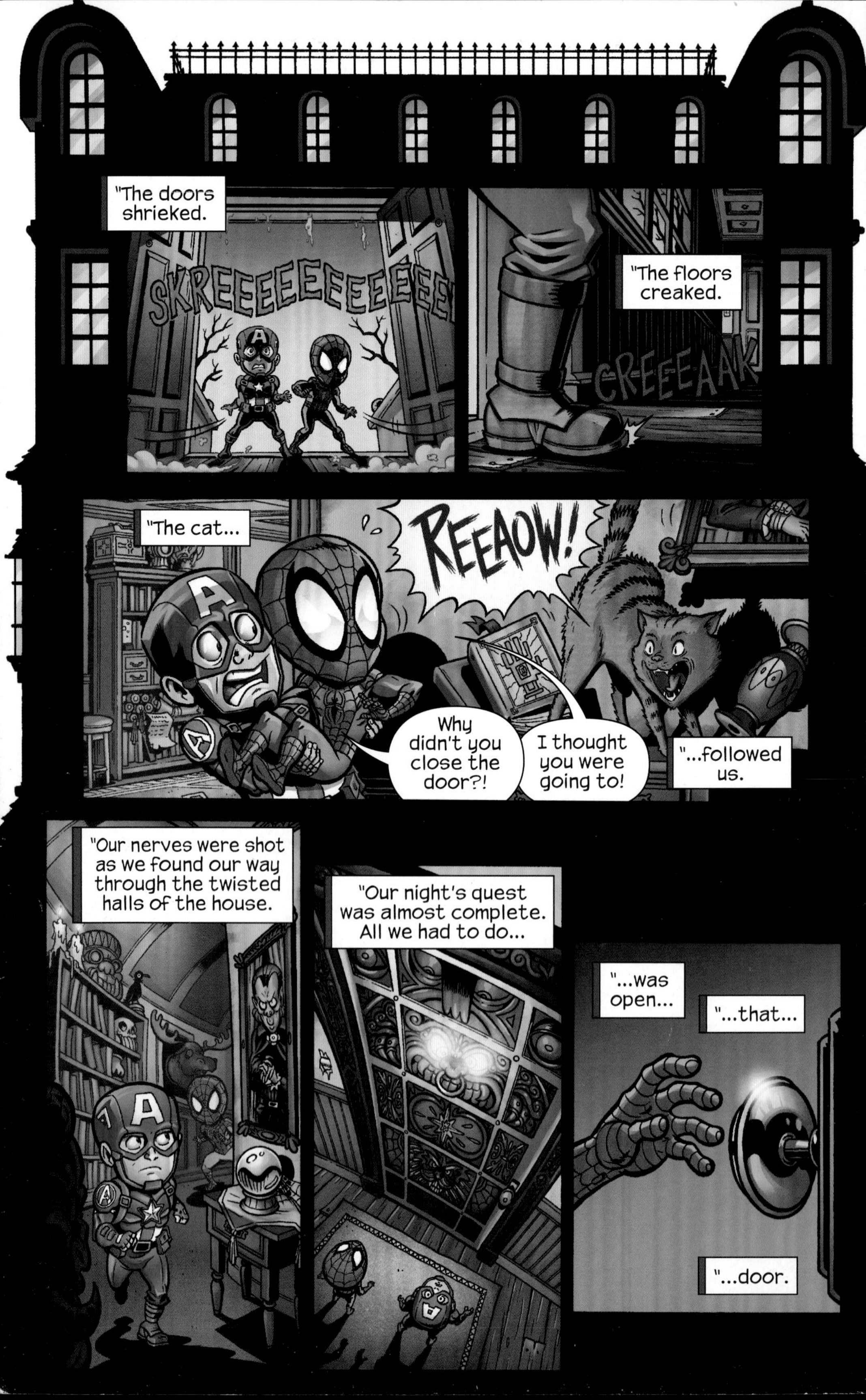
"The doors shrieked.
SKREEEEEEEEEEEEE
"The floors creaked.
CREEEAAK
"The cat...
REEAOW!
Why didn't you close the door?!
I thought you were going to!
"...followed us.
"Our nerves were shot as we found our way through the twisted halls of the house.
"Our night's quest was almost complete. All we had to do...
"...was open...
"...that...
"...door.

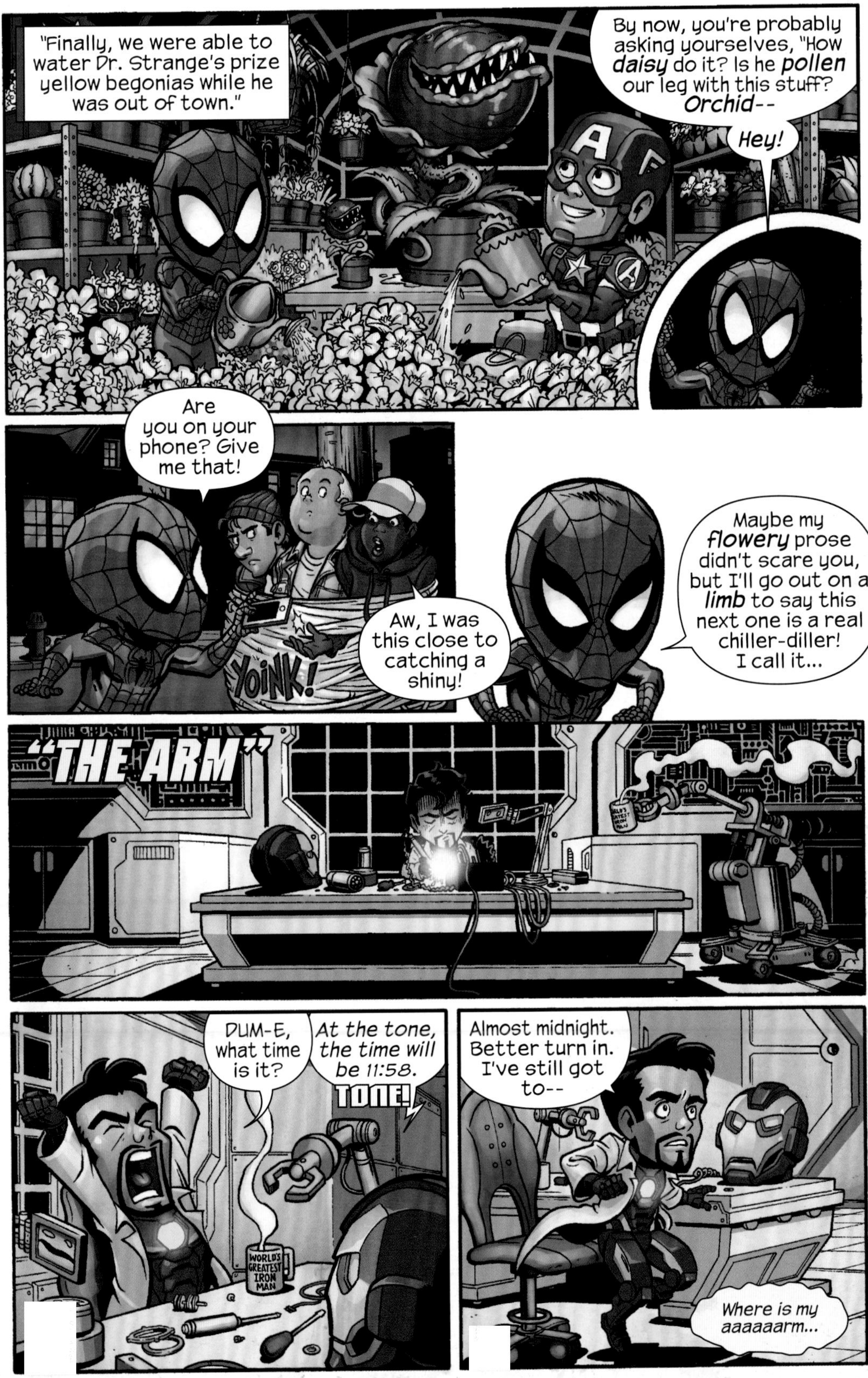
"Finally, we were able to water Dr. Strange's prize yellow begonias while he was out of town."
By now, you're probably asking yourselves, "How daisy do it? Is he pollen our leg with this stuff? Orchid--
Hey!
Are you on your phone? Give me that!
YOINK!
Aw, I was this close to catching a shiny!
Maybe my flowery prose didn't scare you, but I'll go out on a limb to say this next one is a real chiller-diller! I call it...
"THE ARM"
DUM-E, what time is it?
At the tone, the time will be 11:58.
TONE!
WORLD'S GREATEST IRON MAN
Almost midnight. Better turn in. I've still got to--
Where is my aaaaaarm...

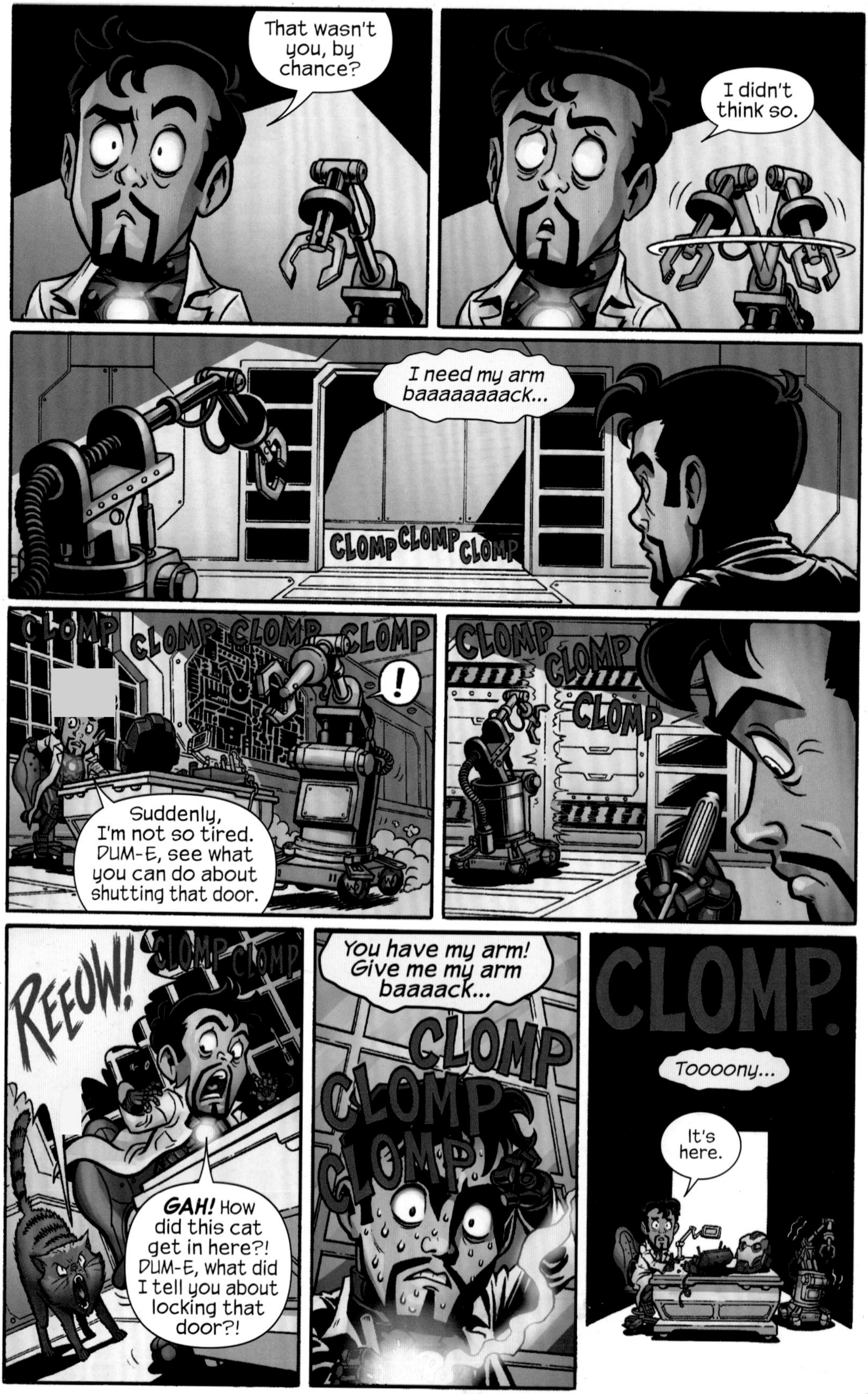
That wasn't you, by chance?
I didn't think so.
I need my arm baaaaaaaack...
CLOMP CLOMP CLOMP
CLOMP CLOMP CLOMP CLOMP
!
Suddenly, I'm not so tired. DUM-E, see what you can do about shutting that door.
CLOMP CLOMP CLOMP
REEOW!
CLOMP CLOMP
GAH! How did this cat get in here?! DUM-E, what did I tell you about locking that door?!
You have my arm! Give me my arm baaaack...
CLOMP CLOMP CLOMP
CLOMP.
Toooony...
It's here.

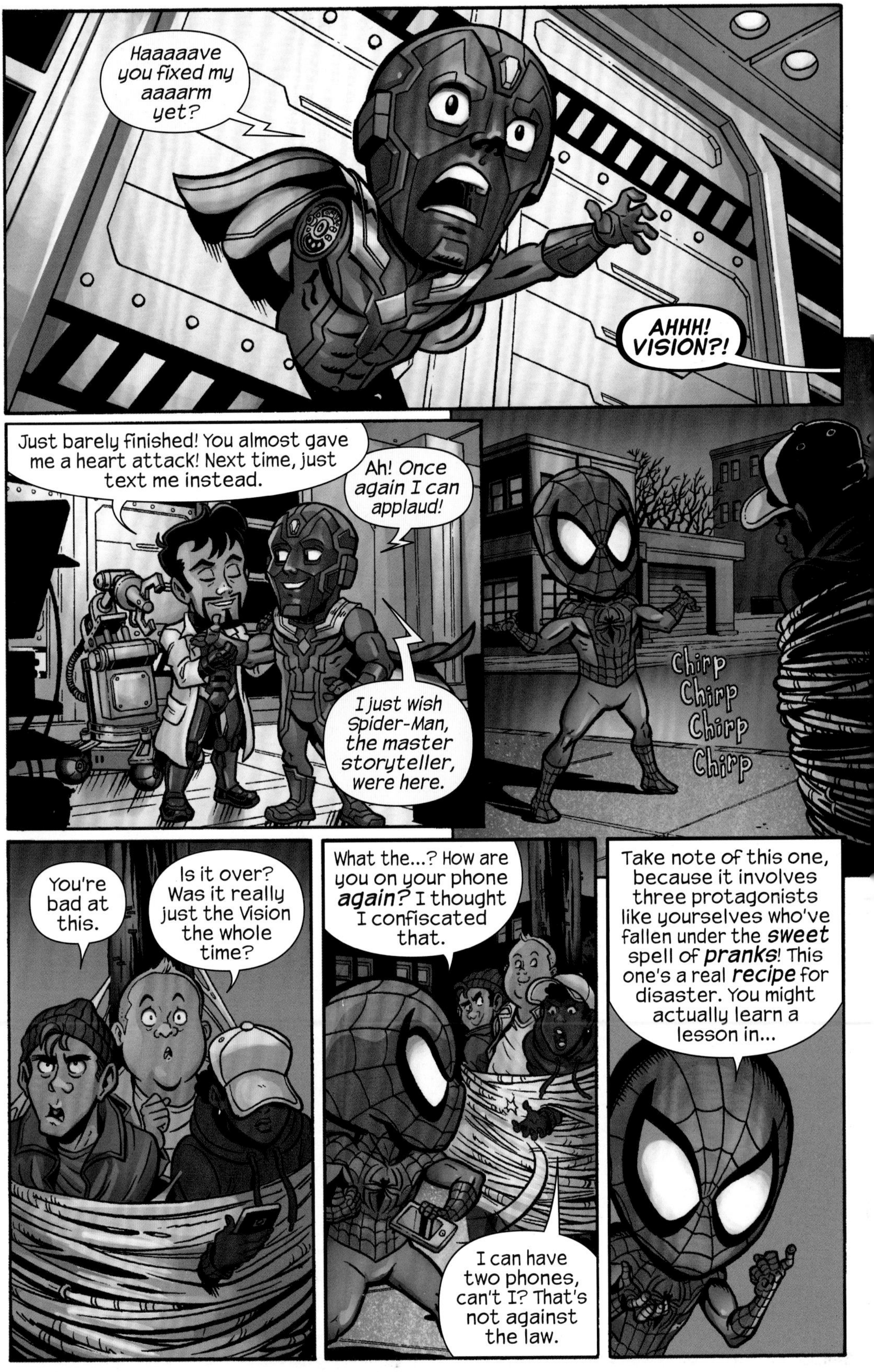

Haaaaave you fixed my aaaarm yet?
AHHH! VISION?!
Just barely finished! You almost gave me a heart attack! Next time, just text me instead.
Ah! Once again I can applaud!
I just wish Spider-Man, the master storyteller, were here.
Chirp Chirp Chirp Chirp
You're bad at this.
Is it over? Was it really just the Vision the whole time?
What the...? How are you on your phone again? I thought I confiscated that.
I can have two phones, can't I? That's not against the law.
Take note of this one, because it involves three protagonists like yourselves who've fallen under the sweet spell of pranks! This one's a real recipe for disaster. You might actually learn a lesson in...

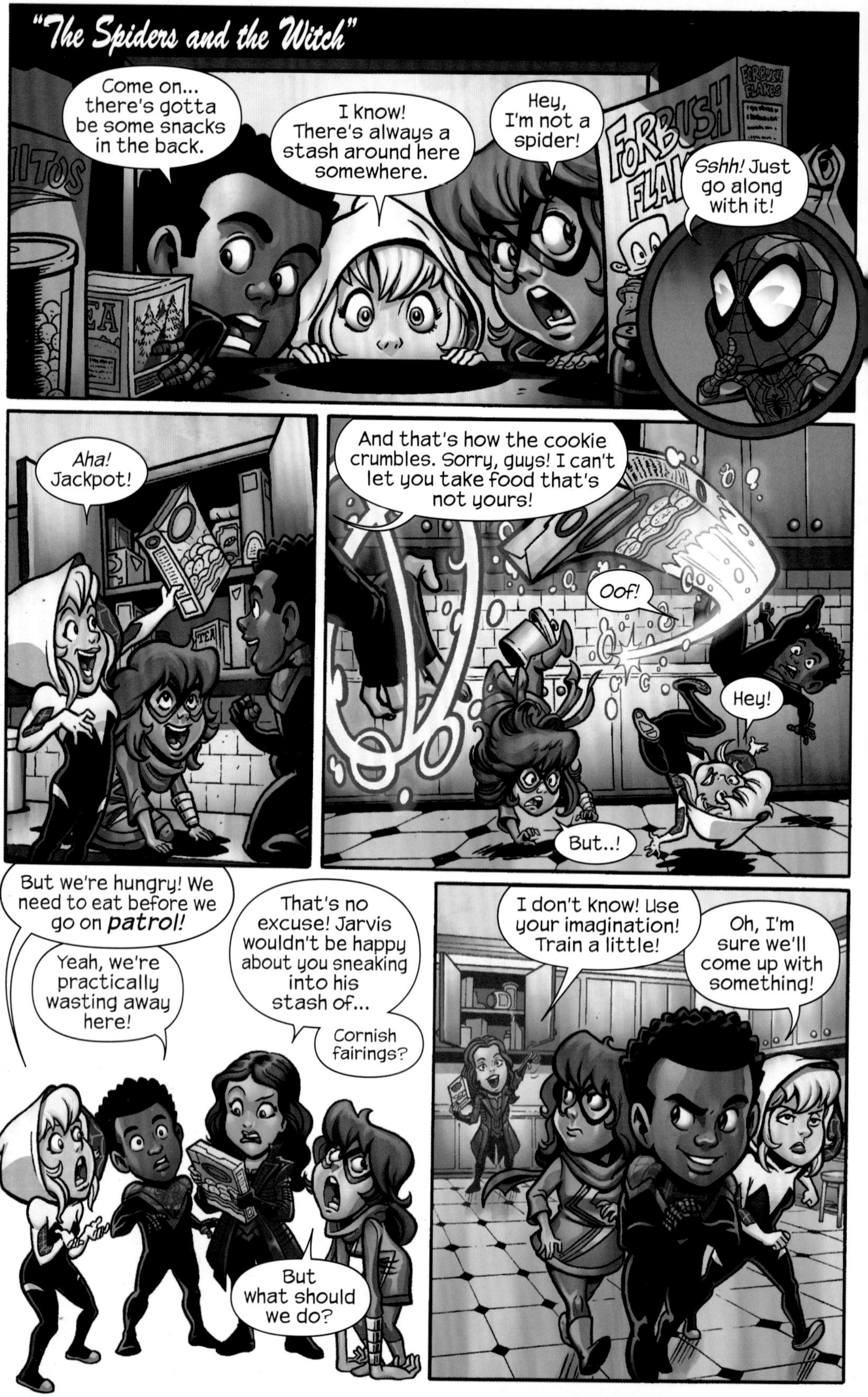
"The Spiders and the Witch"
Come on... there's gotta be some snacks in the back.
I know! There's always a stash around here somewhere.
Hey, I'm not a spider!
Sshh! Just go along with it!
FORBUSH FLAKES
TEA
Aha! Jackpot!
TEA
And that's how the cookie crumbles. Sorry, guys! I can't let you take food that's not yours!
Oof!
Hey!
But..!
But we're hungry! We need to eat before we go on *patrol!*
Yeah, we're practically wasting away here!
That's no excuse! Jarvis wouldn't be happy about you sneaking into his stash of...
Cornish fairings?
But what should we do?
I don't know! Use your imagination! Train a little!
Oh, I'm sure we'll come up with something!

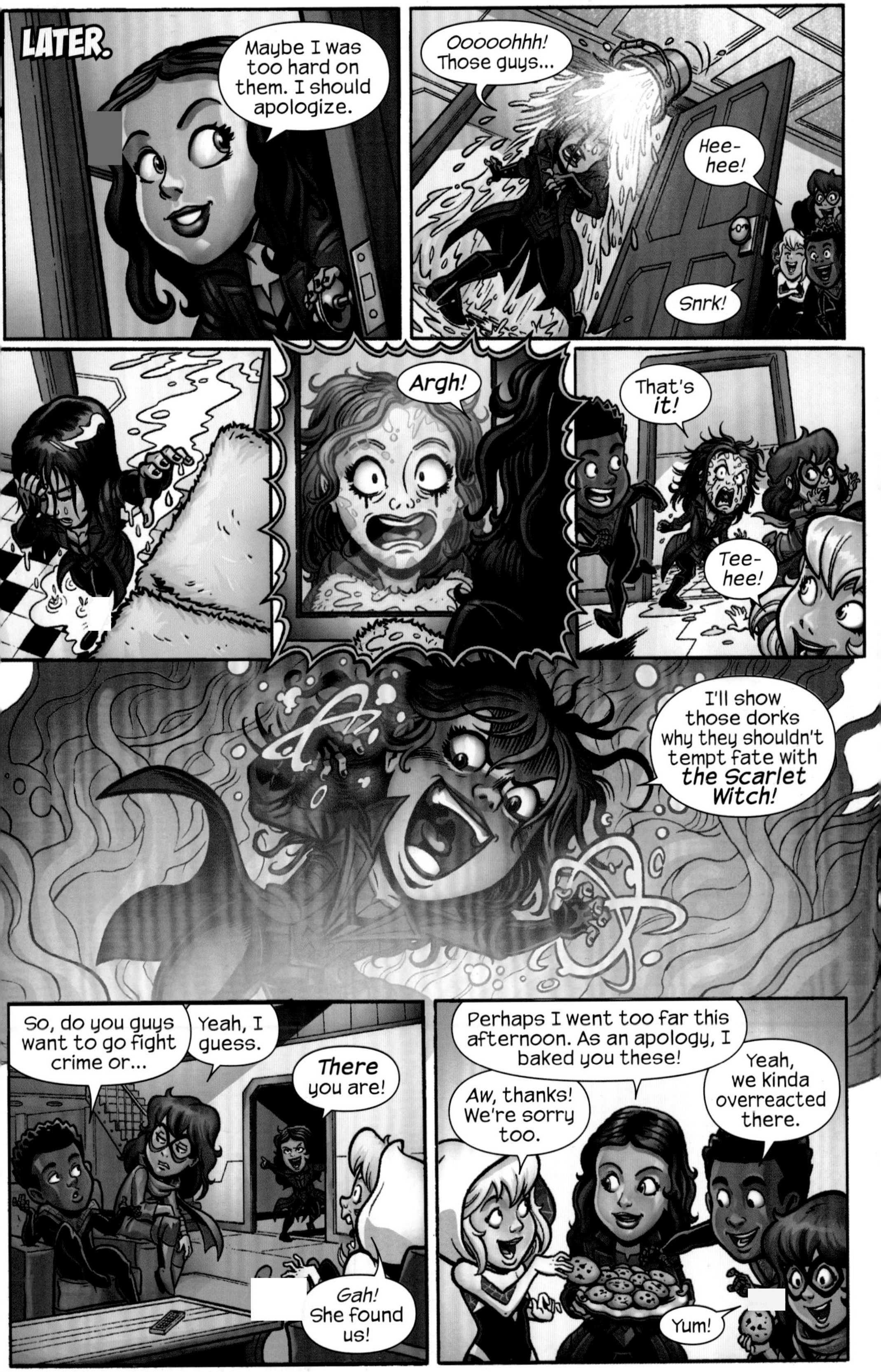
LATER.
Maybe I was too hard on them. I should apologize.
Ooooohhh! Those guys...
Hee-hee!
Snrk!
Argh!
That's it!
Tee-hee!
I'll show those dorks why they shouldn't tempt fate with the Scarlet Witch!
So, do you guys want to go fight crime or...
Yeah, I guess.
There you are!
Gah! She found us!
Perhaps I went too far this afternoon. As an apology, I baked you these!
Aw, thanks! We're sorry too.
Yeah, we kinda overreacted there.
Yum!

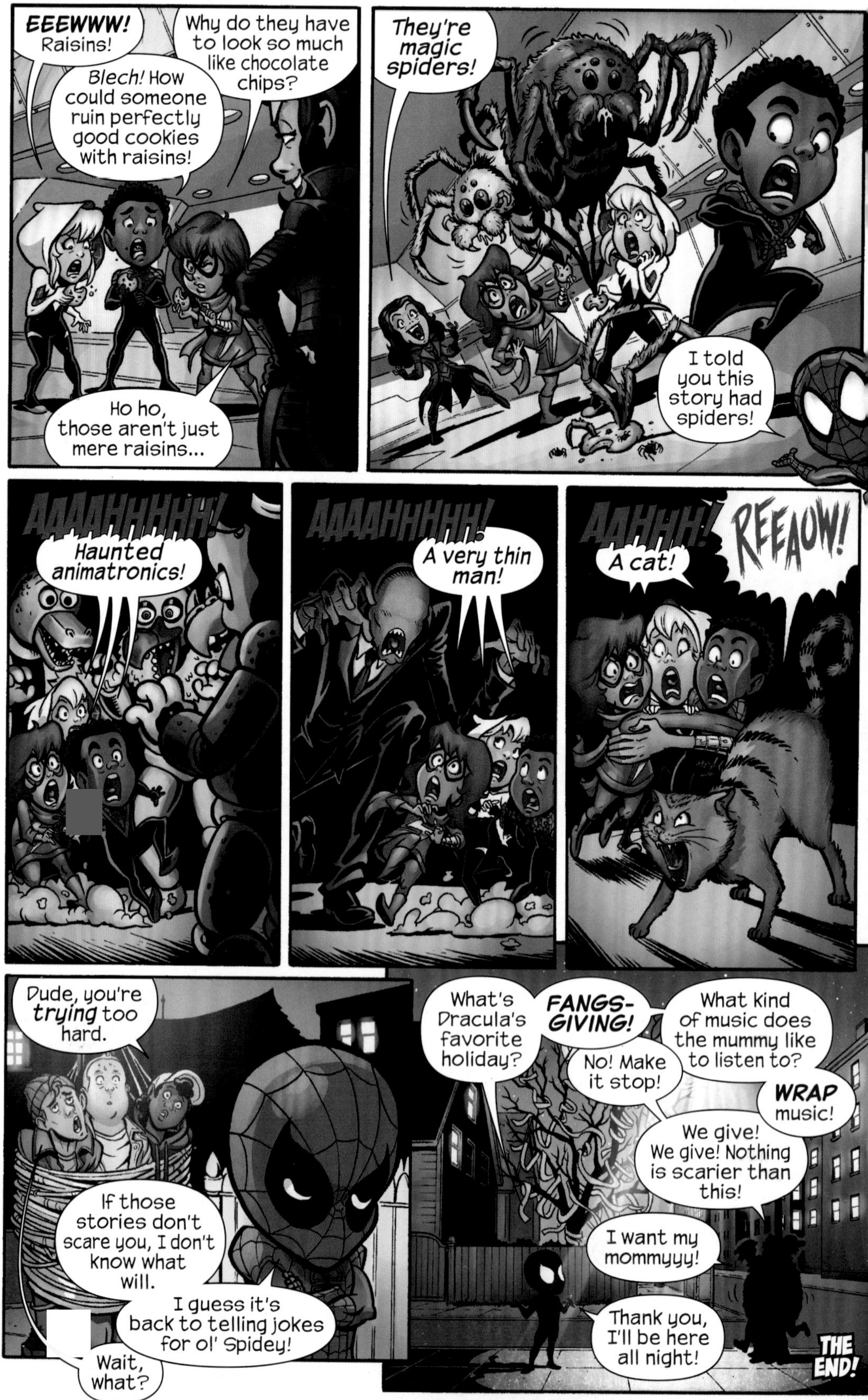
EEEWWW! Raisins!
Blech! How could someone ruin perfectly good cookies with raisins!
Why do they have to look so much like chocolate chips?
Ho ho, those aren't just mere raisins...
They're magic spiders!
I told you this story had spiders!
AAAAHHHHH!
Haunted animatronics!
AAAAHHHHH!
A very thin man!
AAHHH!
A cat!
REEAOW!
Dude, you're trying too hard.
If those stories don't scare you, I don't know what will.
I guess it's back to telling jokes for ol' Spidey!
Wait, what?
What's Dracula's favorite holiday?
FANGS-GIVING!
No! Make it stop!
What kind of music does the mummy like to listen to?
WRAP music!
We give! We give! Nothing is scarier than this!
I want my mommyyy!
Thank you, I'll be here all night!
THE END!

DAILY BUGLE

NEW YORK'S FUNNIEST DAILY NEWSPAPER

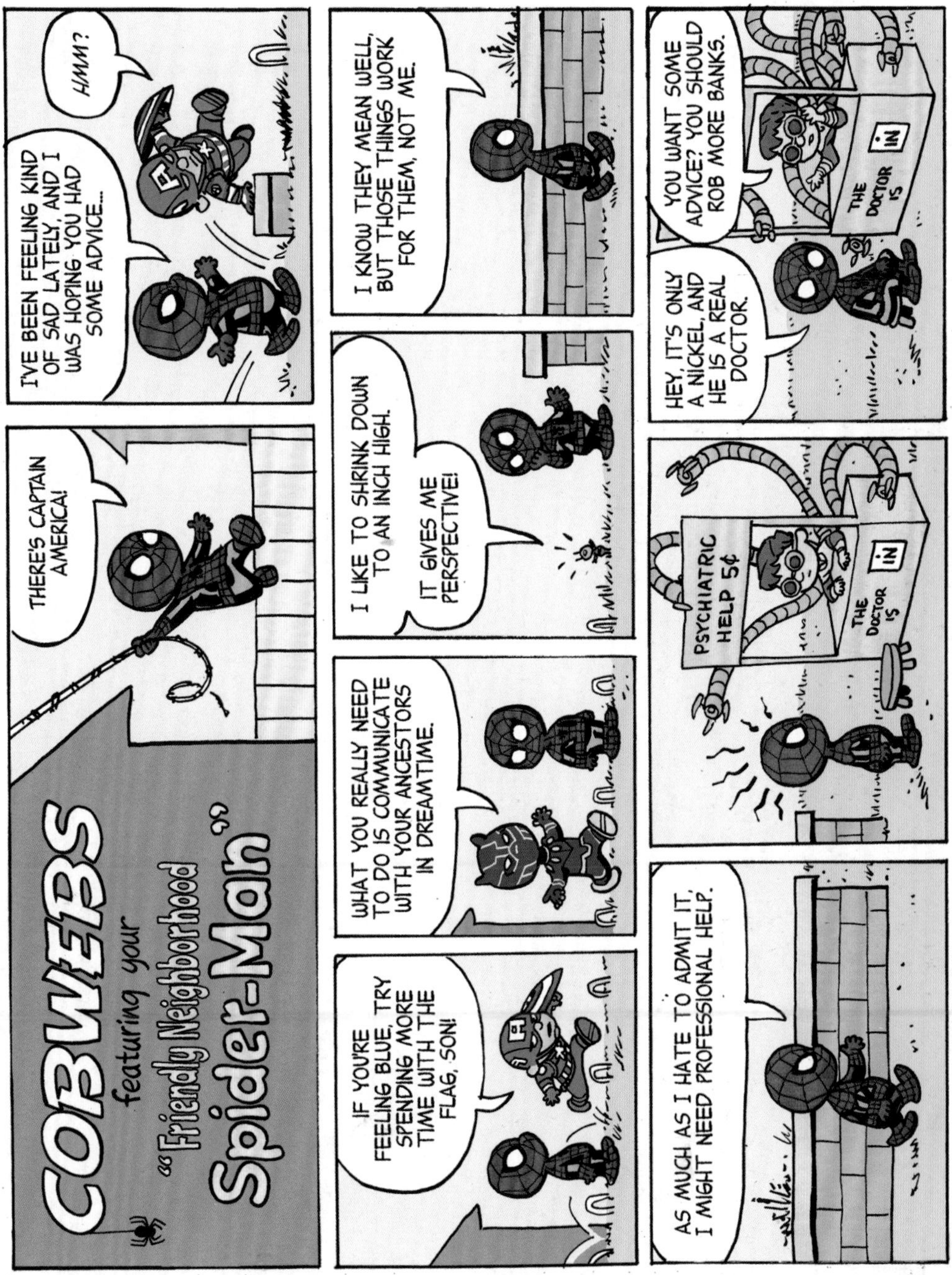
COBWEBS
featuring your
"Friendly Neighborhood Spider-Man"
THERE'S CAPTAIN AMERICA!
I'VE BEEN FEELING KIND OF SAD LATELY, AND I WAS HOPING YOU HAD SOME ADVICE...
HMM?
IF YOU'RE FEELING BLUE, TRY SPENDING MORE TIME WITH THE FLAG, SON!
WHAT YOU REALLY NEED TO DO IS COMMUNICATE WITH YOUR ANCESTORS IN DREAMTIME.
I LIKE TO SHRINK DOWN TO AN INCH HIGH.
IT GIVES ME PERSPECTIVE!
I KNOW THEY MEAN WELL, BUT THOSE THINGS WORK FOR THEM, NOT ME.
AS MUCH AS I HATE TO ADMIT IT, I MIGHT NEED PROFESSIONAL HELP.
PSYCHIATRIC HELP 5¢
THE DOCTOR IS IN
HEY, IT'S ONLY A NICKEL, AND HE IS A REAL DOCTOR.
YOU WANT SOME ADVICE? YOU SHOULD ROB MORE BANKS.
THE DOCTOR IS IN

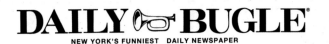

DAILY BUGLE

NEW YORK'S FUNNIEST DAILY NEWSPAPER

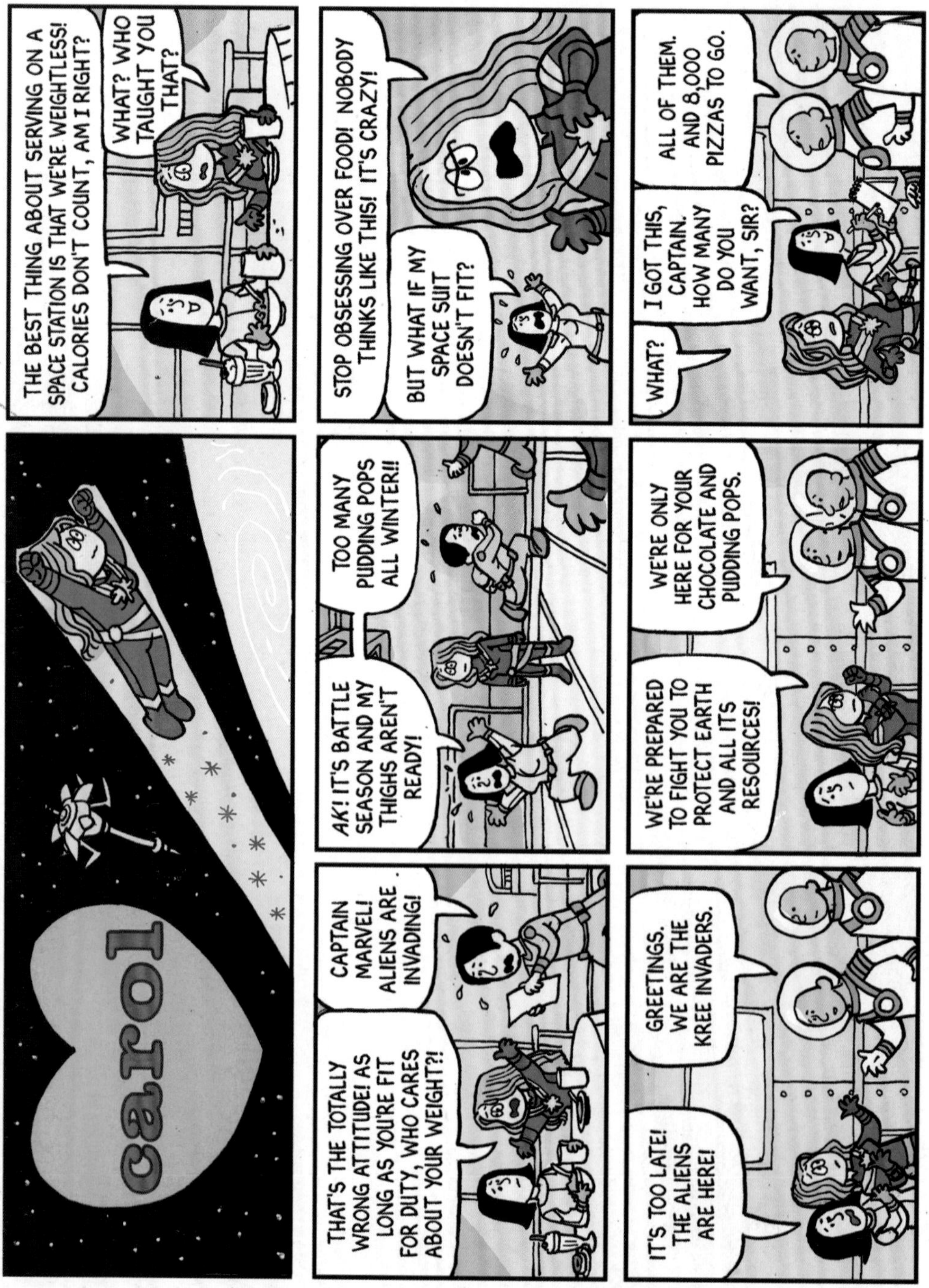
carol
THE BEST THING ABOUT SERVING ON A SPACE STATION IS THAT WE'RE WEIGHTLESS! CALORIES DON'T COUNT, AM I RIGHT?
WHAT? WHO TAUGHT YOU THAT?
THAT'S THE TOTALLY WRONG ATTITUDE! AS LONG AS YOU'RE FIT FOR DUTY, WHO CARES ABOUT YOUR WEIGHT?!
CAPTAIN MARVEL! ALIENS ARE INVADING!
AK! IT'S BATTLE SEASON AND MY THIGHS AREN'T READY!
TOO MANY PUDDING POPS ALL WINTER!!
STOP OBSESSING OVER FOOD! NOBODY THINKS LIKE THIS! IT'S CRAZY!
BUT WHAT IF MY SPACE SUIT DOESN'T FIT?
IT'S TOO LATE! THE ALIENS ARE HERE!
GREETINGS. WE ARE THE KREE INVADERS.
WE'RE PREPARED TO FIGHT YOU TO PROTECT EARTH AND ALL ITS RESOURCES!
WE'RE ONLY HERE FOR YOUR CHOCOLATE AND PUDDING POPS.
WHAT?
I GOT THIS, CAPTAIN. HOW MANY DO YOU WANT, SIR?
ALL OF THEM. AND 8,000 PIZZAS TO GO.

The Villainy Circus

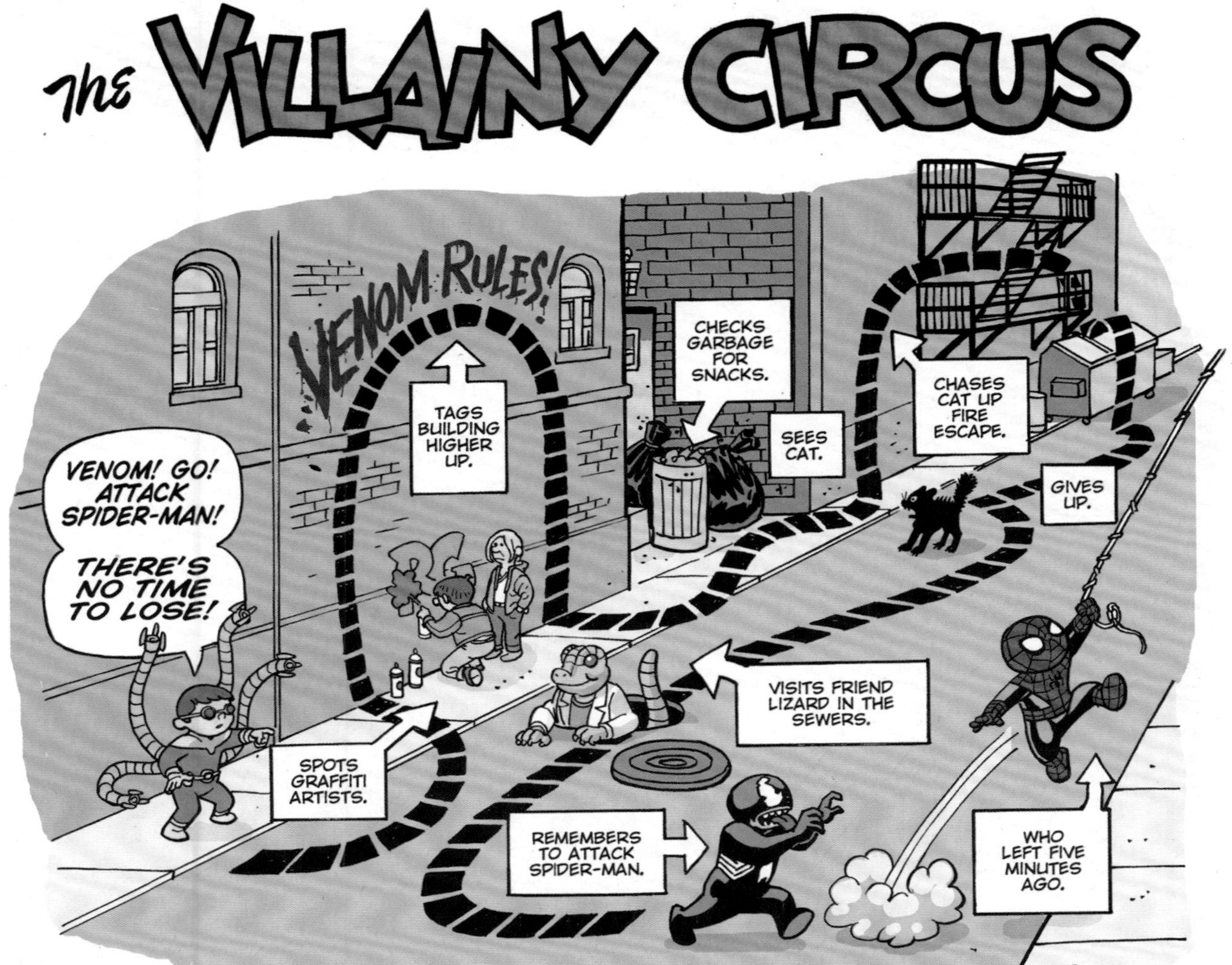

VENOM! GO! ATTACK SPIDER-MAN!
THERE'S NO TIME TO LOSE!
SPOTS GRAFFITI ARTISTS.
TAGS BUILDING HIGHER UP.
VENOM RULES!
CHECKS GARBAGE FOR SNACKS.
SEES CAT.
CHASES CAT UP FIRE ESCAPE.
GIVES UP.
VISITS FRIEND LIZARD IN THE SEWERS.
REMEMBERS TO ATTACK SPIDER-MAN.
WHO LEFT FIVE MINUTES AGO.

DAILY BUGLE

NEW YORK'S FUNNIEST DAILY NEWSPAPER

JUGGLE

THAT JUGGLED-UP WORD GAME!

Unscramble these four JUGGLES, one word per square!

IAMTROOG

IAMGOROT

TOORGMAI

GROOTAMI

Ah, quit yer barkin'.

WHAT THE TREE MIGHT SAY...

Now arrange the circled letters to form the surprise answer, as suggested by the above cartoon.

ANSWER:

Yesterday's |

(Answers tomorrow)

JUGGLES: Vision, Hawkeye, Ultron, Wasp
ANSWER: What Avengers Do: "ASSEMBLE"

Thanos the Menace

"What a day. The teacher taught us how to snap our fingers, and then half our classes were canceled!"

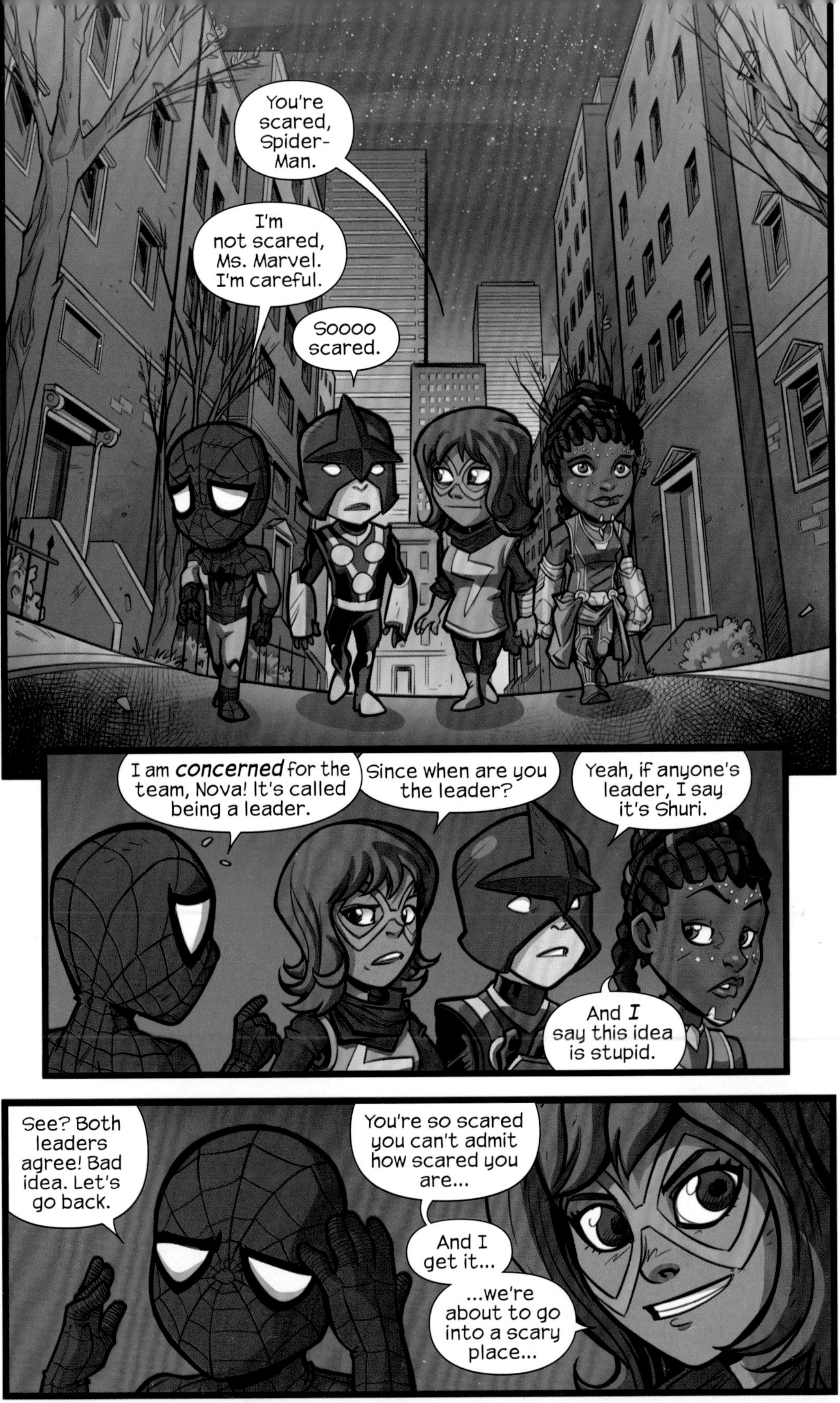
You're scared, Spider-Man.
I'm not scared, Ms. Marvel. I'm careful.
Soooo scared.
I am *concerned* for the team, Nova! It's called being a leader.
Since when are you the leader?
Yeah, if anyone's leader, I say it's Shuri.
And *I* say this idea is stupid.
See? Both leaders agree! Bad idea. Let's go back.
You're so scared you can't admit how scared you are...
And I get it...
...we're about to go into a scary place...

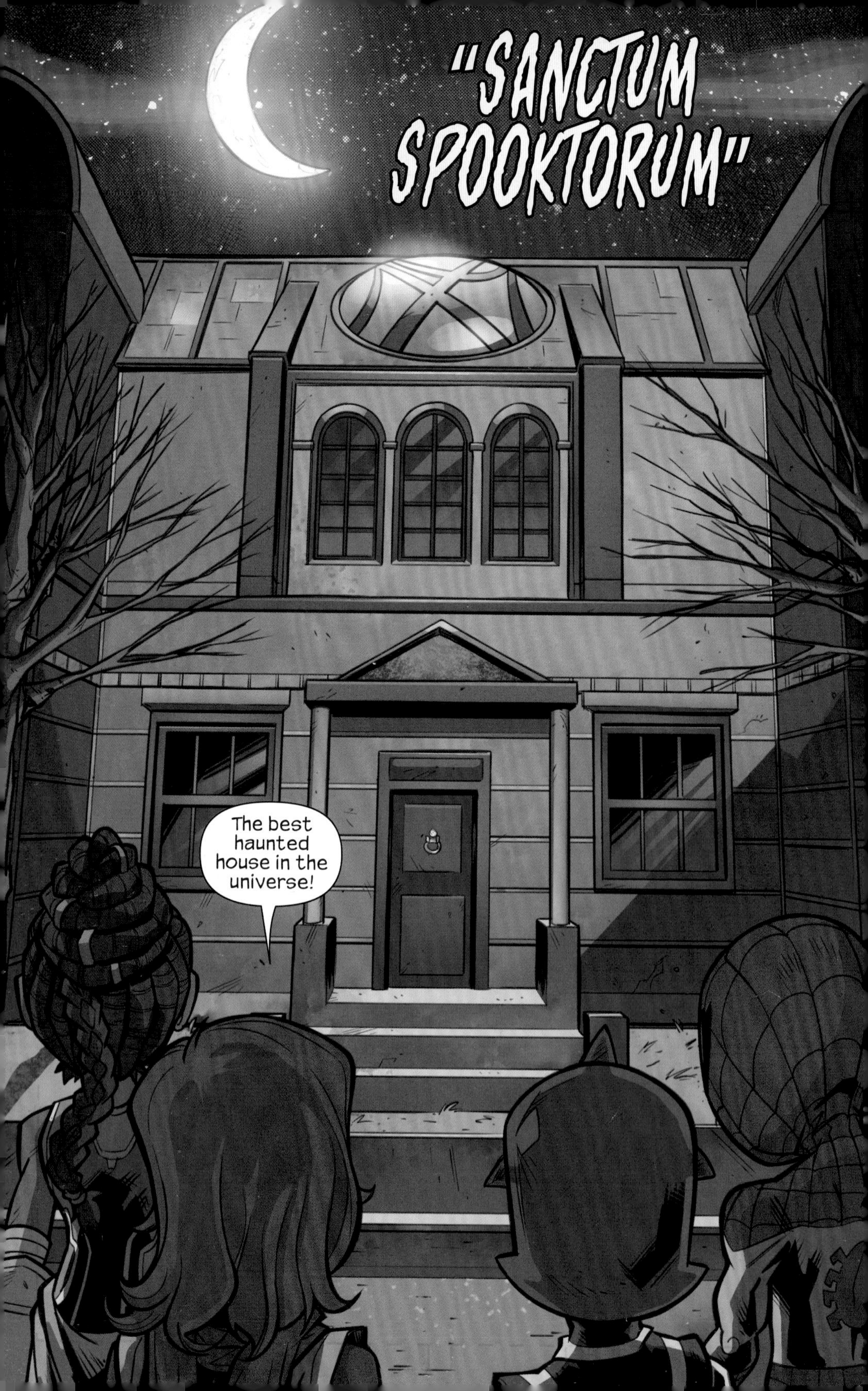
"SANCTUM SPOOKTORUM"
The best haunted house in the universe!

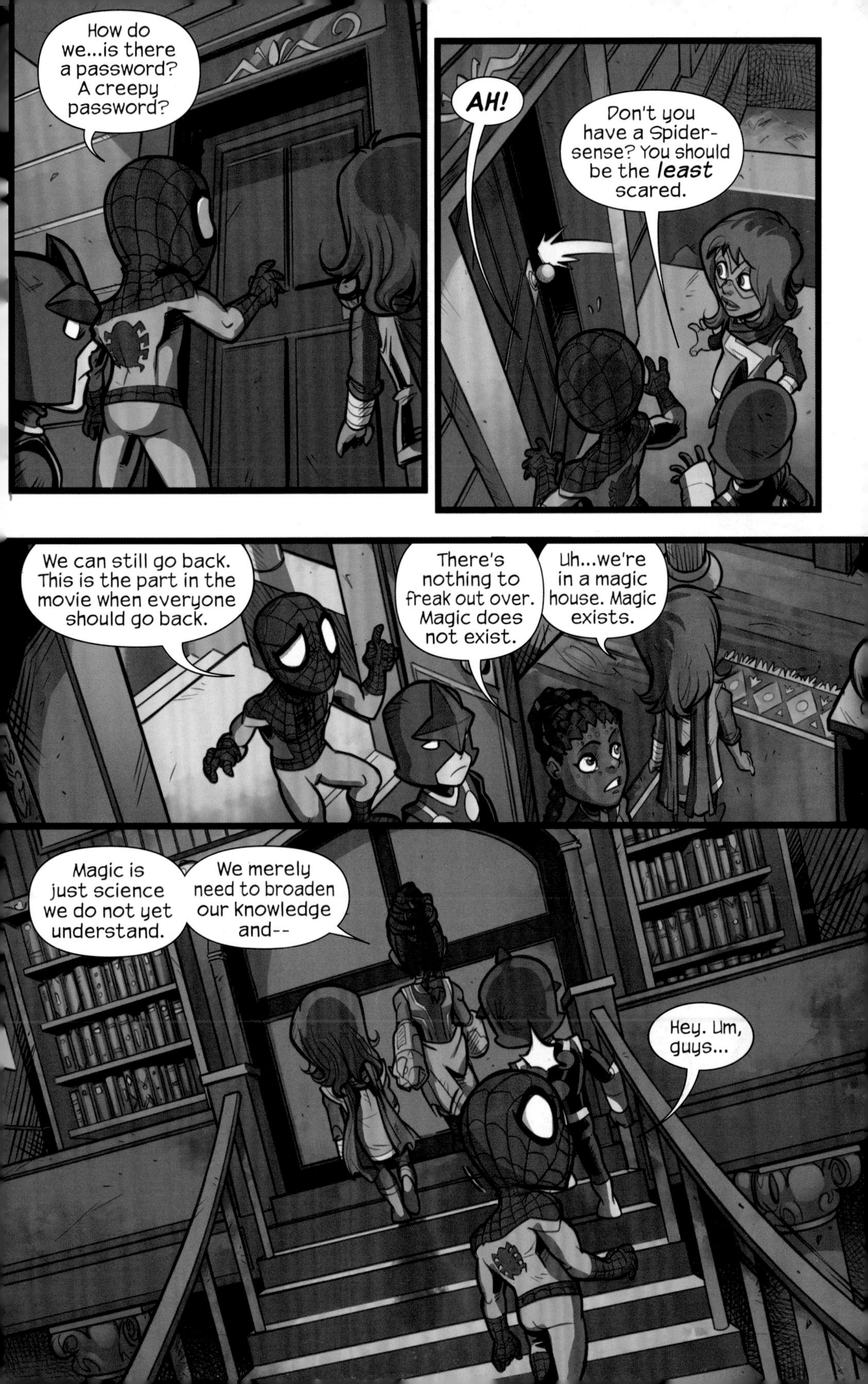
How do we...is there a password? A creepy password?
AH!
Don't you have a Spider-sense? You should be the *least* scared.
We can still go back. This is the part in the movie when everyone should go back.
There's nothing to freak out over. Magic does not exist.
Uh...we're in a magic house. Magic exists.
Magic is just science we do not yet understand.
We merely need to broaden our knowledge and--
Hey. Um, guys...

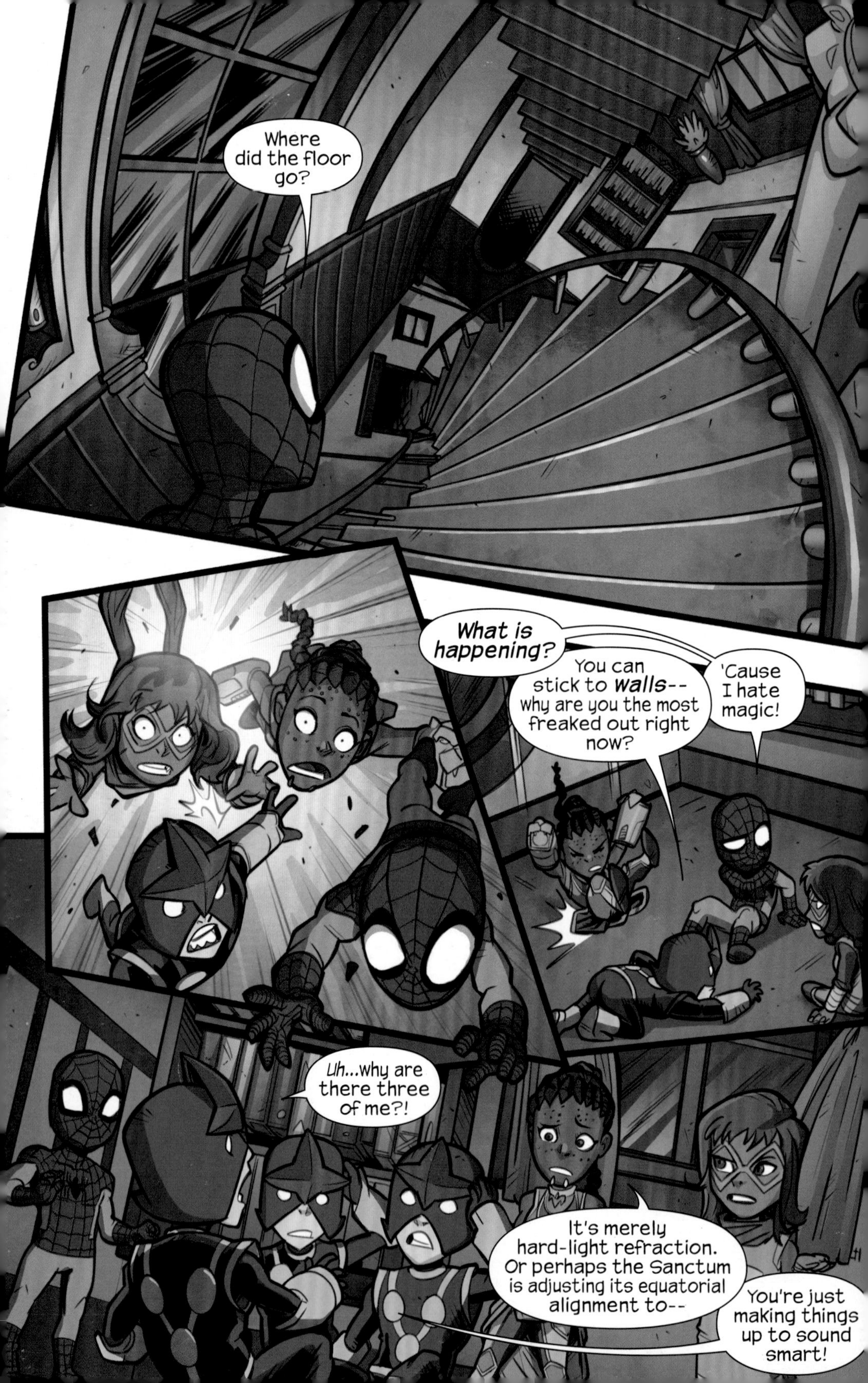
Where did the floor go?
What is happening?
You can stick to walls-- why are you the most freaked out right now?
'Cause I hate magic!
Uh...why are there three of me?!
It's merely hard-light refraction. Or perhaps the Sanctum is adjusting its equatorial alignment to--
You're just making things up to sound smart!

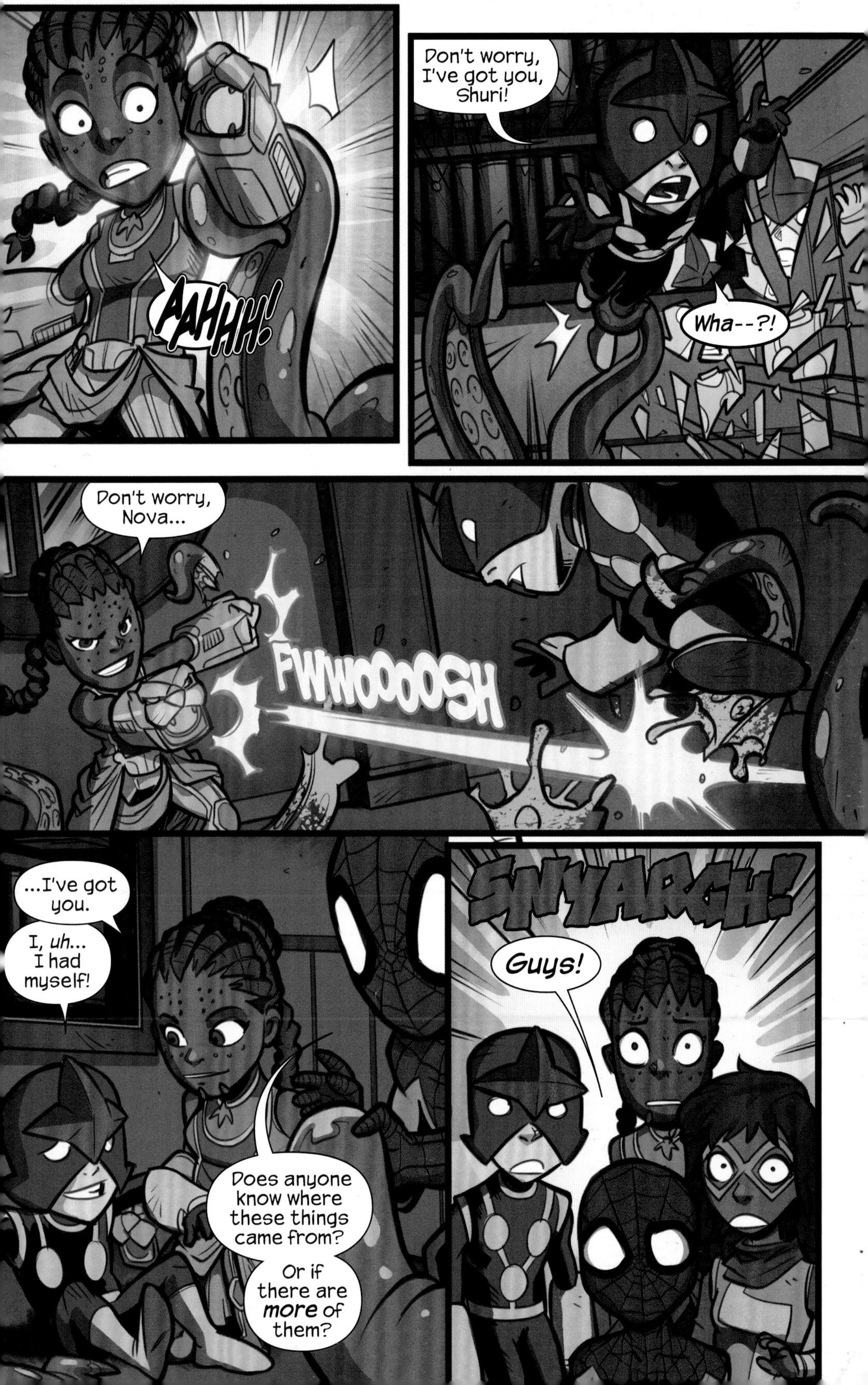

AAHHH!
Don't worry, I've got you, Shuri!
Wha--?!
Don't worry, Nova...
FWWOOOOSH
...I've got you.
I, uh... I had myself!
Does anyone know where these things came from?
Or if there are *more* of them?
SNYARGH!
Guys!

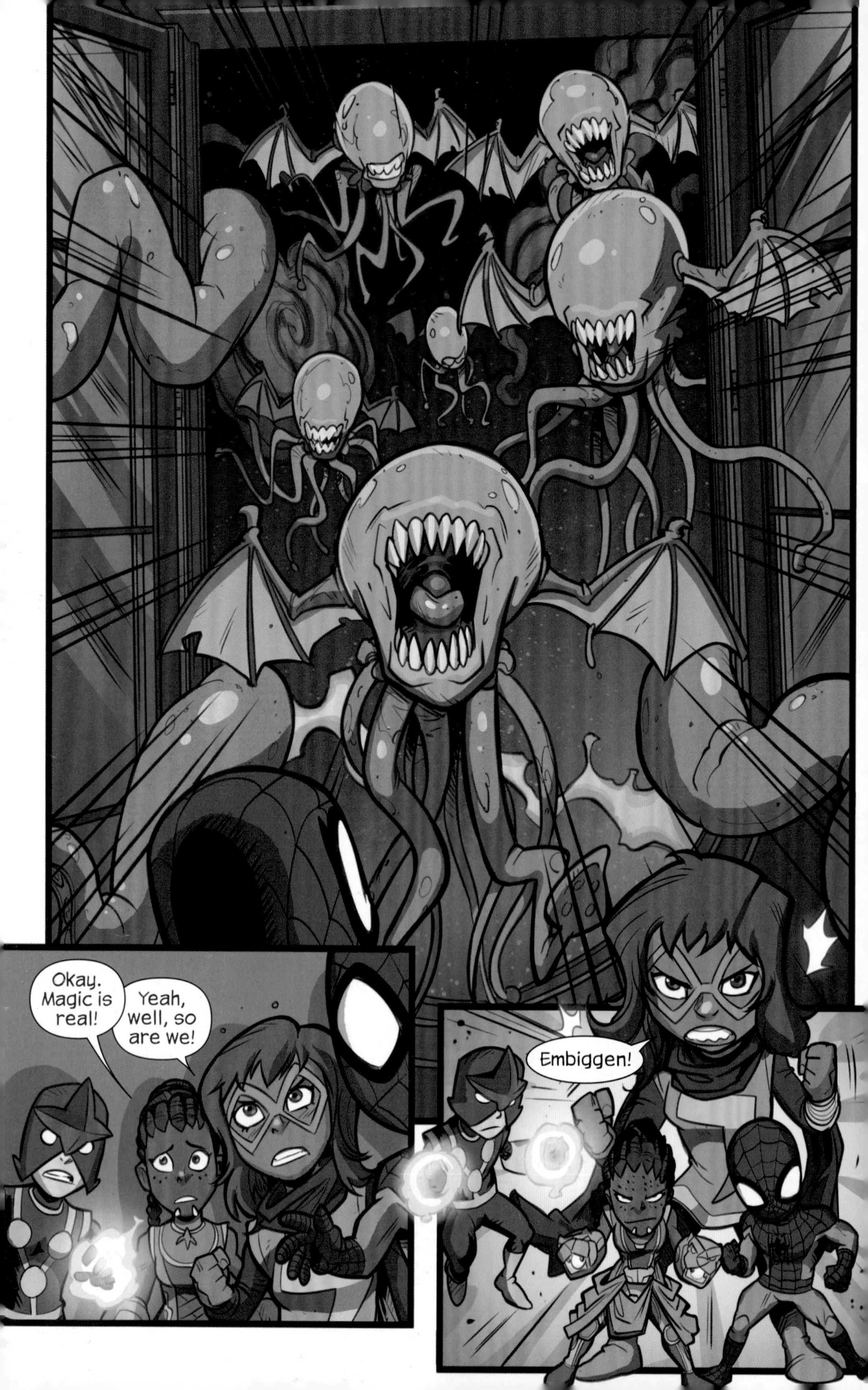
Okay. Magic is real!
Yeah, well, so are we!
Embiggen!

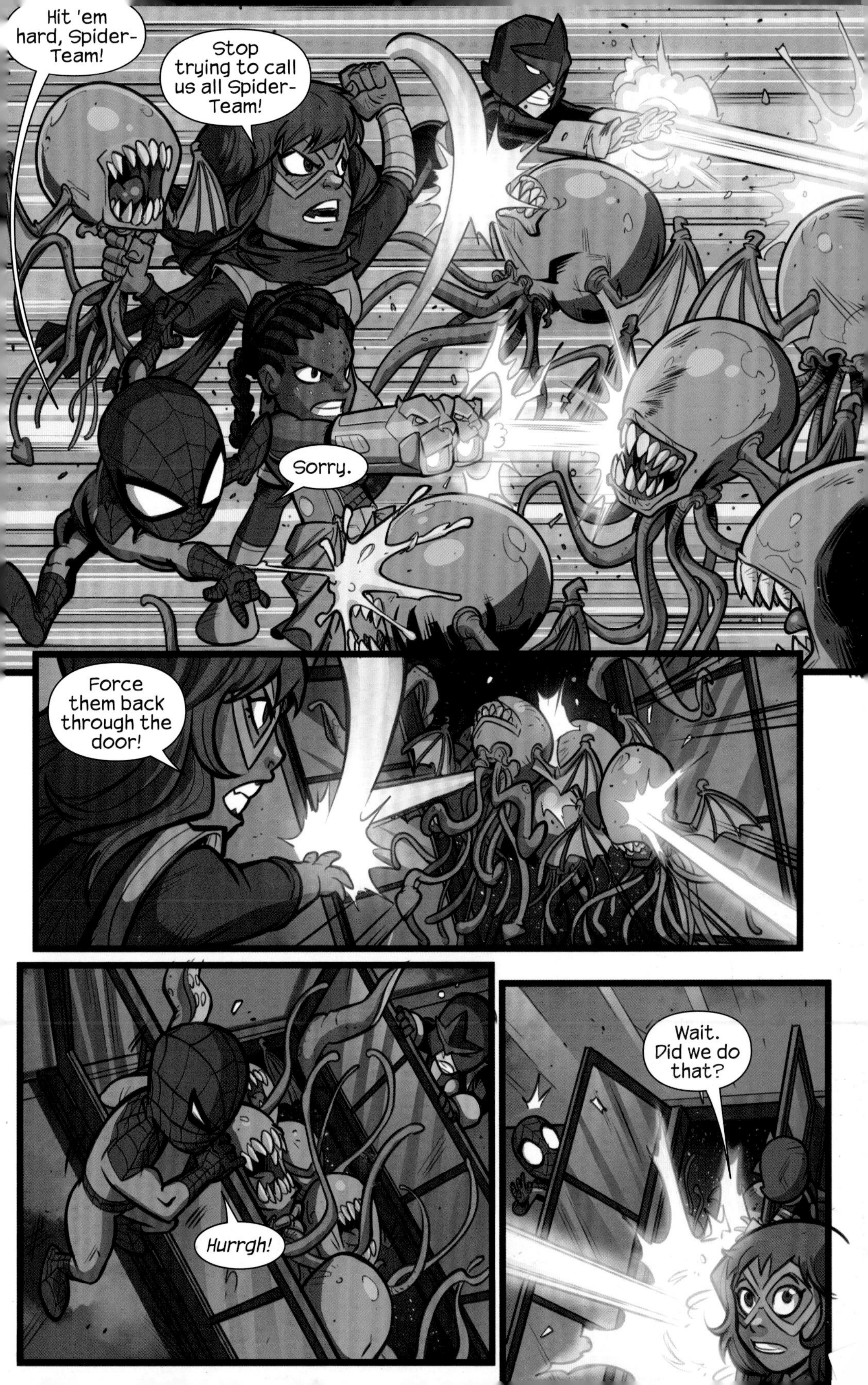
Hit 'em hard, Spider-Team!
Stop trying to call us all Spider-Team!
Sorry.
Force them back through the door!
Hurrgh!
Wait. Did we do that?

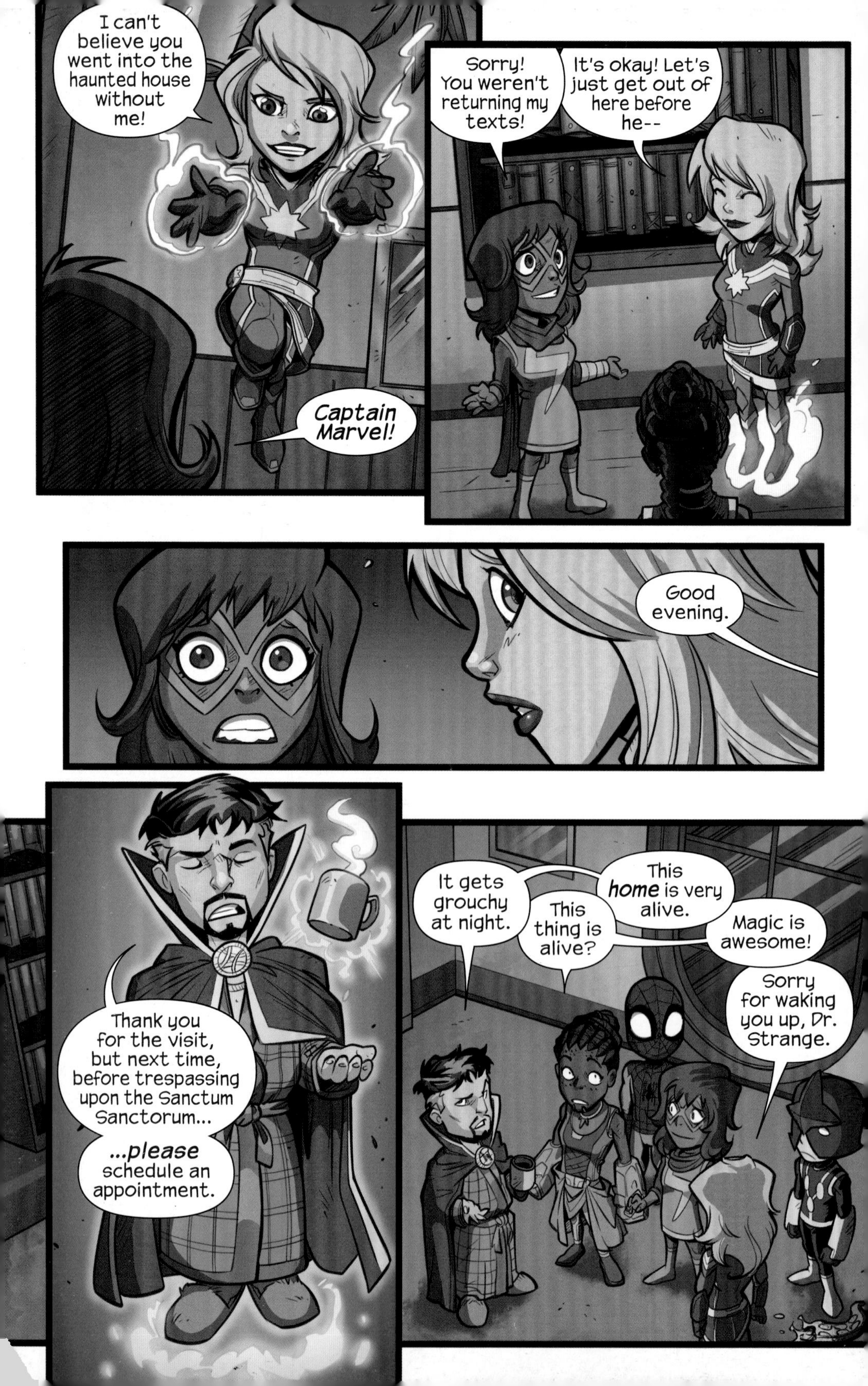
I can't believe you went into the haunted house without me!
Captain Marvel!
Sorry! You weren't returning my texts!
It's okay! Let's just get out of here before he--
Good evening.
Thank you for the visit, but next time, before trespassing upon the Sanctum Sanctorum...
...please schedule an appointment.
It gets grouchy at night.
This *home* is very alive.
This thing is alive?
Magic is awesome!
Sorry for waking you up, Dr. Strange.

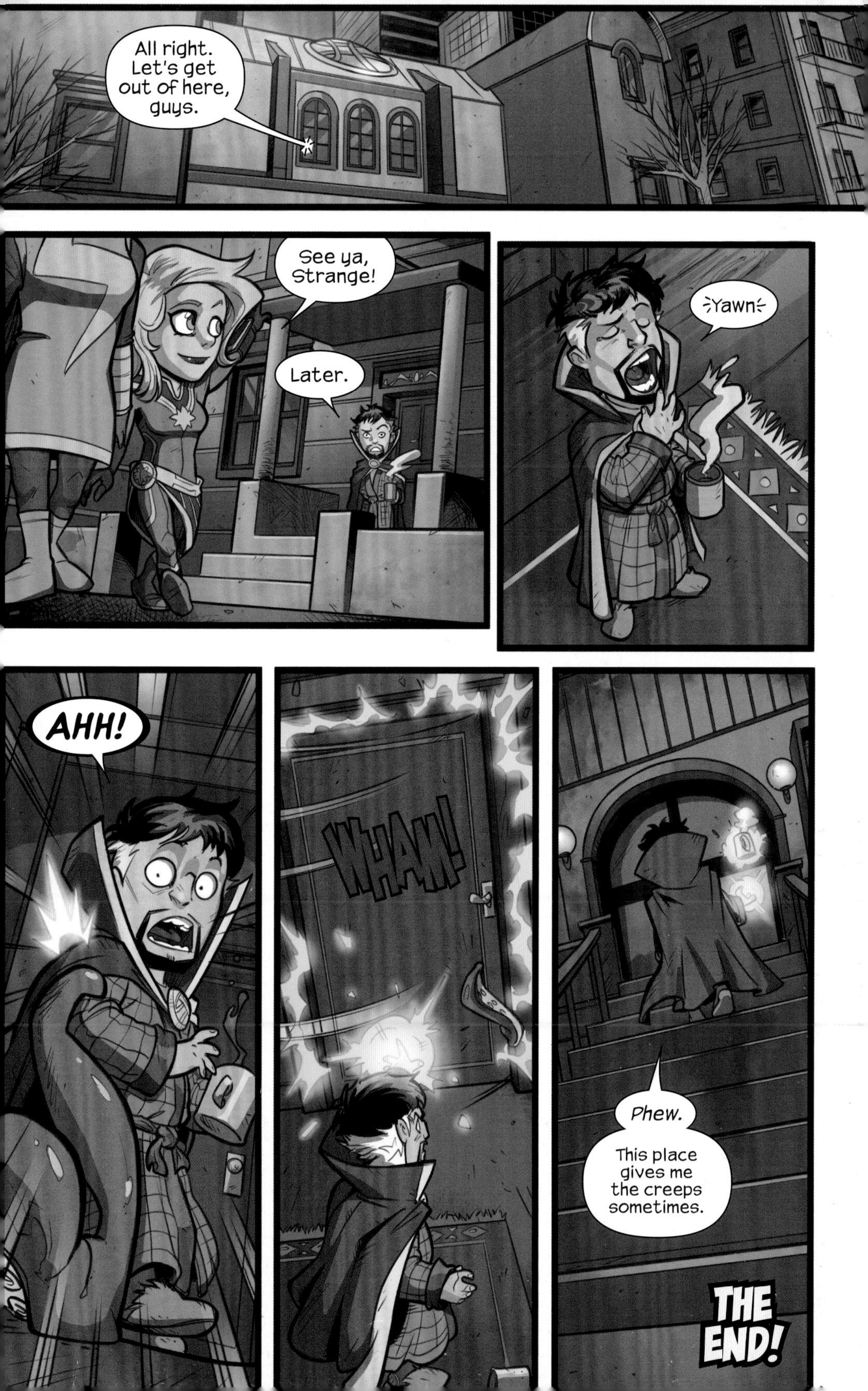
All right. Let's get out of here, guys.
See ya, Strange!
Later.
Yawn
AHH!
WHAM!
Phew.
This place gives me the creeps sometimes.
THE END!

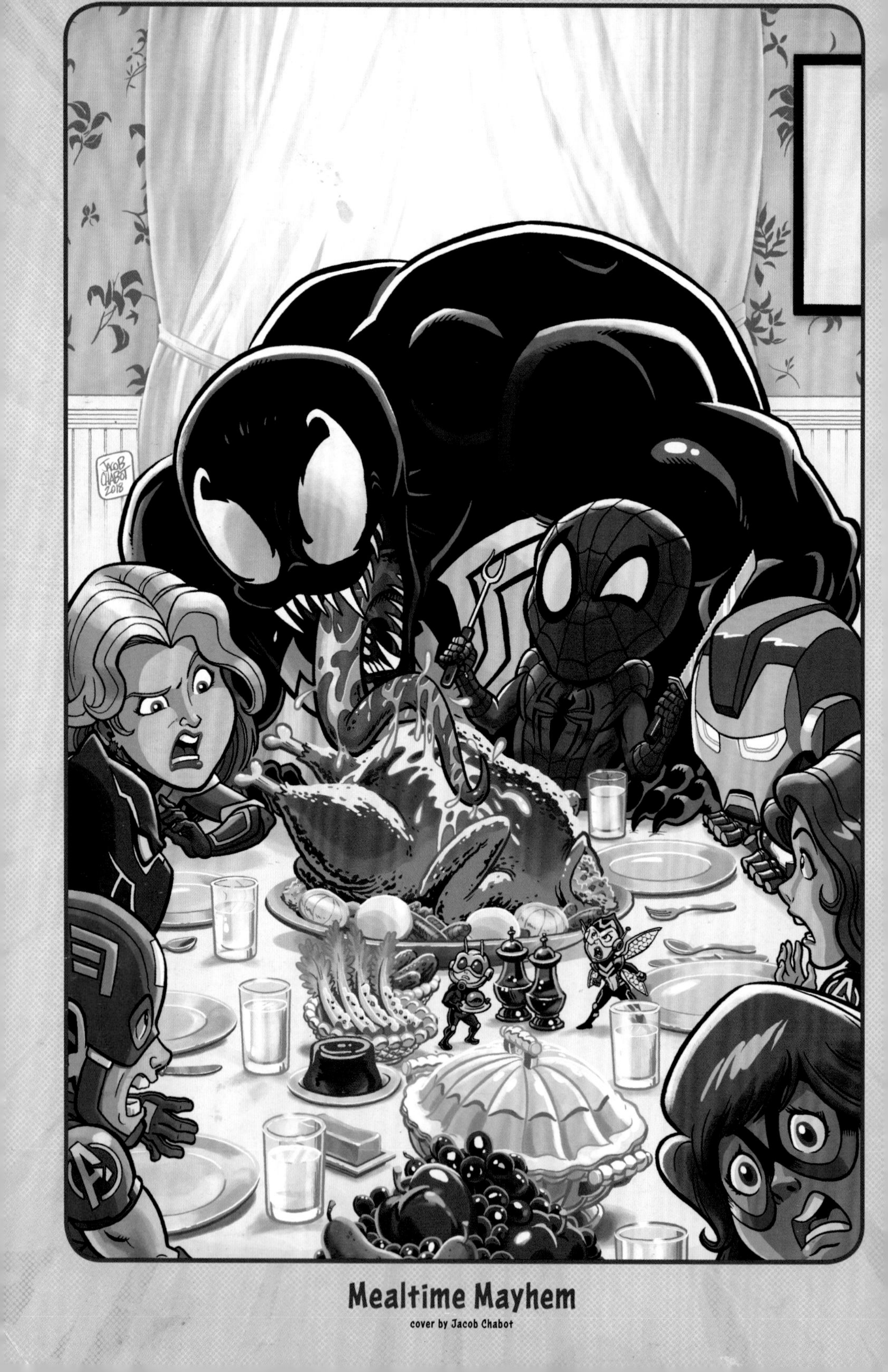
JACOB CHABOT 2018

Mealtime Mayhem

cover by Jacob Chabot

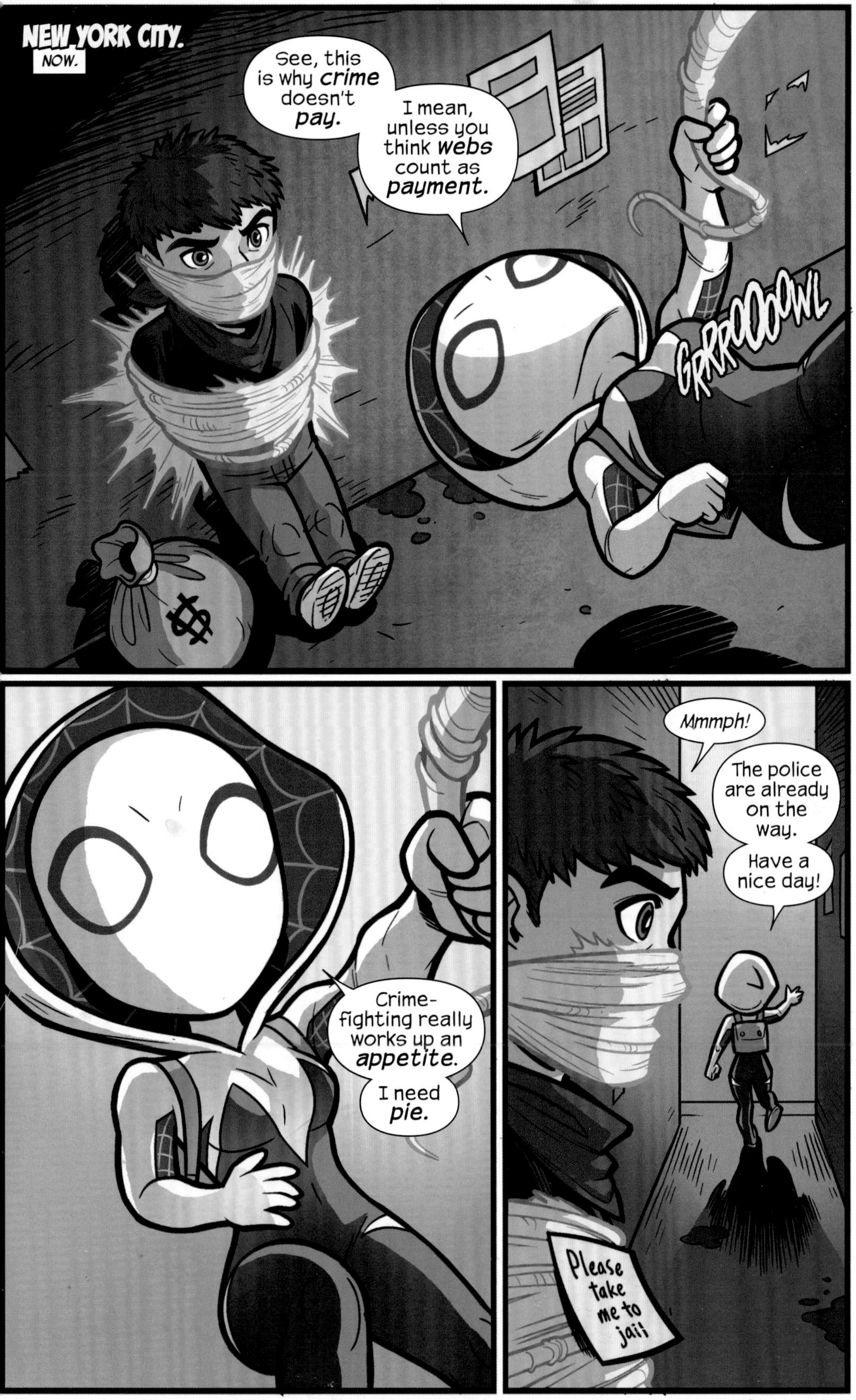
NEW YORK CITY.
NOW.
See, this is why crime doesn't pay.
I mean, unless you think webs count as payment.
GRRROOOOWL
Crime-fighting really works up an appetite.
I need pie.
Mmmph!
The police are already on the way.
Have a nice day!
Please take me to jail

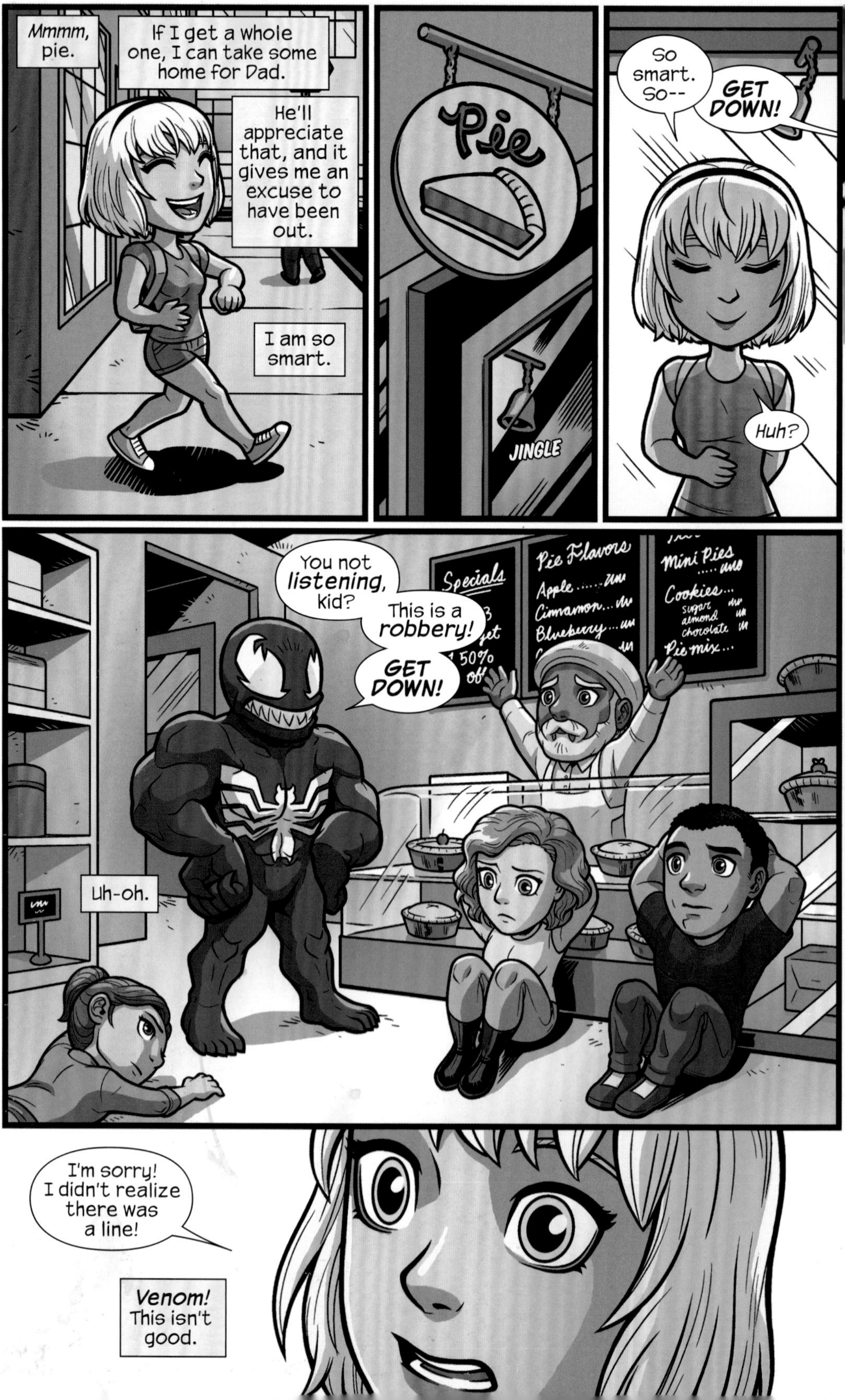
Mmmm, pie.
If I get a whole one, I can take some home for Dad.
He'll appreciate that, and it gives me an excuse to have been out.
I am so smart.
Pie
JINGLE
So smart. So--
GET DOWN!
Huh?
You not listening, kid?
This is a robbery!
GET DOWN!
Specials
Pie Flavors
Apple
Cinnamon
Blueberry
Mini Pies
Cookies
sugar
almond
chocolate
Pie mix
50% off
Uh-oh.
I'm sorry! I didn't realize there was a line!
Venom! This isn't good.

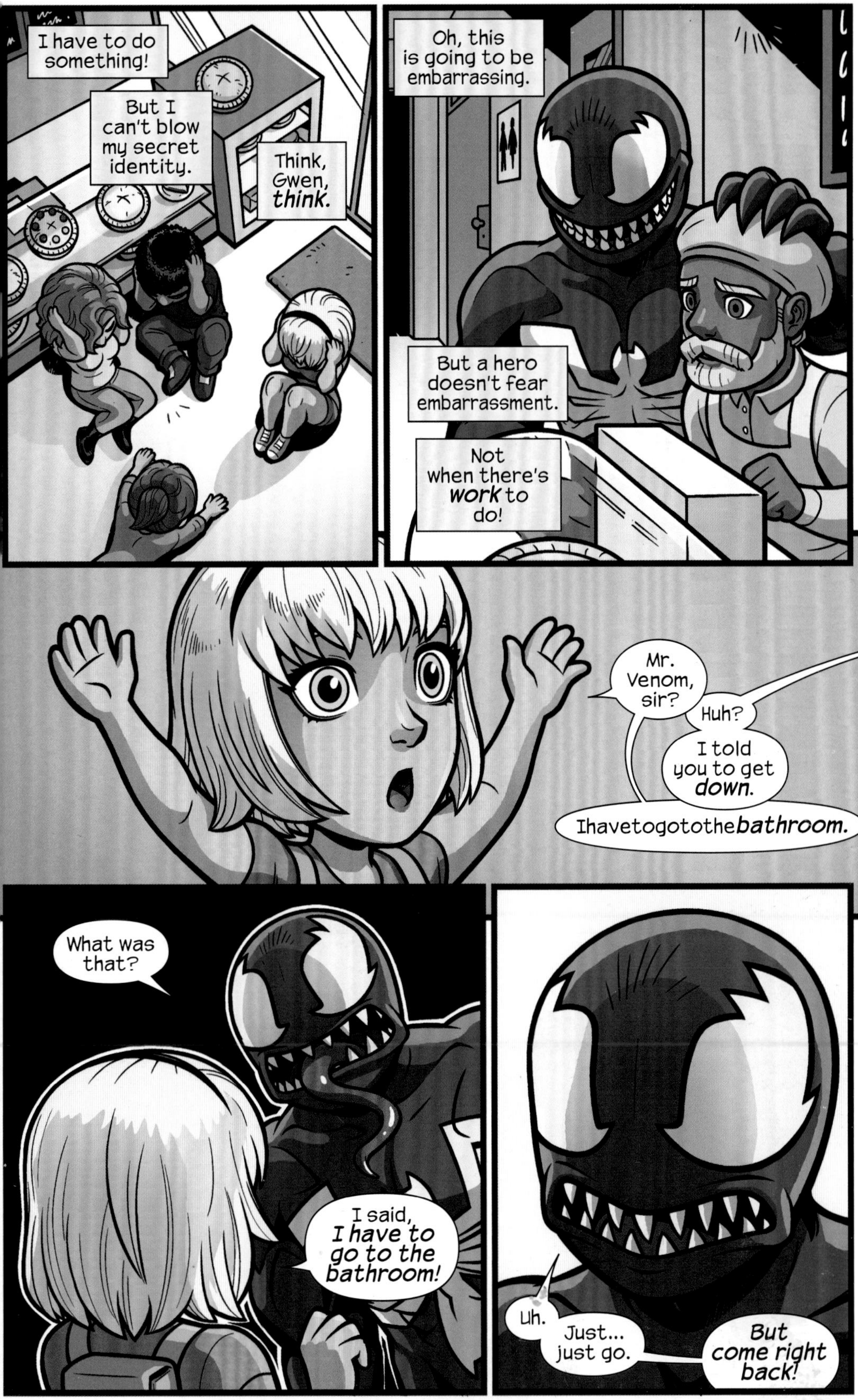

I have to do something!
But I can't blow my secret identity.
Think, Gwen, *think.*
Oh, this is going to be embarrassing.
But a hero doesn't fear embarrassment.
Not when there's *work* to do!
Mr. Venom, sir?
Huh?
I told you to get *down.*
Ihavetogotothe*bathroom.*
What was that?
I said, *I have to go to the bathroom!*
Uh.
Just... just go.
But come right back!

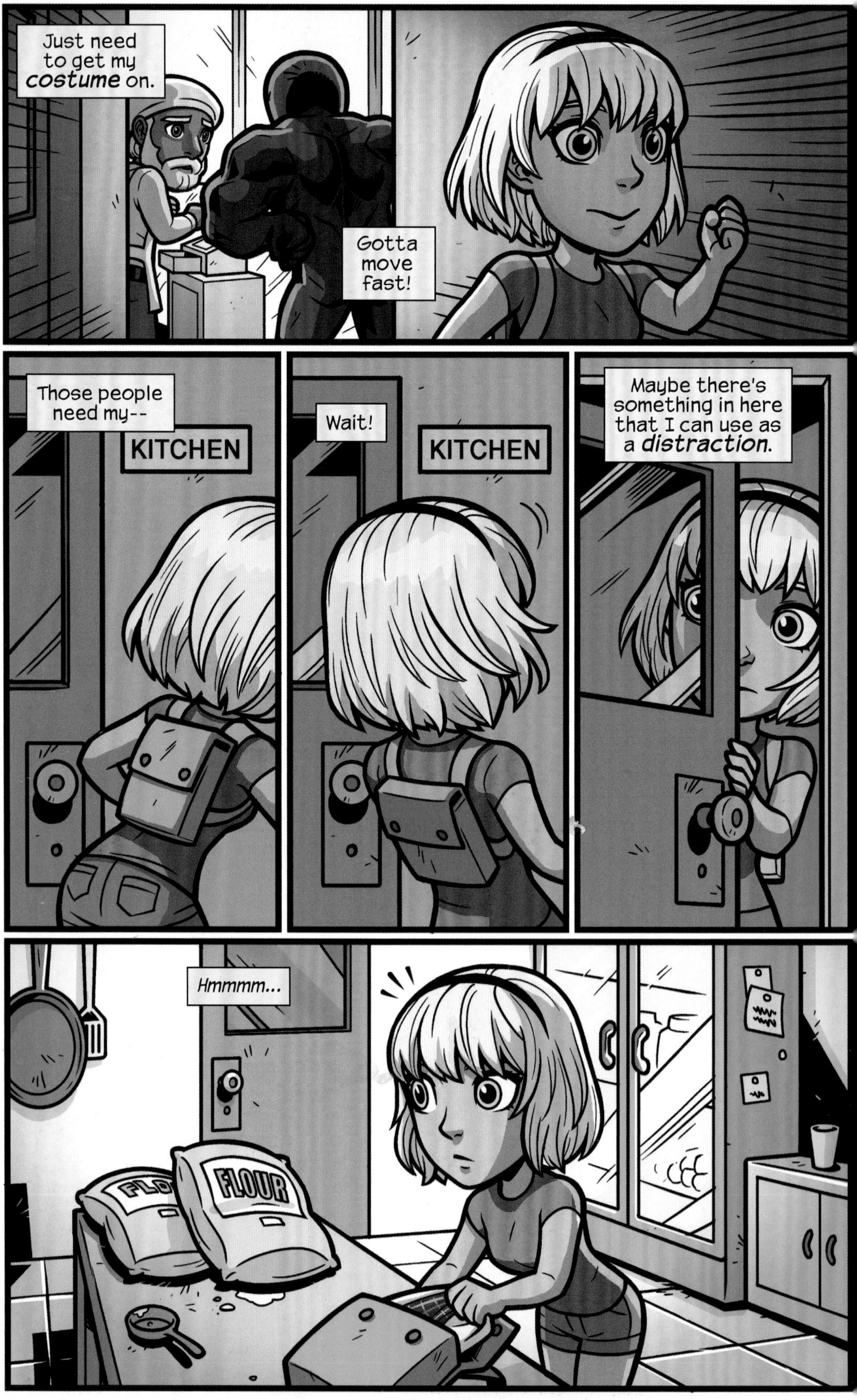

Just need to get my *costume* on.
Gotta move fast!
Those people need my--
KITCHEN
Wait!
KITCHEN
Maybe there's something in here that I can use as a *distraction*.
Hmmmm...
FLOUR
FLOUR

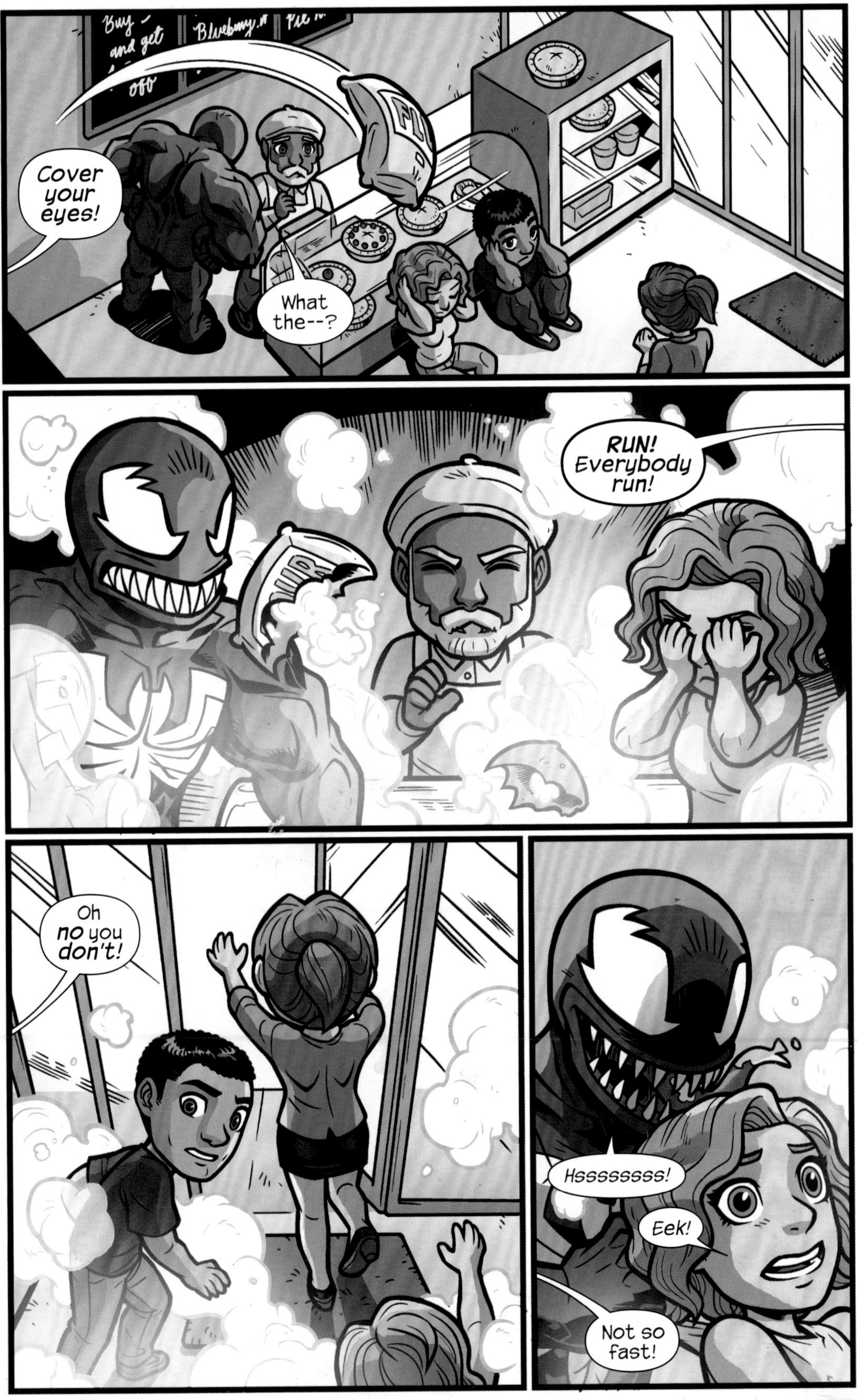

Cover your eyes!
What the--?
RUN! Everybody run!
Oh no you don't!
Hssssssss!
Eek!
Not so fast!

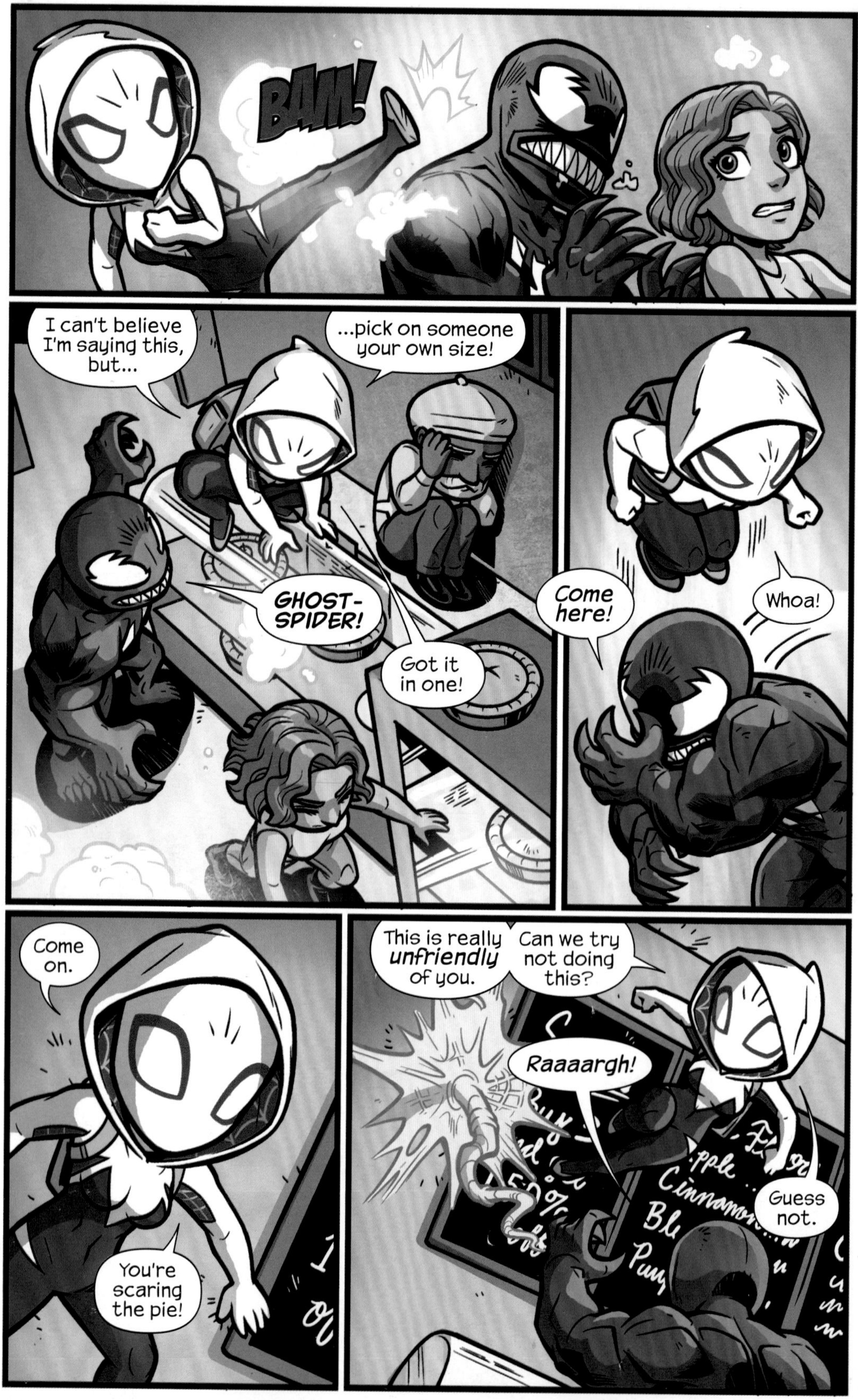
BAM!
I can't believe I'm saying this, but...
...pick on someone your own size!
GHOST-SPIDER!
Got it in one!
Come here!
Whoa!
Come on.
You're scaring the pie!
This is really *unfriendly* of you.
Can we try not doing this?
Raaaargh!
Guess not.

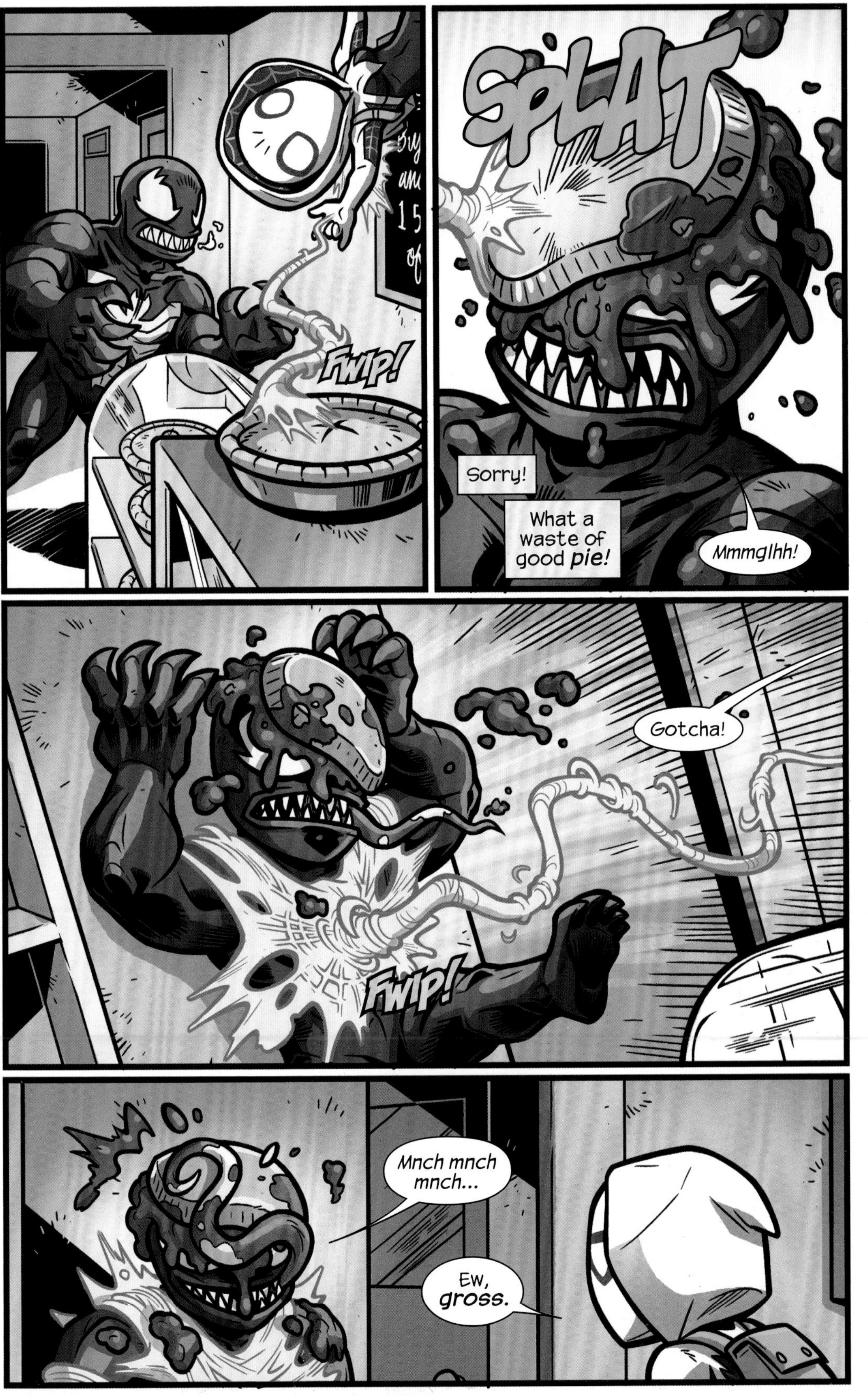
FWIP!
SPLAT
Sorry!
What a waste of good *pie!*
Mmmglhh!
Gotcha!
FWIP!
Mnch mnch mnch...
Ew, **gross.**

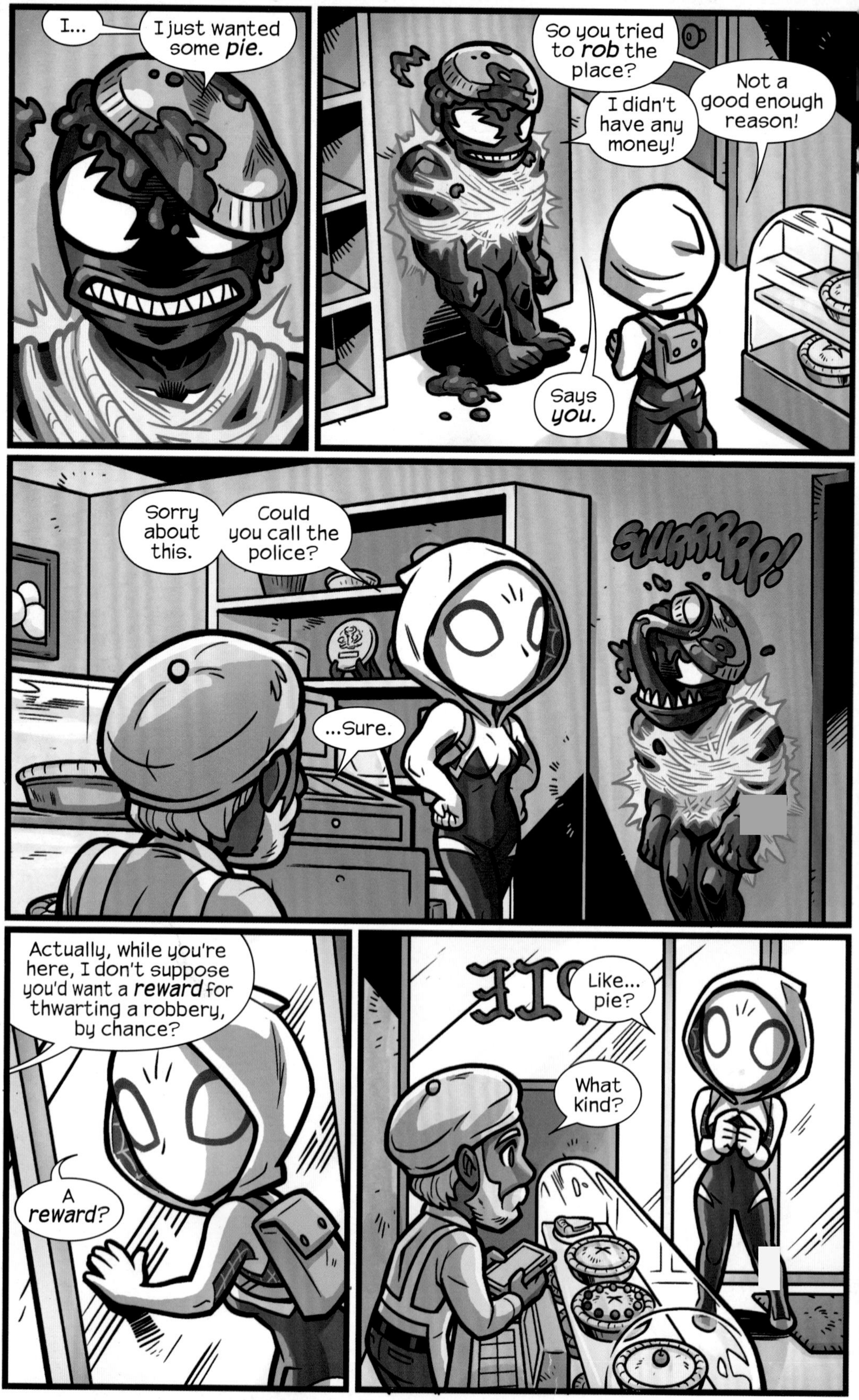

I...
I just wanted some pie.
So you tried to rob the place?
I didn't have any money!
Not a good enough reason!
Says you.
Sorry about this.
Could you call the police?
...Sure.
SLURRRRP!
Actually, while you're here, I don't suppose you'd want a reward for thwarting a robbery, by chance?
A reward?
Like... pie?
What kind?

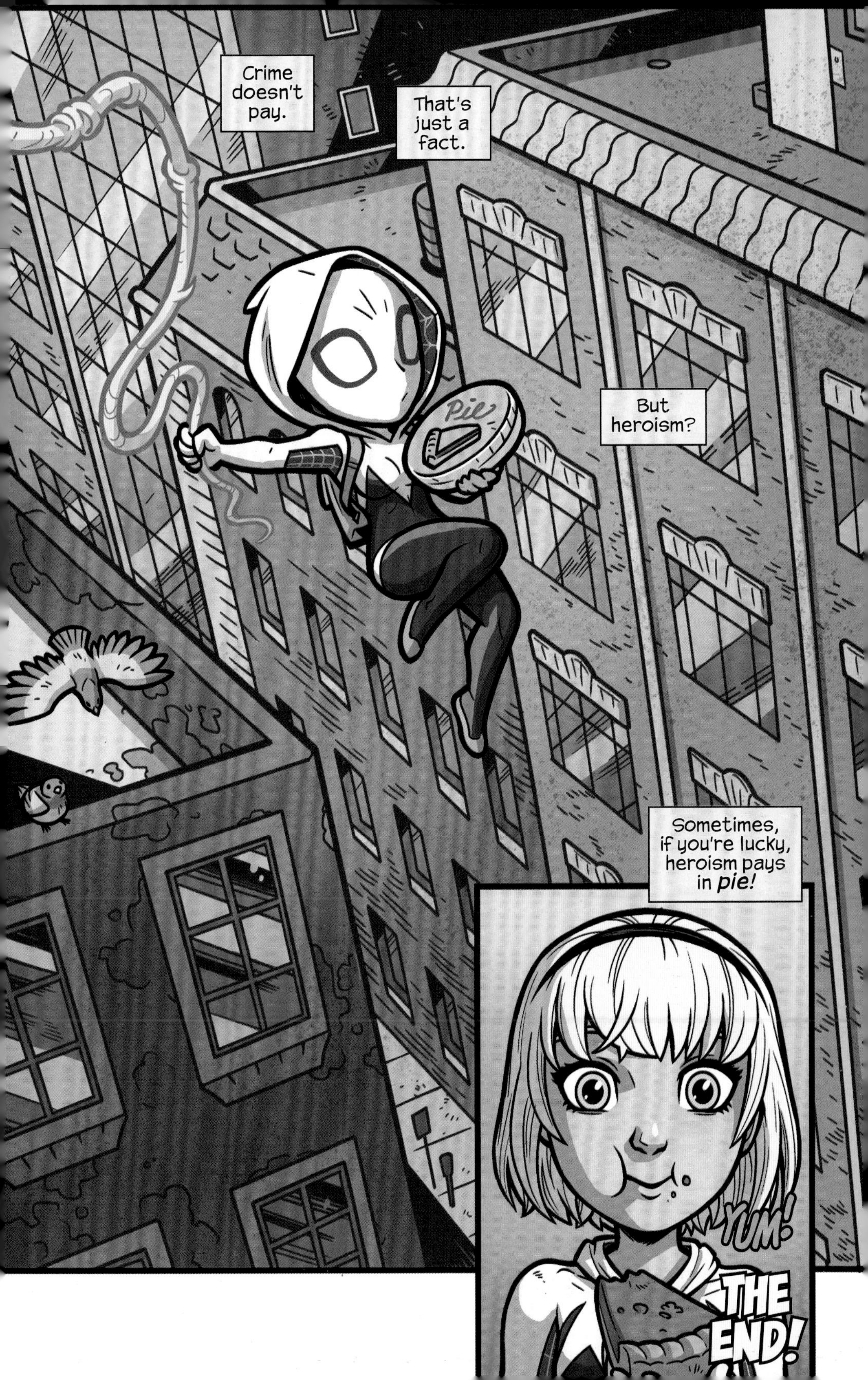
Crime doesn't pay.
That's just a fact.
PIE
But heroism?
Sometimes, if you're lucky, heroism pays in *pie!*
YUM!
THE END!

DAILY BUGLE

NEW YORK'S FUNNIEST DAILY NEWSPAPER

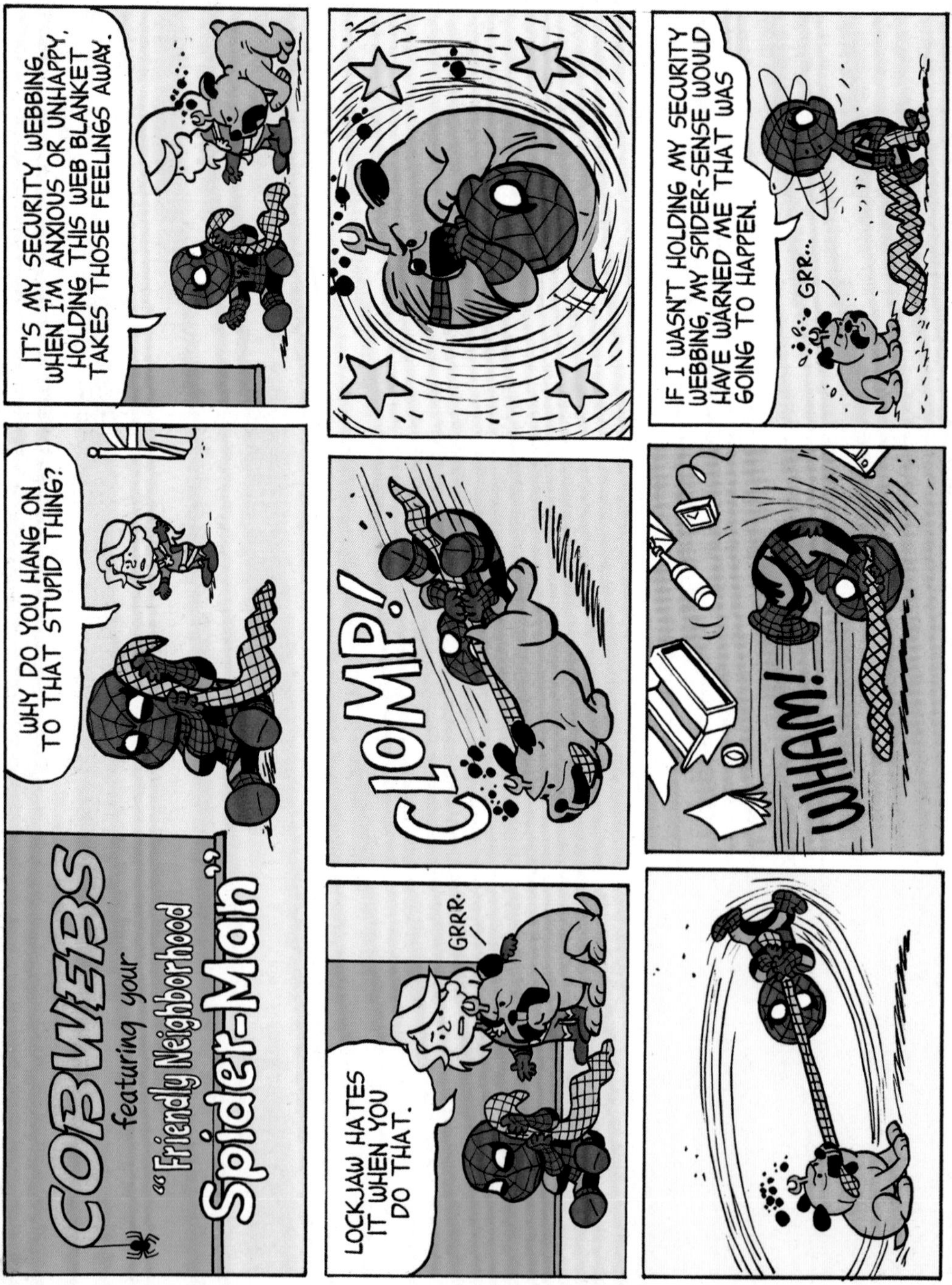

COBWEBS
featuring your "Friendly Neighborhood Spider-Man"
WHY DO YOU HANG ON TO THAT STUPID THING?
IT'S MY SECURITY WEBBING. WHEN I'M ANXIOUS OR UNHAPPY, HOLDING THIS WEB BLANKET TAKES THOSE FEELINGS AWAY.
LOCKJAW HATES IT WHEN YOU DO THAT.
GRRR.
CLOMP!
WHAM!
GRR...
IF I WASN'T HOLDING MY SECURITY WEBBING, MY SPIDER-SENSE WOULD HAVE WARNED ME THAT WAS GOING TO HAPPEN.

DAILY BUGLE
NEW YORK'S FUNNIEST DAILY NEWSPAPER

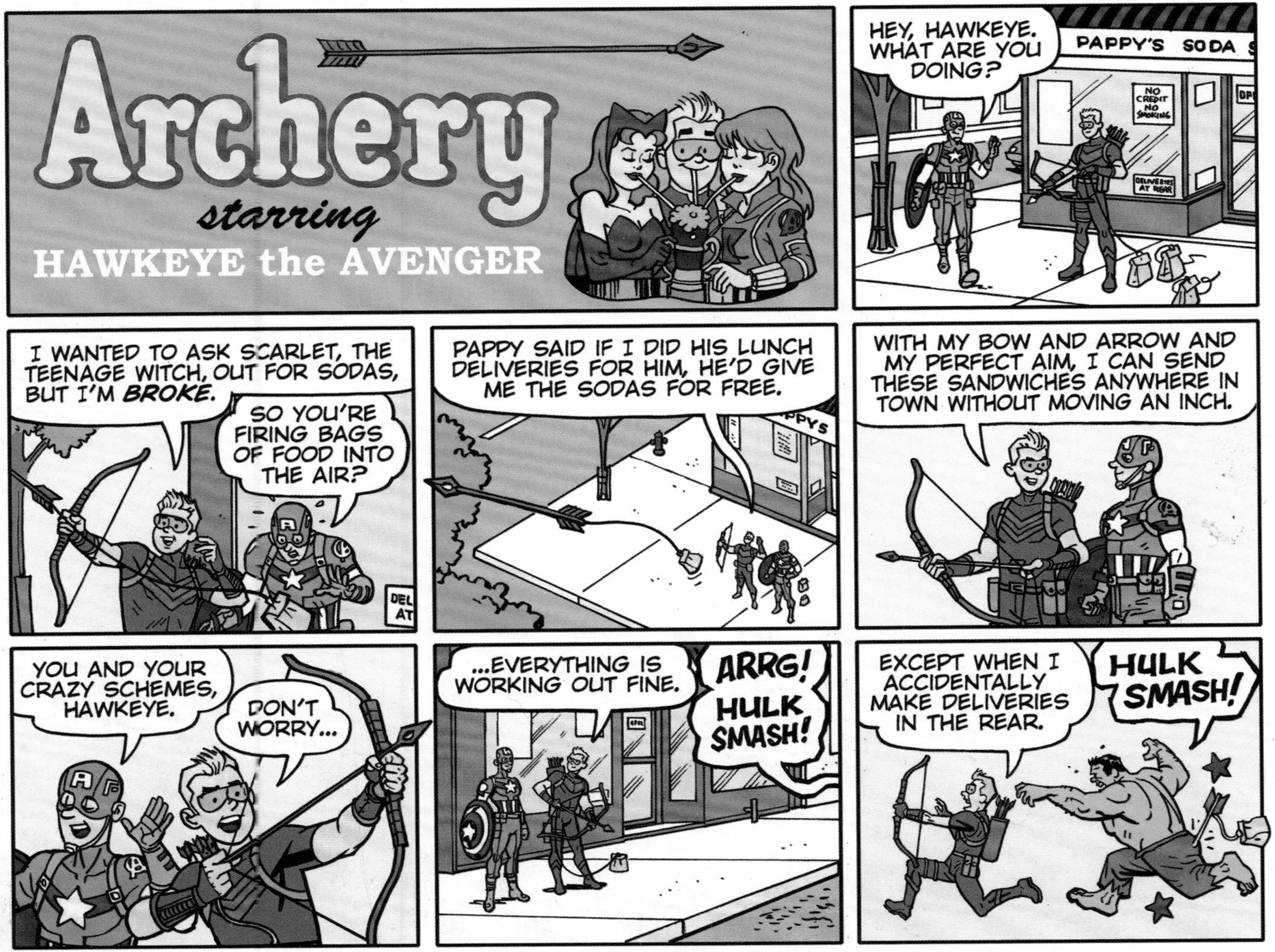
Archery
starring
HAWKEYE the AVENGER
HEY, HAWKEYE. WHAT ARE YOU DOING?
PAPPY'S SODA
NO CREDIT NO SMOKING
DELIVERIES AT REAR
I WANTED TO ASK SCARLET, THE TEENAGE WITCH, OUT FOR SODAS, BUT I'M *BROKE*.
SO YOU'RE FIRING BAGS OF FOOD INTO THE AIR?
PAPPY SAID IF I DID HIS LUNCH DELIVERIES FOR HIM, HE'D GIVE ME THE SODAS FOR FREE.
WITH MY BOW AND ARROW AND MY PERFECT AIM, I CAN SEND THESE SANDWICHES ANYWHERE IN TOWN WITHOUT MOVING AN INCH.
YOU AND YOUR CRAZY SCHEMES, HAWKEYE.
DON'T WORRY...
...EVERYTHING IS WORKING OUT FINE.
ARRG! HULK SMASH!
EXCEPT WHEN I ACCIDENTALLY MAKE DELIVERIES IN THE REAR.
HULK SMASH!

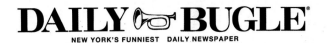

DAILY BUGLE

NEW YORK'S FUNNIEST DAILY NEWSPAPER

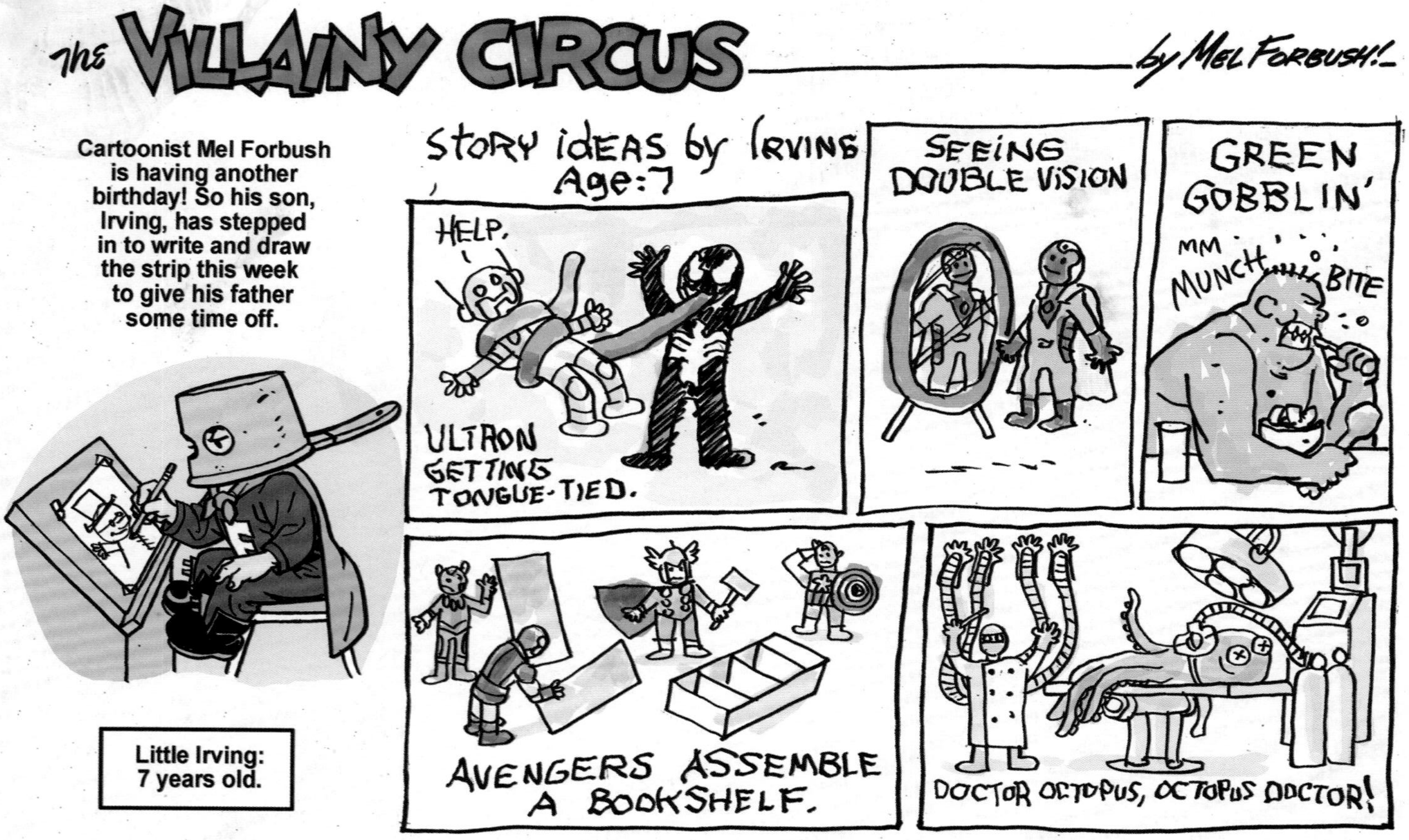
THE VILLAINY CIRCUS
by MEL FORBUSH!
Cartoonist Mel Forbush is having another birthday! So his son, Irving, has stepped in to write and draw the strip this week to give his father some time off.
Little Irving: 7 years old.
STORY IDEAS by IRVING Age: 7
HELP.
ULTRON GETTING TONGUE-TIED.
SEEING DOUBLE VISION
GREEN GOBBLIN'
MM MUNCH BITE
AVENGERS ASSEMBLE A BOOKSHELF.
DOCTOR OCTOPUS, OCTOPUS DOCTOR!

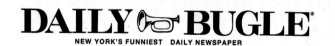

DAILY BUGLE

NEW YORK'S FUNNIEST DAILY NEWSPAPER

J. Jonah's Believe It or Don't!

THERE'S A MAN IN NEW YORK CITY WHO CLAIMS HE CAN STICK TO WALLS LIKE A CAT BURGLAR.
AND YET THE POLICE DO NOT ARREST HIM!!!
IN MOST CIVILIZED COUNTRIES, A MAN WEARING A MASK IS CONSIDERED SUSPICIOUS!!!
NOT ONLY ARE SPIDERS AMONGST THE WORLD'S MOST DEADLY PREDATORS, BUT THEY ARE ALSO NATURE'S UGLIEST BEASTS!!!

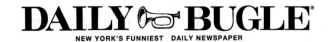

FIND A WORD!

The fun WORD SEARCH game!

C	A	P	T	A	I	N	A	M	E	R	I	C	A
A	V	E	N	G	E	R	S	R	H	I	N	O	S
P	E	T	E	R	P	A	R	K	E	R	X	V	Q
T	H	O	R	H	U	L	K	G	W	E	N	E	U
A	V	E	N	G	E	R	S	A	G	A	I	N	I
I	R	O	N	M	A	N	A	N	D	T	H	O	R
N	O	V	A	C	O	R	P	S	W	E	B	M	R
M	A	R	V	E	L	C	O	M	I	C	S	X	E
A	N	T	M	A	N	T	H	E	W	A	S	P	L
R	O	C	K	E	T	R	A	C	C	O	O	N	G
V	I	L	L	A	I	N	S	B	E	L	O	K	I
E	V	I	L	B	A	D	G	U	Y	S	Z	X	R
L	O	C	K	J	A	W	O	K	O	Y	E	E	L

Today's puzzle is written entirely in the language of the Skrulls, an alien race bent on world domination. Skrulls can shape-shift, so don't be fooled by words you THINK you recognize. You're only looking for the words on the list below.

TRNDW
CVTRGARO
EBMR
NOMXPNK
RHGMC
GSNOEMCIE
MHRNNR
PCNELIO
HROHT

RIUQSA
CARKKHR
XNIHB
RELGIR
TABYY
WIWCEYO
LEVRAM
SOTTALC
CAOLSY

Remember, look backward, forward, up and down, and even diagonally to find words. We helped with the first one to get you started.

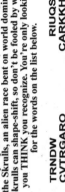

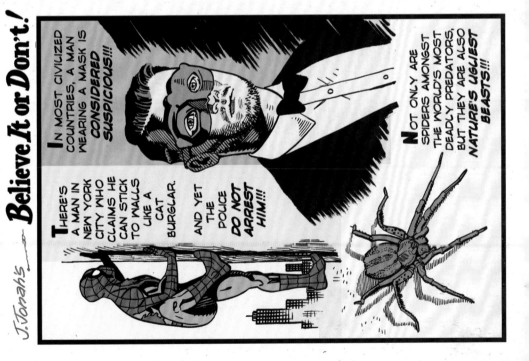

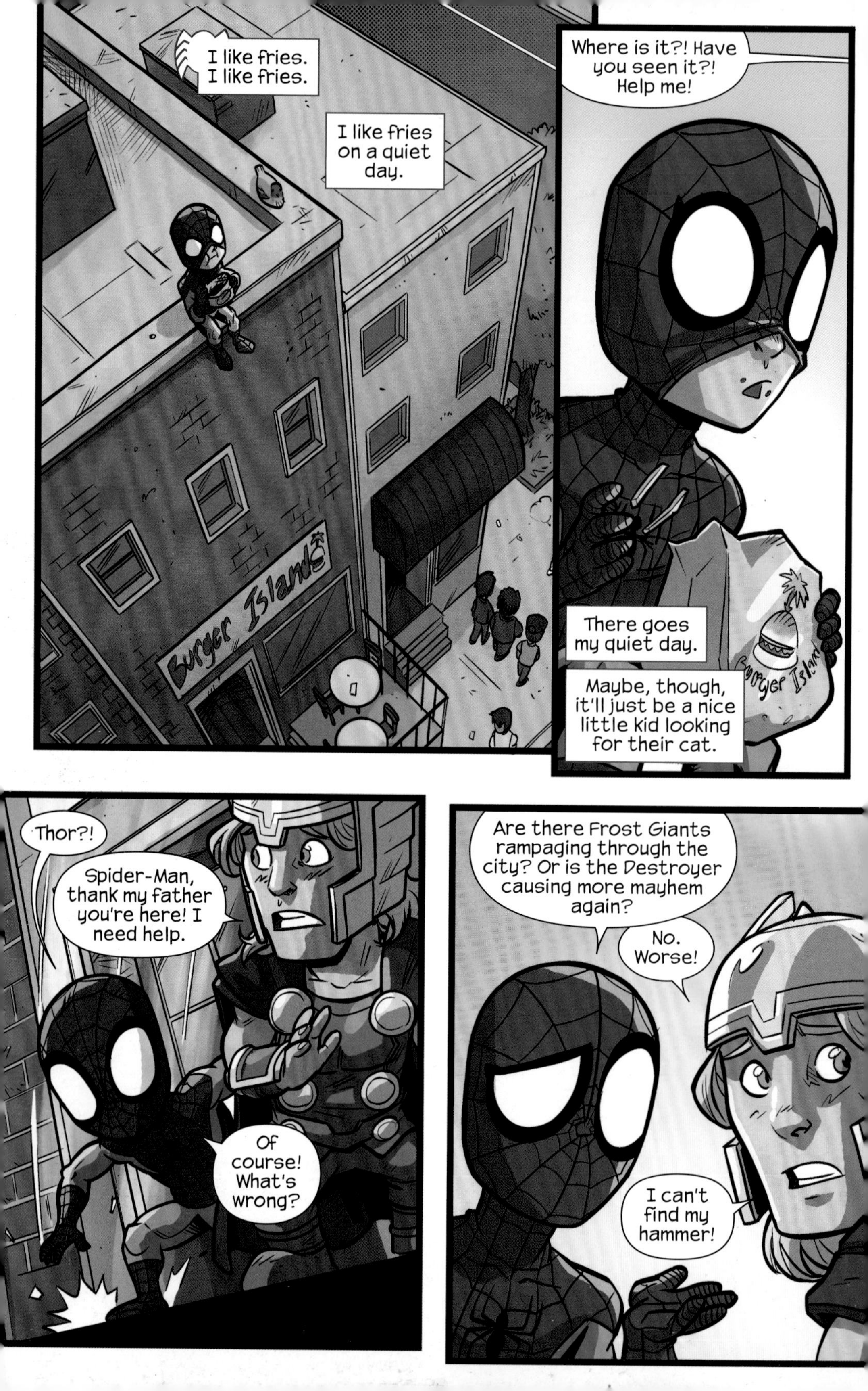
I like fries.
I like fries.
I like fries on a quiet day.
Where is it?! Have you seen it?! Help me!
There goes my quiet day.
Maybe, though, it'll just be a nice little kid looking for their cat.
Thor?!
Spider-Man, thank my father you're here! I need help.
Of course! What's wrong?
Are there Frost Giants rampaging through the city? Or is the Destroyer causing more mayhem again?
No. Worse!
I can't find my hammer!

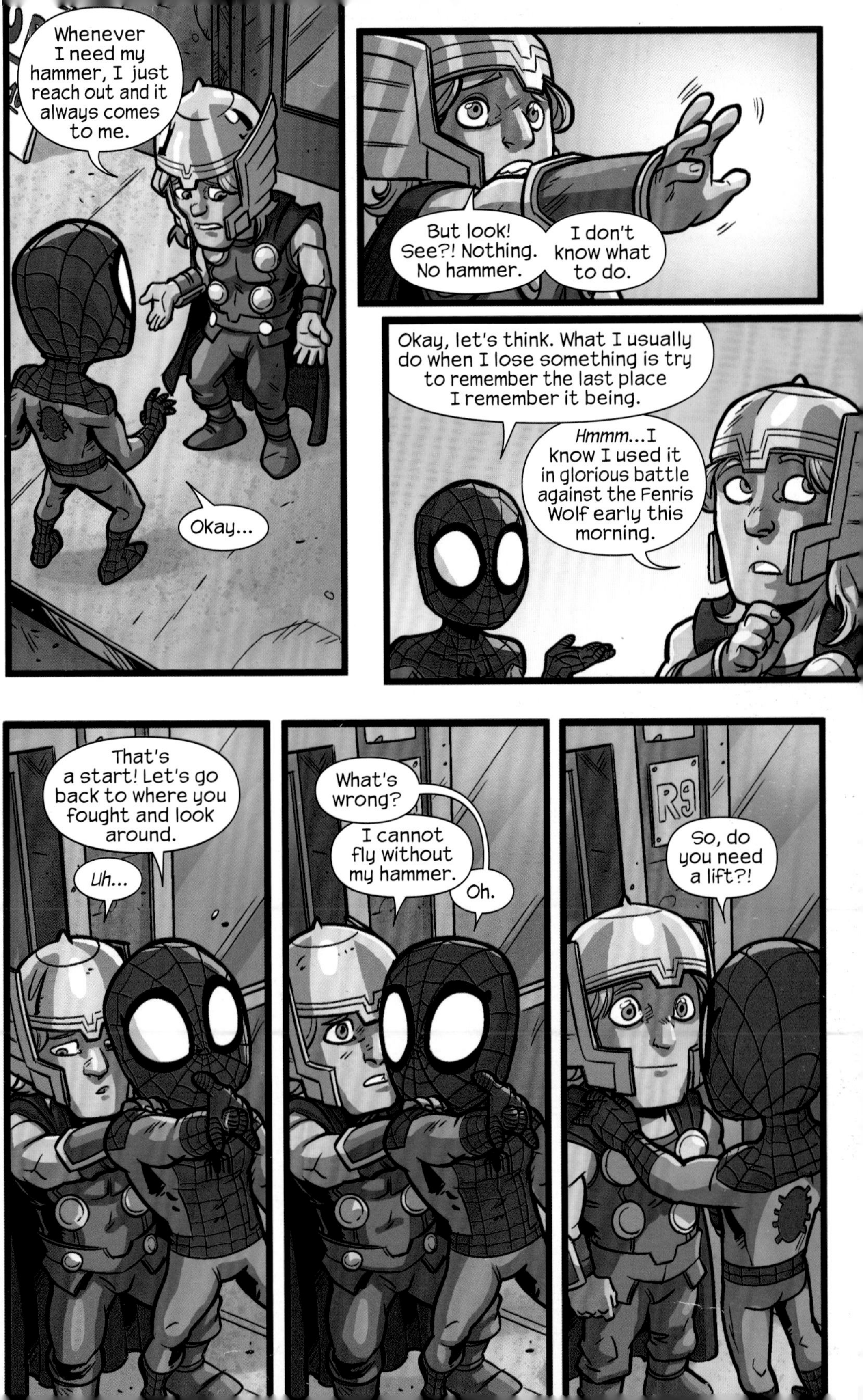
Whenever I need my hammer, I just reach out and it always comes to me.
Okay...
But look! See?! Nothing. No hammer.
I don't know what to do.
Okay, let's think. What I usually do when I lose something is try to remember the last place I remember it being.
Hmmm...I know I used it in glorious battle against the Fenris Wolf early this morning.
That's a start! Let's go back to where you fought and look around.
Uh...
What's wrong?
I cannot fly without my hammer.
Oh.
R9
So, do you need a lift?!

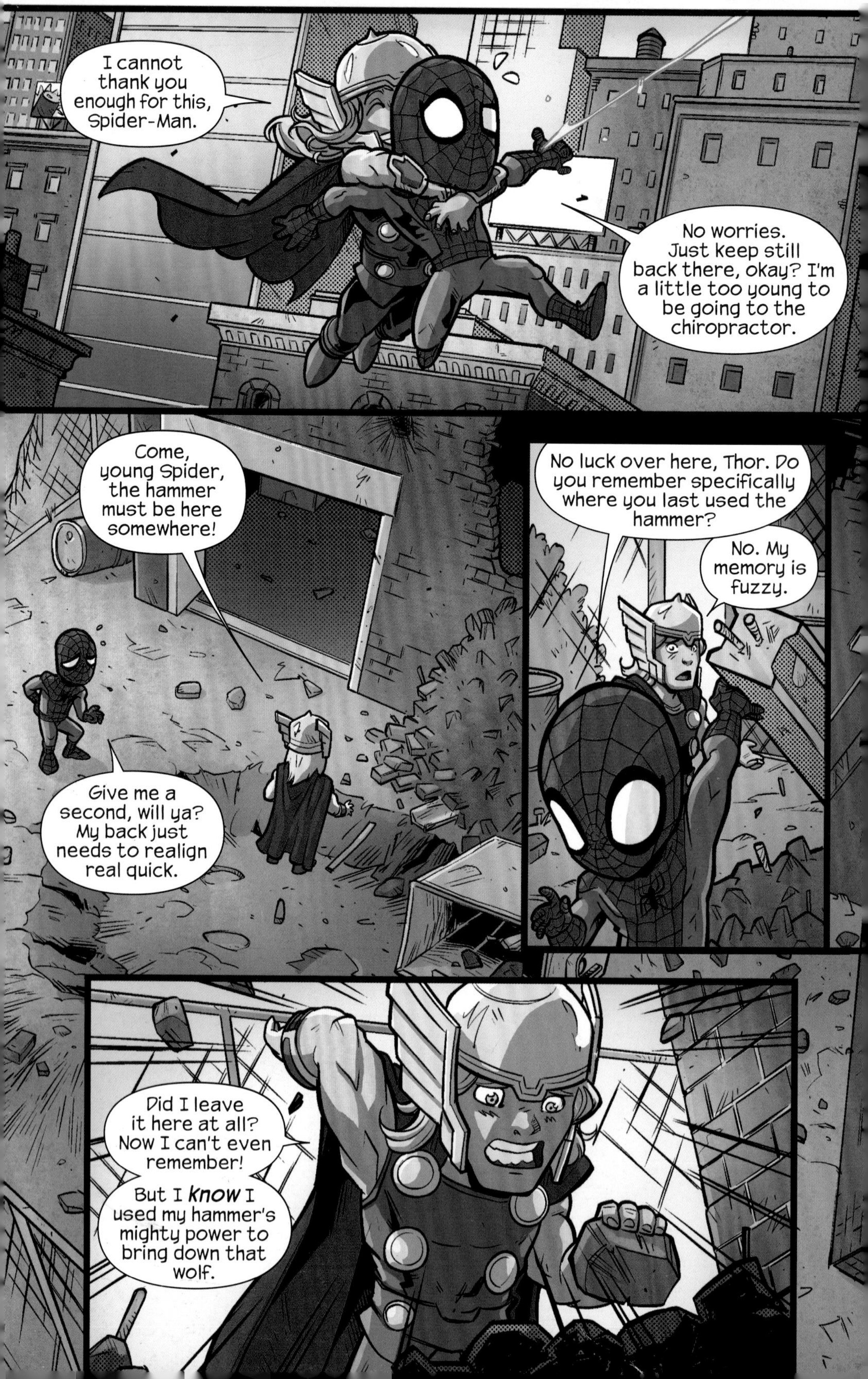
I cannot thank you enough for this, Spider-Man.
No worries. Just keep still back there, okay? I'm a little too young to be going to the chiropractor.
Come, young Spider, the hammer must be here somewhere!
Give me a second, will ya? My back just needs to realign real quick.
No luck over here, Thor. Do you remember specifically where you last used the hammer?
No. My memory is fuzzy.
Did I leave it here at all? Now I can't even remember!
But I *KNOW* I used my hammer's mighty power to bring down that wolf.

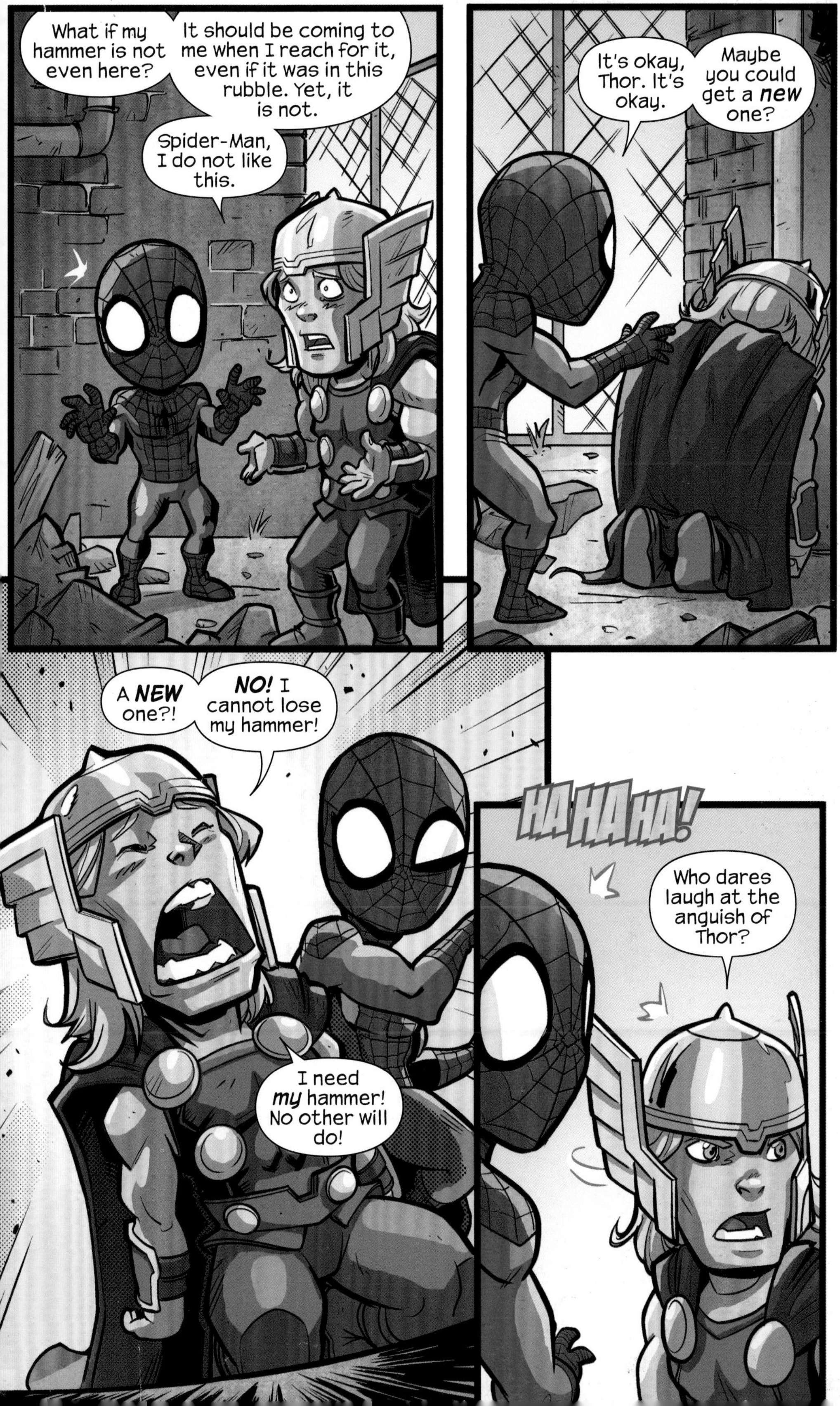
What if my hammer is not even here?
It should be coming to me when I reach for it, even if it was in this rubble. Yet, it is not.
Spider-Man, I do not like this.
It's okay, Thor. It's okay.
Maybe you could get a *new* one?
A *NEW* one?!
NO! I cannot lose my hammer!
I need *my* hammer! No other will do!
HA HA HA!
Who dares laugh at the anguish of Thor?

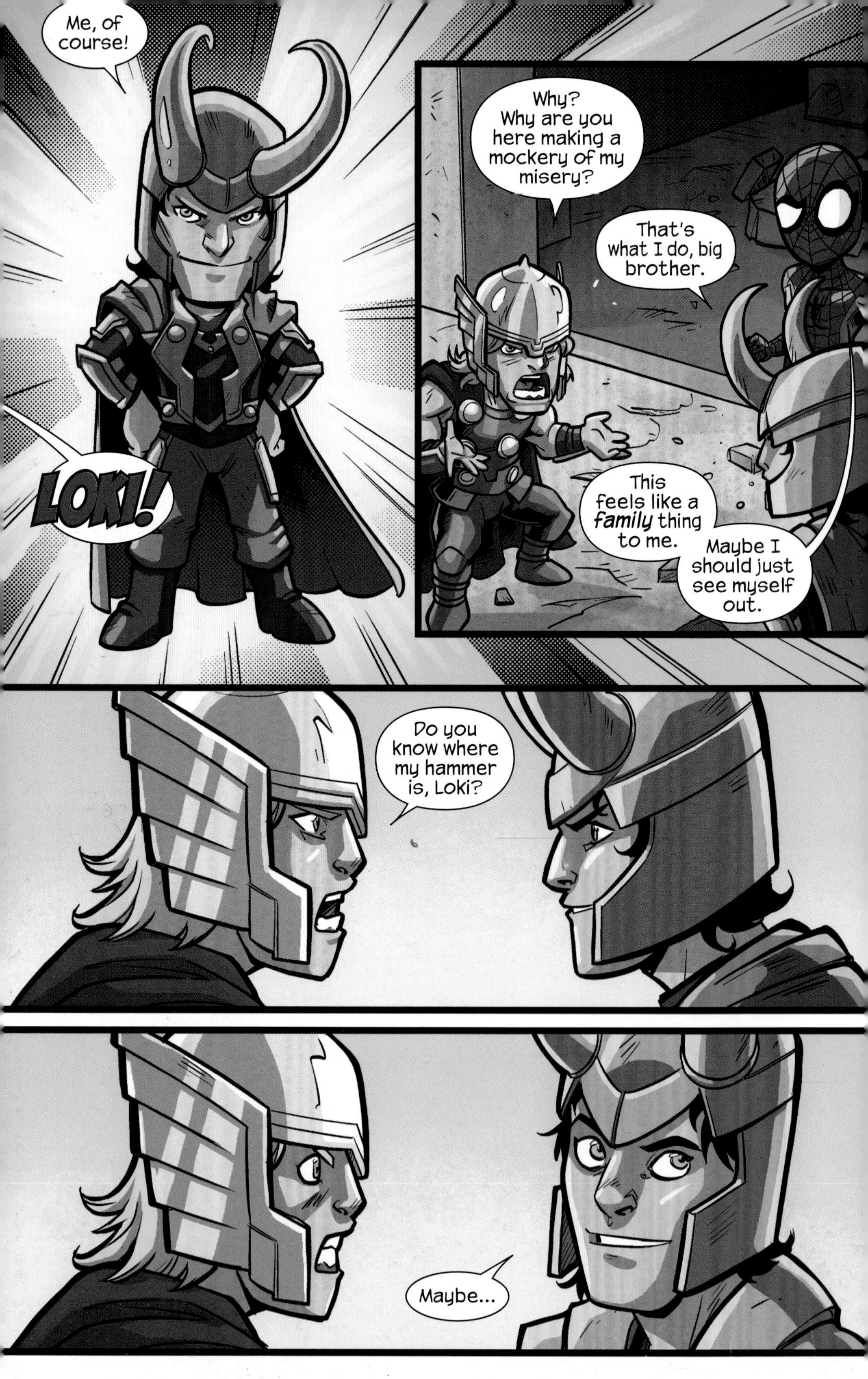
Me, of course!
LOKI!
Why? Why are you here making a mockery of my misery?
That's what I do, big brother.
This feels like a *family* thing to me.
Maybe I should just see myself out.
Do you know where my hammer is, Loki?
Maybe...

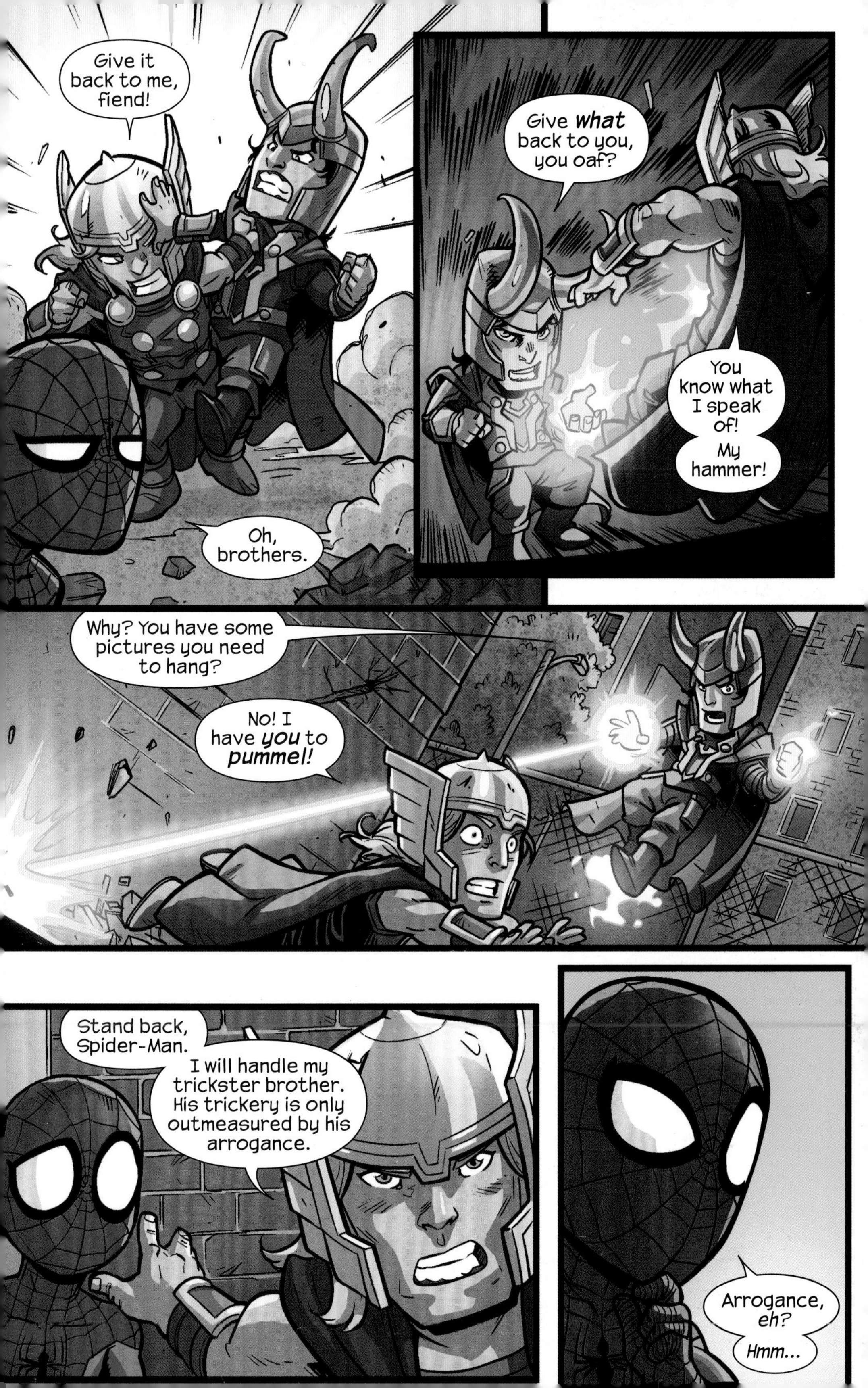
Give it back to me, fiend!
Oh, brothers.
Give what back to you, you oaf?
You know what I speak of!
My hammer!
Why? You have some pictures you need to hang?
No! I have you to pummel!
Stand back, Spider-Man.
I will handle my trickster brother. His trickery is only outmeasured by his arrogance.
Arrogance, eh?
Hmm...

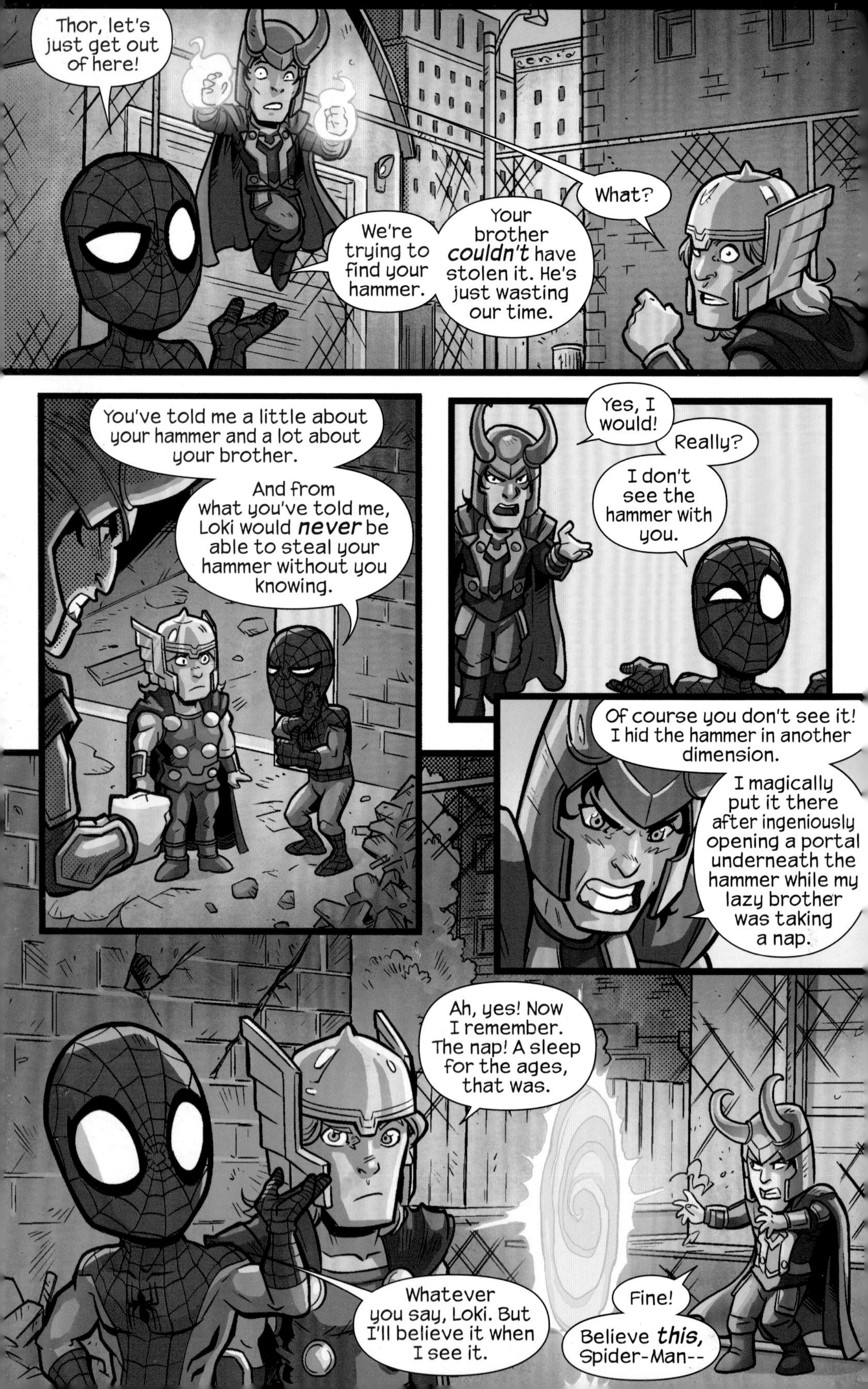
Thor, let's just get out of here!
What?
We're trying to find your hammer.
Your brother couldn't have stolen it. He's just wasting our time.
You've told me a little about your hammer and a lot about your brother.
And from what you've told me, Loki would never be able to steal your hammer without you knowing.
Yes, I would!
Really?
I don't see the hammer with you.
Of course you don't see it! I hid the hammer in another dimension.
I magically put it there after ingeniously opening a portal underneath the hammer while my lazy brother was taking a nap.
Ah, yes! Now I remember. The nap! A sleep for the ages, that was.
Whatever you say, Loki. But I'll believe it when I see it.
Fine!
Believe this, Spider-Man--

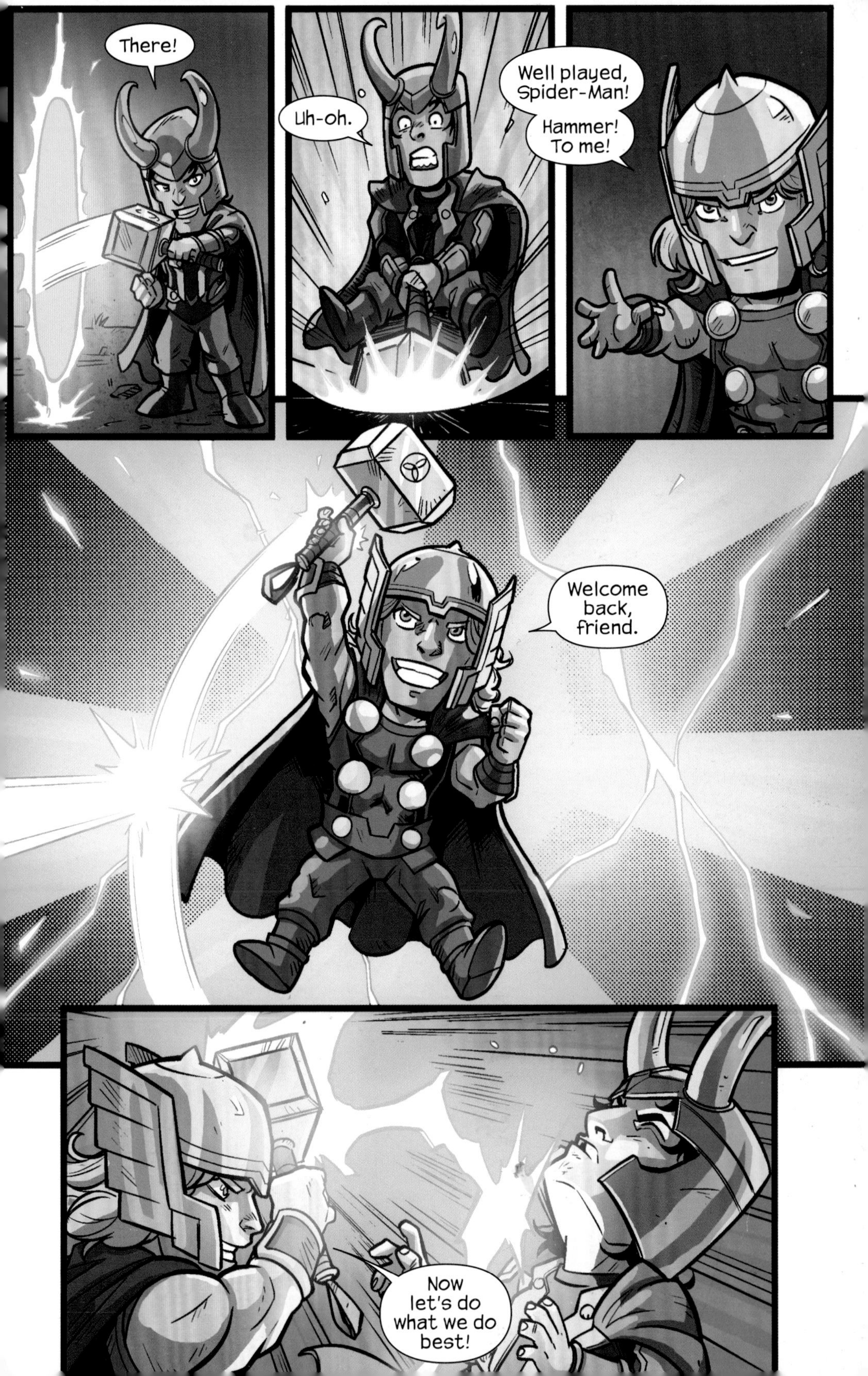
There!
Uh-oh.
Well played, Spider-Man!
Hammer! To me!
Welcome back, friend.
Now let's do what we do best!

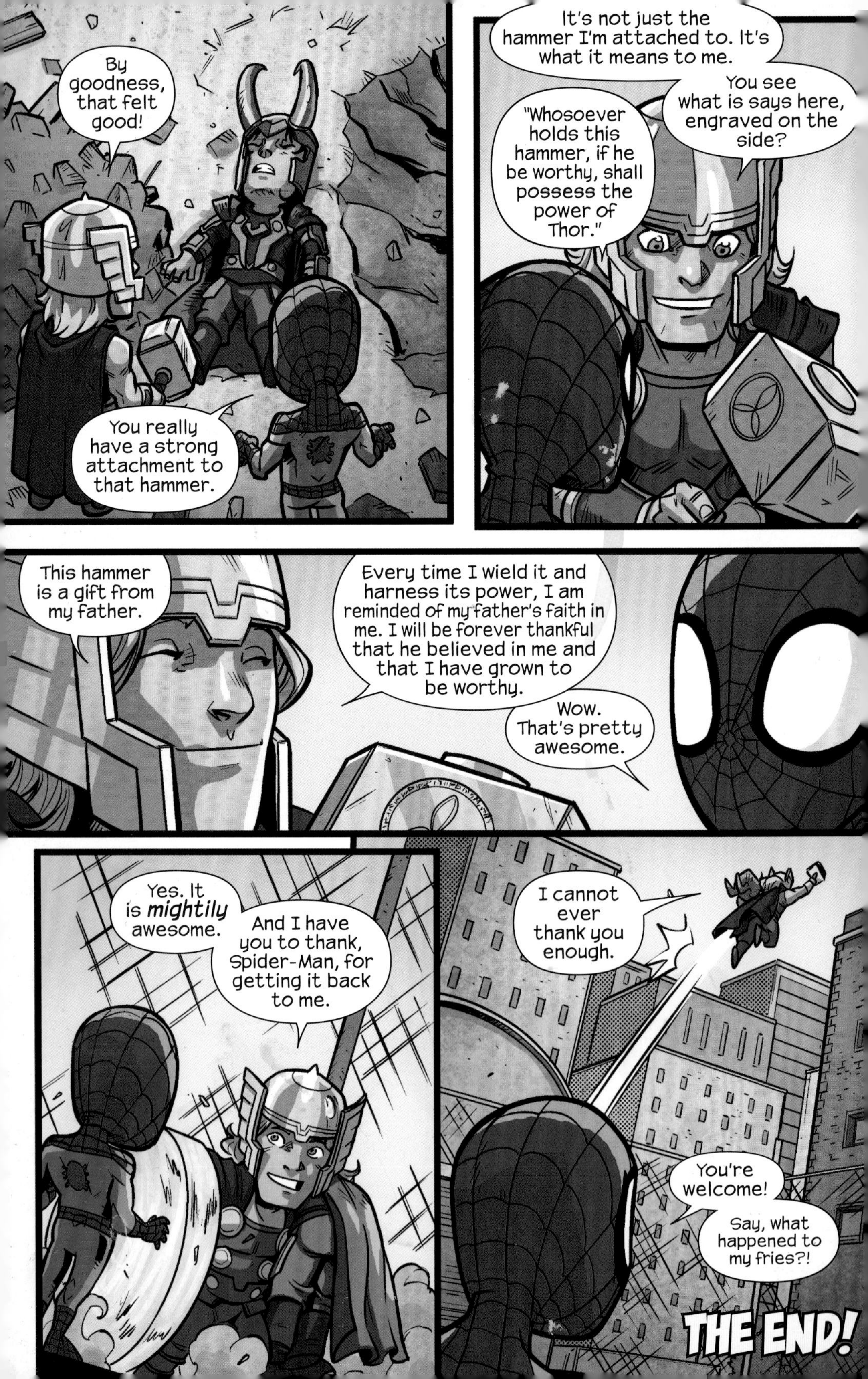
By goodness, that felt good!
You really have a strong attachment to that hammer.
It's not just the hammer I'm attached to. It's what it means to me.
You see what is says here, engraved on the side?
"Whosoever holds this hammer, if he be worthy, shall possess the power of Thor."
This hammer is a gift from my father.
Every time I wield it and harness its power, I am reminded of my father's faith in me. I will be forever thankful that he believed in me and that I have grown to be worthy.
Wow. That's pretty awesome.
Yes. It is *mightily* awesome.
And I have you to thank, Spider-Man, for getting it back to me.
I cannot ever thank you enough.
You're welcome!
Say, what happened to my fries?!
THE END!

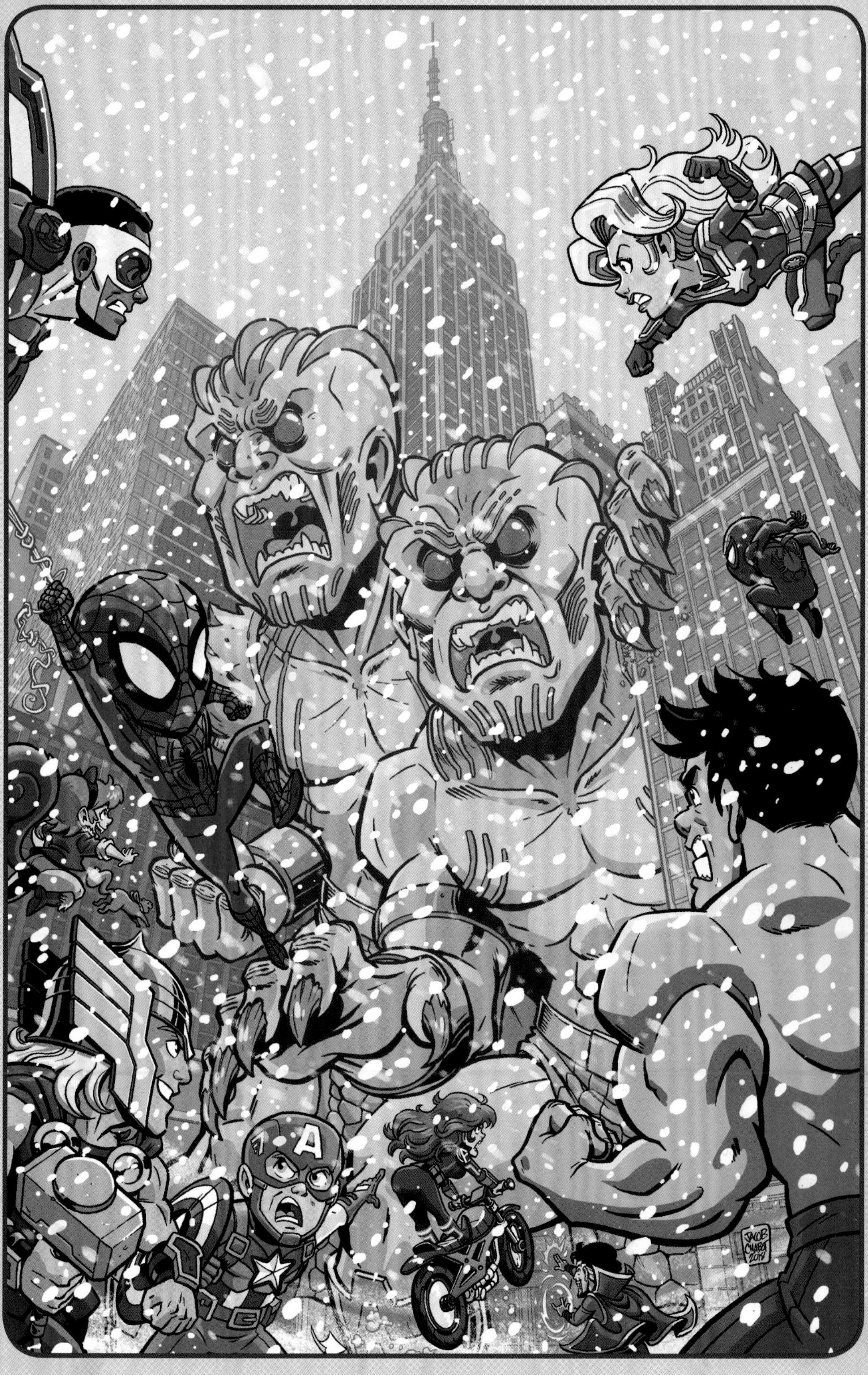
JACOB CHABOT 2019

Frost Giants Among Us

cover by Jacob Chabot

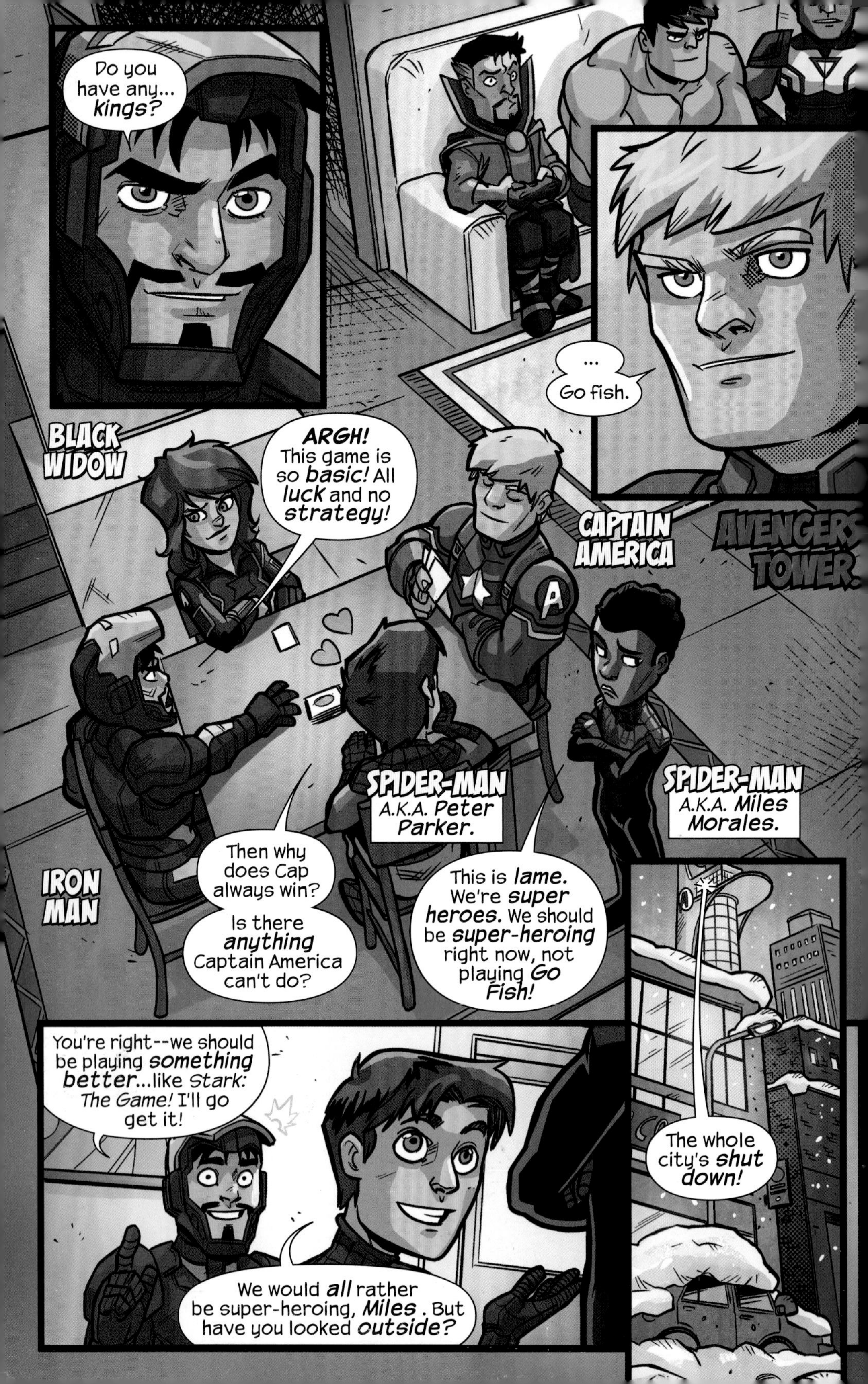
Do you have any... *kings?*
...
Go fish.
BLACK WIDOW
ARGH! This game is so *basic!* All *luck* and no *strategy!*
CAPTAIN AMERICA
AVENGERS TOWER.
SPIDER-MAN A.K.A. Peter Parker.
SPIDER-MAN A.K.A. Miles Morales.
IRON MAN
Then why does Cap always win?
Is there *anything* Captain America can't do?
This is *lame.* We're *super heroes.* We should be *super-heroing* right now, not playing *Go Fish!*
You're right--we should be playing *something better*...like *Stark: The Game!* I'll go get it!
We would *all* rather be super-heroing, *Miles* . But have you looked *outside?*
The whole city's *shut down!*

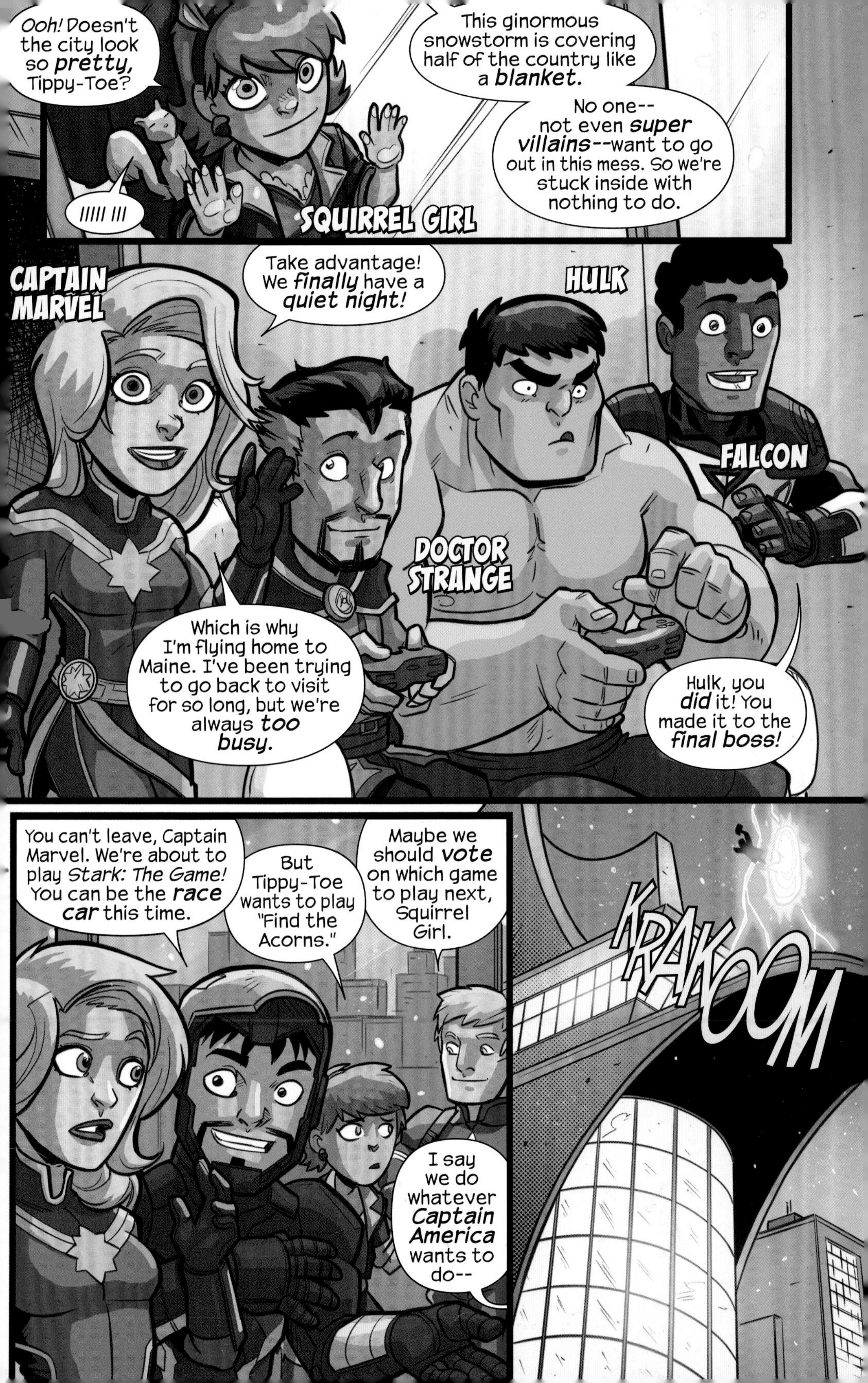
Ooh! Doesn't the city look so pretty, Tippy-Toe?
!!!!! !!!
This ginormous snowstorm is covering half of the country like a blanket.
No one-- not even super villains--want to go out in this mess. So we're stuck inside with nothing to do.
SQUIRREL GIRL
CAPTAIN MARVEL
Take advantage! We finally have a quiet night!
HULK
FALCON
DOCTOR STRANGE
Which is why I'm flying home to Maine. I've been trying to go back to visit for so long, but we're always too busy.
Hulk, you did it! You made it to the final boss!
You can't leave, Captain Marvel. We're about to play Stark: The Game! You can be the race car this time.
But Tippy-Toe wants to play "Find the Acorns."
Maybe we should vote on which game to play next, Squirrel Girl.
I say we do whatever Captain America wants to do--
KRAKOOM

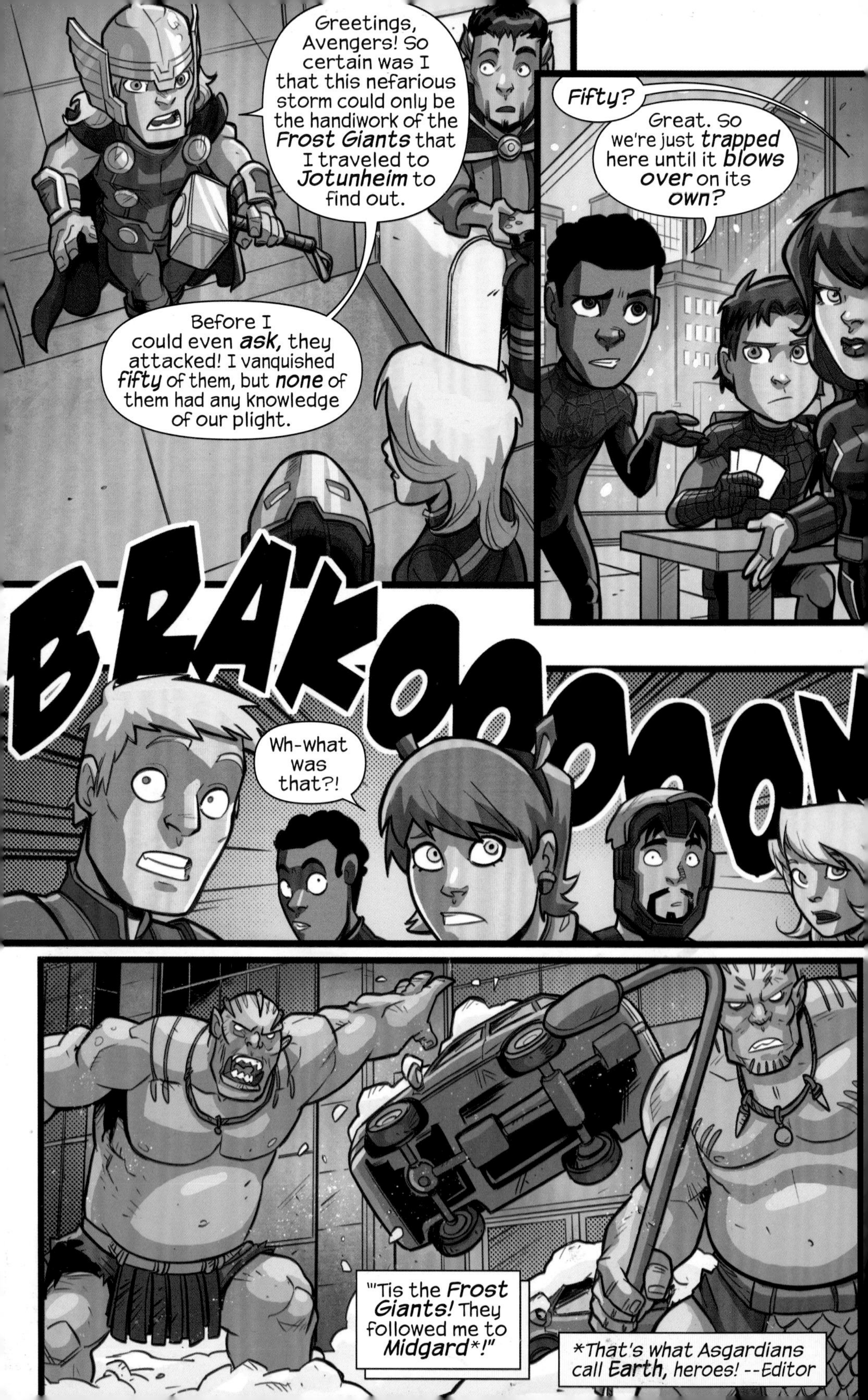

Greetings, Avengers! So certain was I that this nefarious storm could only be the handiwork of the Frost Giants that I traveled to Jotunheim to find out.
Before I could even ask, they attacked! I vanquished fifty of them, but none of them had any knowledge of our plight.
Fifty?
Great. So we're just trapped here until it blows over on its own?
BRAKOOOOOOM
Wh-what was that?!
"'Tis the Frost Giants! They followed me to Midgard*!"
*That's what Asgardians call Earth, heroes! --Editor

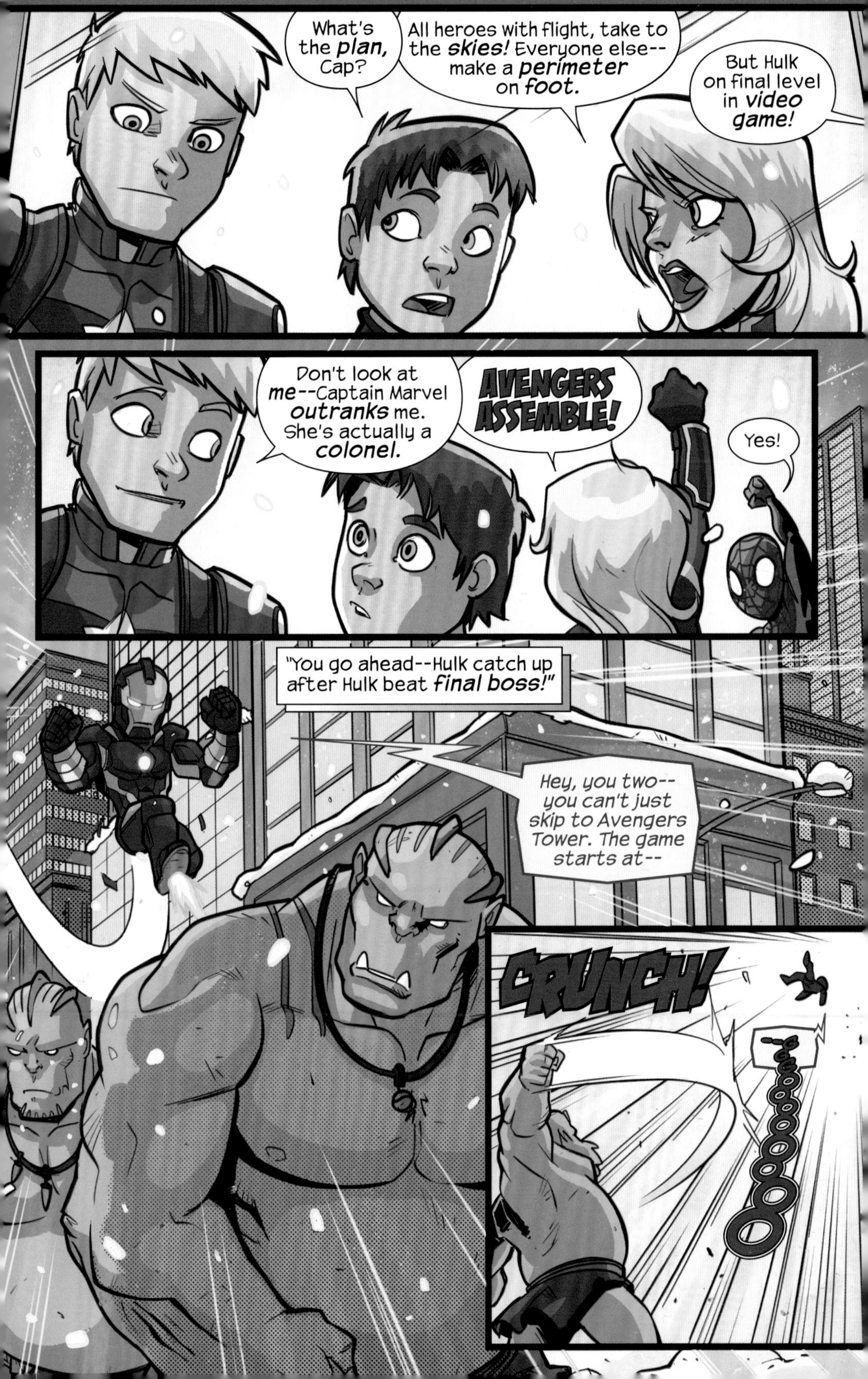
What's the plan, Cap?
All heroes with flight, take to the skies! Everyone else--make a perimeter on foot.
But Hulk on final level in video game!
Don't look at me--Captain Marvel outranks me. She's actually a colonel.
AVENGERS ASSEMBLE!
Yes!
"You go ahead--Hulk catch up after Hulk beat final boss!"
Hey, you two--you can't just skip to Avengers Tower. The game starts at--
CRUNCH!

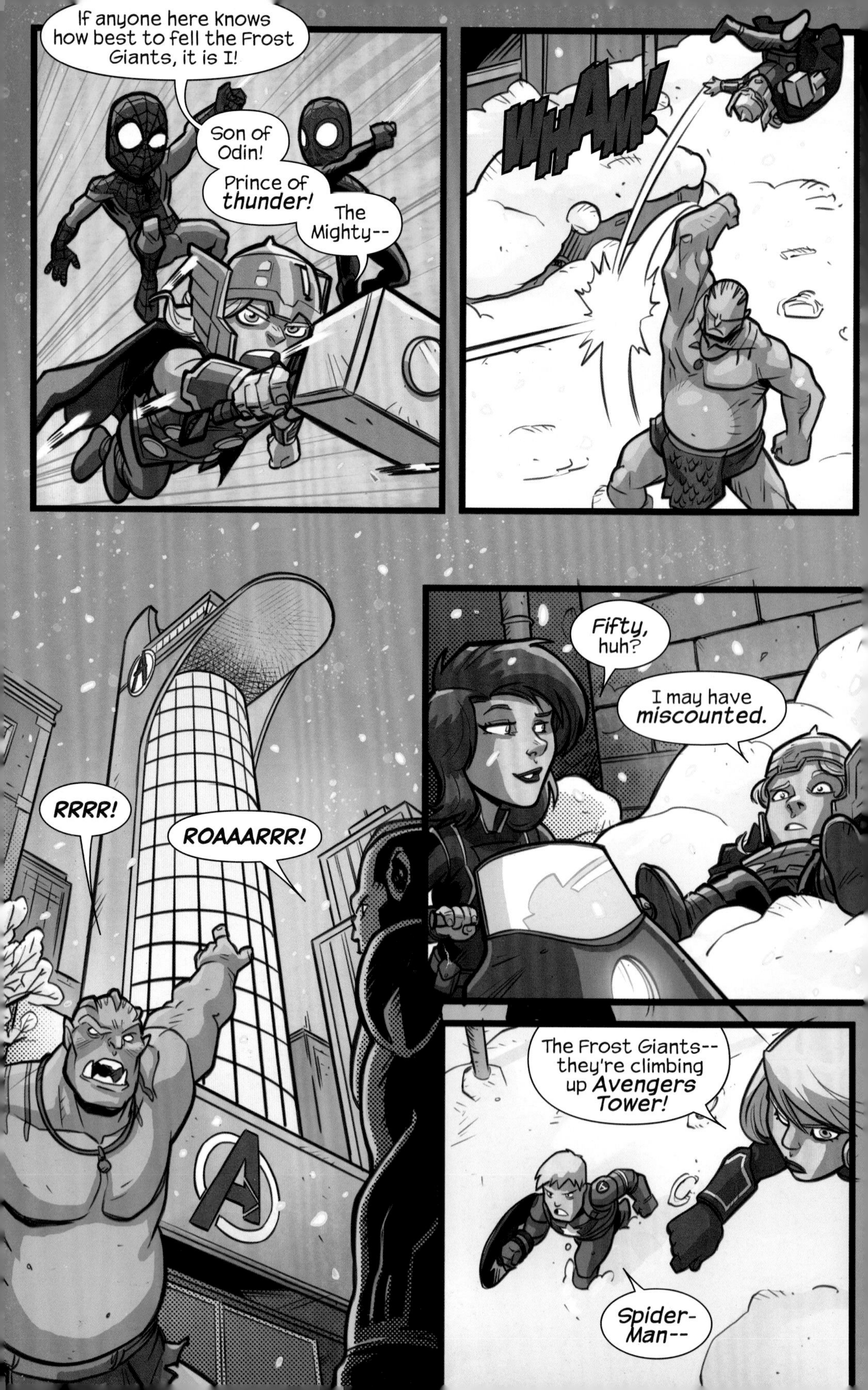
If anyone here knows how best to fell the Frost Giants, it is I!
Son of Odin!
Prince of thunder!
The Mighty--
WHAM!
RRRR!
ROAAARRR!
Fifty, huh?
I may have miscounted.
The Frost Giants-- they're climbing up Avengers Tower!
Spider-Man--

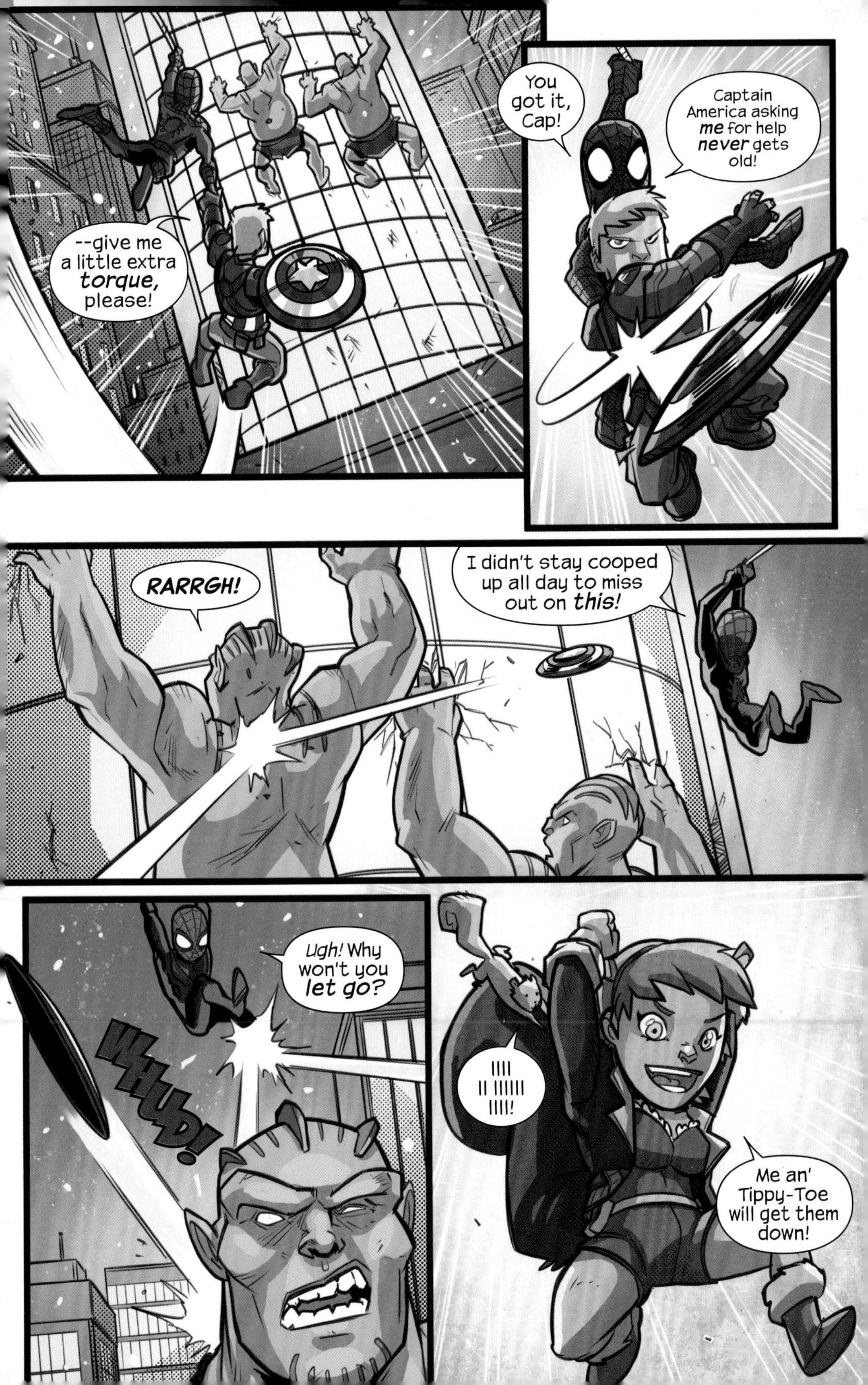
--give me a little extra torque, please!
You got it, Cap!
Captain America asking me for help never gets old!
RARRGH!
I didn't stay cooped up all day to miss out on this!
Ugh! Why won't you let go?
WHUD!
Me an' Tippy-Toe will get them down!

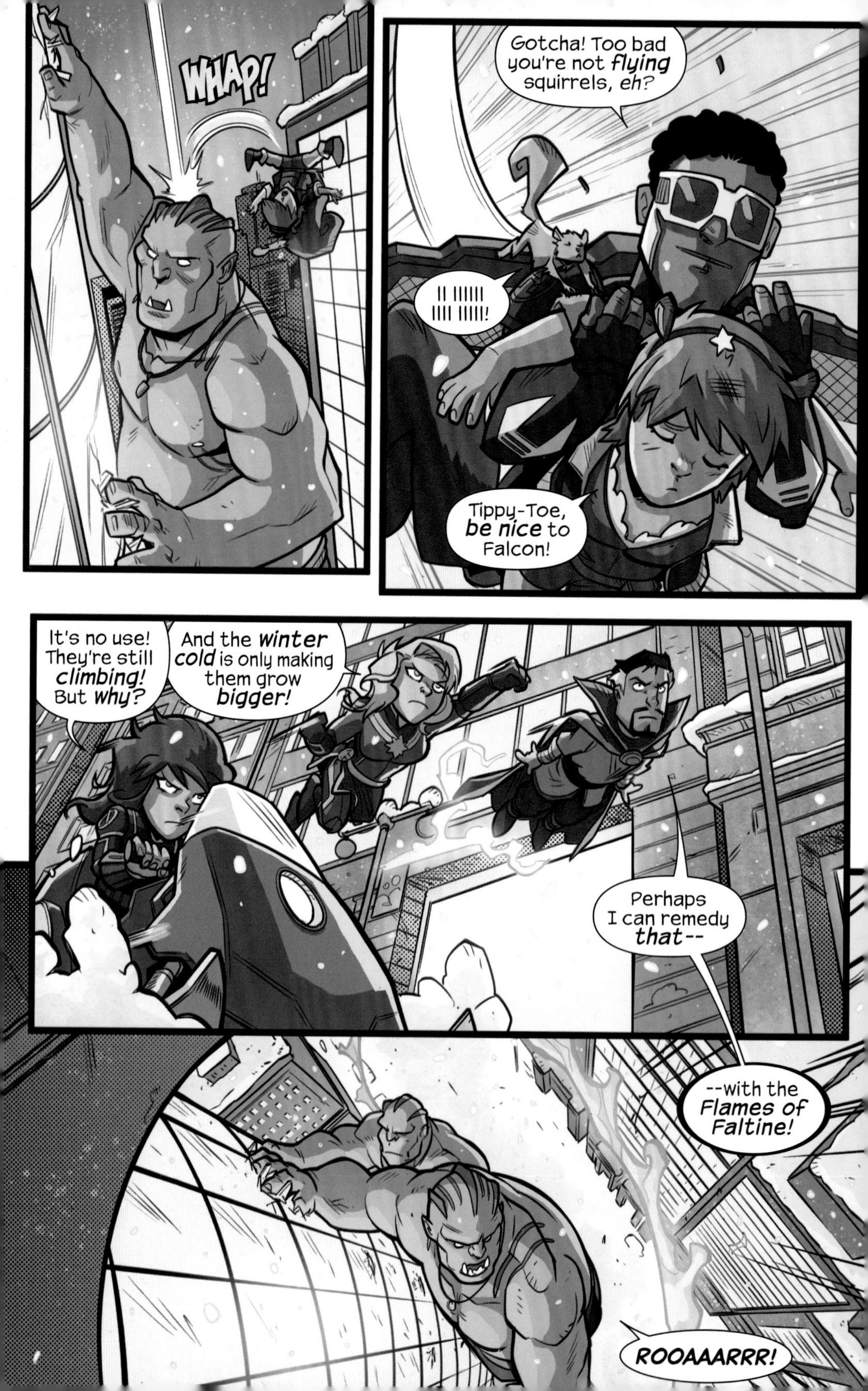
WHAP!
Gotcha! Too bad you're not *flying* squirrels, *eh?*
!! !!!!!! !!!! !!!!!!
Tippy-Toe, ***be nice*** to Falcon!
It's no use! They're still ***climbing!*** But ***why?***
And the ***winter cold*** is only making them grow ***bigger!***
Perhaps I can remedy ***that--***
--with the ***Flames of Faltine!***
ROOAAARRR!

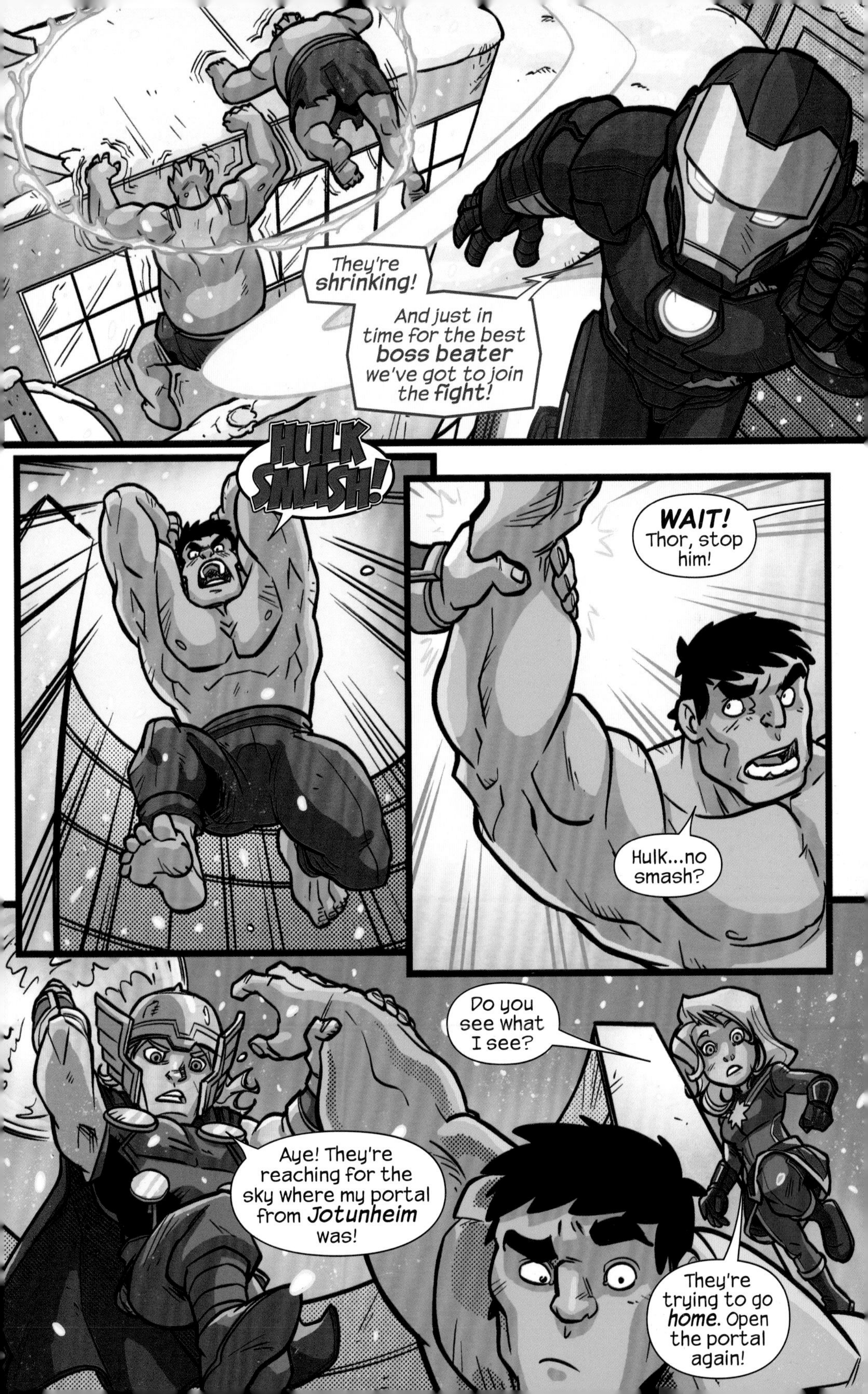
They're shrinking!
And just in time for the best boss beater we've got to join the fight!
HULK SMASH!
WAIT! Thor, stop him!
Hulk...no smash?
Do you see what I see?
Aye! They're reaching for the sky where my portal from Jotunheim was!
They're trying to go home. Open the portal again!

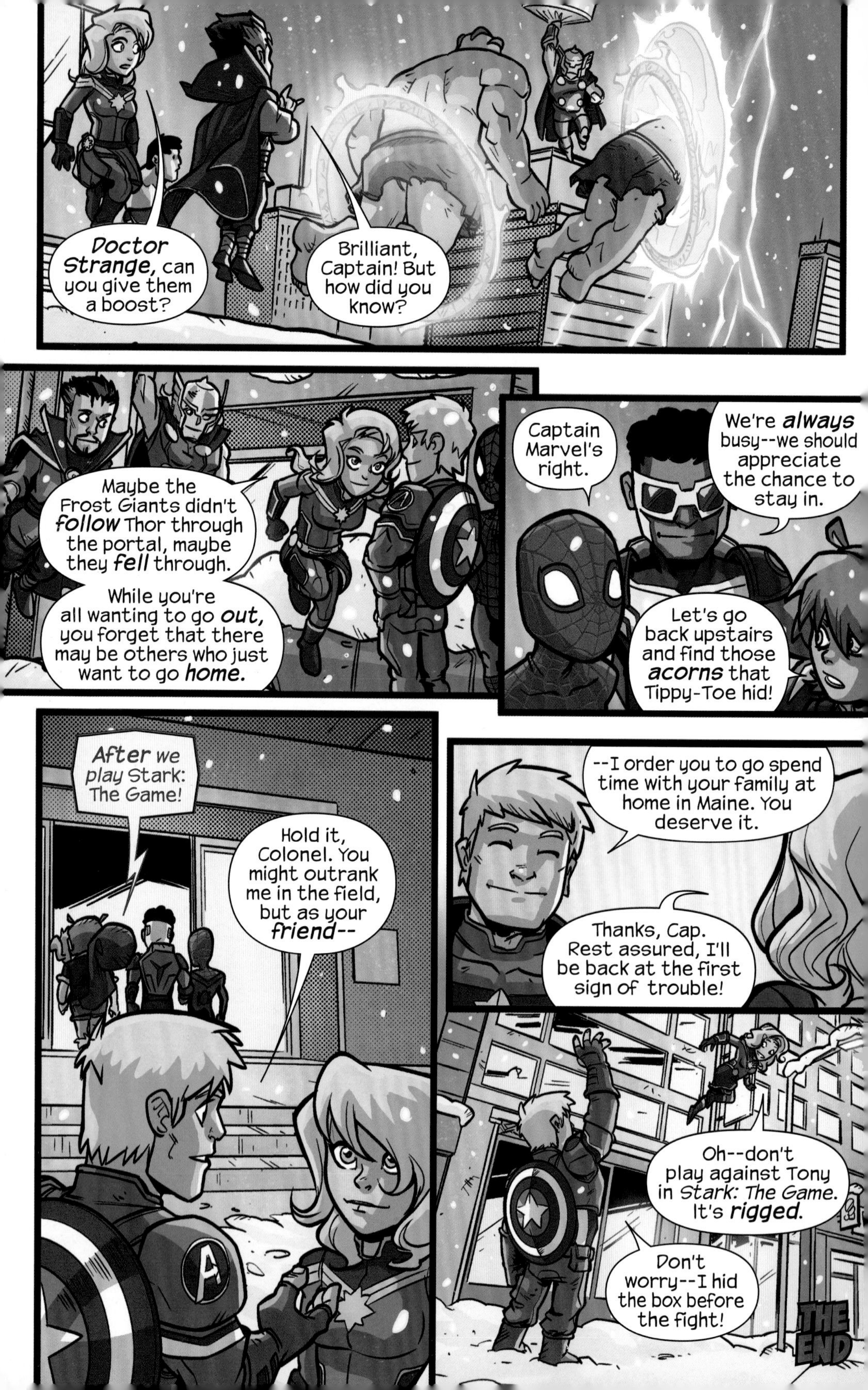

Doctor Strange, can you give them a boost?
Brilliant, Captain! But how did you know?
Maybe the Frost Giants didn't follow Thor through the portal, maybe they fell through.
While you're all wanting to go out, you forget that there may be others who just want to go home.
Captain Marvel's right.
We're always busy--we should appreciate the chance to stay in.
Let's go back upstairs and find those acorns that Tippy-Toe hid!
After we play Stark: The Game!
Hold it, Colonel. You might outrank me in the field, but as your friend--
--I order you to go spend time with your family at home in Maine. You deserve it.
Thanks, Cap. Rest assured, I'll be back at the first sign of trouble!
Oh--don't play against Tony in Stark: The Game. It's rigged.
Don't worry--I hid the box before the fight!
THE END

DAILY BUGLE

NEW YORK'S FUNNIEST DAILY NEWSPAPER

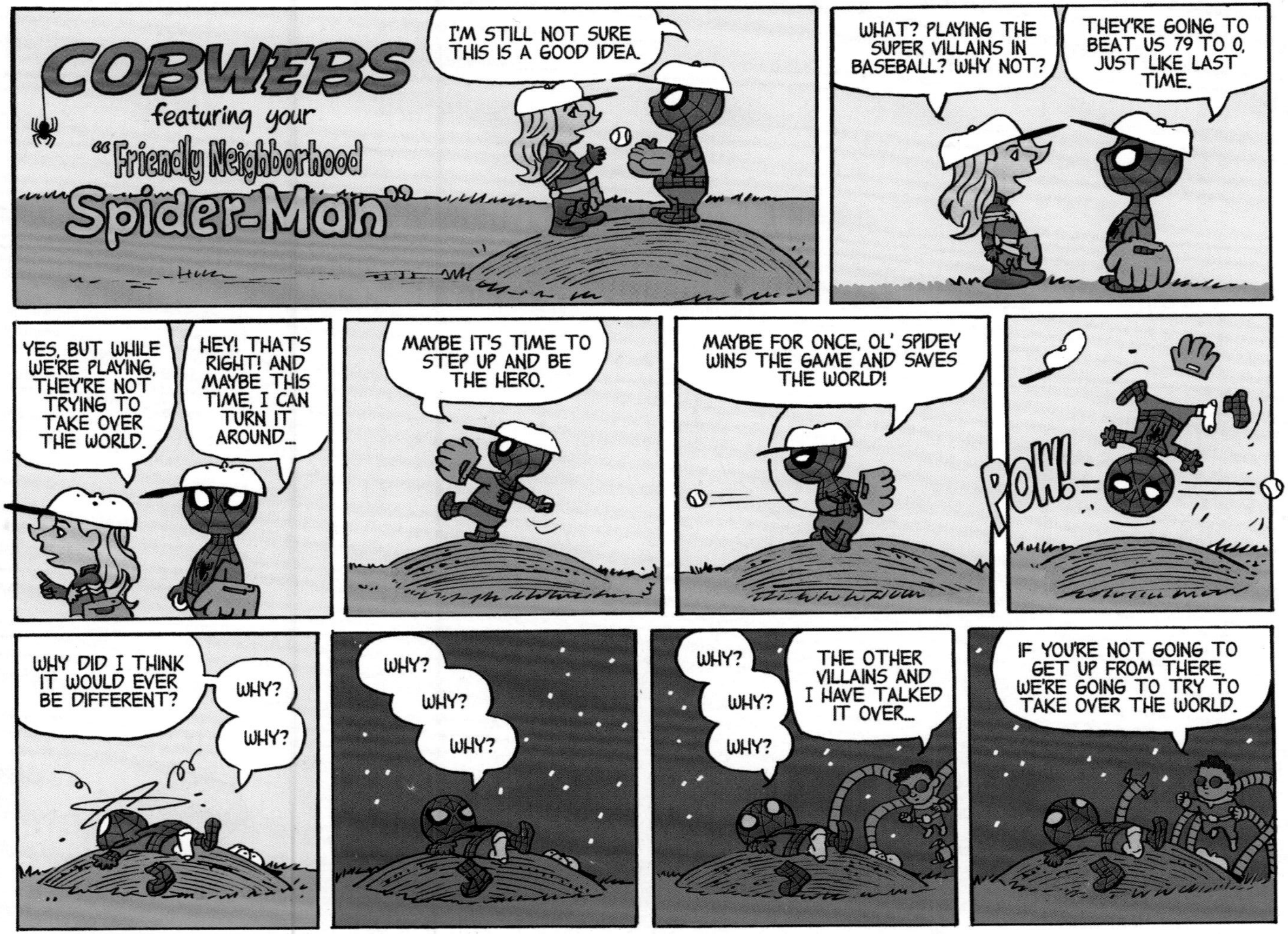
COBWEBS
featuring your
"Friendly Neighborhood
Spider-Man"
I'M STILL NOT SURE THIS IS A GOOD IDEA.
WHAT? PLAYING THE SUPER VILLAINS IN BASEBALL? WHY NOT?
THEY'RE GOING TO BEAT US 79 TO 0, JUST LIKE LAST TIME.
YES, BUT WHILE WE'RE PLAYING, THEY'RE NOT TRYING TO TAKE OVER THE WORLD.
HEY! THAT'S RIGHT! AND MAYBE THIS TIME, I CAN TURN IT AROUND...
MAYBE IT'S TIME TO STEP UP AND BE THE HERO.
MAYBE FOR ONCE, OL' SPIDEY WINS THE GAME AND SAVES THE WORLD!
POW!
WHY DID I THINK IT WOULD EVER BE DIFFERENT?
WHY?
WHY?
WHY?
WHY?
WHY?
WHY?
WHY?
WHY?
THE OTHER VILLAINS AND I HAVE TALKED IT OVER...
IF YOU'RE NOT GOING TO GET UP FROM THERE, WE'RE GOING TO TRY TO TAKE OVER THE WORLD.

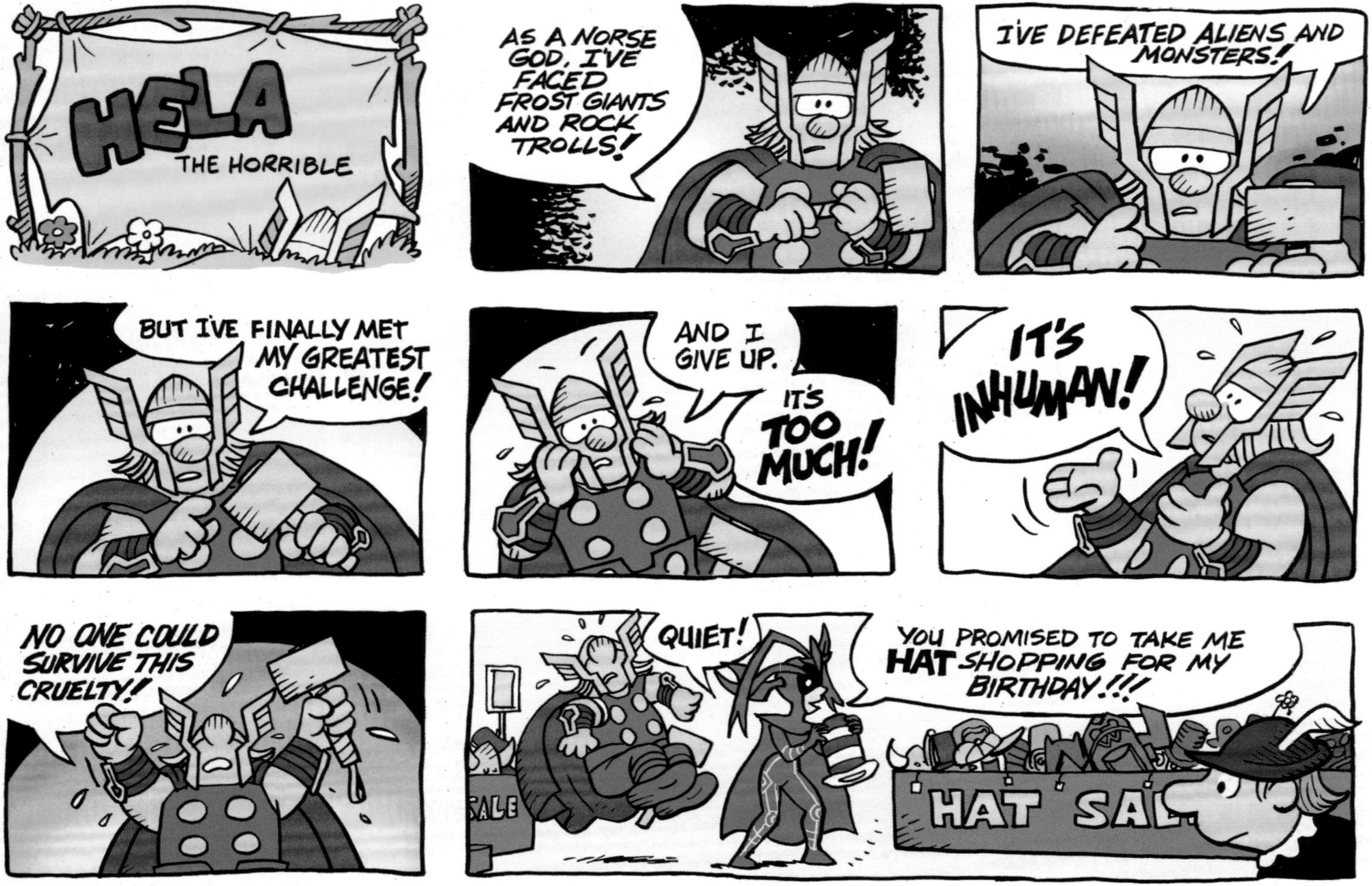
HELA THE HORRIBLE
AS A NORSE GOD, I'VE FACED FROST GIANTS AND ROCK TROLLS!
I'VE DEFEATED ALIENS AND MONSTERS!
BUT I'VE FINALLY MET MY GREATEST CHALLENGE!
AND I GIVE UP.
IT'S TOO MUCH!
IT'S INHUMAN!
NO ONE COULD SURVIVE THIS CRUELTY!
QUIET!
YOU PROMISED TO TAKE ME HAT SHOPPING FOR MY BIRTHDAY!!!
SALE
HAT SAL

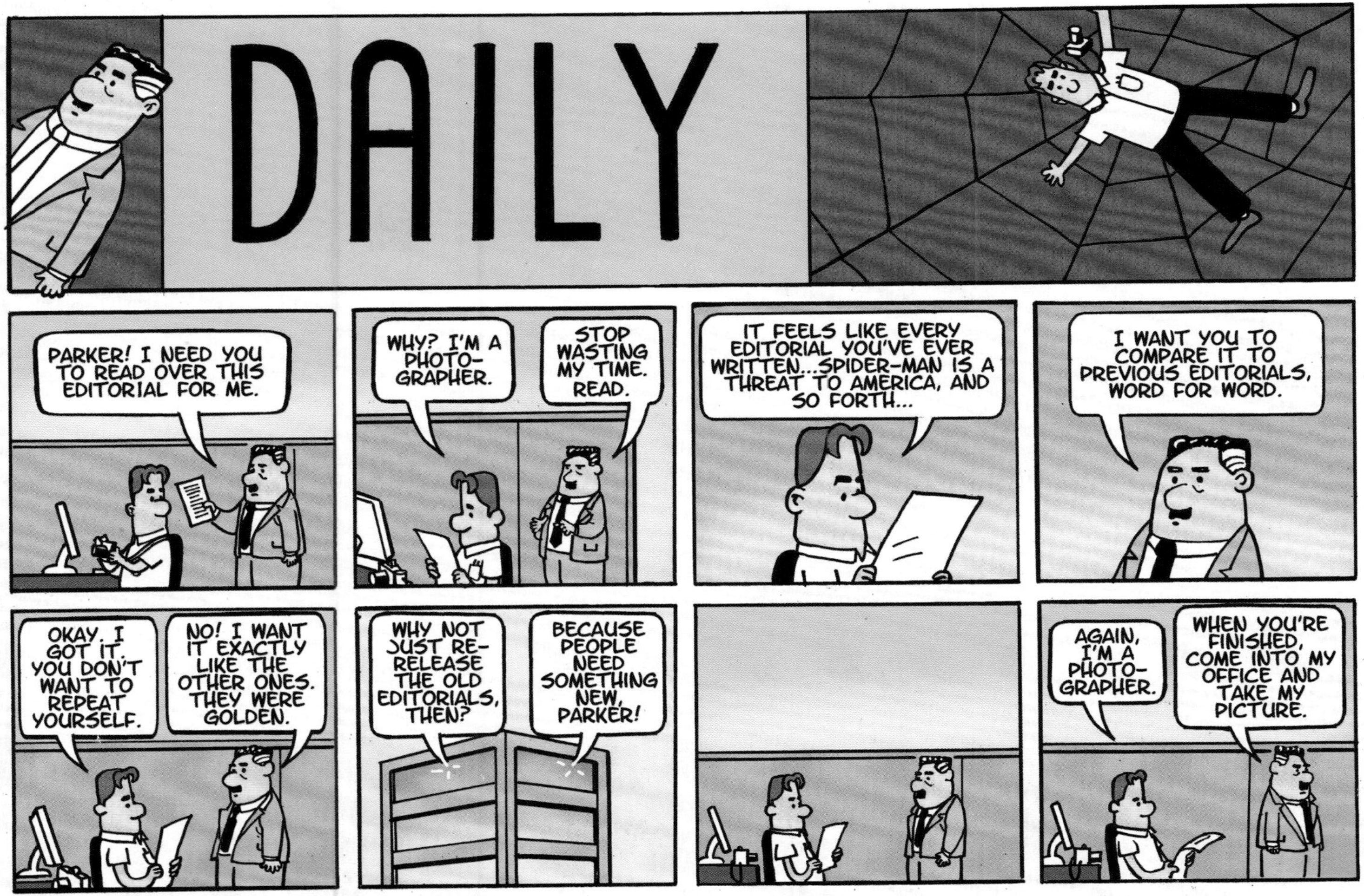
DAILY
PARKER! I NEED YOU TO READ OVER THIS EDITORIAL FOR ME.
WHY? I'M A PHOTO-GRAPHER.
STOP WASTING MY TIME. READ.
IT FEELS LIKE EVERY EDITORIAL YOU'VE EVER WRITTEN...SPIDER-MAN IS A THREAT TO AMERICA, AND SO FORTH...
I WANT YOU TO COMPARE IT TO PREVIOUS EDITORIALS, WORD FOR WORD.
OKAY. I GOT IT. YOU DON'T WANT TO REPEAT YOURSELF.
NO! I WANT IT EXACTLY LIKE THE OTHER ONES. THEY WERE GOLDEN.
WHY NOT JUST RE-RELEASE THE OLD EDITORIALS, THEN?
BECAUSE PEOPLE NEED SOMETHING NEW, PARKER!
AGAIN, I'M A PHOTO-GRAPHER.
WHEN YOU'RE FINISHED, COME INTO MY OFFICE AND TAKE MY PICTURE.

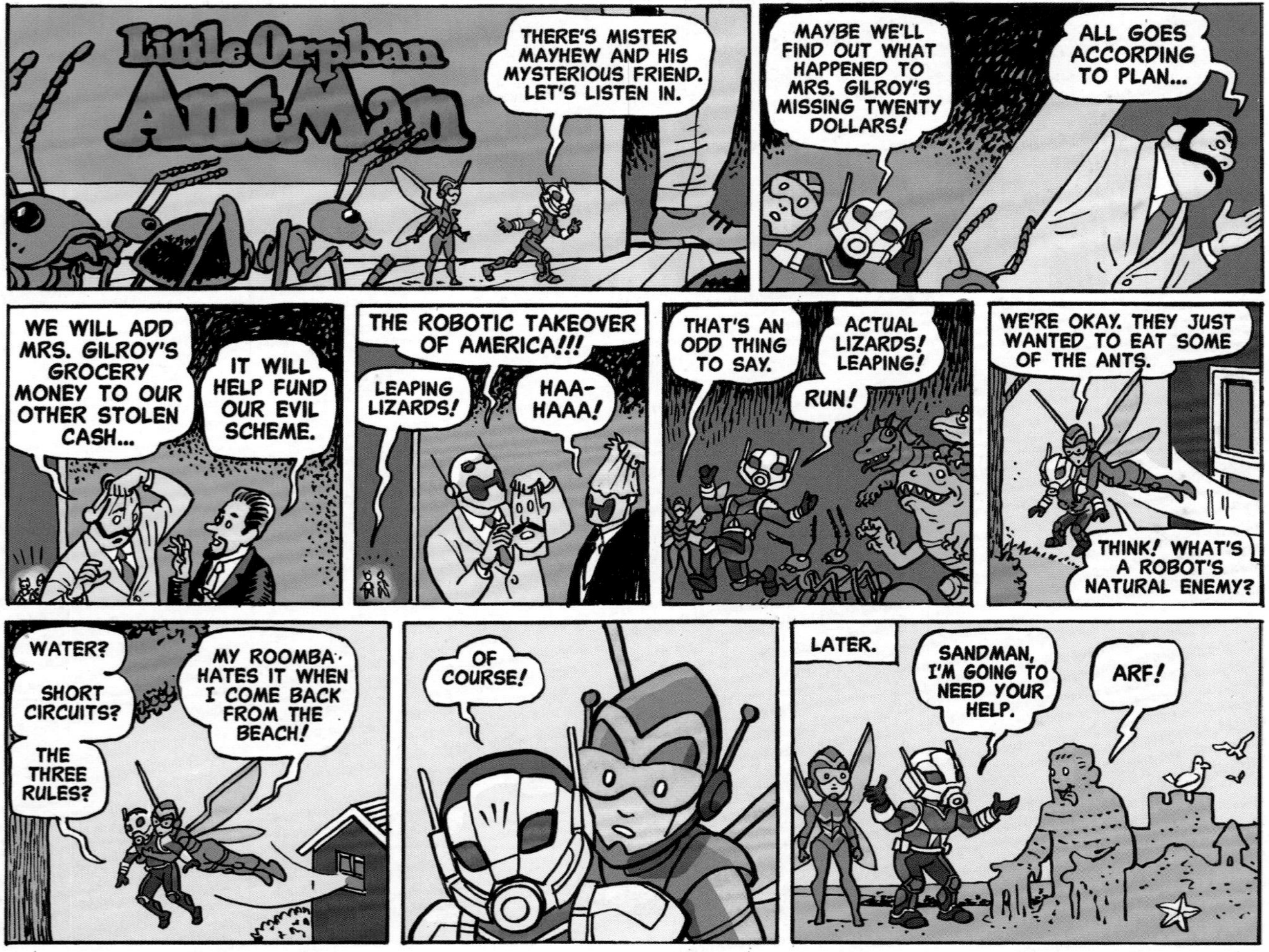
Little Orphan Ant-Man
THERE'S MISTER MAYHEW AND HIS MYSTERIOUS FRIEND. LET'S LISTEN IN.
MAYBE WE'LL FIND OUT WHAT HAPPENED TO MRS. GILROY'S MISSING TWENTY DOLLARS!
ALL GOES ACCORDING TO PLAN...
WE WILL ADD MRS. GILROY'S GROCERY MONEY TO OUR OTHER STOLEN CASH...
IT WILL HELP FUND OUR EVIL SCHEME.
THE ROBOTIC TAKEOVER OF AMERICA!!!
LEAPING LIZARDS!
HAA-HAAA!
THAT'S AN ODD THING TO SAY.
ACTUAL LIZARDS! LEAPING!
RUN!
WE'RE OKAY. THEY JUST WANTED TO EAT SOME OF THE ANTS.
THINK! WHAT'S A ROBOT'S NATURAL ENEMY?
WATER?
SHORT CIRCUITS?
THE THREE RULES?
MY ROOMBA HATES IT WHEN I COME BACK FROM THE BEACH!
OF COURSE!
LATER.
SANDMAN, I'M GOING TO NEED YOUR HELP.
ARF!

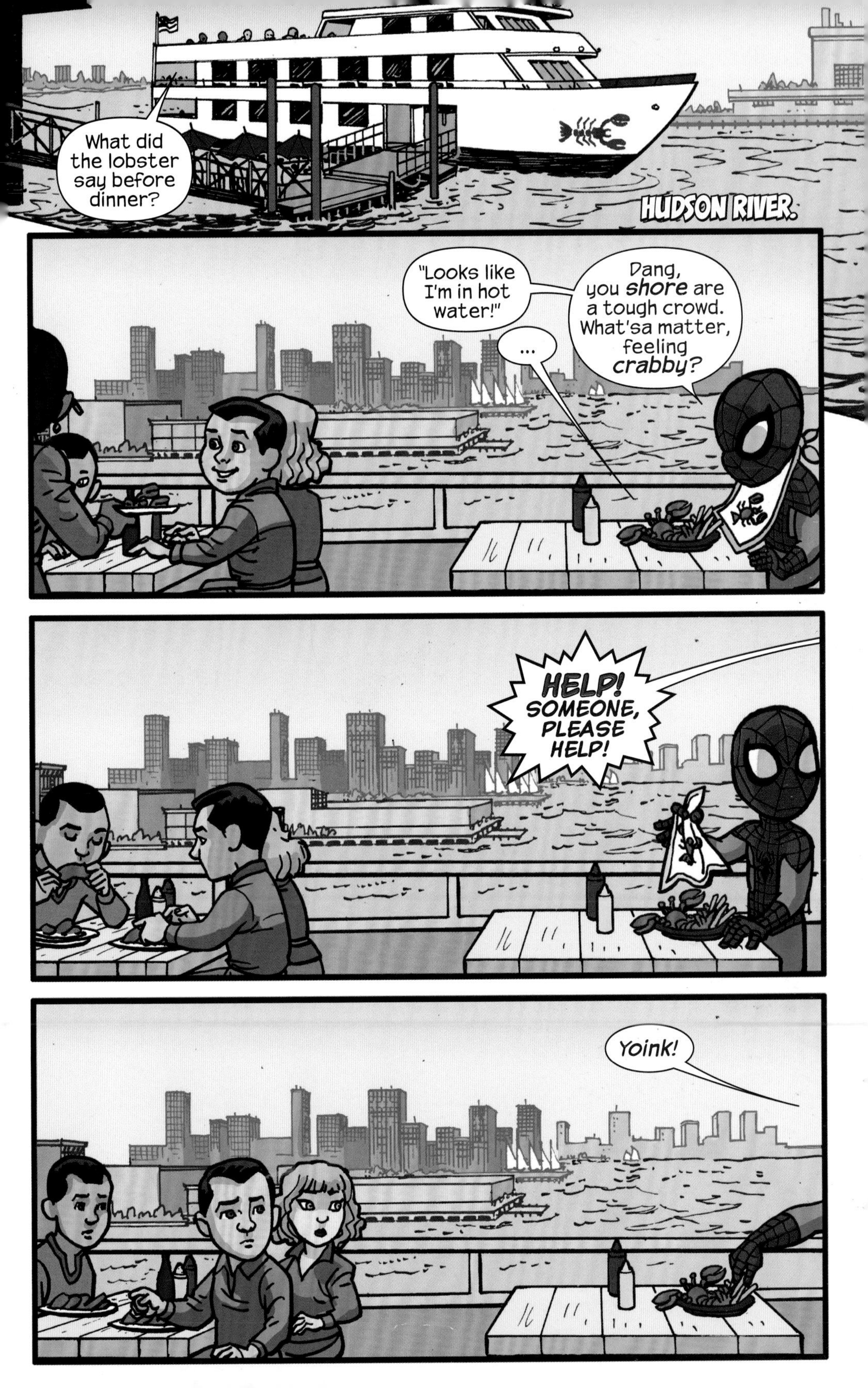
What did the lobster say before dinner?
HUDSON RIVER.
"Looks like I'm in hot water!"
Dang, you shore are a tough crowd. What'sa matter, feeling crabby?
...
HELP! SOMEONE, PLEASE HELP!
Yoink!

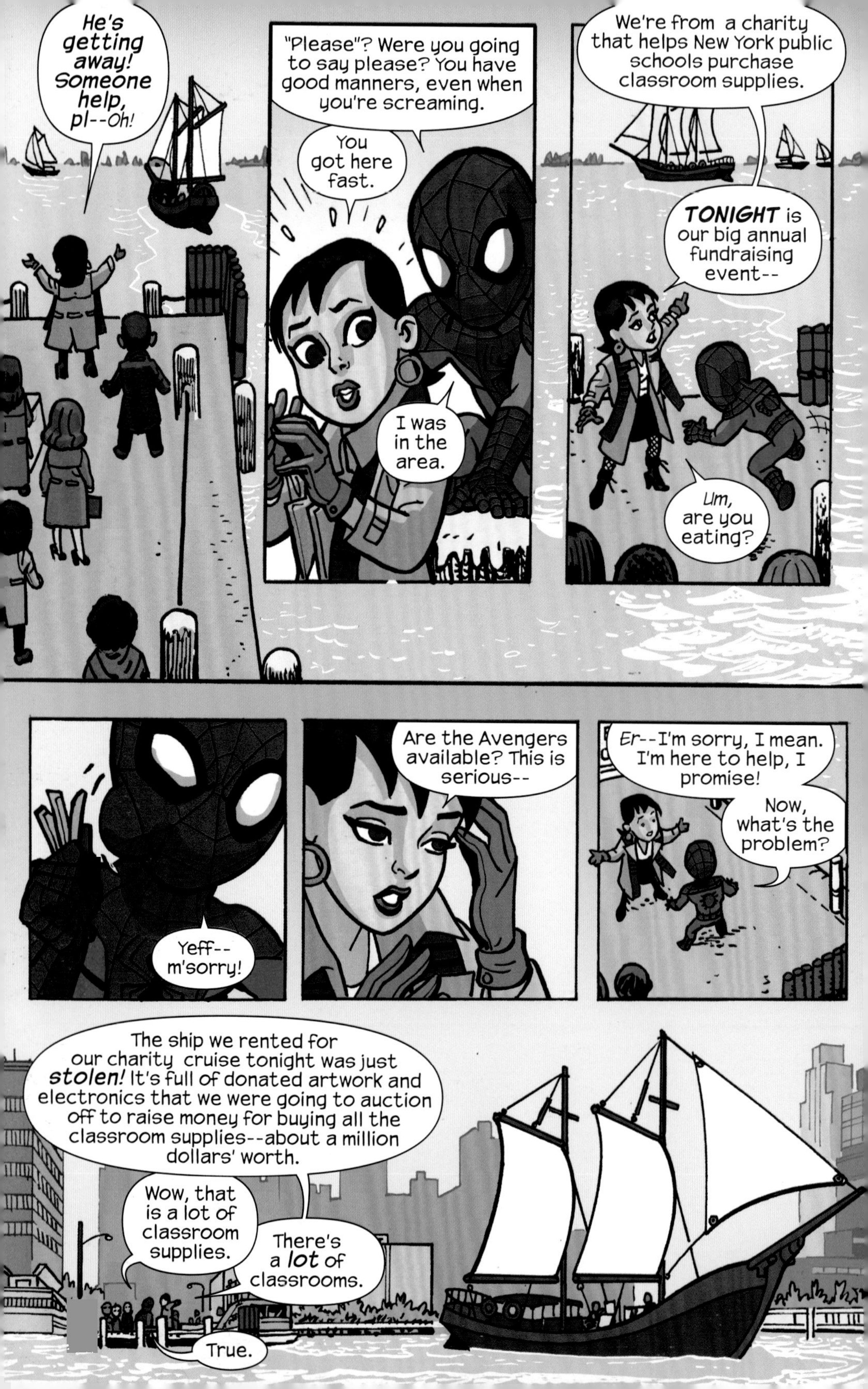
He's getting away! Someone help, pl--Oh!
"Please"? Were you going to say please? You have good manners, even when you're screaming.
You got here fast.
I was in the area.
We're from a charity that helps New York public schools purchase classroom supplies.
TONIGHT is our big annual fundraising event--
Um, are you eating?
Yeff-- m'sorry!
Are the Avengers available? This is serious--
Er--I'm sorry, I mean. I'm here to help, I promise!
Now, what's the problem?
The ship we rented for our charity cruise tonight was just stolen! It's full of donated artwork and electronics that we were going to auction off to raise money for buying all the classroom supplies--about a million dollars' worth.
Wow, that is a lot of classroom supplies.
There's a lot of classrooms.
True.

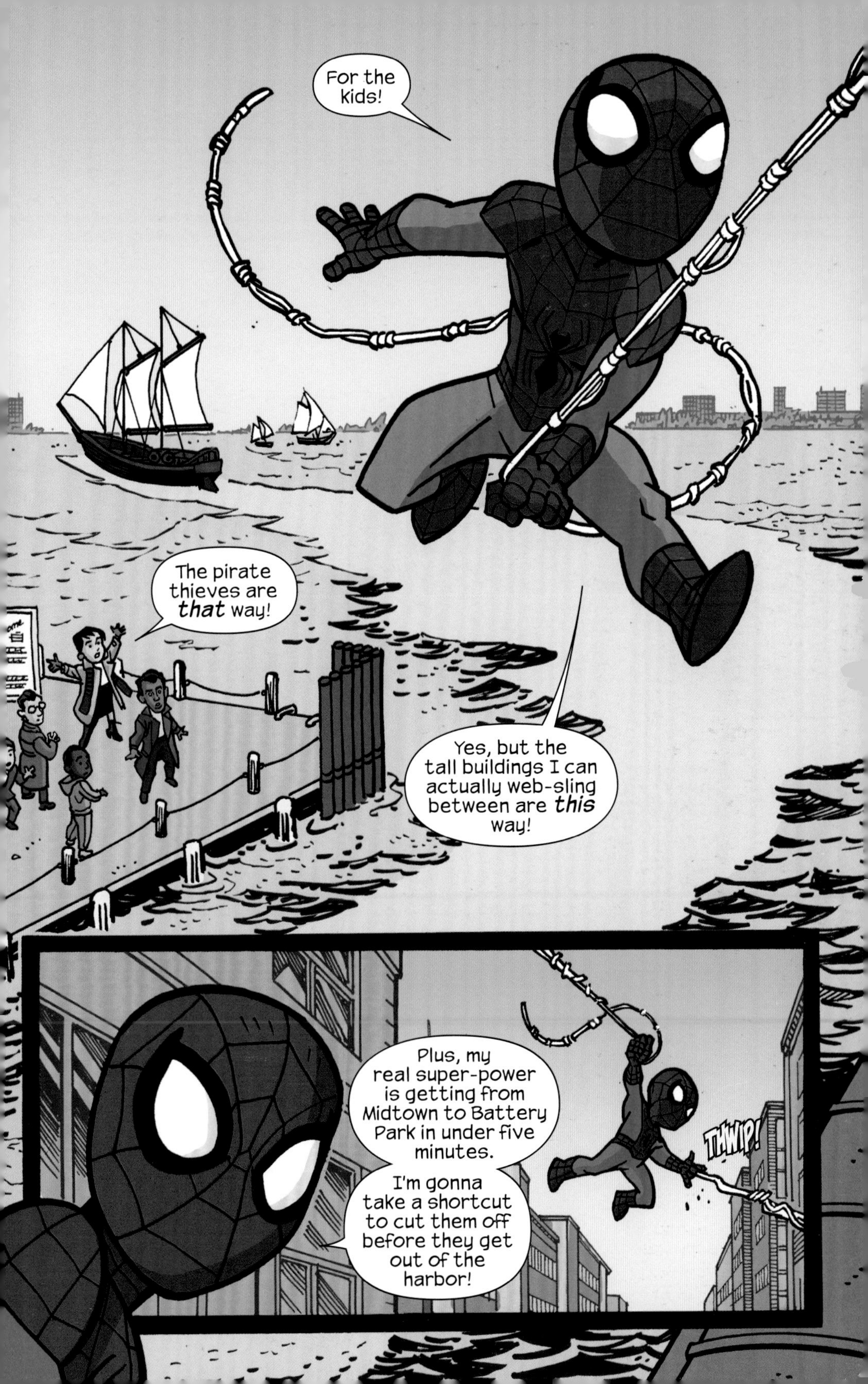
For the kids!
The pirate thieves are *that* way!
Yes, but the tall buildings I can actually web-sling between are *this* way!
Plus, my real super-power is getting from Midtown to Battery Park in under five minutes.
I'm gonna take a shortcut to cut them off before they get out of the harbor!
THWIP!

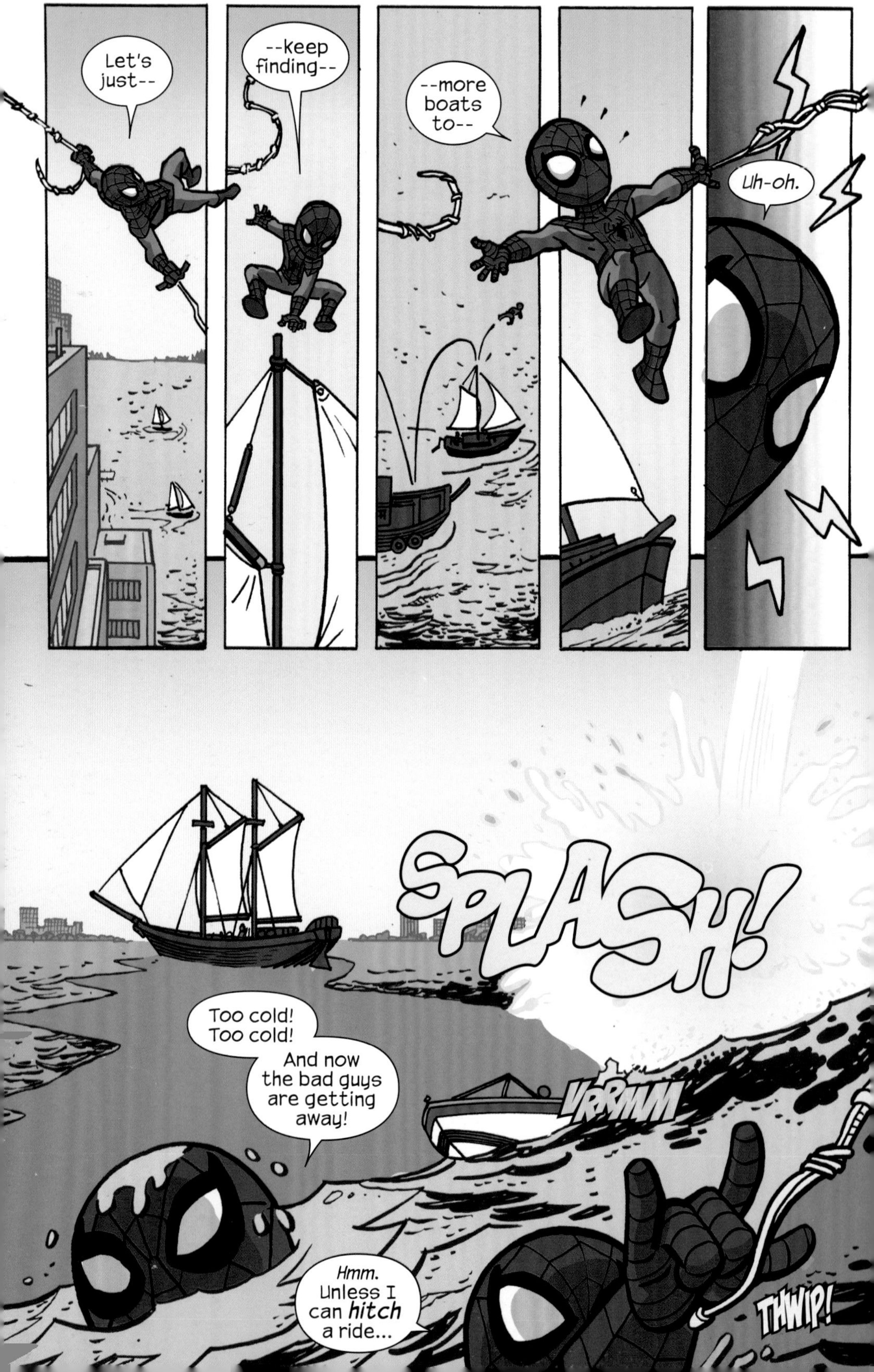
Let's just--
--keep finding--
--more boats to--
Uh-oh.
SPLASH!
Too cold! Too cold!
And now the bad guys are getting away!
VRRMM
Hmm. Unless I can *hitch* a ride...
THWIP!

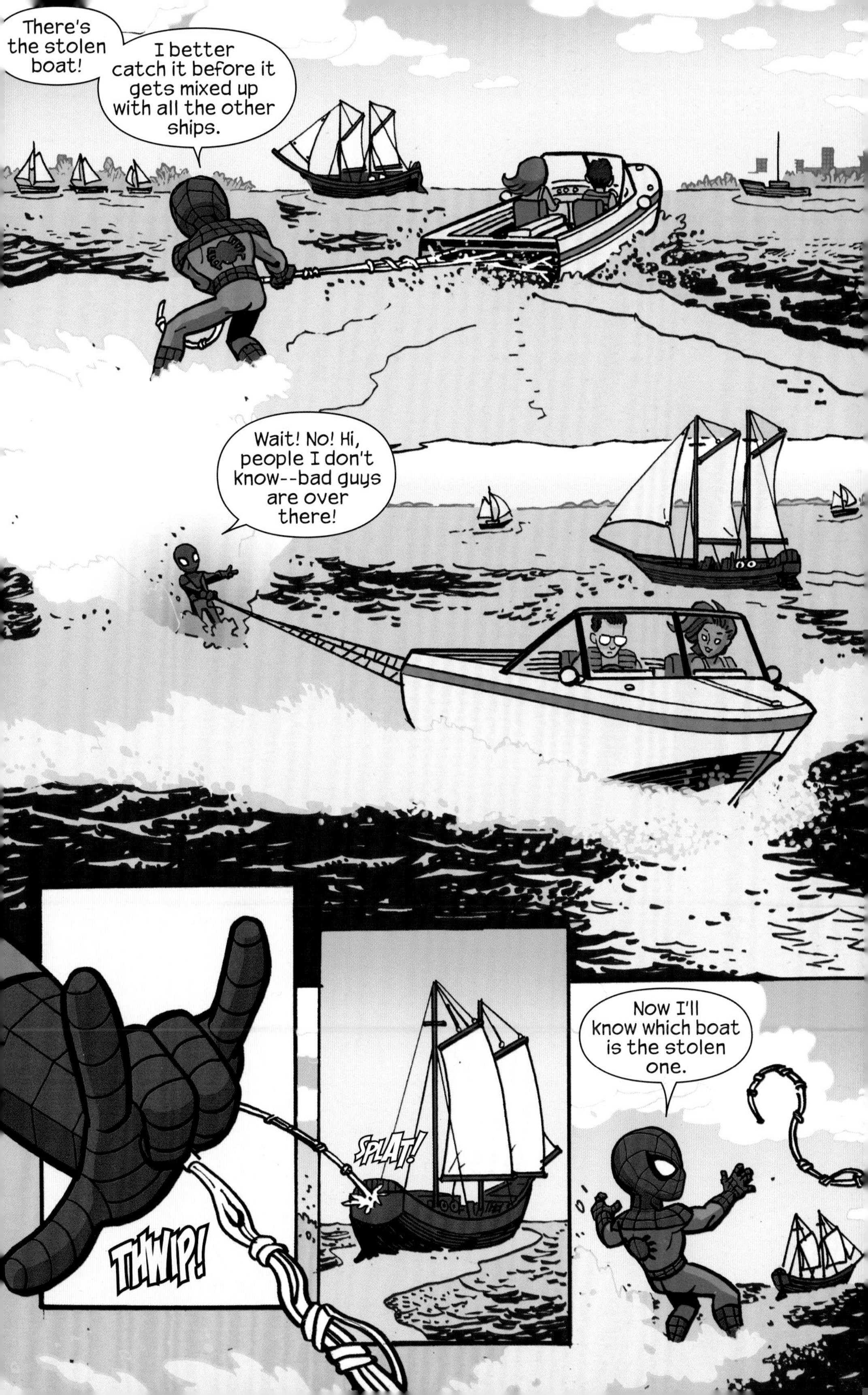
There's the stolen boat!
I better catch it before it gets mixed up with all the other ships.
Wait! No! Hi, people I don't know--bad guys are over there!
THWIP!
SPLAT!
Now I'll know which boat is the stolen one.

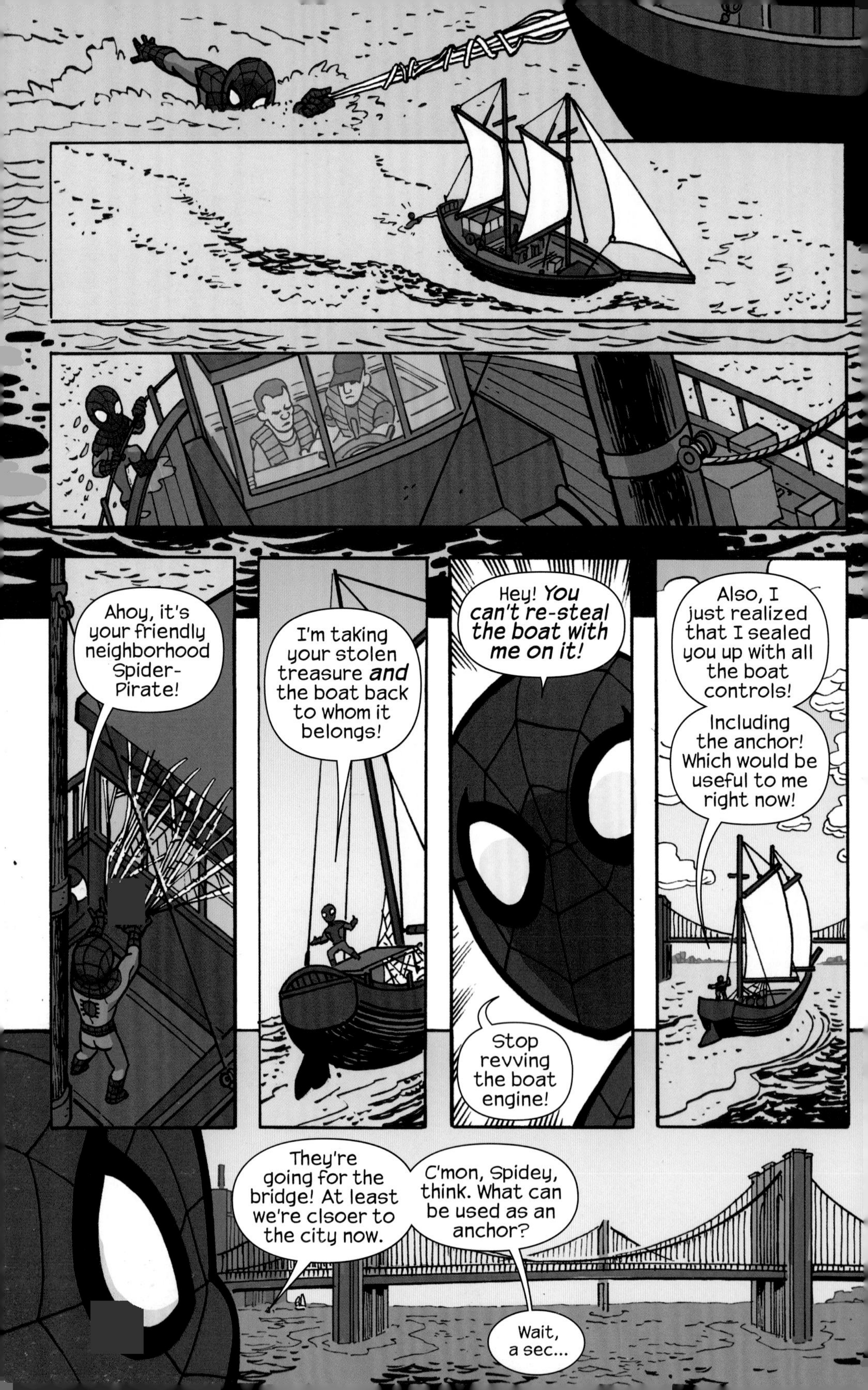
Ahoy, it's your friendly neighborhood Spider-Pirate!
I'm taking your stolen treasure and the boat back to whom it belongs!
Hey! You can't re-steal the boat with me on it!
Stop revving the boat engine!
Also, I just realized that I sealed you up with all the boat controls!
Including the anchor! Which would be useful to me right now!
They're going for the bridge! At least we're clsoer to the city now.
C'mon, Spidey, think. What can be used as an anchor?
Wait, a sec...

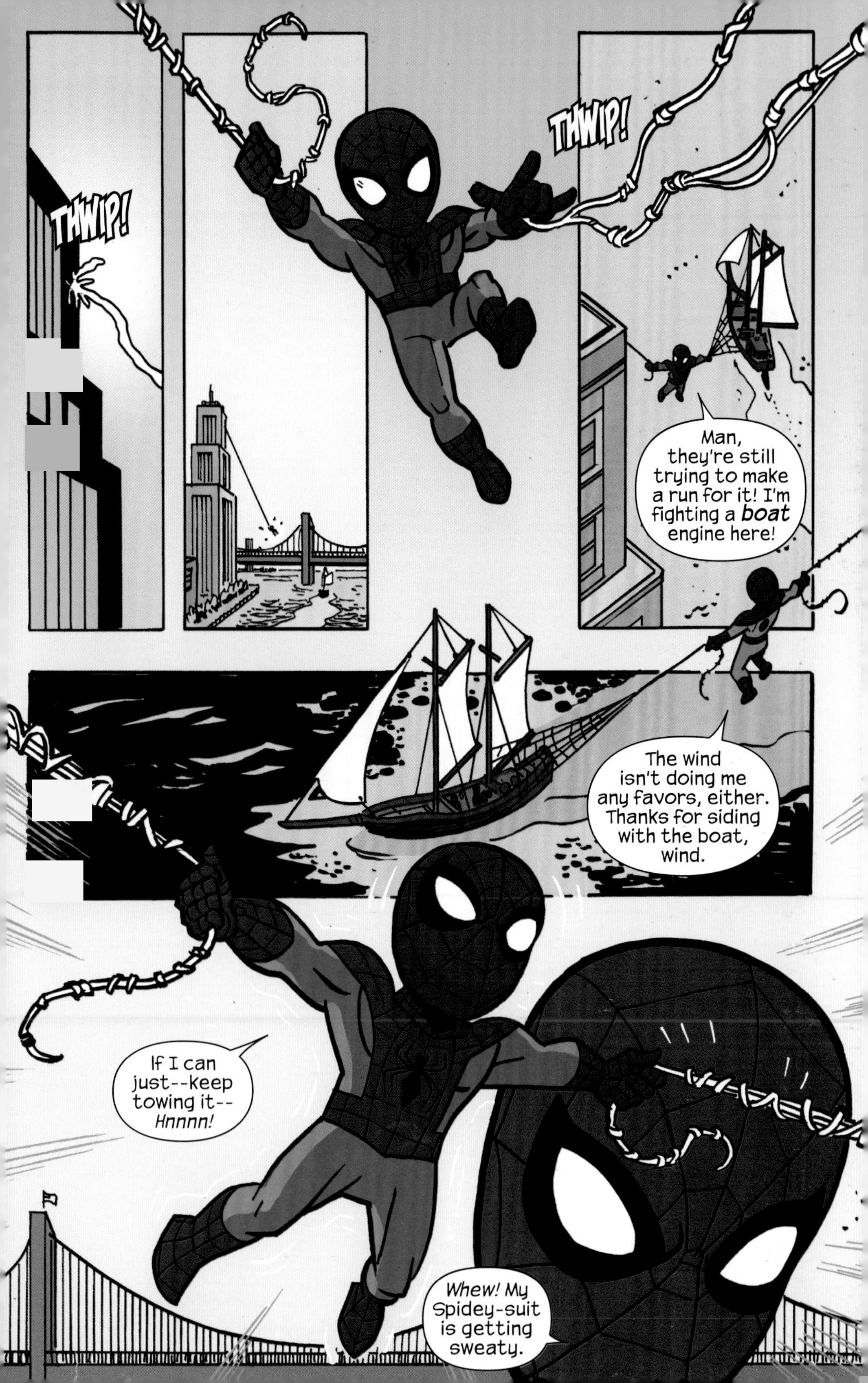
THWIP!
THWIP!
Man, they're still trying to make a run for it! I'm fighting a *boat* engine here!
The wind isn't doing me any favors, either. Thanks for siding with the boat, wind.
If I can just--keep towing it-- *Hnnnn!*
Whew! My Spidey-suit is getting sweaty.

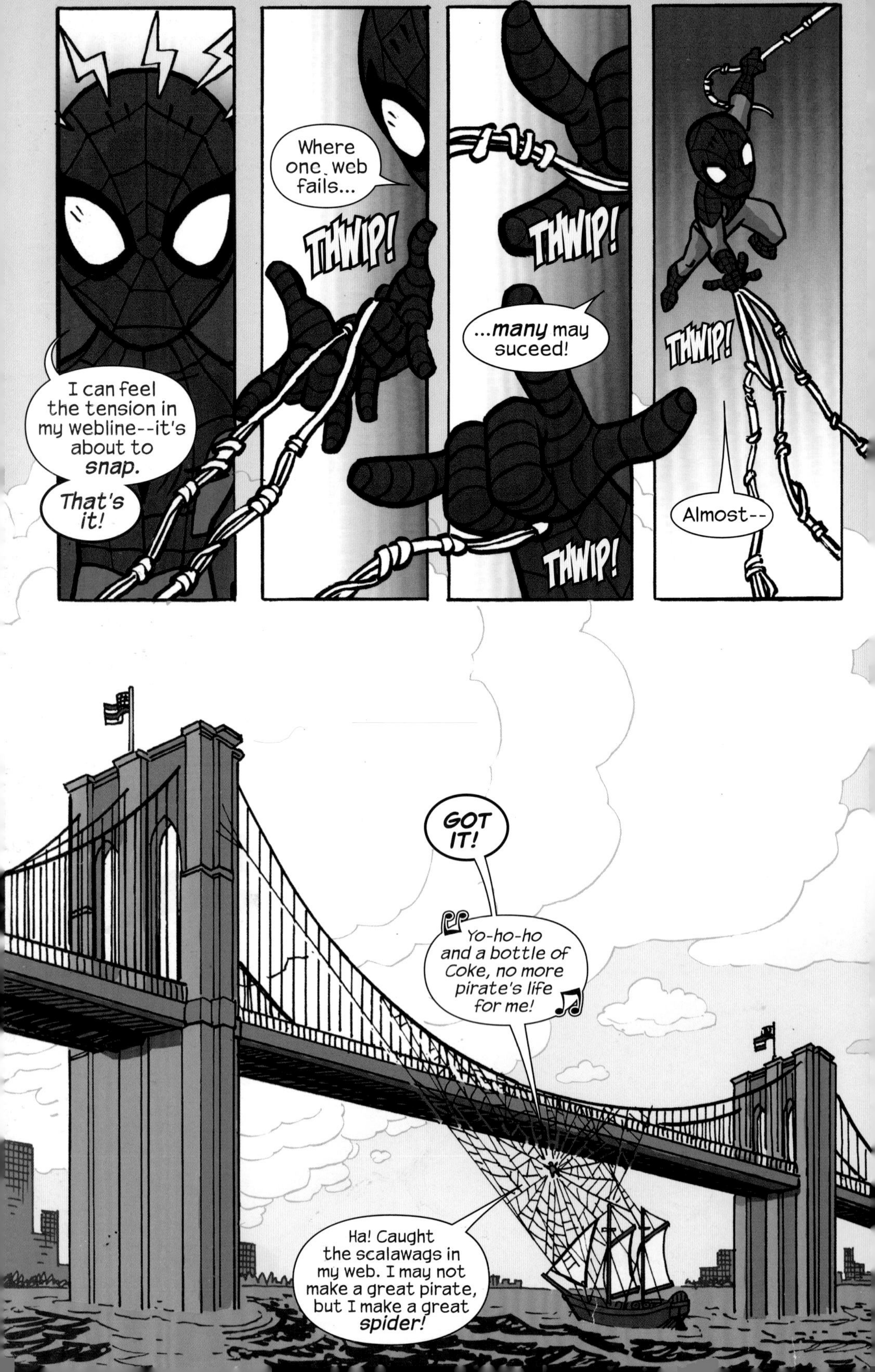
I can feel the tension in my webline--it's about to snap.
That's it!
Where one web fails...
THWIP!
THWIP!
...many may suceed!
THWIP!
THWIP!
Almost--
GOT IT!
Yo-ho-ho and a bottle of Coke, no more pirate's life for me!
Ha! Caught the scalawags in my web. I may not make a great pirate, but I make a great spider!

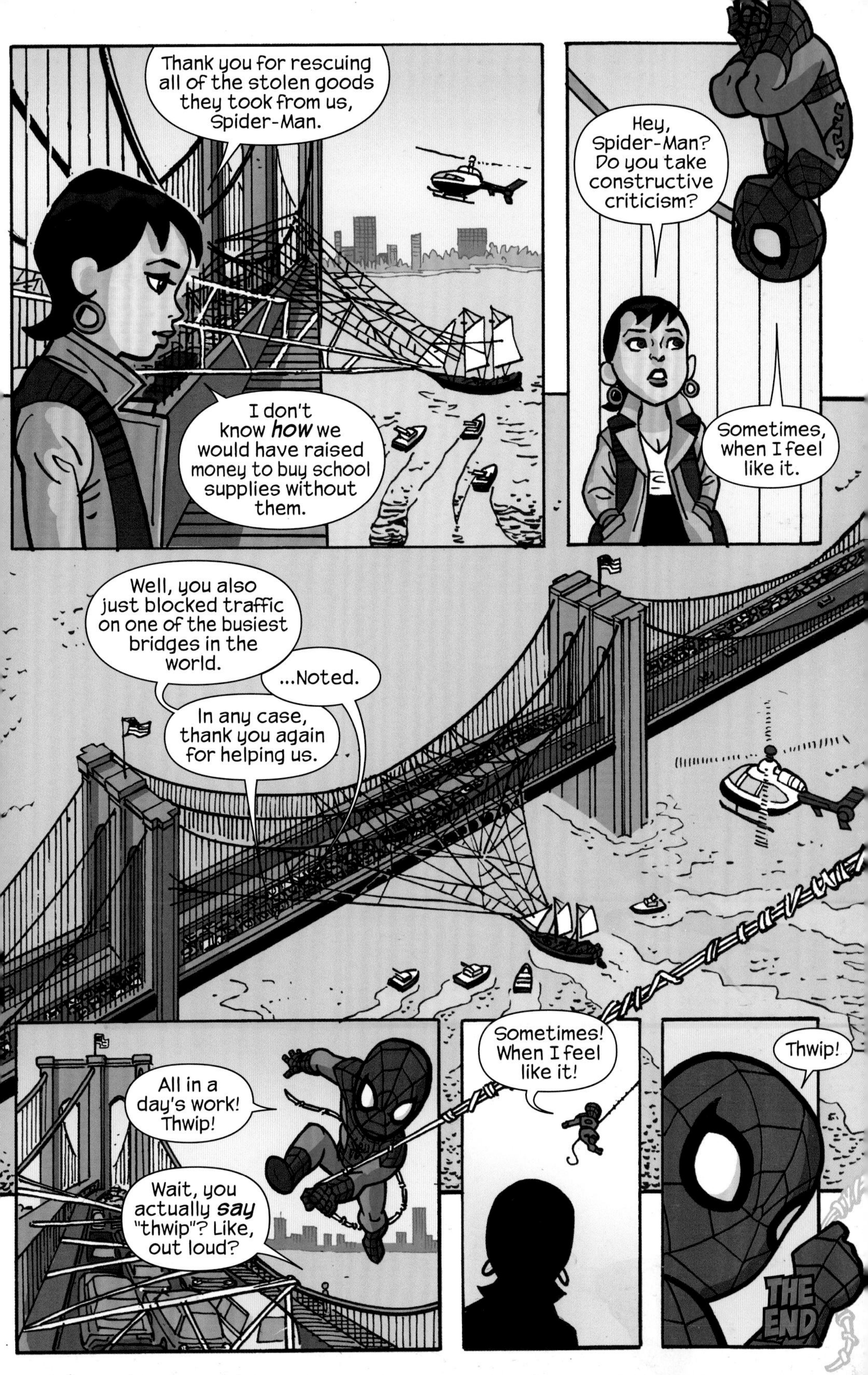
Thank you for rescuing all of the stolen goods they took from us, Spider-Man.
I don't know *how* we would have raised money to buy school supplies without them.
Hey, Spider-Man? Do you take constructive criticism?
Sometimes, when I feel like it.
Well, you also just blocked traffic on one of the busiest bridges in the world.
...Noted.
In any case, thank you again for helping us.
All in a day's work! Thwip!
Wait, you actually *say* "thwip"? Like, out loud?
Sometimes! When I feel like it!
Thwip!
THE END

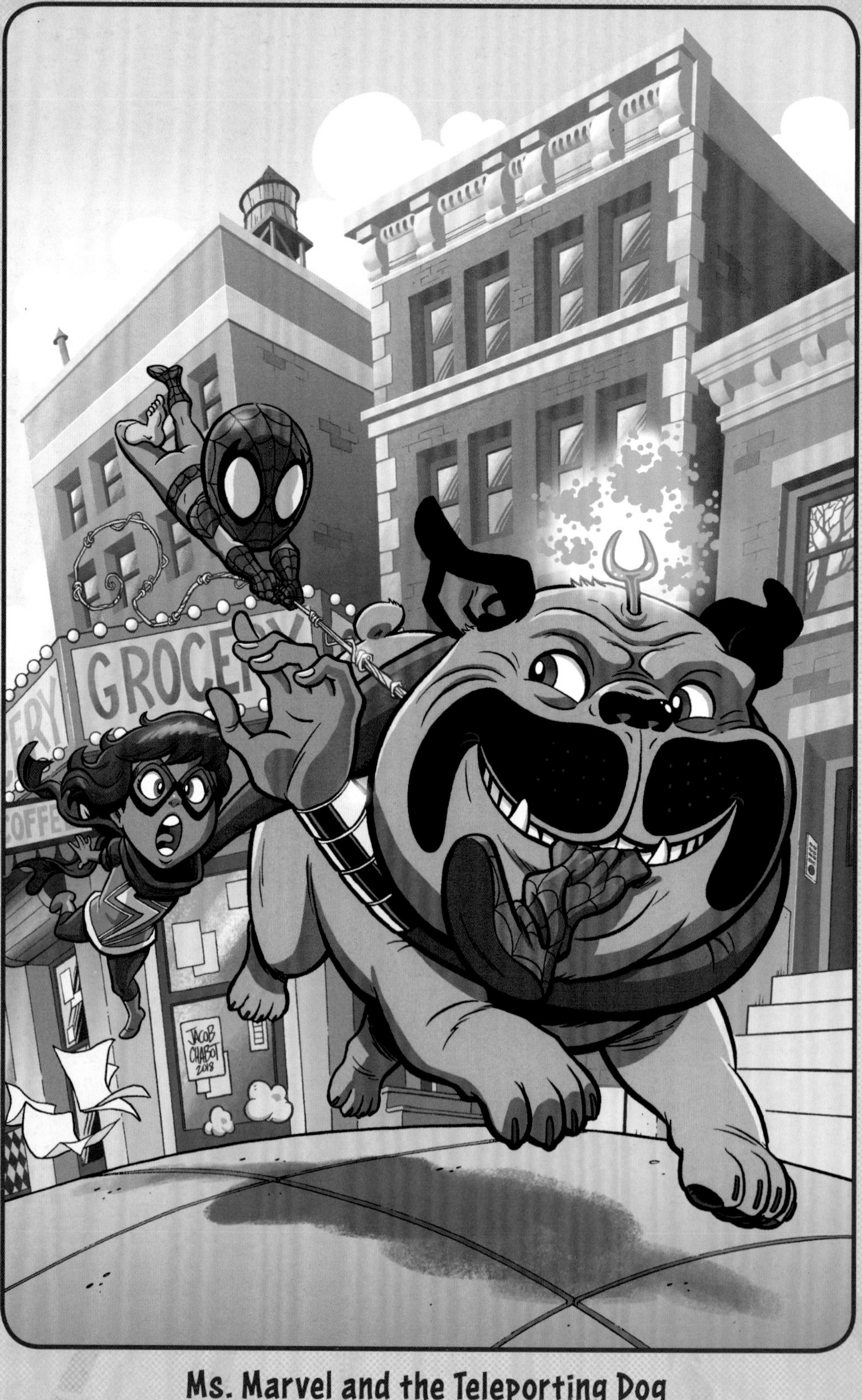
GROCERY
ERY
COFFE
JACOB CHABOT 2018

Ms. Marvel and the Teleporting Dog

cover by Jacob Chabot

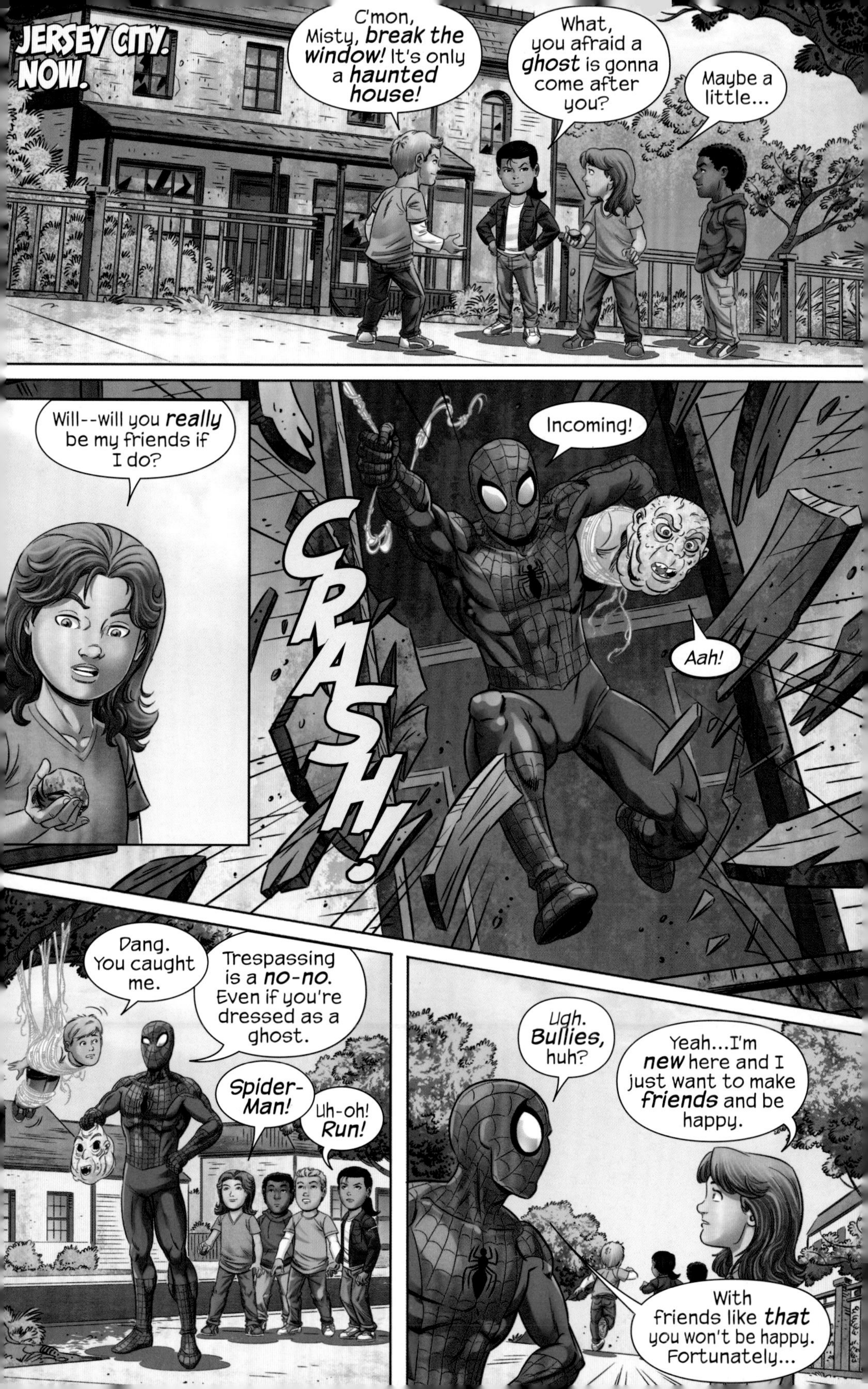
JERSEY CITY. NOW.
C'mon, Misty, break the window! It's only a haunted house!
What, you afraid a ghost is gonna come after you?
Maybe a little...
Will--will you really be my friends if I do?
Incoming!
CRASH!
Aah!
Dang. You caught me.
Trespassing is a no-no. Even if you're dressed as a ghost.
Spider-Man!
Uh-oh! Run!
Ugh. Bullies, huh?
Yeah...I'm new here and I just want to make friends and be happy.
With friends like that you won't be happy. Fortunately...

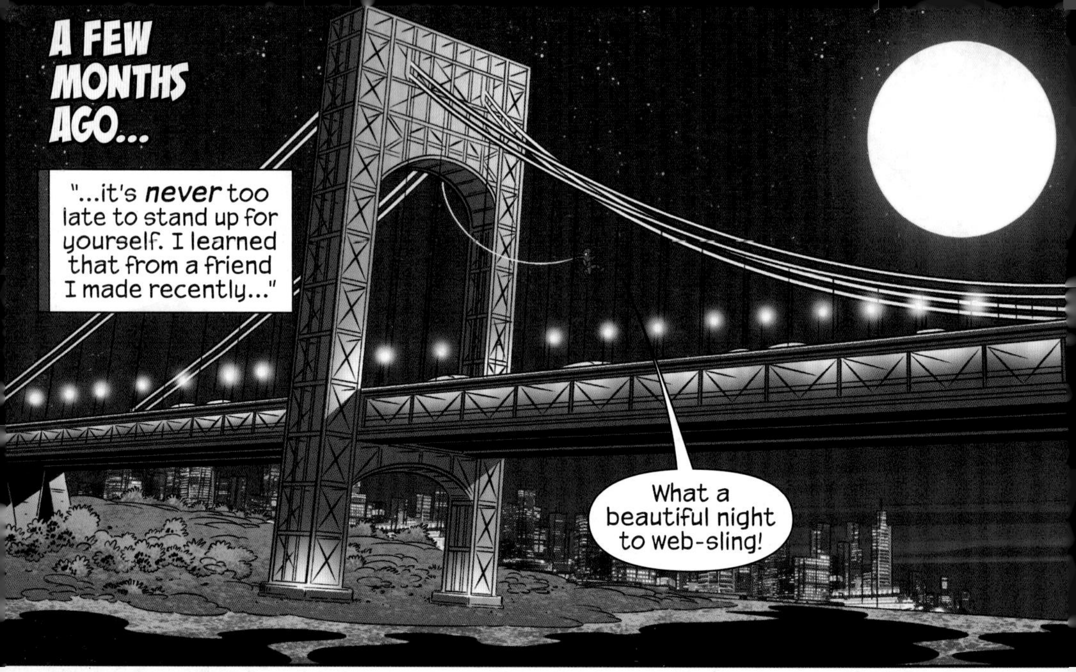
A FEW MONTHS AGO...
"...it's never too late to stand up for yourself. I learned that from a friend I made recently..."
What a beautiful night to web-sling!

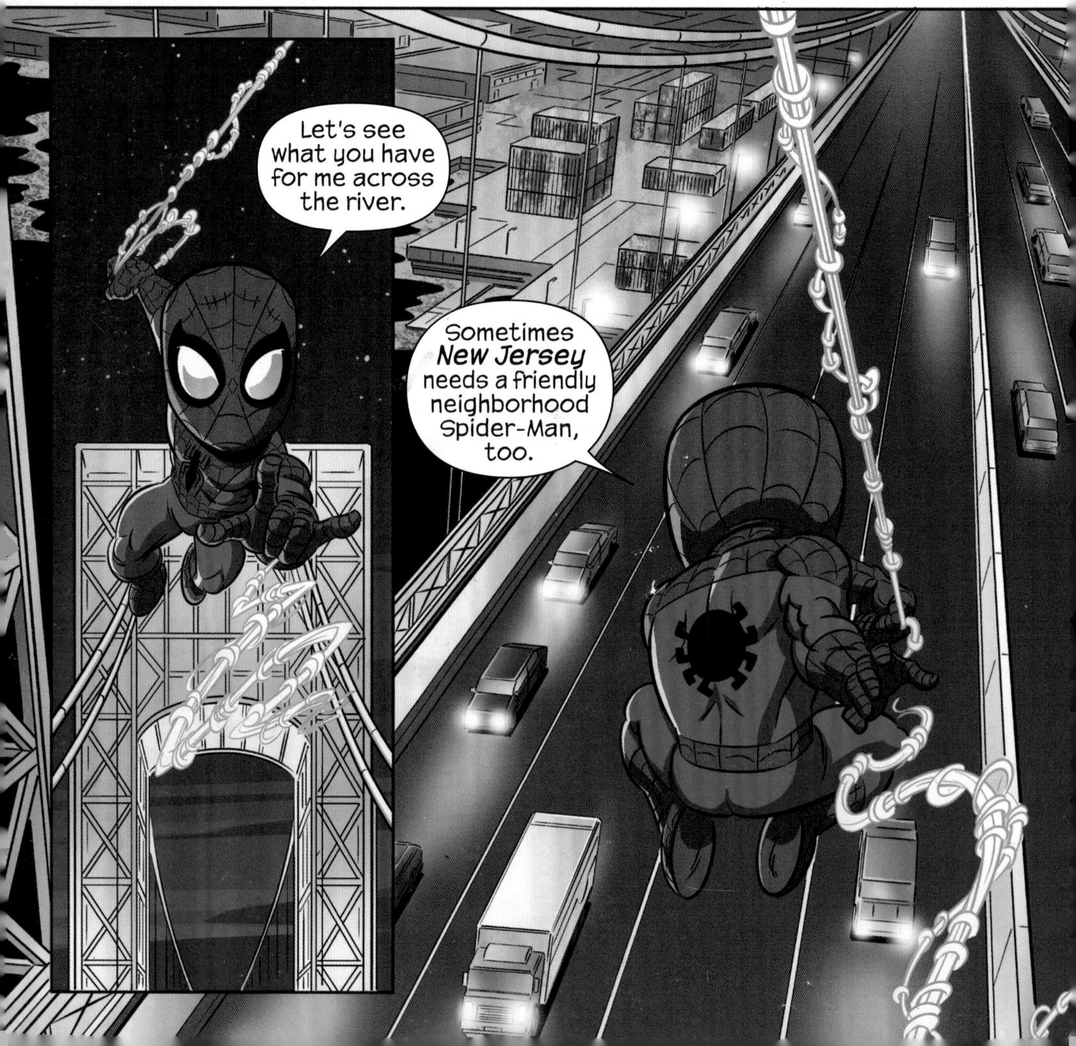
Let's see what you have for me across the river.
Sometimes New Jersey needs a friendly neighborhood Spider-Man, too.

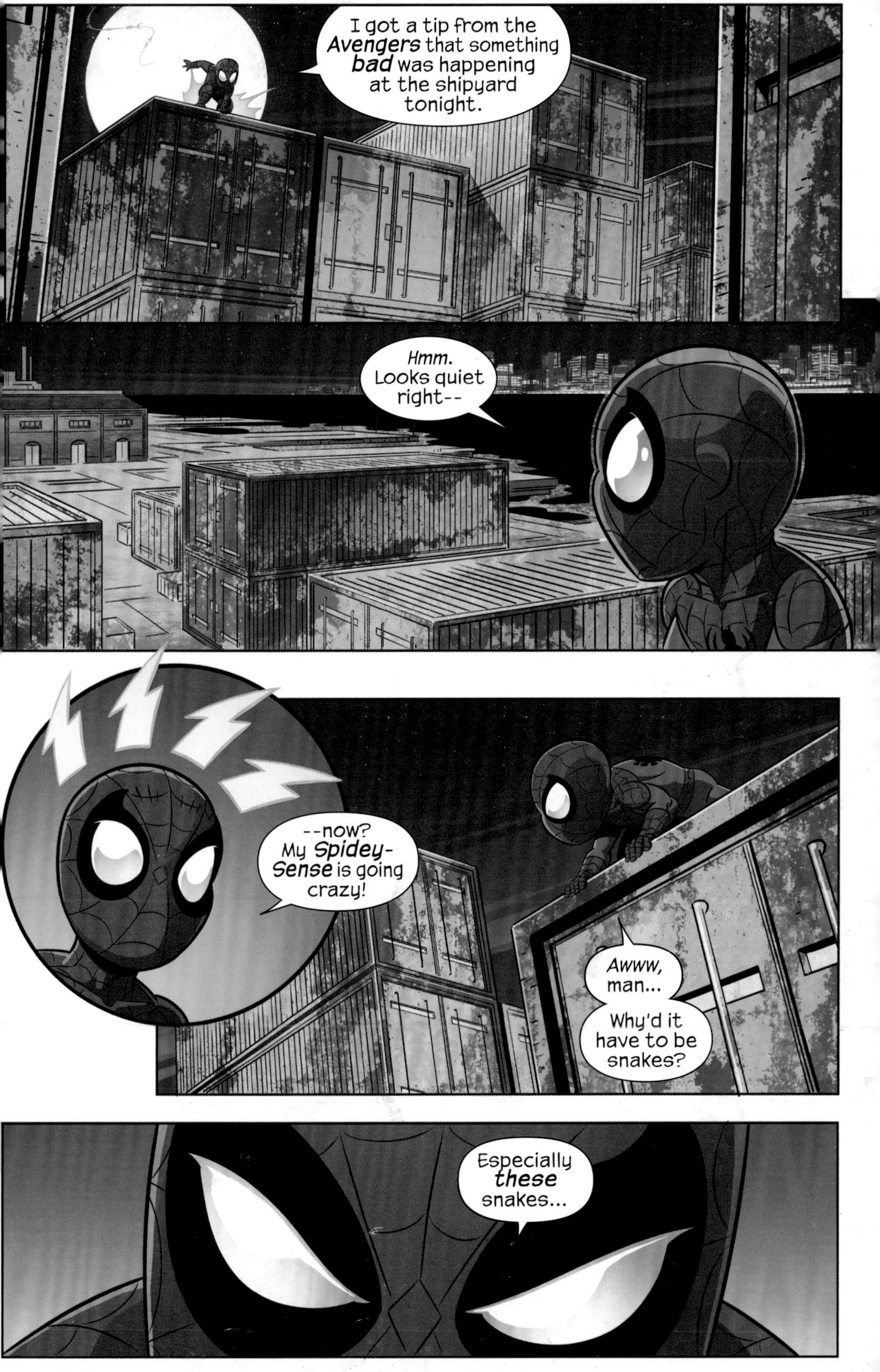
I got a tip from the Avengers that something bad was happening at the shipyard tonight.
Hmm. Looks quiet right--
--now? My Spidey-Sense is going crazy!
Awww, man...
Why'd it have to be snakes?
Especially these snakes...

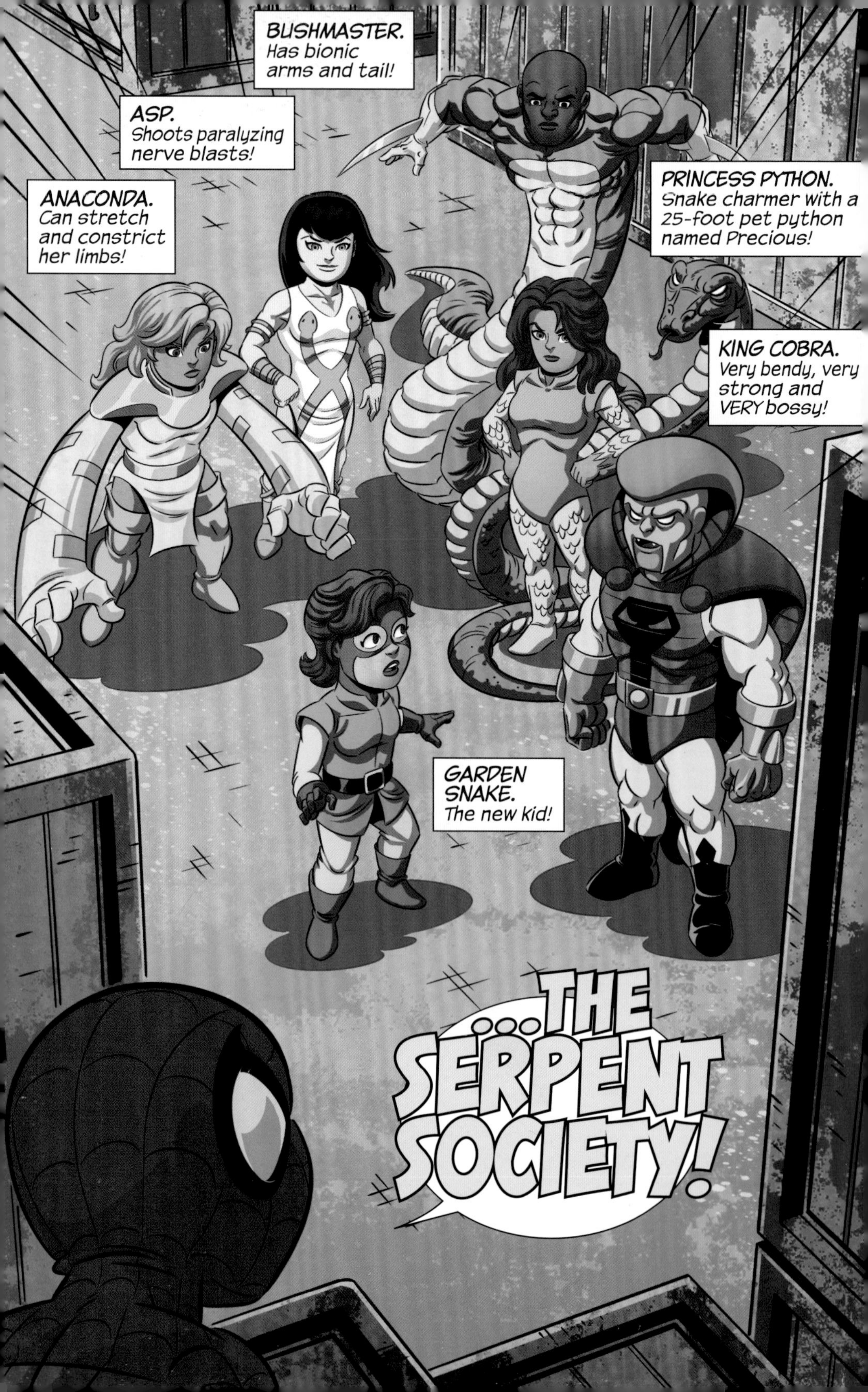
BUSHMASTER. Has bionic arms and tail!
ASP. Shoots paralyzing nerve blasts!
ANACONDA. Can stretch and constrict her limbs!
PRINCESS PYTHON. Snake charmer with a 25-foot pet python named Precious!
KING COBRA. Very bendy, very strong and VERY bossy!
GARDEN SNAKE. The new kid!
...THE SERPENT SOCIETY!

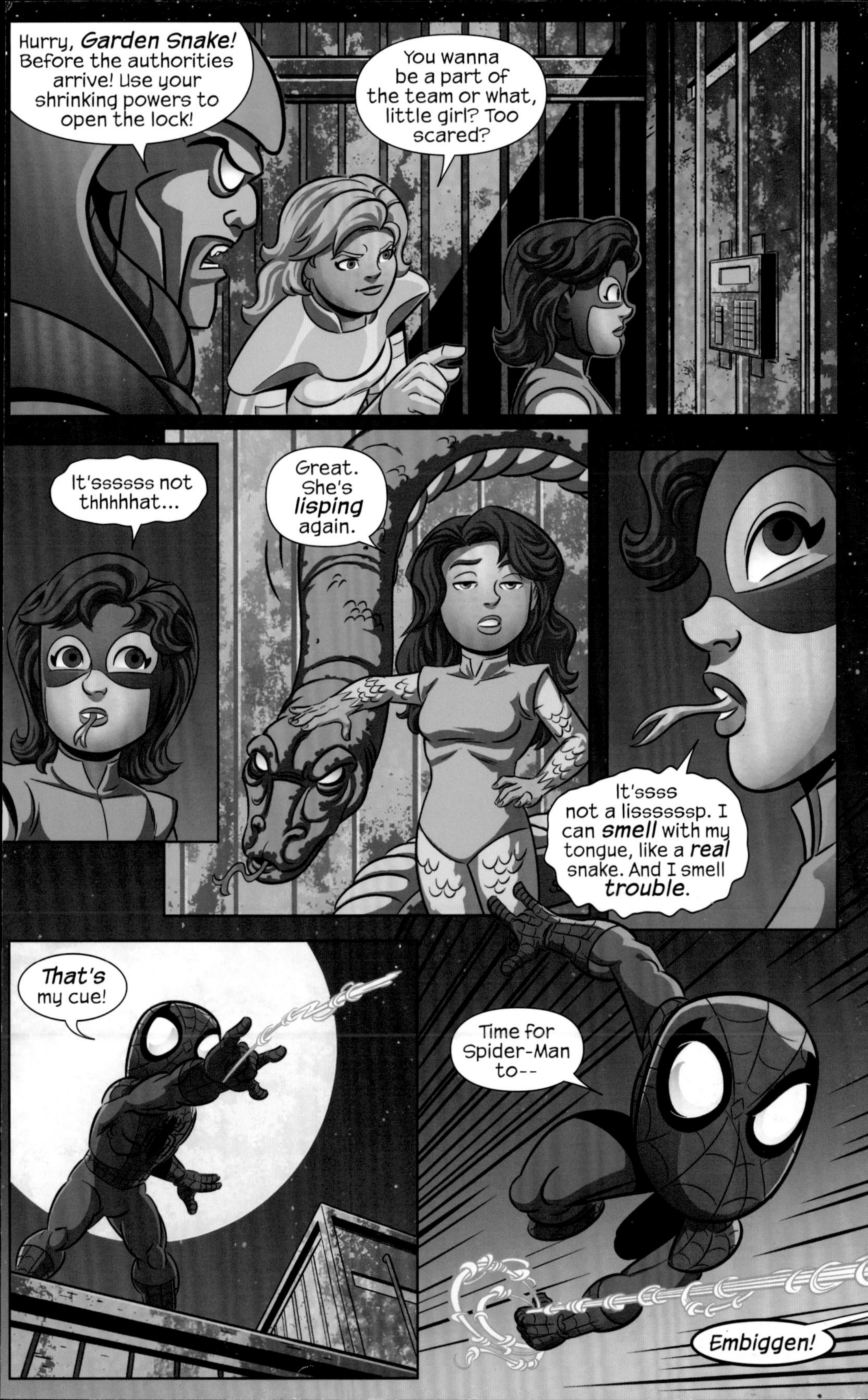
Hurry, Garden Snake! Before the authorities arrive! Use your shrinking powers to open the lock!
You wanna be a part of the team or what, little girl? Too scared?
It'ssssss not thhhhhat...
Great. She's lisping again.
It'ssss not a lisssssp. I can smell with my tongue, like a real snake. And I smell trouble.
That's my cue!
Time for Spider-Man to--
Embiggen!

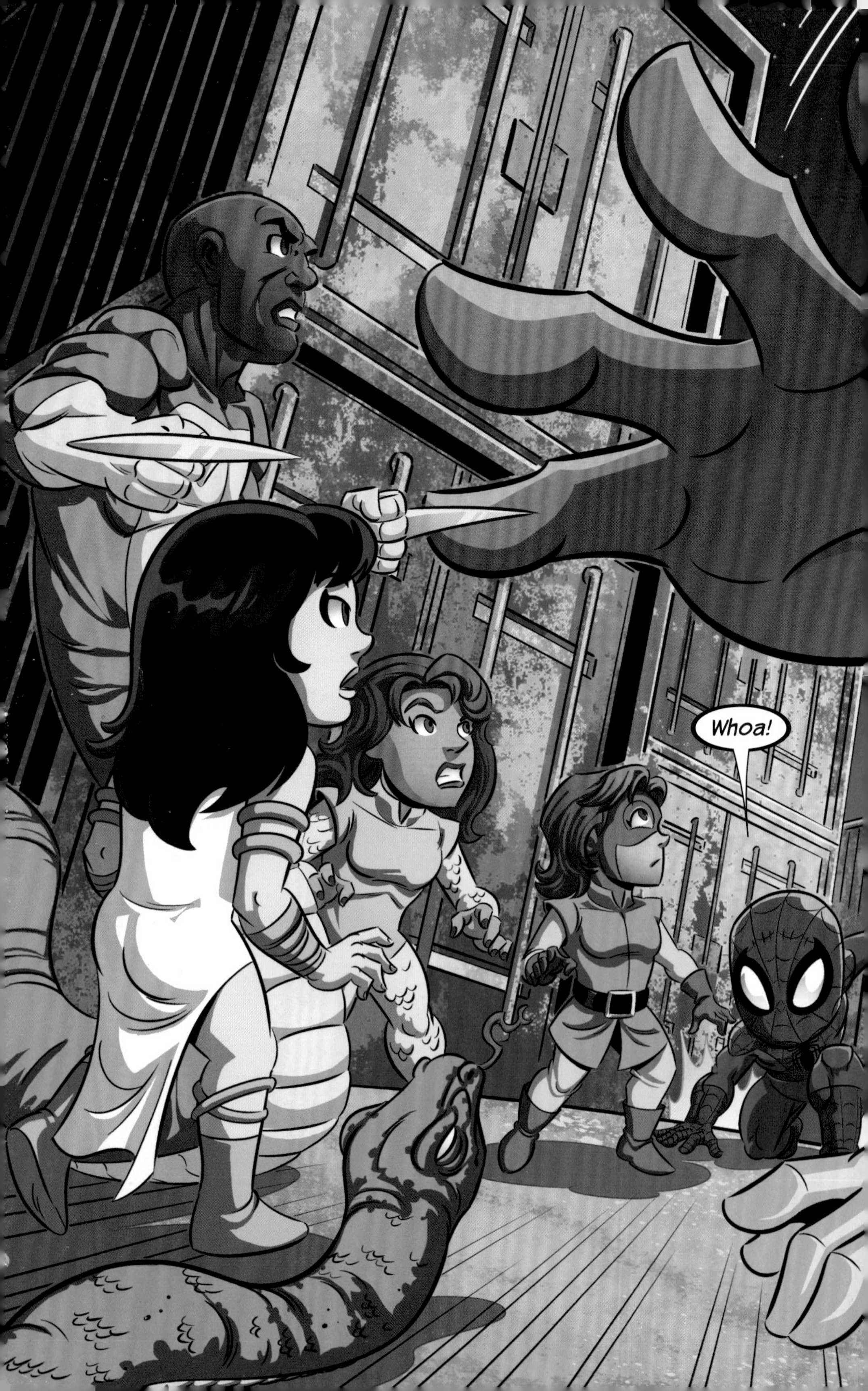
Whoa!

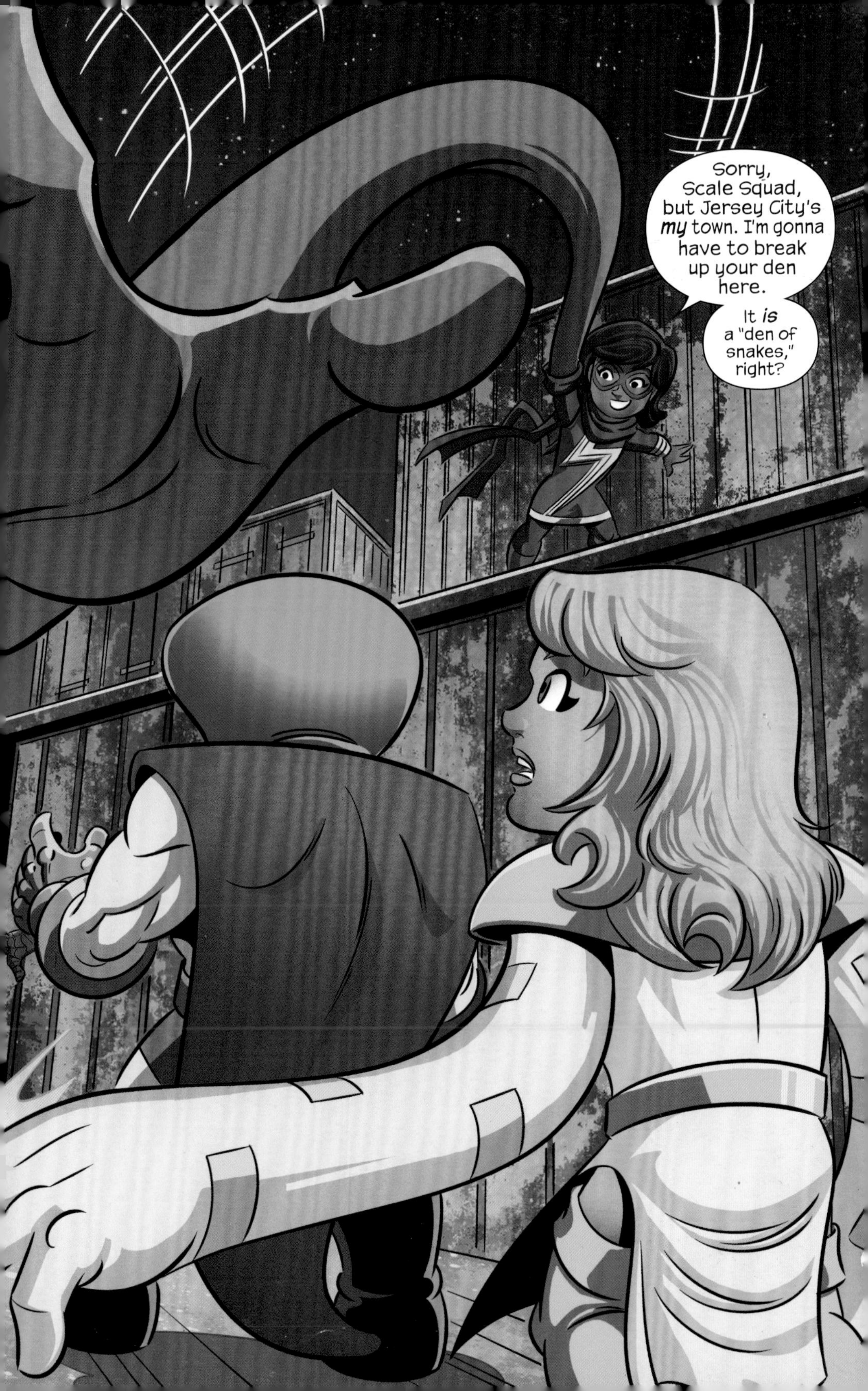
Sorry, Scale Squad, but Jersey City's *my* town. I'm gonna have to break up your den here.
It *is* a "den of snakes," right?

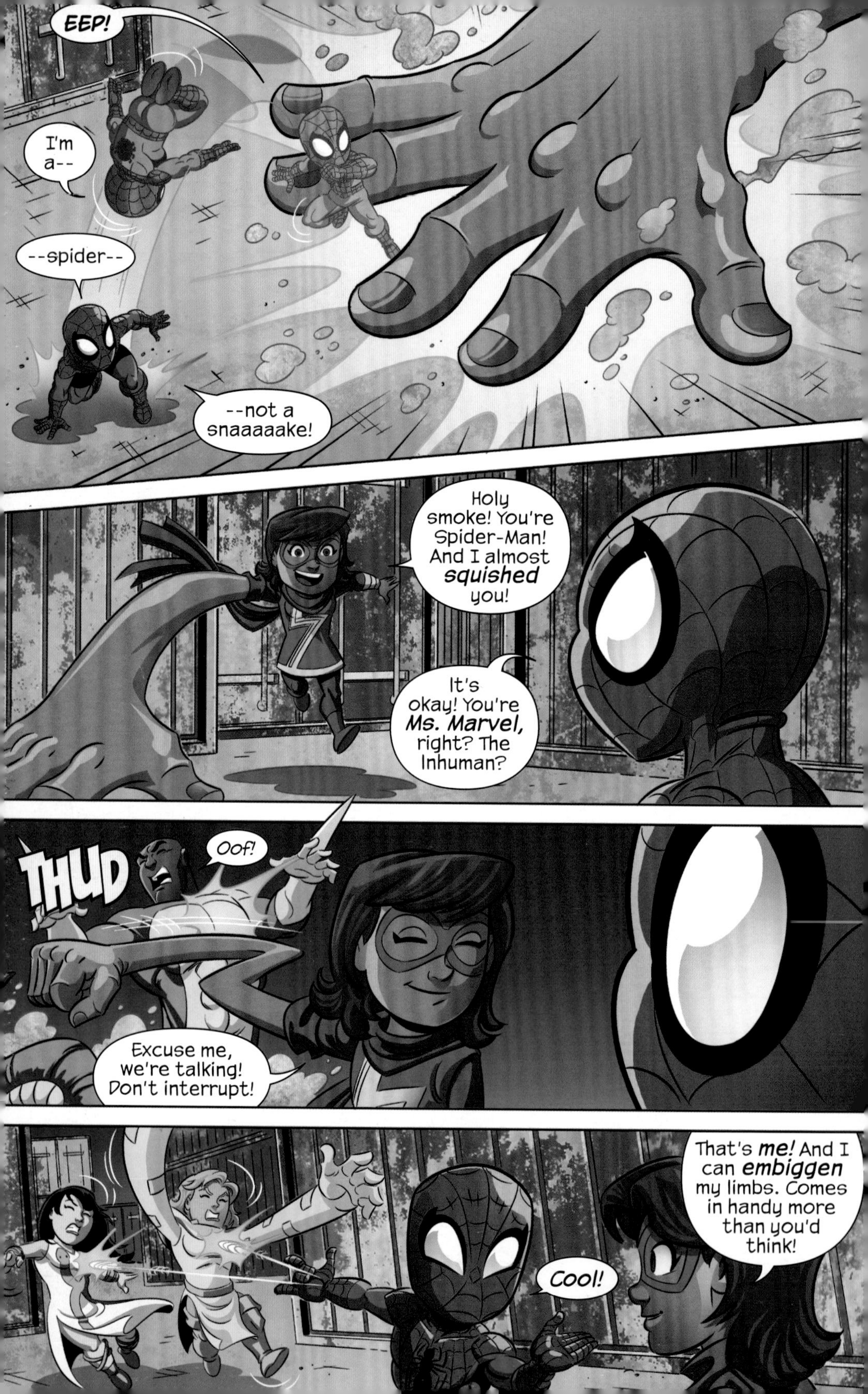
EEP!
I'm a--
--spider--
--not a snaaaaake!
Holy smoke! You're Spider-Man! And I almost *squished* you!
It's okay! You're *Ms. Marvel,* right? The Inhuman?
THUD
Oof!
Excuse me, we're talking! Don't interrupt!
That's *me!* And I can *embiggen* my limbs. Comes in handy more than you'd think!
Cool!

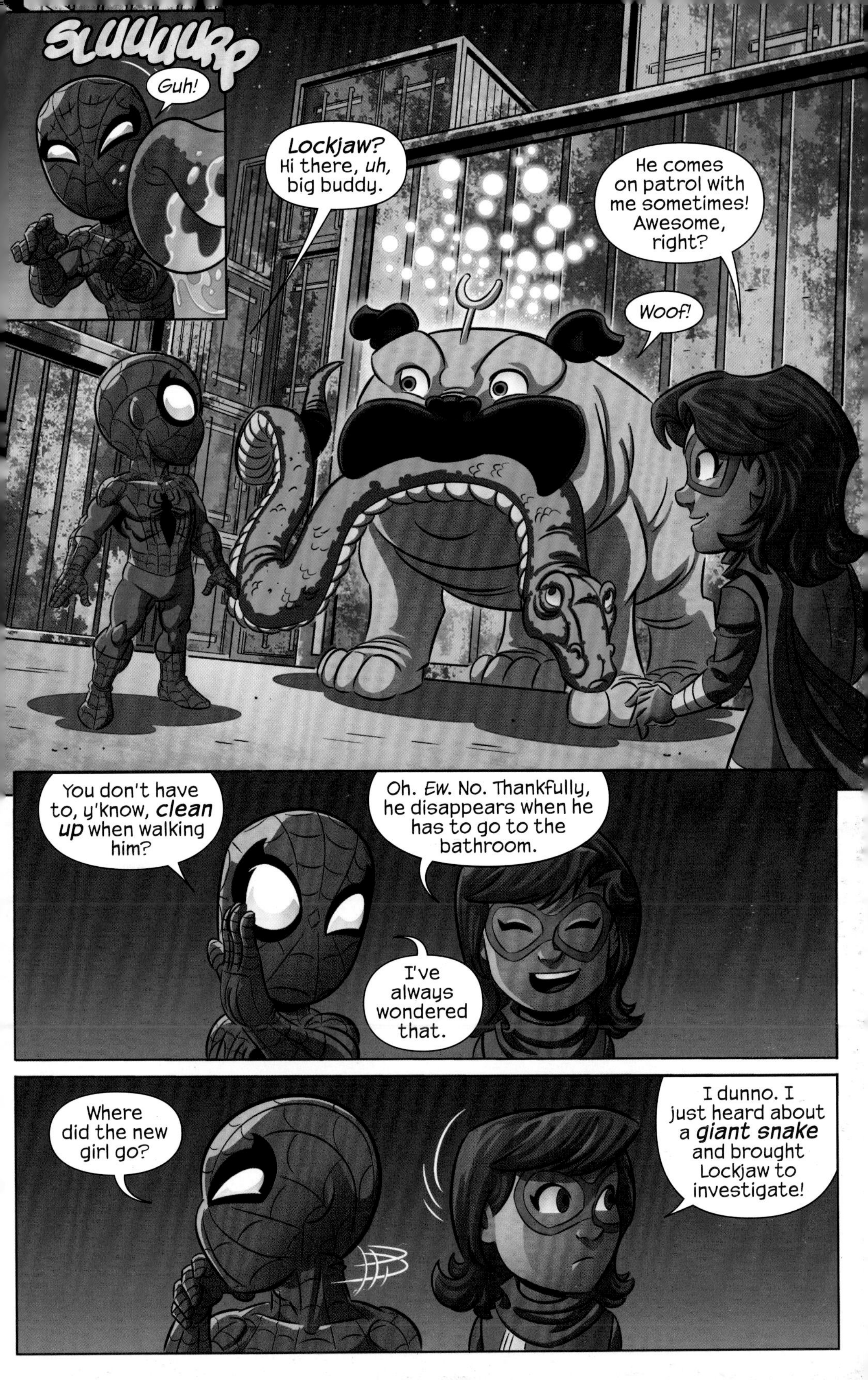
SLUUURP
Guh!
Lockjaw? Hi there, uh, big buddy.
He comes on patrol with me sometimes! Awesome, right?
Woof!
You don't have to, y'know, clean up when walking him?
Oh. Ew. No. Thankfully, he disappears when he has to go to the bathroom.
I've always wondered that.
Where did the new girl go?
I dunno. I just heard about a giant snake and brought Lockjaw to investigate!

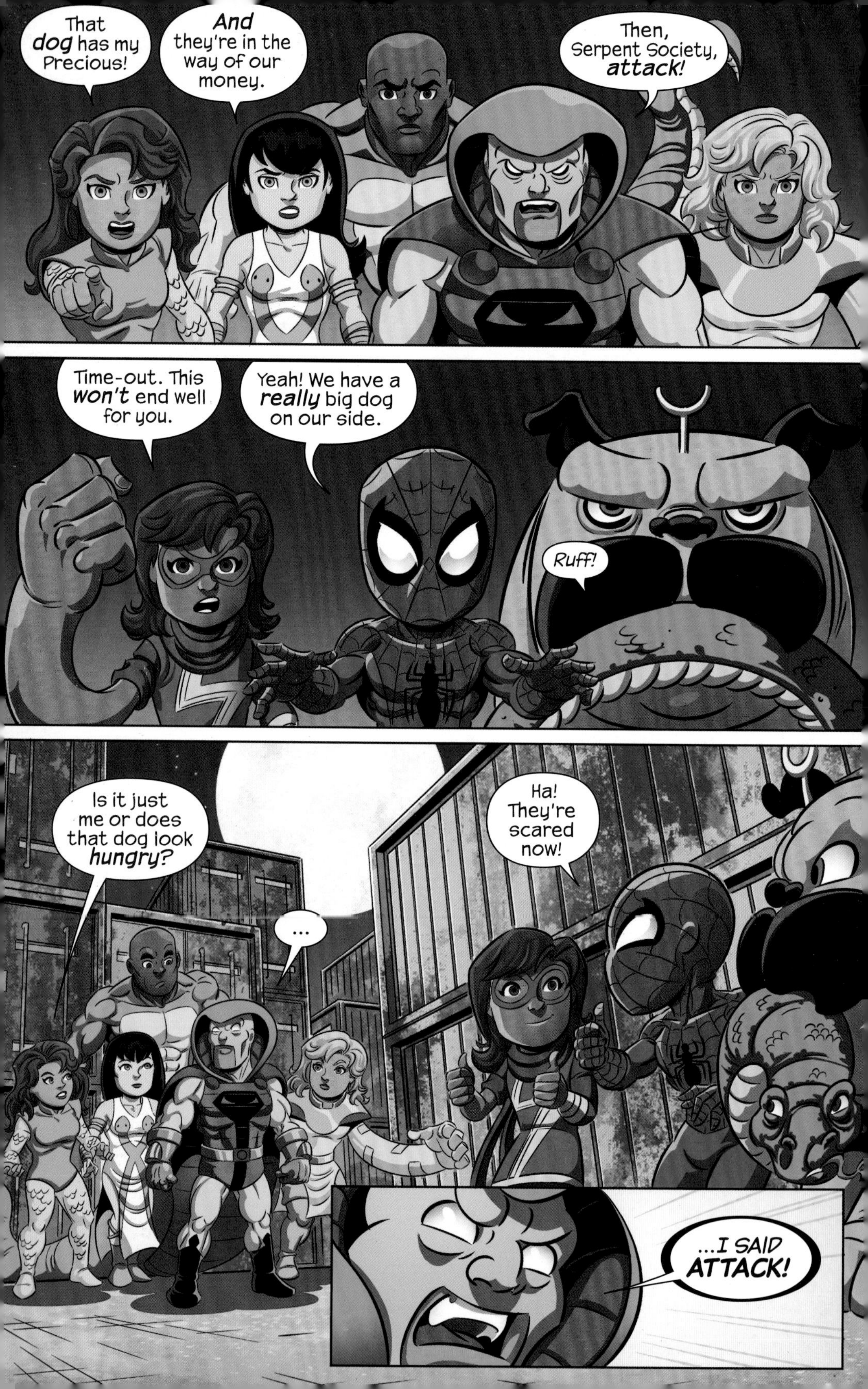
That dog has my Precious!
And they're in the way of our money.
Then, Serpent Society, attack!
Time-out. This won't end well for you.
Yeah! We have a really big dog on our side.
Ruff!
Is it just me or does that dog look hungry?
...
Ha! They're scared now!
...I SAID ATTACK!

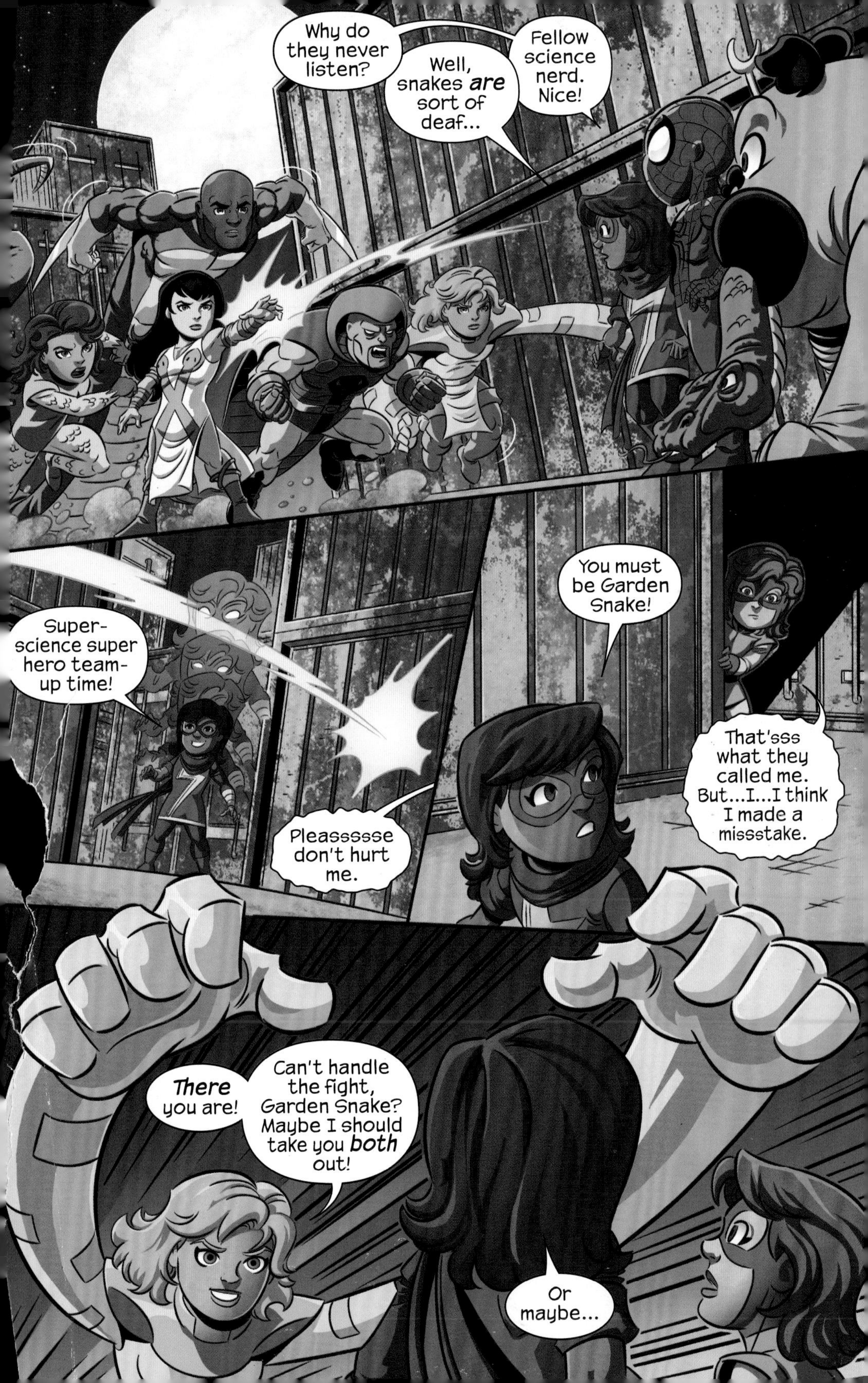
Why do they never listen?
Well, snakes *are* sort of deaf...
Fellow science nerd. Nice!
Super-science super hero team-up time!
Pleassssse don't hurt me.
You must be Garden Snake!
That'sss what they called me. But...I...I think I made a missstake.
There you are!
Can't handle the fight, Garden Snake? Maybe I should take you *both* out!
Or maybe...

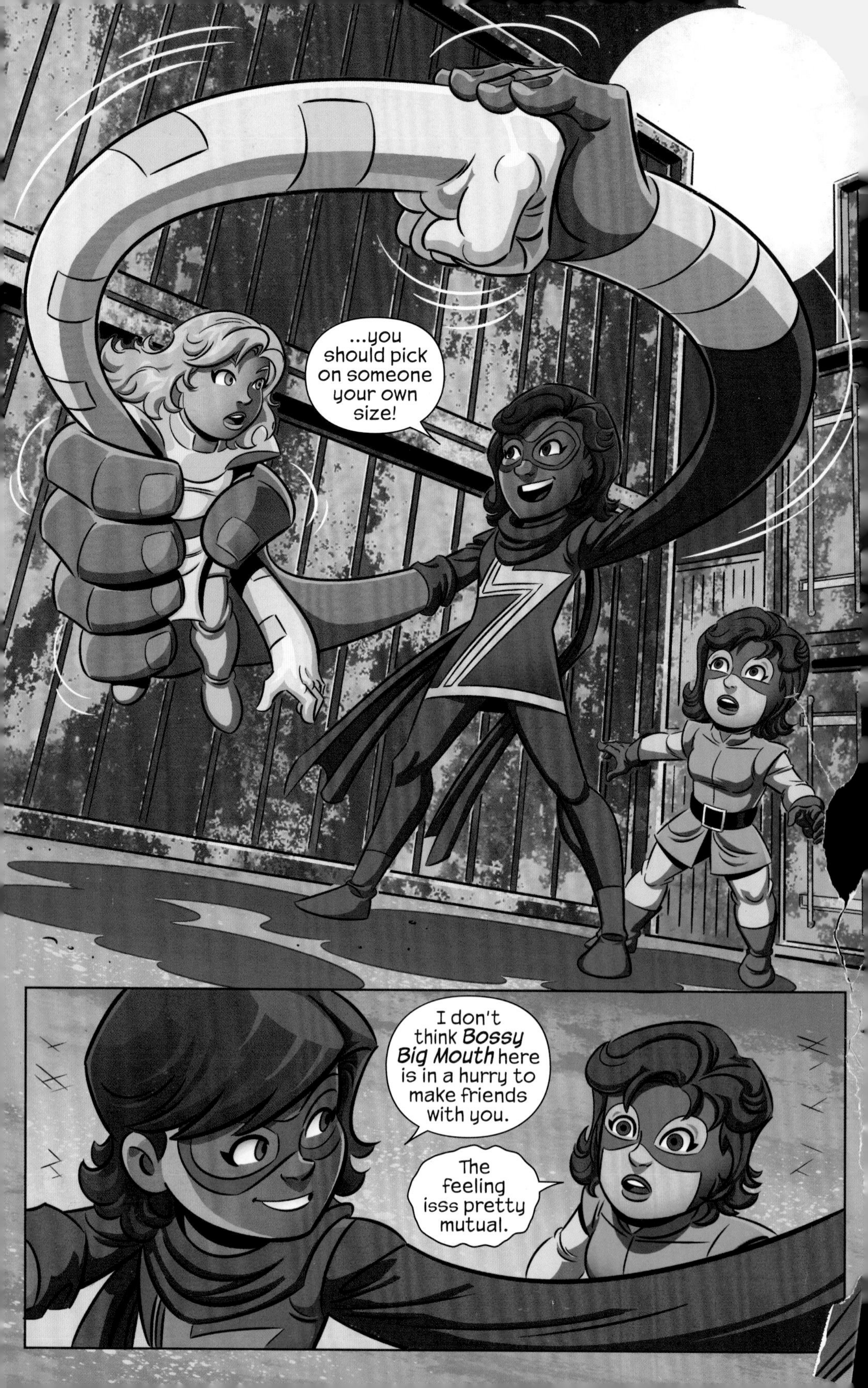
...you should pick on someone your own size!
I don't think *Bossy Big Mouth* here is in a hurry to make friends with you.
The feeling isss pretty mutual.

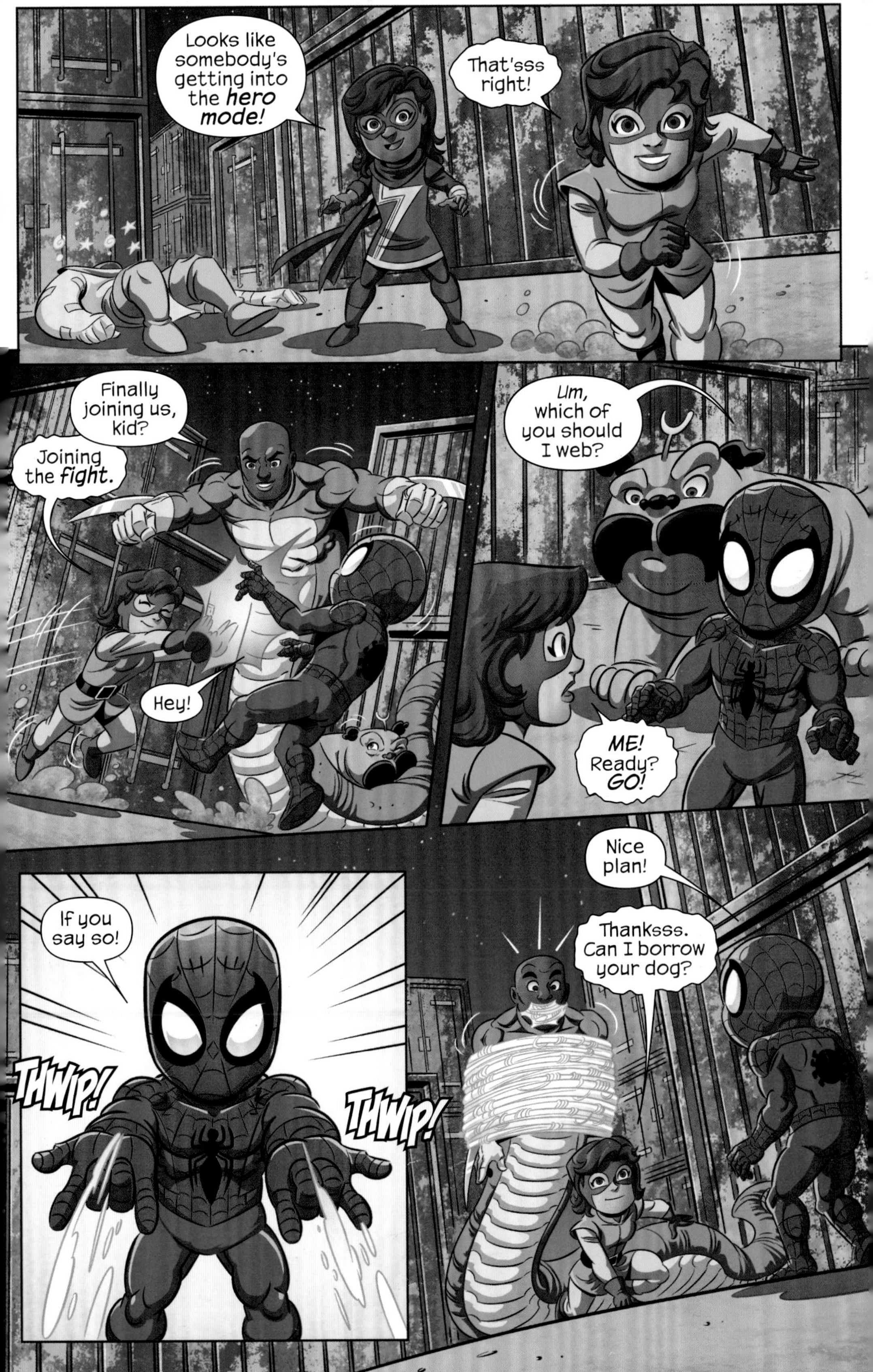
Looks like somebody's getting into the *hero mode!*
That'sss right!
Finally joining us, kid?
Joining the *fight.*
Hey!
Um, which of you should I web?
ME! Ready? *GO!*
If you say so!
THWIP!
THWIP!
Nice plan!
Thanksss. Can I borrow your dog?

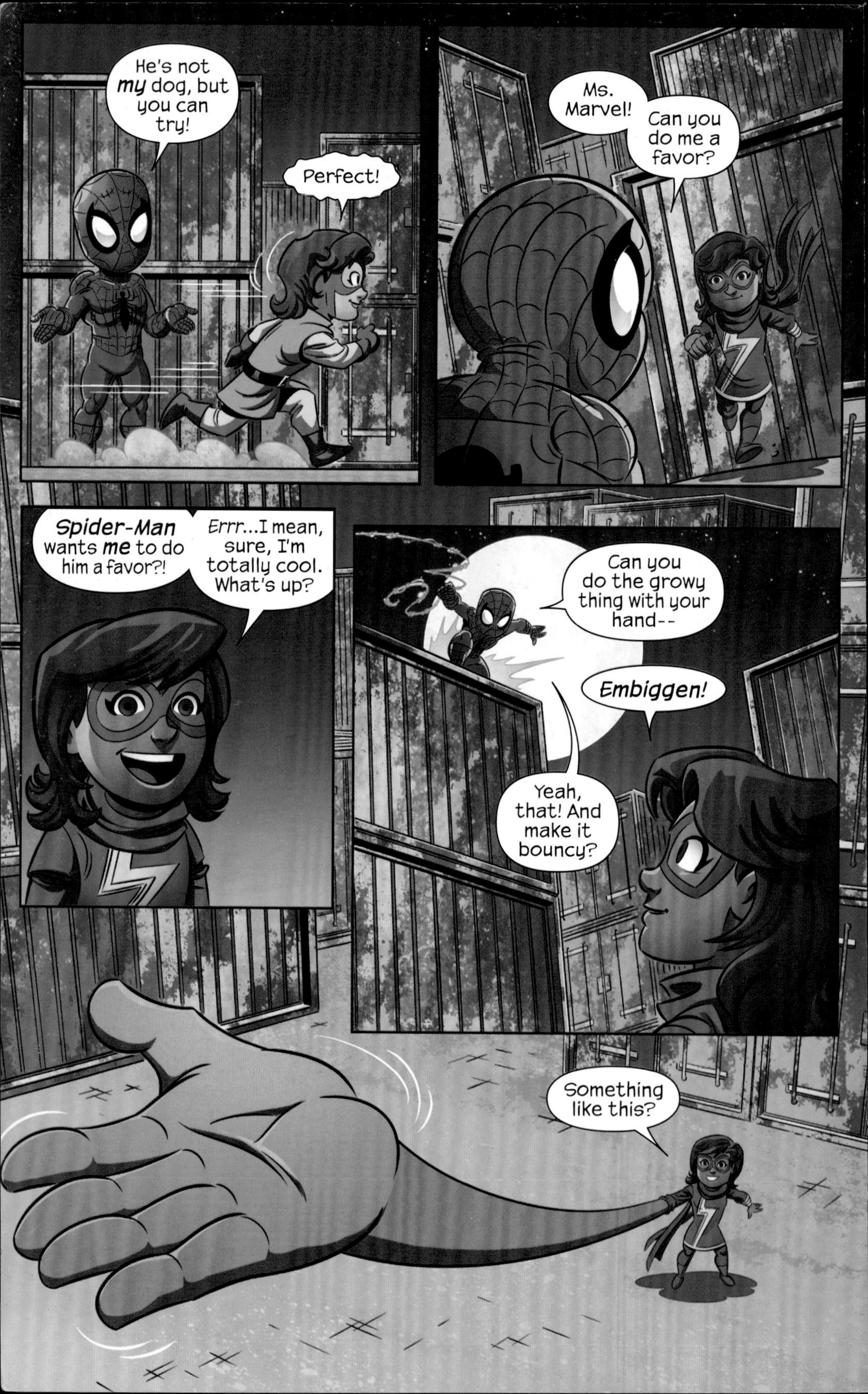
He's not *my* dog, but you can try!
Perfect!
Ms. Marvel!
Can you do me a favor?
Spider-Man wants *me* to do him a favor?!
Errr...I mean, sure, I'm totally cool. What's up?
Can you do the growy thing with your hand--
Embiggen!
Yeah, that! And make it bouncy?
Something like this?

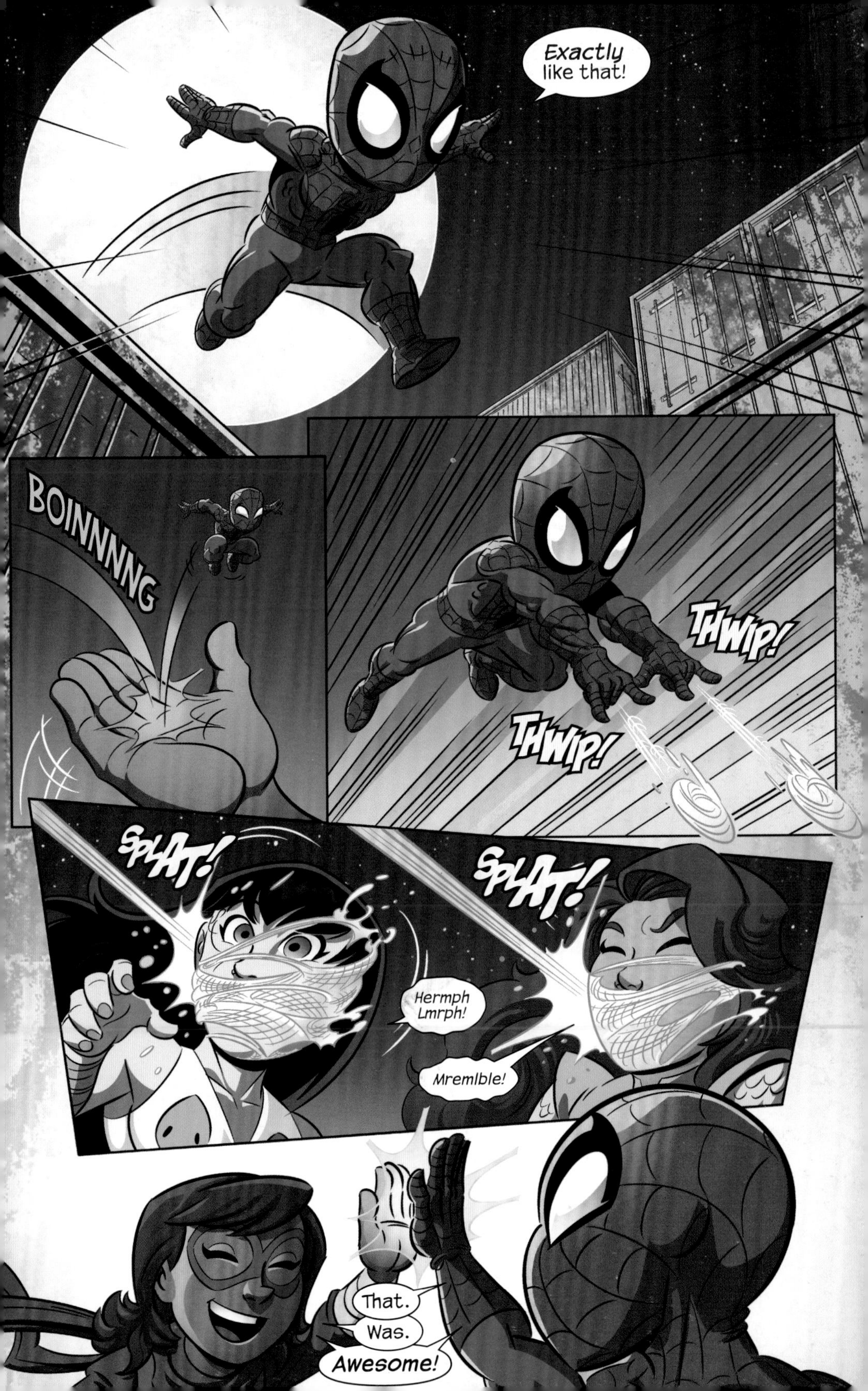
Exactly like that!
BOINNNNNG
THWIP!
THWIP!
SPLAT!
SPLAT!
Hermph Lmrph!
Mremlble!
That.
Was.
Awesome!

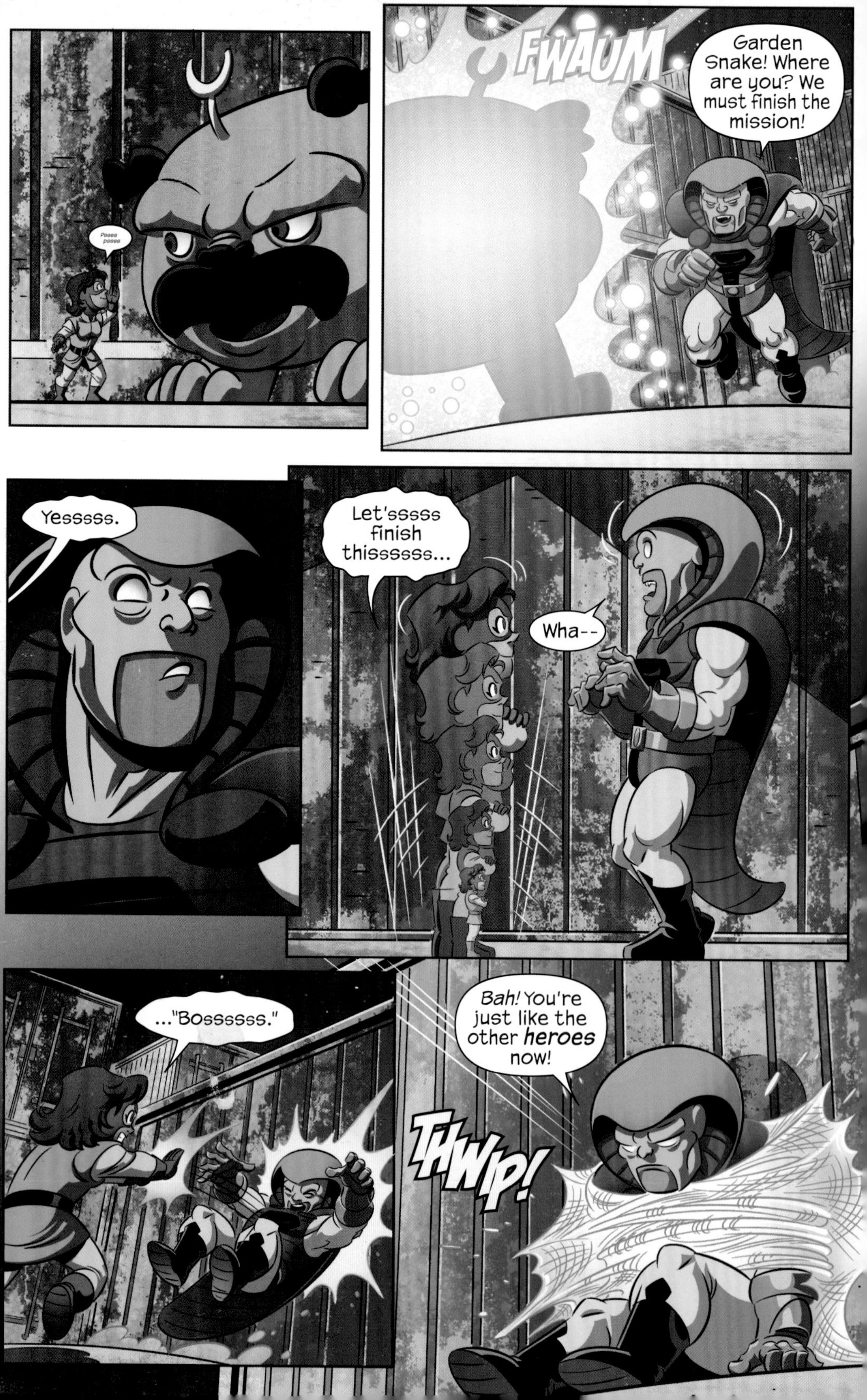
Pssss pssss
FWAUM
Garden Snake! Where are you? We must finish the mission!
Yessss.
Let'sssss finish thissssss...
Wha--
..."Bossssss."
Bah! You're just like the other *heroes* now!
THWIP!

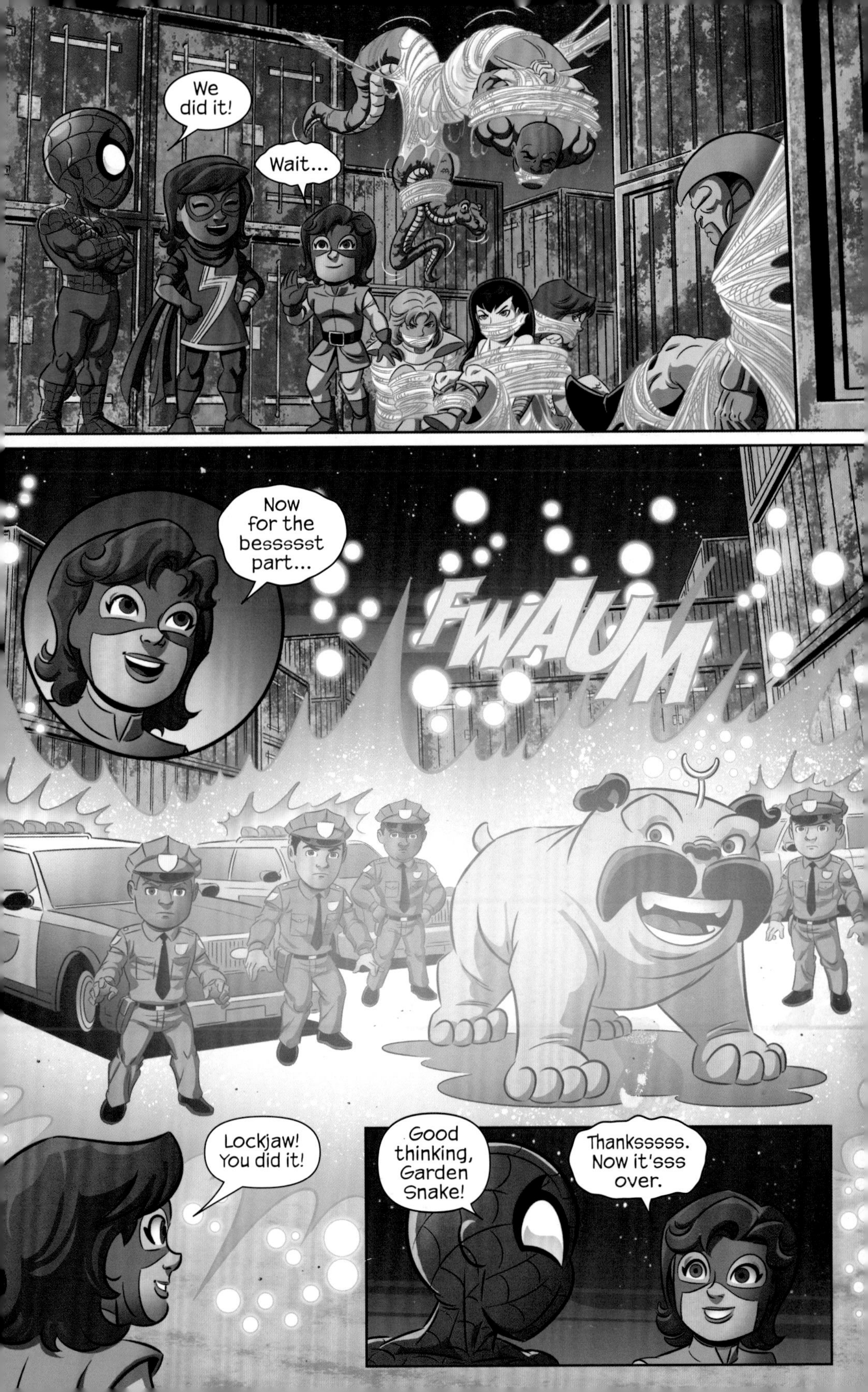
We did it!
Wait...
Now for the besssssst part...
FWAUM
Lockjaw! You did it!
Good thinking, Garden Snake!
Thankssssss. Now it'sss over.

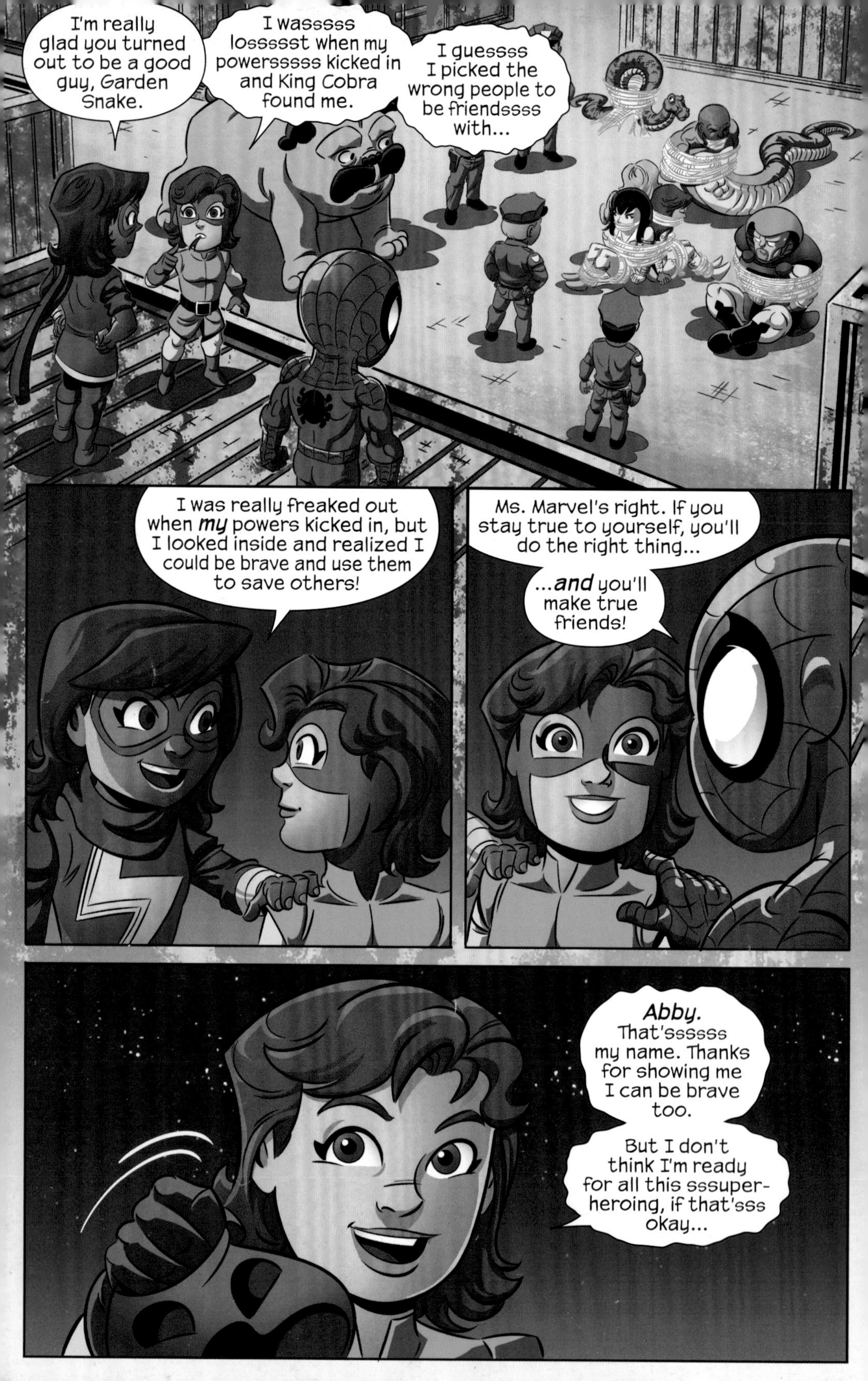

I'm really glad you turned out to be a good guy, Garden Snake.
I wasssss losssssst when my powerssssss kicked in and King Cobra found me.
I guessss I picked the wrong people to be friendssss with...
I was really freaked out when *my* powers kicked in, but I looked inside and realized I could be brave and use them to save others!
Ms. Marvel's right. If you stay true to yourself, you'll do the right thing...
...*and* you'll make true friends!
Abby. That'ssssss my name. Thanks for showing me I can be brave too.
But I don't think I'm ready for all this sssuper-heroing, if that'sss okay...

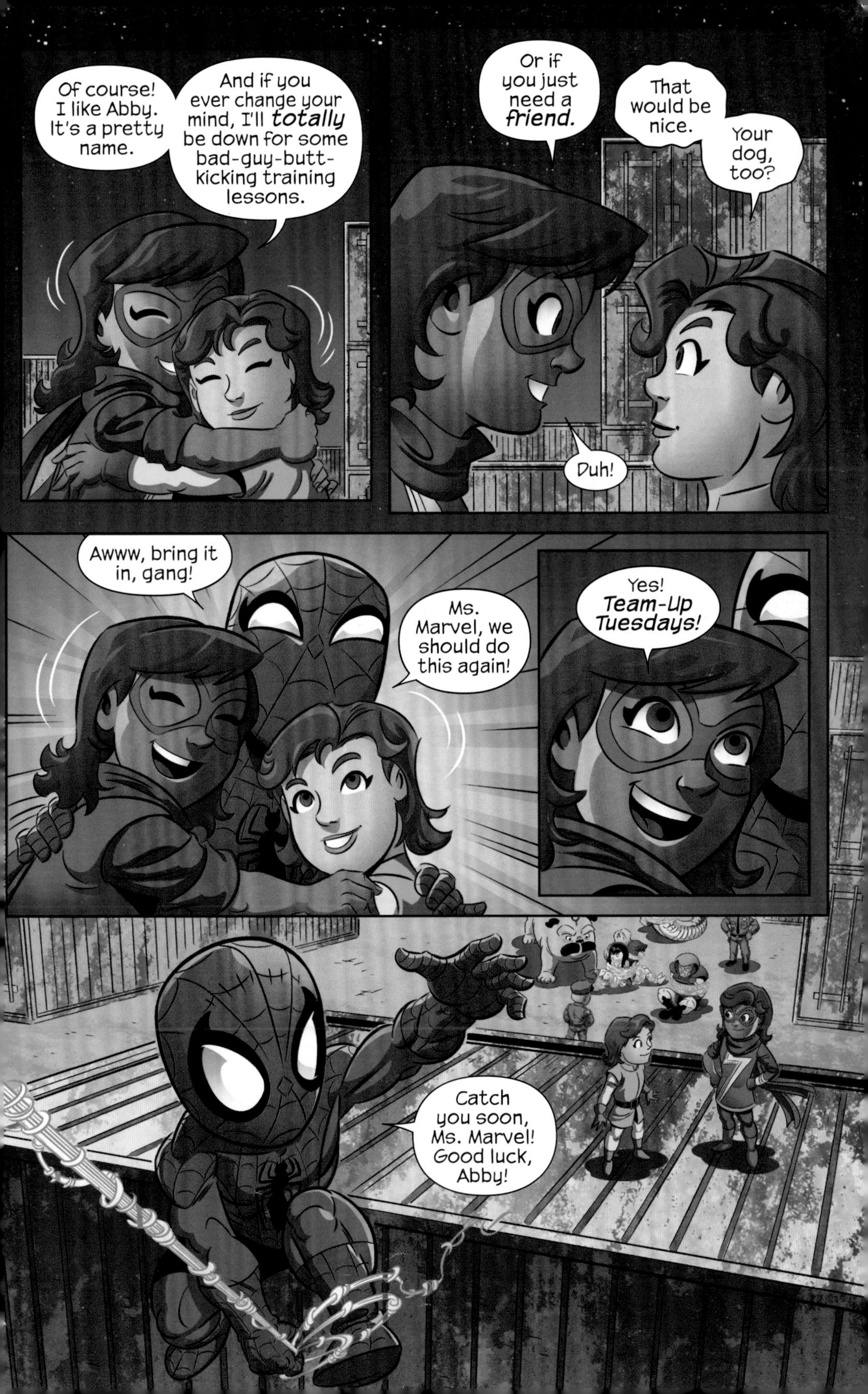
Of course! I like Abby. It's a pretty name.
And if you ever change your mind, I'll *totally* be down for some bad-guy-butt-kicking training lessons.
Or if you just need a *friend.*
That would be nice.
Your dog, too?
Duh!
Awww, bring it in, gang!
Ms. Marvel, we should do this again!
Yes! *Team-Up Tuesdays!*
Catch you soon, Ms. Marvel! Good luck, Abby!

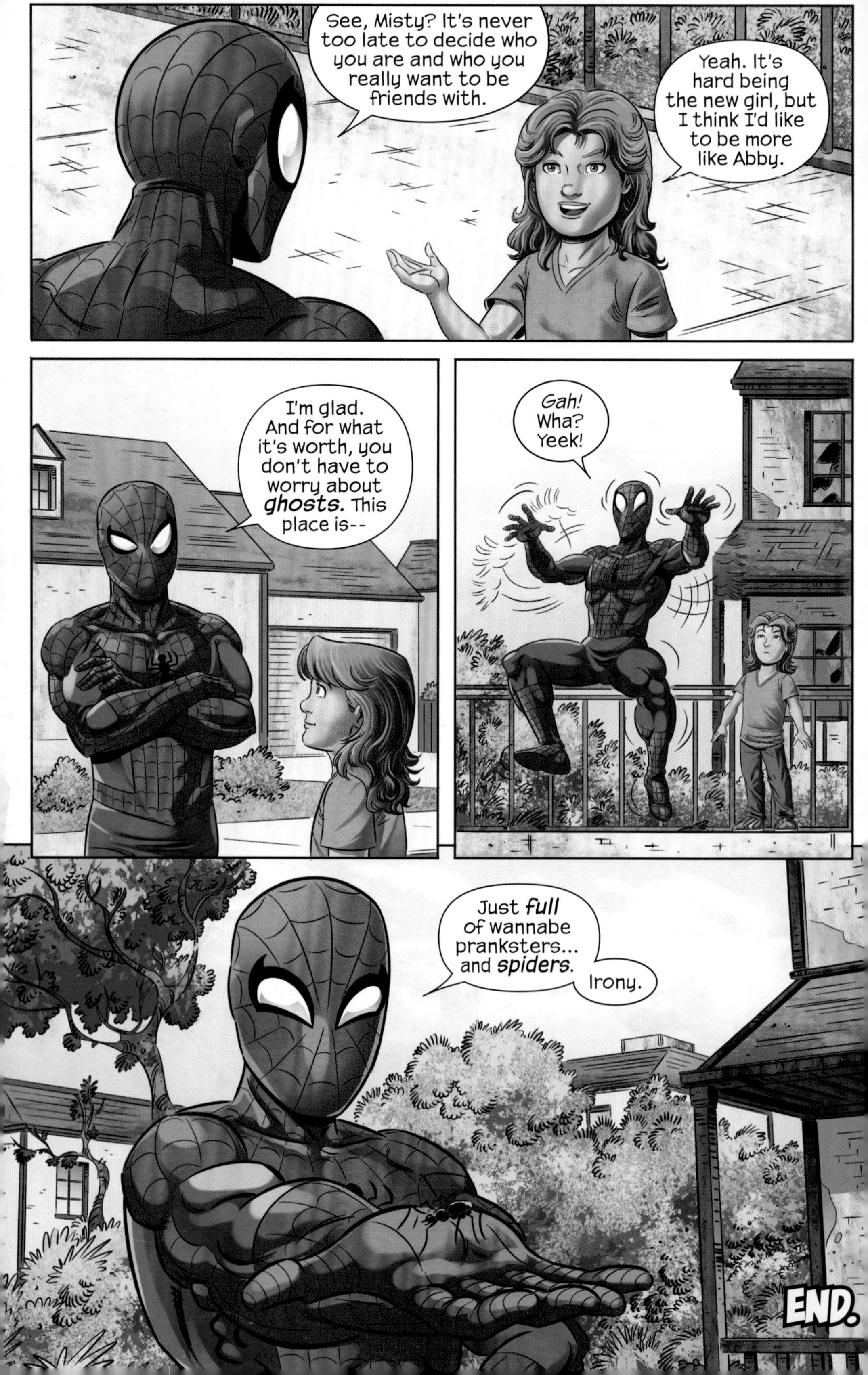
See, Misty? It's never too late to decide who you are and who you really want to be friends with.
Yeah. It's hard being the new girl, but I think I'd like to be more like Abby.
I'm glad. And for what it's worth, you don't have to worry about *ghosts.* This place is--
Gah! Wha? Yeek!
Just *full* of wannabe pranksters... and *spiders.*
Irony.
END.

YOU DON'T NEED A **WEB**STER'S DICTIONARY TO LOCATE **SPIDEY'S FRIENDS**

Find all these spider species:

- BLACK WIDOW
- LYNX
- WATER
- FISHER
- HUNTING
- TURRET
- LIPHISTIID
- WOLF
- GARDEN
- JUMPING
- TRAPDOOR
- CRAB
- TARANTULA
- STICK

```
B T N A R A T R E T T A W S
L A A P T A R H A A T D T C
A C L R E A P J U M P I N G
C L Y E A K R L G N C M U J
X J X H L N A M X K T C H O
B N S I G T N N O H I R A
L I P H O U Y T G C N M
A F H T R O L R B T E G
E D I N E D R A G R A A
C M S F T U R P M R S A
K T T L O C N D T I R H
E C I O R P R O A L E T
G H I W A I E O N C T P
I E D M O H S R P I A N
B L A C K W I D O W O
N O I S S L S I P I L
L T L T E R R U T E T
S A N T L U A R C H E
```

TRUE OR FALSE
SPIDER-QUIZ

THERE ARE 80,000 SPECIES OF SPIDERS
☐ TRUE   ☐ FALSE

SPIDERS USUALLY HAVE 10 EYES
☐ TRUE   ☐ FALSE

SPIDERS HAVE 8 LEGS
☐ TRUE   ☐ FALSE

SPIDERS EAT ONLY SOLID FOOD
☐ TRUE   ☐ FALSE

CRAB SPIDERS CAN MOVE SIDEWAYS AND BACKWARDS
☐ TRUE   ☐ FALSE

SPIDERS PREY CHIEFLY ON INSECTS
☐ TRUE   ☐ FALSE

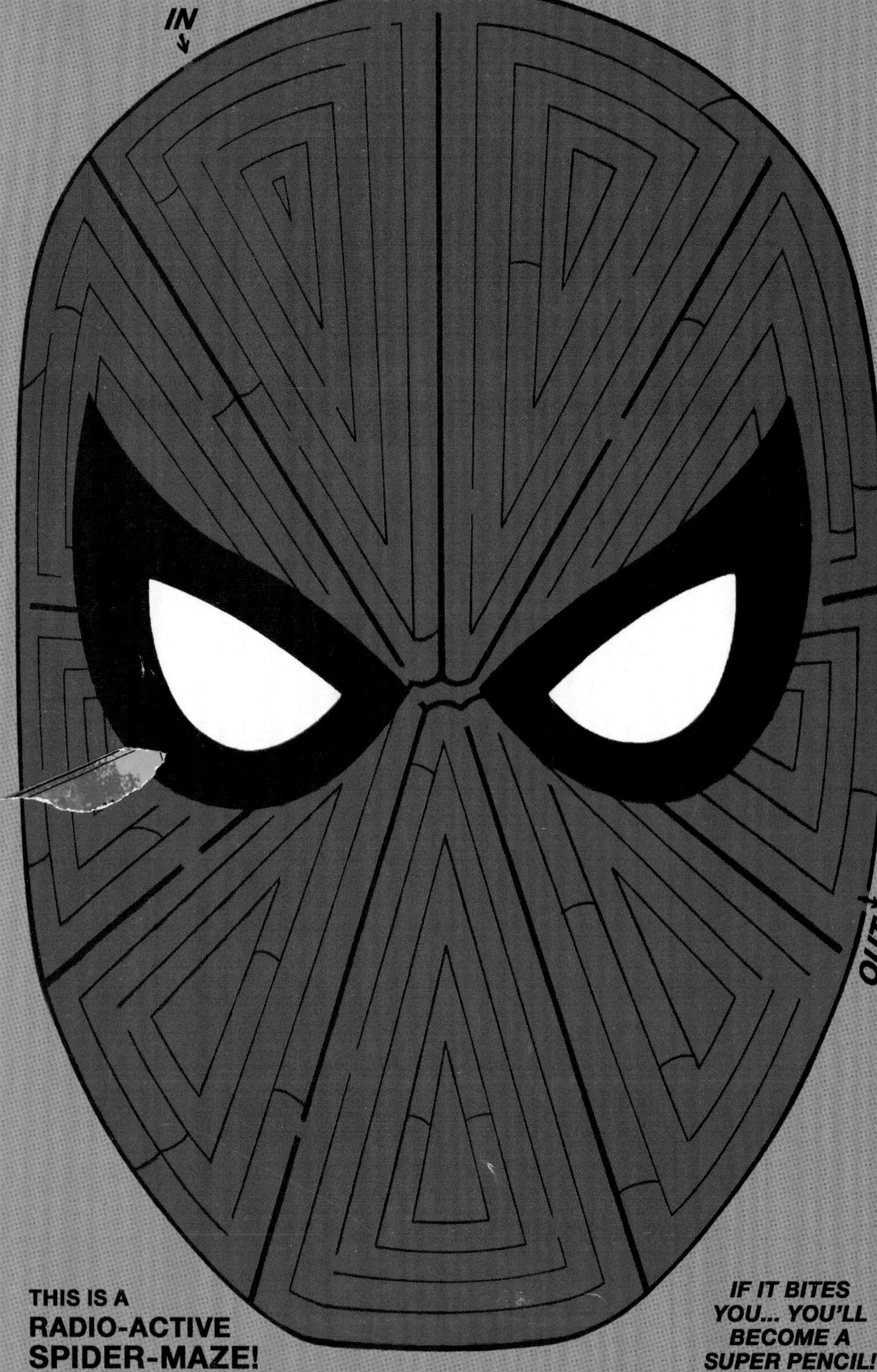

IN
OUT

THIS IS A
RADIO-ACTIVE
SPIDER-MAZE!

IF IT BITES YOU... YOU'LL BECOME A SUPER PENCIL!

YOU DON'T NEED A WEBSTER'S DICTIONARY TO LOCATE SPIDEY'S FRIENDS

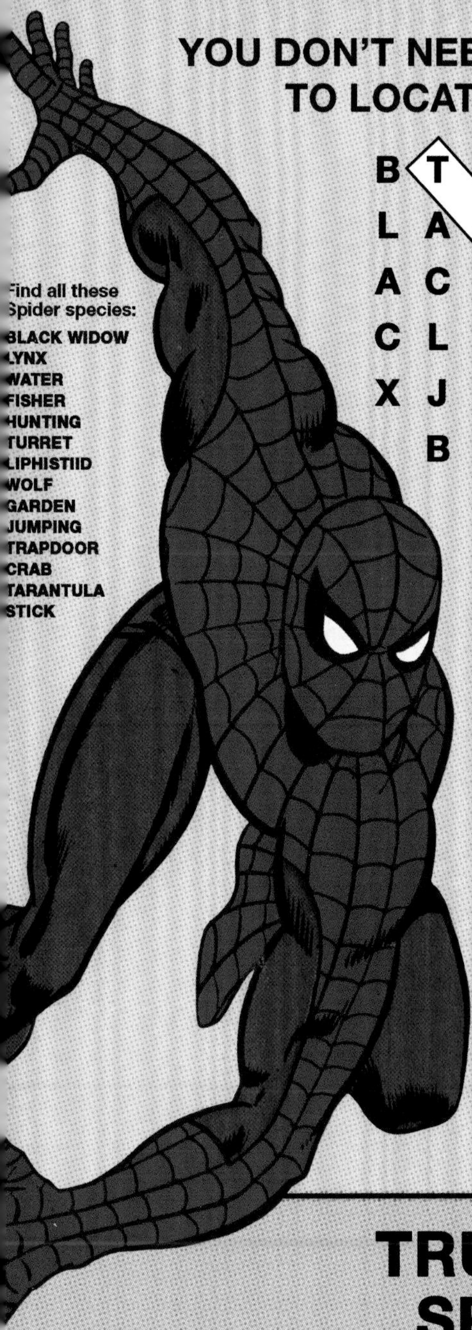

Find all these Spider species:

- BLACK WIDOW
- LYNX
- WATER
- FISHER
- HUNTING
- TURRET
- LIPHISTIID
- WOLF
- GARDEN
- JUMPING
- TRAPDOOR
- CRAB
- TARANTULA
- STICK

B T N A R A T R E T T A W S
L A A P T A R H A A T D T C
A C L R E A P J U M P I N G
C L Y E A K R L G N C M U J
X J X H L N A M X K T C H O
B N S I G T N N O H I R A
L I P H O U Y T G C N M
A F H T R O L R B T E G
E D I N E D R A G R A A
C M S F T U R P M R S A
K T T L O C N D T I R H
E C I O R P R O A L E T
G H I W A I E O N C T P
I E D M O H S R P I A N
B L A C K W I D O W O
N O I S S L S I P I L
L T L T E R R U T E T
S A N T L U A R C H E

TRUE OR FALSE SPIDER-QUIZ

THERE ARE 80,000 SPECIES OF SPIDERS
☐ TRUE ☒ FALSE

SPIDERS USUALLY HAVE 10 EYES
☐ TRUE ☒ FALSE

SPIDERS HAVE 8 LEGS
☒ TRUE ☐ FALSE

SPIDERS EAT ONLY SOLID FOOD
☐ TRUE ☒ FALSE

CRAB SPIDERS CAN MOVE SIDEWAYS AND BACKWARDS
☒ TRUE ☐ FALSE

SPIDERS PREY CHIEFLY ON INSECTS
☒ TRUE ☐ FALSE

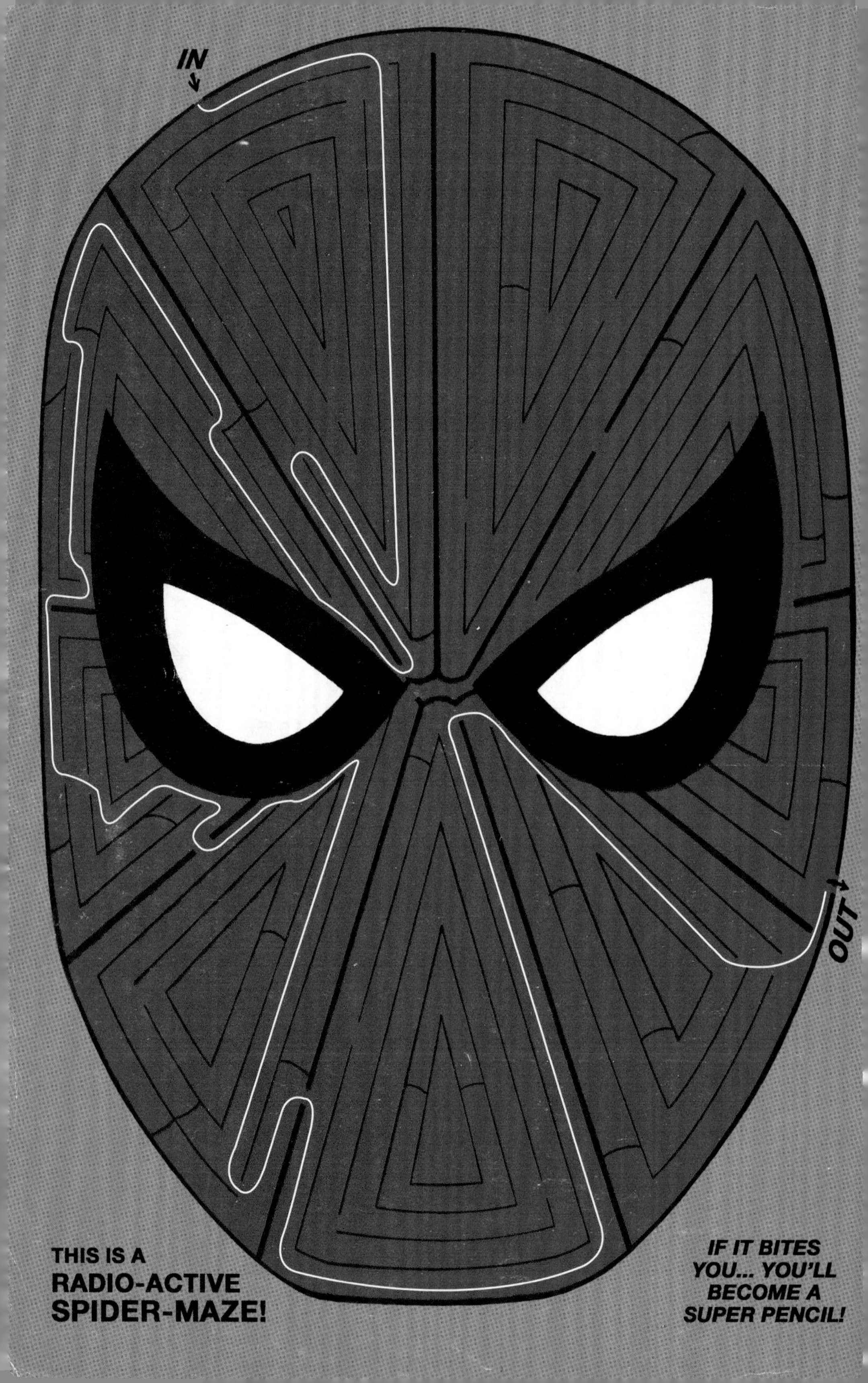
IN
OUT
THIS IS A
RADIO-ACTIVE
SPIDER-MAZE!
IF IT BITES
YOU... YOU'LL
BECOME A
SUPER PENCIL!